"I think the unadorned female form is a lovely thing . . ."

"I have gowns I keep on hand for models, but I doubt they'd fit you," Nic said. "You're a good deal slighter than most of the women I paint. If you can survive till Monday, I know a dressmaker we can visit. Very reasonable and discreet."

I'll bet, Merry thought.

Nic's eyes gleamed as if he'd read her mind. "I, of course, would never force you to wear a stitch. Speaking as an artist, I think the unadorned female form is a lovely thing."

Merry shot a repressive look from beneath her brows, but it only made Nic laugh.

"Little cold for that," she said.

Nic put his elbow on the table and tweaked her nose.

"You forget," he said. "In my house, we stoke the fires."

Also by Emma Holly

BEYOND INNOCENCE

BEYOND SEDUCTION

EMMA HOLLY

JOVE BOOKS, NEW YORK

BEYOND SEDUCTION

A Jove Book / published by arrangement with
the author

Copyright © 2002 by Emma Holly.
Jacket art by Judy York.
Book design by Julie Rogers.

ISBN: 0-7394-2573-0

A JOVE BOOK®
Jove Books are published by The Berkley Publishing Group,
a division of Penguin Putnam Inc.,
375 Hudson Street, New York, New York 10014.
JOVE and the "J" design
are trademarks belonging to Penguin Putnam Inc.

PRINTED IN THE UNITED STATES OF AMERICA

To my fantabulous editor, Christine Zika,
for asking me to go beyond.

To my never-say-die agent, Roberta Brown,
for her humor and her steely nerve.

I am grateful, ladies, more than I can say!

Prologue

"YOUR DAUGHTER *WILL* MARRY MY SON," SAID AL-
thorp.

He stood by the parlor window, stout and sure, his chill
gaze betraying the ruthless nature at his core. Despite the
thickening of his figure, he was as handsome as he'd been at
twenty-nine. The cut of his morning coat was impeccable, his
posture both casual and assured.

Few would guess he was an object of scorn among the circle to which he had always aspired.

The sight of him in her home—in her life—made Lavinia
Vance, celebrated duchess to the duke of Monmouth, want to
rake her nails down his cultured face. Instead, she smoothed
the skirt of her tightly laced brocade gown. Her skin glowed
beside the *terre D'Egypte* red and the long cuirass bodice
made her curves seem more imperial than ever. She looked
her fashionable best, but rather than experiencing her usual

satisfaction at the fact, she found herself wishing she felt as confident as she looked.

Judging by the amusement in his eyes, Althorp was aware of her emotions. He stepped closer, lifting his arm as if to touch her cheek. When she shrank instinctively back, he merely smiled. His hand fell to her arm.

At the touch, a memory came: her own fingers stroking the dun-brown birthmark on his back as they lay in a rumpled hotel bed. He'd been magnetic then, strong and attentive, and so much more intelligent than most of her husband's friends. It had seemed the height of injustice that they snubbed him simply because his father had been in trade. A baronetcy bought with coal, they sneered, the ink on the title barely dry. Hurting back then herself, she'd wanted to kiss his wounds and make them better, never dreaming how coldly he'd use her sympathy to control her—in bed and out. She could not believe the things she'd done, the things she had enjoyed.

Repelled, she turned her head away. If only she could erase that much-regretted time!

Too close to evade, Althorp's breath stirred her hair. "I remember when you welcomed my caress, when you could not do enough to please me."

"That"—she lifted her chin—"was a lapse of judgment of which I am not proud."

"Tut-tut, Lavinia. Insults gain you nothing. You know you have more to lose than I should our former relationship be exposed."

She shook free of him, part of her wondering as always if he were bluffing. Exposing himself as an adulterer would hardly further his son's ambitions—or, rather, his ambitions for his son; Lavinia doubted Ernest himself aspired so high.

But the doubt remained unspoken. She did not dare test Althorp's determination. Given the paucity of the baronet's support among the peerage, if Lavinia's husband didn't help Ernest stand for the House of Commons, chances were no one with leverage would. If her enemy's dreams of paternal grandeur were dashed, would he hesitate to return the favor?

She could not deny she had more to lose than he did. Her position in society was the culmination of her every hope. If the truth became known, at the very least her husband would banish her to Scotland. For his wife to have had an affair with a man he believed to be his friend . . . Geoffrey's pride would not allow that to go unpunished.

Satisfied he'd made his point, Althorp folded his arms and regarded her from under heavy, half-lidded eyes. Still in his hand, the brim of his black silk top hat rested against his side. It was an exquisite creation, neither too high nor too low, with a crisp, curving rim. The duke did not own one so fine.

"My son is going to be prime minister," he said with the sureness she'd come to loathe. "And your husband, his future father-in-law, is going to start him on that road. He'll have to if he doesn't want people to think his precious Merry has married down. All you have to do is push your idiot daughter into my son's arms."

Lavinia laughed at his claim, an edge of hysteria in the sound. She *had* pushed, to an extent that shamed her. Moreover, she'd made certain her daughter would have no other suitors for her hand. As plain as she was, as outspoken as she was, Merry herself had sabotaged her prospects well enough. Thanks to Lavinia, however, every mother with a son knew what a hellion she was and how she'd be certain to shame any family she married into. Lavinia had disguised her purpose with mournful sighs—no one would think her an unnatural mother—but the few men who had shown a glimmer of interest had thus been scared away.

If only manipulating Merry were as easy.

"I don't dare push her any harder," she said, her fingers twined into an involuntary knot. "She'll only dig her heels in if she feels cornered."

Her plea fell on deaf ears. Althorp dropped his arms and tapped his hat against his trouser leg. The flutter of the paler cloth was a telling sign of his impatience.

"I've given you a year," he said, "and twice she has refused him. For God's sake, my son is not a monster. He is a good-looking, intelligent, well-mannered young man. Your husband approves. And from what I can see, your daughter does not despise him."

"She thinks he'll try to control her."

"She needs controlling!" Althorp exclaimed, then lowered his voice. "Put your foot down, Lavinia. And have your husband put down his. The girl has to marry someone. You and I both know it had better be my son."

Lavinia sensed he was in earnest. She looked down at the hands she'd clutched together in unconscious prayer. Her gloves were creased, and damp inside with fear. With all her heart, she wished she weren't a coward. Surely nothing was more despicable than pandering one's daughter for the self-ish preservation of one's place.

"I need more time," she said.

Althorp caught her chin and raised it in an iron grip. The squeeze of his bare fingers was intimate and hot. "One month," he said. "My son is planning to ask her again on New Year's Eve. By New Year's Day I want to hear they are betrothed."

He released her and turned, not saying good-bye or even nodding. He simply pulled on his gloves and strode from the room.

He knew she had no choice but to do precisely as he asked.

Alone once more, an unladylike sweat prickled beneath her breasts. Her heart beat against her stays as if it longed to escape the bonds of flesh. For a moment, she allowed the dark deliverance to whisper its temptations in her ear. But what sort of haven would Death be to a sinner like herself? No haven at all, she thought. And why should she surrender when much of her life was still so sweet? She was the duchess of Monmouth: a social force. She had her house and her clothes and her handsome sons. Her husband had in later years become if not a lover, at least a friend. These were precious gifts she would not willingly leave behind.

Her hands curled into fists. Somehow she had to change her daughter's mind. Then they could all go on with their lives. But how to do it—how?—when the foolish chit would rather be a spinster than a bride.

_1_ ❧

NICOLAS CRAVEN, FAMOUS ARTIST AND INFAMOUS libertine, slouched in the wing-backed leather chair as if he did not ever intend to rise. His paisley brown robe of flowing silk was tied at his trim, hard waist. Beneath this he was naked. In the interest of warmth, a snifter of brandy, mostly full, lay cradled against his chest. A coal fire burned behind the grate on which his slippered feet were propped. Its steady glow lit keen, saturnine features. His eyes were smoke, his jaw as sharp as steel. A pianist would not have scorned his hands. His voice was another matter. In contrast to this lean, dark elegance, it was as hoarse and graveled as if he spent his days shouting on the docks.

That impression was misleading. Nicolas Craven barely had to whisper to draw attention. He was a genius, people said, better than Leighton or Alma-Tadema, not that either of those luminaries would have conceded their position. In any case, people listened when Nic spoke, whether out of respect for his talent or fear of his occasionally cutting wit he did not care. He only cared that they leave him alone when he was tired.

As he was tonight.

He'd completed his latest commission. The bursts of manic activity—elation, frustration, nights spent with brushes clamped between his teeth and paint-stained fingers plunged in his hair—had ceased as if he'd grabbed the clapper of a big bronze bell. His body rang with the echoes of his exertion, emptied out and exhausted. But he would rest now. The portrait was done. Monmouth had come to collect it that morning and pronounced himself pleased, though Nic doubted the duke saw more than a fraction of what the painting said.

He had caught the man.

Hell, he'd caught half the British peerage: their befuddlement at the changing times, their pomposity and self-indulgence, their earnest belief in their ability to save the world . . . as long as the world wanted to be saved in a manner they approved of.

His mouth curled in ironic self-disgust. No point looking down his nose at them. No matter how Nic lived, his blood was just as blue.

Not that he could blame his sins on that.

He turned his gaze to the window, to the jungle of foliage that hid his cozy home in St. John's Wood. A winter fog, thick as cat's fur, had crept out from London to swallow this artist's enclave to the north. He could barely make out the ivy that grew across the glass, obscured as it was by the ashy haze. The mix of chocolate and silver was extraordinary, soft as velvet. If Nic hadn't been too lazy to move he'd have reached for his pastels. That something so foul could be so beautiful he could only marvel.

He was actually considering getting up when a tap on the library door saved him from the effort. At his grunt, his butler, Farnham, entered with a tray of food and coffee. As always, Nic had dismissed the servants in the emotional low water that followed his painting fits. Since this particular low water had come during the holidays, Nic was a popular man. Holiday or no, per usual, Farnham had not hied himself away. The older man had been a sergeant in the Crimea. His sense of duty was stronger than that of the other staff—stronger, in fact, than his employer's.

"Your dinner, sir," he said, just as if Nic had ordered it. He removed the brandy decanter in order to place the meal on the little table at Nic's side. Then he waited. Nic knew the butler wouldn't leave until he saw him eat.

He lifted the hefty beef-and-pickle sandwich and took a bite. "There," he said. "Satisfied?"

Without comment Farnham poured a steaming cup of coffee and set it on a saucer. The smell alone was enough to clear Nic's head—at least until Farnham slid a fat white envelope between the dishes.

"You'll be wanting your mail, sir."

Nic snorted, his mouth full of savory bread and beef. Farnham knew that for a lie as well as he did. This particular letter had been following him around the house all week, appearing beside his plate at breakfast, peeping from the pocket of his coat. Nic had ignored it with a determination honed by years of practice. Unfortunately, unlike Nic, Farnham didn't believe in putting off till tomorrow what one would rather not face today.

With a grimace, Nic put down his coffee and took the envelope. It *had* been a week. His commission was finished, his mind as serene as it ever was. Surely he was ready to open the damn thing now. What was there to fear, after all? The contents of his mother's correspondence were invariably the same.

"I'll leave you to it then," said Farnham as Nic's thumb slid under the flap.

The letter was as he'd expected. A brief expression of hope for Nic's well-being—omitting, of course, any mention of his work—then straight to a summary of the myriad tasks she had undertaken since her last report. The sheep, the fields, the drainage in the village ditch: all had been seen to with his mother's trademark efficiency. She was the strongest, most managing person he knew, and yet behind each proof of competence lay an unspoken accusation.

These responsibilities are yours, Nicolas. Yours. Never mind she would resent the mildest interference, she still behaved as if his failure to bestir himself were an affront. "What's more," she continued, "the boy needs the steadying influence of a male. He's nearly fifteen. I can no longer guide him as I should."

Guide him. Nic snorted. More like *rule.* Skimming to the end, he crumpled the page and tossed it into the fire. A smaller note remained, which had been tucked inside the other.

Nic opened it. Against his will, his heart began to rap more swiftly against his ribs. The note was from the boy, the usual update on his progress at school. The tone was formal. The boy always called him "sir." Never volunteered more than the impersonal, nor asked questions he'd learned would not be answered. Unlike the dowager marchioness, the boy was far too sharp to inquire when Nic would visit. Nic had seen him twice in his life: once shortly after his birth and again when he was four. At the time, the boy's resemblance to Bess had been too wrenching to make Nic eager to repeat the experience.

Some memories were better left to lie.

He ran one finger over the spiky loops of ink. Despite the stiff language, he fancied he could read the boy's character in the scrawl. Bright. Impatient. True to his friends. Fonder of sport than he was of schooling but, apparently, from one comment he let slip, a budding admirer of Trollope.

Nic smiled at that. With an impulsive movement at odds with his former languor, he opened the drawer in the table at his side. As he'd expected, Farnham had stocked it with writing materials. Using the arm of the chair as a desk, he scribbled a response.

Dear Cristopher,
Am doing well, though busy with work. Should you need anything for which you would prefer not to ask the marchioness, feel free to write my man of business.

He bit the end of his pen and reread what he'd written. His eyes strayed to the nearest rank of shelving. A small flutter of satisfaction warmed his breast. Yes, he did have a leather-bound set of *The Eustace Diamonds*. The pages, bright with gold leaf, hadn't yet been cut. The boy might have read the novel, of course, but not in such handsome form. Rising, he pulled out the first volume and opened it to the frontispiece. The pen was still in his hand. He should write something, shouldn't he? Otherwise, the gift would seem too cold even for him.

He pondered a moment.

"Thought you might like this," he wrote, then hesitated over what to sign. "Your father" would probably please the boy, but Nic wasn't sure he could force that appellation through the nib. He could sign himself "Northwick" he supposed, but that, too, seemed insufferable. In the end, he simply wrote "Nicolas" and, just in case, added a twenty-pound note. Warm, it was not. He had no wish, however, to promise more than he could give.

THE MANSION IN KNIGHTSBRIDGE HUMMED WITH THE pleasure of its guests. The holidays had never come so grandly as they did to these lofty rooms. Hundreds of beeswax tapers lit them, all banded with crimson bows. Every door was a faerie forest of fresh-cut pine. The scent of sugared negus and French perfume drifted like incense through the heated air. Bosoms glowed, jewels glittered, and trains like satiny peacock's tails swept inlaid marble floors. The sweet melancholy of a Chopin nocturne was nearly drowned by laughter.

When the clock in the hall struck midnight, no one showed the least desire to leave.

One reveler stood apart from the cries of "Happy New Year." In the relative quiet of the blue salon, a slender, freckled woman with hair like a scrub brush of red-gold wire stared intently at a portrait of the host. The picture had been hung that morning above the mantel, and ever since Merry

Vance, only daughter of the duke of Monmouth, had been haunted by what it said.

Mind, there was nothing wrong with the thing. The likeness was exacting, the execution skilled. The artist had posed her father standing behind the desk in his study, with one hand resting on a globe and the other steepled lightly over a well-thumbed copy of the London *Times.* A soft golden light, like the end of an autumn day, angled down from a nearby window to diffuse over the rich black wool of his coat sleeve. At the very limit of the wedge of slanting sun, a small felt lion lay toppled on its side. The lion was a toy from Merry's childhood, treasured by a father who had four sons and just one daughter. The sight of it lying there, half in the light, half out, struck her with the force of a strange and uncomfortable portent. Indeed, the whole picture made her squirm.

Her father appeared vigorous, his stance confident, his jaw firm. But there was something in his eyes: a look Merry had never noticed and now could not imagine how she'd missed.

How did I get here? the look said, and, *What has happened to the world I used to know?*

In that moment, for the first time in all her twenty years, she thought of her father not as Her Father but as a person like herself. Despite his title and his wealth, despite being a citizen of the mightiest empire on earth, he, too, was capable of doubt. In one way, the realization scared her but, in another, it made her even more determined to control her destiny.

When she was her father's age, she did not want to know regret.

Ten more years and I'll be free, she thought. That's when the estate left in trust to her by her grandmother would be handed into her care. She could live as she pleased then, answerable to no one but herself—but only if she managed to stay unwed.

A husband, she knew, would not support her secret plans.

A whisper of orange-scented silk warned Merry she had company. Her best friend, Isabel Beckett, now Lady Hyde, laid a delicate, white-gloved hand upon her shoulder. Both girls were fair, but where Merry was as wiry as a jockey, Isabel was pleasingly plump. Pretty, too, with fashionably wavy hair and skin as smooth as cream. They'd attended the same finishing school, two incorrigible pranksters. Merry couldn't count the times her friend's batting golden lashes had gotten them out of trouble. As Isabel joined her in gazing at the portrait, her expression was one of amusement.

"They say he spent three months seducing Lady Piggot."

"What!" gasped Merry, far from ready to face this news.

Isabel giggled. "Not your father, silly. Nicolas Craven. The artist. Did you get to meet him while he was here?"

Merry shook her head. "I only caught a glimpse of him in the hall. He was all over paint and wild-eyed—like a refugee from Bedlam. I don't think he even noticed I was there."

"Probably caught up in his Art," said Isabel, nodding sagely. "Mother claims he's a terrible rake. Says no decent woman would sit for him."

"Well," Merry retorted, "he is not a very efficient rake if it took him three months to seduce Lady Piggot."

"No one says she wasn't willing to give in sooner. Apparently, he likes to savor his conquests." The newly married Isabel licked her upper lip. "Morsel by morsel, as it were."

"Hmpf." Merry ignored a rush of warmth through her inner regions. "Likes them panting after him, I'll bet."

"I wouldn't mind panting. My husband is almost as boring as your fiancé."

"Ernest is not my fiancé."

"Good as," Isabel countered. "You know your parents have their hearts set on the match."

Merry did know this, and had known it long before he began proposing. Ernest Althorp was the son of a neighboring landowner, now employed as her father's secretary. Growing up, he'd been her refuge from her brothers: calm when they were impetuous, sympathetic when they teased.

Not that she had ever considered marrying Ernest. He was like a brother to her, and a stuffy brother at that. Besides which, his father's baronetcy was hardly a match for her father's dukedom. Merry cared less for such matters than her friends, but if one had to be leg-shackled, one did not want to sink! Her father, however, thought him "sound." Her mother just plain adored him. Whenever Merry spent time with her, thankfully not often, she found an excuse to sing Ernest's praises. Merry was beginning to think the duchess had a *tendre* for him herself. Most of all, though, her parents thought Ernest was precisely the steadying influence their wild young daughter needed. *Time you settled,* her father liked to say. *Trade those horses of yours for a husband.*

Merry shuddered. Trade her freedom for a yoke, more like. Ernest was as conservative as he was steady.

"At least he isn't fat," said Isabel, whose own husband was portly. "And at least you like him."

But liking him made it worse. Merry knew she didn't have the meanness to defy him the way she would a bully. Nor did she like him enough. Once upon a time, Merry had been in love. She'd been young, and it hadn't ended well, but the experience had taught her how deeply her passions could be stirred.

Stymied, she stared at Nicolas Craven's painting as if it held the secret to her fate. The candlelight caught a hairline crack in the gilded frame. That will be my life, she thought, if I can't fend Ernest off.

"Nothing has been decided," she said aloud.

"Will be soon," warned her friend. "I'd be surprised if old Ernest doesn't propose again tonight. Your brothers have been winking at him all evening."

"Argh," said Merry, suspecting she was right.

Isabel laughed and squeezed her waist. "Shall I hide you in the broom cabinet the way I used to do at school?"

"No," Merry sighed. "It's time I let them all know where I stand."

MERRY'S ELDEST BROTHER, EVELYN, HIS WIFE INDISPOSED by her latest pregnancy, had the dubious honor of ensuring his little sister did not languish by the wall. Even at a fam-

ily party Merry wasn't one to gather beaus—though her following had not always been so sparse.

When she first came out, she'd had her share of admirers,
enough to feel a flush of anticipatory pleasure before a ball.
At one point, after Ernest's first proposal, she'd thought she
might someday say yes to someone else—until she'd realized no one else would ever ask.

Apparently, when males reached a certain age, they lost
their tolerance for female frankness. Overnight it seemed
her opinions were not as valid as their own. They forgot
she'd been raised by a respected member of Parliament and,
what's more, had a brain. Where once they'd marveled at
her ability to take a fence, now they held her horsemanship
in disgust. What they'd praised in a girl, it seemed they
could not stomach in a woman.

Beauty might have saved her, or charm, but she had neither. She'd lived too much of her life in the footsteps of her
brothers. Even if she'd wanted to simper, she wouldn't have
known how.

And now men her age cut their eyes away when she
passed, as if to see her was to be tainted. To hell with them,
she'd think each time it happened. To hell with them all.

Only her love of dancing induced her to suffer the indig-
nity of being partnered by her brothers.

On this evening, contrary to his usual custom of chattering her ear off, Evelyn maintained a grinning silence
through the waltz. When the last strains faded, he led her off
the ballroom floor to the palm-lined alcove that held the
punch tables. There, two more of her brothers waited with
matching smirks. Merry's heart sank to her stomach. Isabel
was right. Ernest was planning to propose. Obviously, the
man didn't know better than to share his secrets with her siblings.

She sighed in exasperation. Her brothers were three
handsome peas in a pod. Like her, they had light-brown
eyes, fair, freckled skin, and Grandmother Vance's kinky
red-gold hair—though only Merry had to wear it long
enough to turn into a bird's nest by itself. True, Evelyn had,

since the birth of his second child, cultivated an unfortunate pair of side whiskers, but the less said on that the better.

"So," she said, nonchalantly ladling herself a cup of heated wine, "come to roast me?"

"Nothing of the sort," said James, her second married brother. She hadn't seen him in months, not since his wedding. Like Evelyn, he glowed like a horse who'd been eating rich. His wife, too, was newly breeding.

Neither brother had wasted a moment ensuring their brides would be trapped at home.

"We like Althorp," he added. "We're happy for you."

She sipped her sugared port and tried not to wish it were a whiskey. "I've no idea why you'd be happy, since I'm determined to turn him down just like before."

"Seriously," said James.

"Seriously," echoed Evelyn. "Why won't you marry him? He can ride—"

"And shoot—"

"And he's always good for a loan."

Peter's contribution to the chorus dashed her last hope for support. Still unmarried and a mere two years older than herself, he'd helped her into and out of more scrapes than the others put together. Admittedly, her debut had put a distance between them—she'd had to be a bit of a lady at least—but lately, with the older boys gone from the house to start their families, she and Peter had grown close again.

Unfortunately, her repeated refusal of Ernest Althorp, who'd never been anything but kind to Peter, exceeded even his patience. "Come on, Mer," he said, "haven't you humiliated him enough?"

The accusation stung but she fought to keep a steady voice.

"I'm glad you like Ernest," she said. "I like him myself. But I hold the firm opinion we should not suit as man and wife."

Her brothers goggled at her, clearly unable to comprehend what she was saying.

"Is it because he isn't as rich as we are?" Evelyn asked.

"Of course it isn't. How could you think that!"

"Then it's got to be that his father hasn't got a proper title—which shouldn't worry you, by the by, because you know if you two marry, Father will sponsor him for the Commons, no matter if he does think Ernest isn't cut-throat enough to play top-drawer politics. He'd have more standing as an MP."

"I don't care about Ernest's standing. At least, I wouldn't if I loved him."

Evelyn pulled a face. "Don't tell me you're still in love with Greystowe. That was ages ago and he's a married man."

"I'm not in love with anyone," she assured him through gritted teeth, though she wasn't certain that was true. Edward Burbrooke, the earl of Greystowe, was a political ally of her father. She still blushed when she remembered how she'd thrown herself at him as a chit of seventeen. He'd fallen for Florence Fairleigh: sweet, pretty, womanly Florence Fairleigh. No one since had stirred Merry the way he had, which was probably just as well. Her reckless streak hadn't abated much in the intervening years.

"Good," said Evelyn, his voice gruff. "Didn't like seeing my sis down in the doldrums."

Touched, Merry squeezed his arm. This was why she loved the big, overprotective dolt; why she loved all her oafish brothers. Evelyn, of course, could not quit while he was ahead.

"Althorp would never lift a hand to you, you know. Not even if you deserved it."

Merry let this implication pass. "It's not me I'm worried about. It's Ernest."

"Well, you can start worrying now," James warned, "because that's him coming through the crowd."

Merry turned and pasted on what was probably a sickly smile. Oblivious to the undercurrents surrounding his approach, Ernest beamed at her and waved, a tall, solid figure with a head of smooth blond hair. As usual, his evening clothes didn't quite fit his muscular form. Despite his lack of sartorial splendor, he was attractive: country healthy, country clean. Women turned when he passed, but Ernest never saw. He was a man without mystery, his strides sure, his eyes just a trifle shy.

"Merry," he said, clasping her hands with a fervor he did not usually display.

"Ernest," she answered.

His eyes crinkled happily at her tone. He couldn't have known the softness was born of pity.

AS IT HAPPENED, SAYING NO TO ERNEST WAS NOT as harrowing as she'd feared. Apart from stiffening like a man before a firing squad, her friend took her refusal as he took everything: with good grace and a minimum of fuss.

"Are you certain?" he said. They sat alone in the conservatory, beneath the lantern-lit shadows of the palms. "Your mother led me to believe you might accept."

Merry wrinkled her nose. Did the duchess actually think Merry had heeded her gushing praise? "Er, no," she said. "Nothing's changed my mind. I care for you, Ernest, but I'm convinced we wouldn't pull well together. You know how I am: always wanting my own way. I'd drive you to drink within the year."

A muscle bunched in Ernest's jaw. "You could try to change."

"And you"—she nudged his shoulder with her own—"could try to meet another girl. I'm like an old shoe for you. I might pinch, but you're used to me. You'd rather not stir yourself to find a better fit."

"I like you," he insisted, "and I know I'd be good for you."

This, of course, was the problem. Like everyone else, he thought he could fix her, and thought she ought to be grateful for the help. Frowning, she kicked her heels within her skirts.

"You can do better," she said.

"If it's about the rumors, I don't believe a one of them."

"Rumors?" Merry blinked in surprise.

"I heard someone say—" he began, then pressed his lips together. "Never mind. It's nonsense. I know what you would and wouldn't do. So if you're trying to be noble by refusing me . . ."

"No." She covered his hand. "I'm refusing because I truly don't wish to marry you, because I don't wish to marry anyone. That's not going to change, no matter how many times you ask."

He pursed his mouth as if he wanted to argue, but all he said was, "Very well. If you're certain that's what you want."

She was certain, more than ever. Despite her regret at the hurt she might have caused, she left him with a sense of profound relief. Even Ernest could not mistake her this time. Her pride might prick at being left with no suitors at all, but if that earned her the right to live as she pleased, she would swallow every drop of pride she had.

And all she had to do was convince her parents they ought to let her.

AS SOON AS THE DUCHESS SAW ERNEST, AN ICY dread spread through her chest. She'd been so hopeful this time, so careful, even enlisting Peter to plead his case. Ernest had been good to Peter at school, his protector in the first years, his financial savior in the last. Were it not for his guidance, Peter might never have learned to stay out of debt. More than anyone, Merry's favorite brother knew Ernest's strengths. If his endorsement could not sway her, Lavinia did not know what voice of reason could.

"I'm sorry," Ernest said with a resignation that made her want to slap him. "I wish I had better news."

She swallowed against the panicked pounding of her heart. "I'm sure you did your best, dear. We'll simply have to try harder next time."

Ernest wagged his golden head. "She doesn't want there to be a next time."

"Of course she does." Hands clenched, Lavinia felt one of her nails snap inside her glove. "She's simply being stubborn. You and I both know marrying you is the best thing that could happen."

"I can't force her."

"Force her!" Lavinia's laugh was as sharp as cracking ice. "Darling, the girl doesn't know what's good for her. Come now." She patted his slumping back. "If you love her, she's worth a fight."

He stared at her, mute and miserable, as different from his father as he could be. Normally, she was glad for this; Ernest's decency eased her guilt. Tonight, though, she wished he had a fraction of his sire's Machiavellian spine.

"I'll speak to my husband," she said. "I'm sure between the two of us we can sort our daughter out."

As she returned along the passage to her guests, Lavinia spotted Althorp in the smoking room with her husband and a circle of other men. Behind the clouds of tobacco they were laughing, deep and rough, the way men will when women are not around. To her eyes Althorp stood out like a wolf among sheep, sleeker, slyer, more dangerously focused in his will. A second burst of laughter swelled. The resentment she felt at their ability to enjoy themselves was sharp.

No doubt Althorp had told one of his vaguely meanspirited jokes. He had a gift for that: making one laugh when one should not.

She couldn't help seeing that the other men, while amused, regarded Althorp more coolly than did her husband.

Geoffrey looked up just then and flashed her a happy grin.

Fool, she thought—though how could he know to distrust this friend and country neighbor? Her husband was not stupid but neither was he suspicious. The depths of Althorp's deceit were beyond his capacity to imagine.

Seeing his expression falter, she forced herself to smile and mime regret that she could not stop. In truth, she had not the nerve. She didn't want Althorp to read her most recent failure in her eyes.

As she left, her enemy's gaze fell like a weight upon her back.

*   *   *

THE STRENGTH OF HER FATHER'S FURY TOOK MERRY by surprise. She was so used to her mother's scolds she barely heard them. And why should she, when time and again her doting papa took her side? Alas, he did not take her side tonight, the measure of his anger being that he could not wait till morning to upbraid her, but must burst into her sitting room while old Ginny was combing out her hair.

"Merry," he said, his barrel chest swelling with indignation, "Lavinia tells me you refused Ernest's suit. Again."

To Merry's dismay, her mother swished stiffly in behind him. Her father wore his old quilted smoking jacket, but the duchess had not changed from her formal gown. The bodice hugged her in a daring plunge of blood-red silk.

"Ginny," said the duchess, with a nod for the startled maid.

Ginny had once been her mother's nurse and was now so arthritic her chores took twice as long as they should. Despite this, she was too attached to the family to accept their offers to pension her off. Merry feared if her parents ever pressed the issue, Ginny would go into a decline.

As might she. After all, a nearly blind, nearly deaf maid could be quite convenient.

Accustomed to ignoring the elderly servant, her father spoke as if she were not there.

"Well," he said, "is it true? Did you turn Ernest down?"

"Yes, Papa," she admitted and looked meekly at her hands. She meant to disarm him, but the appearance of humility seemed to anger him even more.

Or perhaps the presence of his wife made him want to look too strong to bend.

"Don't 'yes, Papa' me," he snapped. "Who else do you think will offer for you? Even the fortune hunters will give up. You're a hellion and everyone knows it. And don't think I haven't heard about that stunt you pulled last week. Riding hell-for-leather in Hyde Park. In breeches no less!"

"It was a dare, Papa," she explained, wishing she could speak to him alone. "None of your sons would have declined it."

"You're not one of my sons! You're my daughter. I've indulged you, no doubt. Given you too much rein. But, by God, I'm putting my foot down now. You'll marry Ernest Althorp or I'll know the reason why!"

"But I don't love him," she said, a tremor in her voice.

Her father's face turned the color of a brick. "Love has nothing to do with it. You simply can't stand the thought of a man having the right to tell you what to do. It's unnatural, Meredith, for a woman to be so willful. Do you want to end up a spinster? Do you want to die alone?"

"I'm only twenty."

"Twenty and impossible!" He threw up his hands and addressed the coffered ceiling. "I thought your moping after Greystowe was bad, but this! This is the limit, to refuse Ernest Althorp, a good, solid man who positively dotes on you."

"Does he, though, Papa?" Merry couldn't help but ask. "Everyone says he adores me, but I think he's more interested in pleasing his father than marrying me. When I turned him down, he hardly even argued."

"Good Lord, Merry. Allow the man some pride. Just because he doesn't turn your idiocy into a scene from the opera doesn't mean he doesn't care."

Merry swallowed, vaguely aware that Ginny's gnarled old hands had settled sympathetically on her shoulders. "I don't want a scene from the opera. I just—I just want—"

"Yes?" prompted her father with a sarcasm he'd never turned on her before. "I'd dearly love to hear what my fastidious daughter wants."

She tried to remind herself of what she'd seen in his portrait: the insecurity, the sense of being powerless in the face of change. He only wanted to protect her. That was the reason for his ire. She squared her shoulders and forced herself to meet his glare. She would speak to him as if they were alone, as if her mother weren't standing there, judging every word.

"I want a husband who'll let me be myself," she said, for once speaking nothing but the truth. "I don't want to be a bird in a cage; I want to be a woman in the world. Free to come and go. Free to read and think and speak just as I please. Dear as Ernest is, he wouldn't let me do that. You said it yourself, Papa. He has his pride. I know it sounds terrible to you, but I'd rather never marry than have to live as a proper wife."

Her declaration seemed to stun him. "What about children? Don't you want a family of your own?"

"I don't know that I do. Maybe with the right man. But until I find him"—she ventured a coaxing smile—"I can always borrow James's and Evelyn's. Their wives seem to pop out new ones every year."

"Merry," he said and shook his head from side to side.

Despite his concern, she sensed a weakening of his will. Praying inside, she clasped his big, broad hands: hands that had tossed her in the air and always caught her, hands that had paddled her when she misbehaved and ruffled her awful hair when she made him laugh. He had spoiled her and she loved him for it.

But her mother was determined not to let him spoil her now.

"Darling," she said to Merry, her hand on her husband's coat. The duke shook himself as if her touch had woken him from a dream. "You know this decision does not affect you alone. Think of the scandal to the family, to your brothers and their wives should their youngest sister stay on the shelf. Really, dear, if we thought you'd find the paragon you describe we might allow it, but it's time we all faced facts. If you don't marry Ernest, you will not marry anyone."

Merry had known everyone thought this, but no one had said it to her face. How much it hurt was hard to believe.

"I'm sorry for the inconvenience to my siblings," she said, with a quaver she could not overcome. "But I'm not afraid to be alone. Better a spinster than a slave."

"A slave," repeated her father. He eased his hands from her pleading grip. "Is that what you think I've made your mother? Is that what you call your brothers' wives?"

"Of course not, Papa." She flushed at the truth of the accusation. "I only meant—"

"Your father and I have discussed this," her mother broke

in, her palm still bracing her husband's back. "For your own good, we are determined to save you from yourself."

"But—"

"For your own good," she repeated, her jaw as firm as iron. "We're giving you a week, Meredith, to reconsider your position. At the end of that week, if you have not come to your senses, we shall put your horses on the block."

"No," Merry protested, the shock like a kick to her gut. Not her horses. Not Flick and Sergei and her new Arabian mare. She tried to catch her father's gaze but he would not meet her eye.

"That's not all," her mother added, her voice so low Merry knew old Ginny could not hear. "Once your horses are gone, we're going to make some changes in the staff. We're going to hire a real lady's maid, one who can keep you on a lead."

"No," she said, a whisper this time. The thought that they'd find her a keeper didn't bother her half as much as the thought of losing Ginny. "You can't, Papa. I don't believe it."

Her father cleared his throat. "You know what you have to do if you want to stop it."

Still not looking at her, he strode to the threshold and paused. "A week," he said, and pulled the door shut behind him.

The fire crackled in the silence as his footsteps faded down the hall. Merry's face was hot and a pulse beat raggedly in her neck. Tears burgeoned behind her eyes but she fought them back. She was not going to cry. She was not.

But she almost did when her mother stroked her cheek. Merry's senses must have been more disordered than she thought, because her mother's fingers seemed to shake. Her tone was caressing. "It's for your own good, darling. Truly, it is."

Merry pressed her lips together. She could not speak for fear of saying the unforgivable. As if she sensed her turmoil, Ginny's brush resumed its careful stroking of her hair.

"Perhaps you should leave now, Lavi," the maid said

with the familiarity and the tenderness of one who knew the family well. "Give everyone a chance to settle down."

Lavinia started at the sound of her voice, but did not disagree. "Yes," she said dazedly, "perhaps I should."

Merry did not release her tears until her mother had left the room. Even then, she struggled to contain her angry sobs. She had never liked crying, not even as a child.

"Don't you worry," said Ginny, her strokes as steady as a stable lad currying a horse he meant to soothe. "Sometimes a creature has to follow its heart. Sometimes its nature doesn't give it a choice."

Her words made Merry's tears fall all the harder. Her own mother didn't understand her as well as her dear old nurse. She couldn't believe her father would really let Ginny go. Simply couldn't. Not if she lived a hundred years.

Which left her with one conclusion.

Her mother was the evil genius behind her father's stand.

A NIGHT OF RESTLESS SLEEP HADN'T SHAKEN Merry's conviction. Her father hated punishing her, even when she deserved it. So now she had no choice. She had to change her mother's mind before she could change her father's. No matter how long the odds, this was a challenge from which she could not shrink.

Not surprisingly, she found the duchess closeted with her dresser. The changing tides of fashion were the chief concern of her mother's life. When Merry proved not only indifferent but a poor frame on which to hang an elegant gown, Lavinia had lost most of her interest in her daughter. *She's a fencepost,* she'd lament to anyone who'd listen. *Gets it from her father's side.* And then she'd run her hands down her own more generous curves, as if anyone could possibly doubt her claim.

Merry didn't think her mother did this to be cruel. She simply could not conceive of a life where anything mattered

more than being perfectly turned out. To be fair, were it not
for the duchess's efforts, Merry knew she'd be considered
even plainer than she was. And her mother could be affec-
tionate, in her absentminded way, though Merry was
tempted to forget that now.

When she entered the suite, Lavinia was standing before
a cheval glass. Her dresser, a woman even more ancient than
Ginny, was known only as Madame. She rarely spoke, English or French, but was, despite her age, a genius with a
needle. Merry's mother would order her gowns cut by Worth
in Paris, then have them stitched at home. This was not for
economy's sake; Lavinia scorned such schemes. She had
Madame sew her clothes because the woman could fit a
dress like a second skin.

At the moment, she and the seamstress were draping
lengths of cloth across her bosom, apparently seeking the
ideal color for a gown.

"The emerald plaid camel hair, I think," said Lavinia,
"with the matching silk for the bodice and underskirt."

"The color is good," Madame agreed with an inscrutable
pursing of her lips.

"Mother?" said Merry, before the two could continue
what was sure to be a long discussion.

Lavinia spied her in the mirror. "If you're here to ask me
to intercede with your father, there's nothing I can do. He is
the head of this household. Besides, I agree with him. Remember how glum you were when James and Evelyn wed?
Imagine how you'll feel when Peter marries and all your
friends have families, too. Women need occupation. And
don't tell me you want to be one of those female postal
clerks. Even you couldn't be that mad."

Merry hoped her mother couldn't hear her grind her
teeth. "I have a plan," she said, struggling to sound pleasant
and self-assured. "I've had one for years."

Her mother raised her brows, but before she could respond the butler knocked on the open door. "Pardon, Your
Grace. Sir Patrick Althorp has just sent up his card."

Her mother went so pale Merry feared that she would
faint. She recovered with a toss of her well-coifed head.

"For goodness sake!" she exclaimed, her cheeks now brightly pink. "Can't you see I am not at home to visitors? Tell the baronet I'll see him later."

And she dismissed the butler with a wave of her elegant hand.

"Is something wrong?" Merry asked, surprised by her response. Lately, the duchess and Ernest's father had been as thick as thieves. The duke didn't seem to mind, but sometimes Merry wondered at his unconcern. She herself did not like the man. He was too watchful, she thought, like a serpent about to strike. "Have you and Sir Patrick fallen out?"

Her mother exhaled loudly but did not confirm this budding hope. Instead, she swapped the green plaid she'd been holding for a deep magenta satin. The color looked fine to Merry, but both Lavinia and Madame immediately shook their heads. Once the offending bolt was set aside, her mother's reflection met her eyes. "You were speaking of a plan?"

"Yes," Merry said, trying to gather her powers of persuasion. "Once I come into Grandmama's money, I want to breed Arabians. I'm sure I can make a go of it. You have to admit I have every qualification I could need."

"Every qualification but one," said her mother. "As far as I know, you have yet to grow a penis."

The shock of this blunt speech tied Merry's tongue. "I don't . . . I don't need a penis to . . ."

"Merry." Her mother silenced her spluttering retort. "Be reasonable. First of all, you won't receive that trust for ages. And second, what man would marry a woman who ran a stud?"

"But I don't want to marry. That's what I've been saying all along."

"You *think* you don't want to marry, but believe me—"

Merry covered her face and fought a scream.

"Believe me," her mother continued, "you'll feel differently when you're thirty and all alone."

Merry sensed this was not the moment to mention her plan to have affairs. Being unmarried did not, after all, mean living like a nun. "I won't feel differently," was all she said as she let her hands drop to her sides. "I know you and Papa only want me to be happy, but I'm sure I wouldn't be happy as Ernest's wife."

"Nonsense," her mother scoffed. "Ernest Althorp is a perfectly nice boy. And far from repulsive. Good manners. Good teeth. Strong as an ox. Plus, I've always liked blond men."

Then why don't you marry him, she thought, but was shrewd enough to keep the words inside.

"Come now," said her mother, her tone light, her expression strangely hard. "You're being overly romantic, which I never thought of as one of your faults. Trust me, a love match is not the least bit like a novel."

"I don't care about a love match. I care about being free."

"Free?" Her mother's laugh was anything but joyful. "Dearest, only whores and rich widows are truly free."

"You don't understand," Merry said.

"I do," her mother insisted. "I simply don't agree."

After that, there was nothing to say.

UNDER LEADEN SKIES, MERRY GALLOPED HER MARE flat out across the Knightsbridge grounds, pushing the horse until steam rose from her flanks and clods of turf flew out from her pounding hooves. Even this did not soothe her. How could it, when Flick, the horse she'd bottle-fed as a foal, might soon be carrying a stranger?

There had to be a way to get her father to retreat. She couldn't surrender, not when surrendering meant making both herself and Ernest wretched.

On the other hand, could she really forego the greatest pleasure of her life? Give up her horses? Let them pass out of her care? Worse, could she risk old Ginny's future?

Damnation. If only her mother weren't so immovable! Merry wasn't sure she had the right to make her father choose between his daughter and his wife. Nor—which was worse, if she was honest—was she certain his decision would come down on her side.

She slowed Flick to a walk, her breath coming as heavily

as the mare's. Clearly exhilarated, the horse frisked underneath her. What spirit she had! And how horribly Merry would miss her! She wished Evelyn and James hadn't left for the country, though she knew they did not support her position. Her whole family was against her, every one.

Without their help, she didn't know what she could do.

ISABEL AT LEAST PROVIDED A DISTRACTION. SHE was full of news when Merry saw her that afternoon. Her father-in-law had died unexpectedly and her husband was now an earl.

"Which makes me a countess," she said, sounding strangely wistful. Sprawled on her back on Merry's four-poster bed, she wore a gray and black bias-striped walking dress. The hem of the overskirt, fetchingly draped and piled, was trimmed with tasseled braid. Even Lavinia had clucked in appreciation as she passed. Isabel's current pose would not do the outfit good, but at the moment she did not care.

Merry sat beside her on the bed. "You're not happy about being a countess?"

"Oh, I suppose I'm happy. I didn't really know Andrew's father, so I can't pretend I'll miss him. But we'll be in mourning just forever. As it is, I barely snuck out of the house wearing this. It's as gloomy as a crypt, Mer. All the mirrors covered. All the drives muffled in straw." Wrinkling her nose, she plucked at her handsome gown. "I'm too young to wear crape."

"I don't know, I think black makes you look ethereal."

Isabel grinned and covered Merry's hand. A moment later, she remembered her complaints. "We're leaving for the estate the day after tomorrow. It's in Wales, Merry. Wales! Some unpronounceable, godforsaken place. Lord knows how long we'll be there. According to Andrew, his father was a cheeseparing old goat who let the place go to ruin. It'll take ages to put things in order the way he wants."

"But surely *you* don't have to stay all that time."

Isabel blushed and busied herself straightening the tassels on her sleeve. "Andrew says he doesn't sleep well anymore unless I'm with him." Her color deepened at Merry's snort. "Yes, I know. I said he was fat and boring, and he is, except . . ."

"Except?"

"Except it is rather comforting to have him close at night, holding me, you know."

Merry could imagine few things less comforting than being held all night by a controlling prig like Andrew Beckett. With an effort, she held her tongue. "Well," she said resignedly. "It looks as if we'll both be prisoners of rectitude for a while."

Isabel hummed in sympathy, then wagged the tips of her black kid shoes. "Merry, I was wondering, are you certain you don't want to marry Ernest Althorp?"

"Not you, too," she groaned. "I'm glad you're content, Isabel, but surely you know that wouldn't be the case for me. Or for Ernest. Can you imagine him trying to put me on a check-rein? We'd be at each other's throats."

"I suppose," Isabel conceded and rolled up onto her elbow. "I simply don't see how you're going to get your parents off your back. Of course, you could keep me company at Caerna-whatsis. Nothing much to do there, you understand, but Andrew's father kept a decent stable and at least you'd have a respite from your mother's scolds."

"You didn't see her face. She's never going to let this go, no matter how long I stay away. What I should do is pretend to go with you, then run off to join the music hall. After that, even Mother would have to give up on marrying me."

"Ha ha," said Isabel, "as if you could even sing."

Merry had meant the idea as a joke, but now it sparked a thought. "Wait," she said. "I know what we need, what both of us deserve."

"I'm sure I don't want to know," said her friend, but her eyes were immediately alight. She was not, apparently, a proper countess yet.

"A prank," said Merry, her blood beginning to hum with anticipation, "like we used to play at school. One last hurrah before our families skewer us on the stake of respectability."

Both she and Isabel were sitting up now, clasping each

other's hands. "Nothing too dangerous," Isabel cautioned, "and nothing we'll be caught at."

"Cross my heart," Merry assured her. "No one will know but you and I."

THE ESCAPADE COULD NOT HAVE GONE BETTER. The music hall in Soho had held a number of middle class families, even a few unattended females like themselves, all outfitted respectably—including the ones they suspected of being women of ill repute. Indeed, Merry and Isabel were underdressed, clad as they were in clothes borrowed from their maids.

The program, too, was all they could desire: a humorous *pose plastique* with men dressed as Greek goddesses reenacting the Judgment of Paris, a bawdy but not indelicate skit called "The Spare Bed," and a number of surprisingly talented singers, the last of whom had pretended to search the audience for a husband.

Merry hummed the refrain about *single young gentlemen, how do you do* as the hired hansom cab dropped them off before Merry's house. Happily, its high brick wall shielded them from sight. The hour was late, the streets nearly empty. Wanting to make sure her friend was safe, she escorted Isabel to her carriage.

The smart five-glass landau waited in the narrow lane between the Knightsbridge house and its nearest neighbor. Once inside, Isabel would pull the shades and change into her own dress, now completely black, while hiding any irregularities of fastening beneath her coat. Then she'd return home to her unsuspecting husband. He, bless him, was under the impression she'd been visiting an ailing friend.

As she invariably did at the end of a prank, Isabel grew fearful. "Be careful," she begged as Merry handed her up the carriage step. "Don't linger in the lane. It's foggy tonight. I want you to go straight to your door."

"I will," Merry promised, and kissed her friend's cheek.

Chuckling to herself at Isabel's nerves—for what could go wrong now?—she pressed a gold sovereign into the coachman's palm. "Take care of her," she said, though the driver and she both knew she meant *take care not to tell.*

With a nod and a grin, he flicked the reins across the horses' backs. Merry watched them pull away. From the sound of it, the leader needed his shoes picked, but that was nothing the Beckett's groom couldn't handle when they got home.

Shrugging off the concern, she followed the long brick wall to the servant's sidegate.

The man must have been waiting in the shadows. She neither saw nor heard him when he grabbed her from behind, hooking her neck and waist to drag her forcibly off the footpath.

A second of frozen shock delayed her scream. That was enough for the man to get his palm across her mouth. She struggled then, violently, but her strength was no match for his. He cursed under his breath when she kicked his shin, but other than that he did not speak.

He seemed quite focused on what he meant to do.

Whatever that was, it involved pulling her around the corner toward the street. He must have a vehicle there, she thought, or perhaps he intended to knock her out and stuff her in a cab. She'd look like a drunken maid out with her gent. No one would give them a second glance, especially here, where the houses were spread out and set back on their grounds.

Her heart hammered in her chest, her mind racing, her nose filled with the stench of tobacco and rank male sweat. She flailed for a hitching ring in the wall, but the man didn't give her a chance to grab it. Then she spied the golden circle of a streetlamp up ahead. If she screamed there and struggled very hard, someone would have to look out and see.

At least, she prayed they would. Oh, if only she'd left right away, or had the carriage wait somewhere else. She didn't know what this man wanted but she could guess. And maybe what he wanted was worse than what she guessed.

She could die tonight.

Sickness rose in her belly. She had to swallow to keep it

down. His silence, his intentness was unnerving. She would have felt better if he'd threatened her, but the only noise he made was the heavy soughing of his breath.

She tried kicking him again but her legs were tangled in her skirts.

Bloody things, she thought. Bloody, bloody stupid things.

He had her off her feet now. Her heels didn't even drag. The hand he'd clamped around her waist was making it hard to breathe. Or maybe the effect was simply fear. She felt like a doll as he carried her, not a person at all. But she couldn't think about that now. Not about slit throats and bloody knives. They had almost reached the lamppost. She had to take her chance.

She pretended to sag in her captor's arms, then bucked wildly as they hit the edge of misty light.

She managed a shriek, short and high, before the man slammed her scarf-wrapped skull against the brick. The cheap wool was no shield. Spots bloomed before her eyes, but she knew she could not afford to swoon. Frantically, she blinked her vision clear.

Then she saw it, a second figure running toward them down the street, a man in an Inverness coat. He shouted as he ran: "Hey! Hey there!"

The man who held her shoved her aside. He turned to escape but the second man grabbed him. They scuffled with their coats flapping—her captor's short, her rescuer's long. Their arms grappled for purchase like wrestlers at a fair. With a boarlike grunt, her attacker smashed his forehead into Long Coat's. Long Coat let go and drove his fist into the other's belly.

The uppercut was a prize winner. Merry could hear the *oof* from where she huddled against the wall. Her attacker dropped to his knees, gasping, then scrambled to his feet and ran away. The gaslight caught a slice of his face, coarse and unfamiliar. Then he disappeared into the murky night.

The whole fight hadn't lasted more than a minute.

"You all right, miss?" asked a kind, breathless voice.

Merry forced her chin away from the spot where it was

tucked into her chest. The voice belonged to Long Coat, her rescuer. She was shaking too much to answer, almost too much to nod.

How odd that was: now that she was safe she could not move.

"I'm afraid he got away," the man said. Gingerly, he touched his bloodied forehead. "Stunned me a bit. Guess his head was harder than mine."

His grin was wide and slightly wry. Merry's lips twitched, but couldn't quite form a smile. Her rescuer seemed to understand. "There," he said comfortingly, crouching down beside her. "Had a scare, didn't you?"

"Y-yes," she said, the answer shaken by the chattering of her teeth.

"Only natural. You sit a minute and catch your breath. Then I'll see you safely to where you're going."

He smelled different from the other, clean and soapy and faintly of—she wrinkled her nose—yes, he smelled faintly of linseed oil.

Just as she realized who he must be, he offered an un-gloved hand. She laid hers in its palm, where he covered it very gently. His hands weren't the largest she'd ever seen but they were graceful and they felt strong. The strangest sensation rippled through her, perhaps the strangest of the night, as if her whole being wanted to yield itself to his care. Nothing could have been further from her nature, and yet she could not deny the intensity of the response.

This, she thought, is how other women feel about their men.

"I'm Nicolas Craven," he said, calling her back from her distraction, "at your very humble service."

"Merry," she replied dazedly, then shook herself. "Mary, er, Colfax."

"Well, Mary Colfax, do you think your legs are steady enough for me to escort you home?"

She nodded, but they weren't because when he helped her up, she almost fell back down. She would have, in fact, if he hadn't caught her against his chest.

"Hm," he said with a gravelly chuckle, "perhaps we were a bit too optimistic."

His hold wasn't what she expected from a supposedly notorious rake. Under the circumstances, it was as polite as it could be. As soon as she found her footing, his hands moved from her back to her elbows. They stood in the outermost arc of the lamplight, his gaze quiet and considering on her face.

"Was it someone you knew?" he asked softly.

Her eyes widened. "No," she said, shocked by the suggestion that she'd know someone who would hurt her. "No, I've never seen that man in my life. He just grabbed me and—" She shuddered. "I don't think he knew who I was, either. I was simply there at the wrong time."

The painter's lips formed a thin, harsh line. "That makes me sorrier then."

"Sorrier?"

"That I let him get away."

"Oh," she said, her shudder returning.

Seeing it, he chafed her shoulders through her coat. His eyes twinkled reassuringly. "There. I've gone and spooked you, which I never meant to do to such a pretty spark of gold."

Merry's hand flew to her disordered hair. Gold it might be, but hardly pretty. In spite of herself, she had to squelch a tiny flare of female pride. Surely he was only being kind.

But he wasn't. The tip of his index finger drew a line across her brow and down her cheek, the touch a shimmer along her nerves. Without warning, her face prickled with sensitivity: her lips, the tip of her nose, the delicate skin around her eyes. She tried to recall if she'd ever felt the like, then stopped when she realized her mouth was hanging open.

Amazingly, her rescuer seemed lost in admiration.

"Look at these bones," he murmured, his gaze following the path of his featherlight caress. "Look at this gorgeous skin. I'd pay a guinea a day to paint you, love, and consider the coin well spent."

"Paint me!" She almost choked on the words. "You want to paint *me*?"

He tugged a curl from beneath her scarf, testing it between his thumb and finger. His mouth curved in a smile. "Yes," he said. "Do you think your employers would give you time away?"

But look at me, she wanted to say. I'm plain as a pikestaff. What idiot would want to paint me? The obvious hope in his eyes was all that kept the words inside.

Well, that and her ludicrous longing to believe him.

"I assure you," he said, misinterpreting her silence, "I am who I say. I just came from that house over there, to change a broken frame. Here." He rummaged inside the caped woolen sweep of his winter coat. "Here's my card."

Somewhat befuddled, Merry peered at it in the lamplight. "Nicolas Craven, Artist," said the tiny black letters, followed by an address in St. John's Wood.

"I believe you are who you say," she admitted, not yet ready to accept the rest.

"Then you'll ask your employers' permission to pose?"

She shook her head, more in wonder than refusal. A thought was beginning to form: what it would mean if she said yes, how it might change her value on the marriage mart. What had Isabel's mother said? *No decent woman would sit for him.*

As if sensing her hesitation, Mr. Craven jerked his chin toward her parents' house, a rise of Georgian marble behind the wall. "Is this where you work? For the Vances? I could speak to them, if you like. Make sure the job wouldn't endanger your position."

The offer, kindly as it was meant, restored her common sense. Even supposing she had been a maid, her mother would never tolerate the presence of a servant who'd sat for the infamous Nic Craven—no more than she'd tolerate one with followers. That his manner held nothing of lechery would not matter; his reputation would be sufficient to condemn her.

All the more reason to agree, hissed the little devil in her ear. You'd ruin yourself but good if you let him paint you.

Besides which, if he's as much a gentleman as he seems, you might not have to ruin yourself in truth.

Caught by indecision, she looked at him, really looked, for the first time since her rescue. From her glimpse of him in the house, she knew he was slender and untidy. Now she saw he was also handsome. Never had she seen a man with eyes so wonderfully expressive. One moment they twinkled boyishly. The next they were ironic. The humorous stretch of his mouth made her want to smile along. His bones were as fine as he'd claimed hers were. His nose, narrow and aquiline, was entirely without flaw. His jaw might have been too sharp for beauty, but it lent his face a strength it would otherwise have lacked. All of which came together to form a visage both individual and attractive.

And knowing. That most of all. She could see it in his eyes. This man had plumbed the secrets she'd always wanted to explore. This man had tasted freedoms she could only dream of. A face like Nicolas Craven's promised things.

Merry could imagine how it might make a woman weak.

"I can't," she said with true regret. The devil on her shoulder groaned, but she could not accept his offer, not even if she could devise a way to keep it secret from her parents. A daughter's reputation reflected on her family. No matter how angry Merry was, hers didn't deserve to be treated with so little consideration.

"Don't say you can't," coaxed Mr. Craven, the plea a sweet temptation. "Say you'll think about it. An artist doesn't find such inspiration every day."

Oh, how she wanted to believe him! Her hand clenched around his card, the pull to accept a palpable force. Her chest ached with it, and something deeper, something only one man had ever called from her before.

"I can't," she said again, then slipped inside the gate before his charm, and her foolish susceptibility, could make her turn around.

*   *   *

"I WANT PROGRESS," ALTHORP INTONED, "NOT promises."

Like dragon's breath, his words formed puffs of white in the misty predawn air. He'd instructed Lavinia to meet him in Rotten Row, inside the Albert Gate. The Serpentine was frozen, of course, but they were spared the hordes of skaters by the earliness of the hour. Only the groundskeepers threatened their less than splendid isolation.

Lavinia didn't know if Althorp thought he'd been seen too often in her house or if he simply wanted to prove his power to order her about. Either way, the furtive, solitary trip to get here had done nothing to calm her nerves. She hadn't dared use their carriage and had been forced to go on foot. No doubt her reckless daughter would have thought nothing of the walk, but every shadow, every sound had Lavinia jumping in her skin. Fighting to steady herself, she clutched her hands inside her sealskin muff.

"I've put events into motion," she said. "It's only a matter of time."

"You've threatened," corrected Althorp, his voice like curdled scorn. "You've pleaded, you've lied, and you've spread a fair amount of gossip. Beyond that, I have yet to see you act."

"I shall act. I had to warn her. To give her a chance."

"A chance to do what: talk your husband round? Even I know your daughter better than to think a warning will suffice. Dismiss the maid, Lavinia. Only that will teach her you mean what you say."

His arm rose and his large gloved hand formed a V against her neck. His hold was so firm she could barely swallow.

"You're hurting me," she whispered.

"Am I?" His eyes glittered strangely in the fog, watching her mouth, watching his hand. His color was suddenly higher, his breath more swift. "You used to like when I did this; used to melt like butter in July."

"Patrick." His Christian name wrenched from her. She hadn't meant to use it, not ever, not again. The slip seemed to satisfy his urge to shame her. He smiled and dropped his arm.

He was gone before she could protest, before she could plead with him to escort her safely home.

Coward, she thought, her chin quivering on the verge of tears. She had never hated herself more than when she knew she would obey his every word.

ALWAYS AN EARLY RISER, MERRY WAS HALF DRESSED by the time the maid came in with a tray of tea and biscuits. She was young; new, Merry thought without surprise. In a household like theirs, the staff was subject to frequent change. This, to Merry's mind, was all the more reason to cherish an old retainer like . . .

The thought ground to a halt as an awful suspicion formed. She closed the book she'd been reading and rose from her chair.

"Where's Ginny?" she demanded, the words as sharp as striking hooves.

She willed the maid to tell her Ginny was in bed with an ache or a creaky knee. Instead, the girl cut her eyes away like someone who does not want to break bad news. She fussed with the arrangement of the tray. "Er, I'm not sure who you mean, Lady Merry."

"Don't lie to me," Merry snapped, her hand flashing out to catch the maid's retreating arm. The girl trembled, her eyes showing white. Merry forced her voice to soften. "I'm not mad at you. I understand why you don't want to tell me. But I really need to know where Ginny is."

"I—" said the maid, then cleared the nervousness from her throat. "I heard she's been let go, sent off to her sister in Devon."

"What? This morning?"

"Yes, Lady Merry. Mr. Leeds put her on the first train out of St. Pancras. Your mother—begging your pardon—didn't even give her time to pack. Said her things'd be sent after."

Merry released the maid's wrist and thrust both hands

through her tousled hair. Ginny was gone. Shoved on a train like a sack of bad potatoes.

She stood and paced to the window, needing air, no matter how cold.

Her mother had fired Ginny.

And Papa had let her do it.

This changed everything.

If her parents could do this to an innocent, to an elderly woman who'd never done anything but serve them faithfully and well . . .

They didn't deserve her consideration, didn't deserve the love that even now twisted painfully in her heart.

A rip sounded as Merry inadvertently tore her green satin drapes.

The maid gulped back a frightened whimper. "Shall I— Will you be wanting my help to finish dressing?"

For a moment, Merry could not answer: she was so caught up in what this meant. When her mind cleared and she once again saw the agitated maid, her decision was already firm.

"Yes," she said. "Please lay out the dark-brown habit with the velvet trim."

The maid bobbed a shaky curtsey and withdrew. Merry scarcely noticed. She knew what she had to do, down to the smallest detail, as if she'd been planning it all along.

First, though, she was going to give the best performance of her life. Otherwise, the duchess would not believe she meant to visit Isabel in Wales, where—so Merry would claim—she intended to contemplate the error of her ways. She'd protest and she'd plead, but mostly she'd be shaken. She'd imply she might well marry Ernest Althorp on her return.

Once that ground was laid, she'd give Isabel a stack of letters to mail on her behalf, carefully composed to demonstrate the progressive weakening of her will. Thankfully, her mother was an incurious correspondent. In her supreme self-absorption, she wouldn't think to ask for details about either her daughter or her supposed hosts. A mention of the weather or some dull specific regarding the earl's assumption of his duties would have her eyes glazing with indifference. Only signs of remorse would catch the duchess's attention, only hints of capitulation. And if her mother should make demands or probe, Isabel could fake Merry's hand well enough to dash an appropriately evasive postscript.

Add to this a trunk full of clothes "for Wales" and her mother would be convinced her daughter was where she said.

Merry knew her friend would love the scheme, if only for the spice it would add to her long, dull days in mourning black.

Her sole regret was that Ernest, even more than her mother, was sure to believe the lie.

FARNHAM LET NIC SLEEP TILL NOON, AT WHICH
point he must have lost patience with his master's sloth. The
evening before had been bad enough: having to pry him from
his bed just to change that broken frame for the duke of Monmouth. Nic hadn't wanted to go, but he supposed he was glad
Farnham forced him, even if he had sat for an hour afterward
at the police station, waiting to give a description he sincerely doubted anyone wanted to follow up. London's bob-
bies couldn't be bothered investigating crimes that hadn't
happened. Nor had they been pleased by his refusal to reveal
the victim's name. Why they expected him to, he couldn't
guess. They knew as well as he a servant could be dismissed
for sillier reasons than having the misfortune to be attacked.

Nic wondered if Farnham would let him sleep if he knew
his master had been a hero.

Deciding it wasn't worth finding out, he shaded his eyes

as the butler threw open the drapes. Sadly, the precaution was unnecessary. The fog lingered, curling against the windows.

Nic groaned at the gloom that enfolded him at the sight. He hated winter in London. Hanging would be better than waking up to this.

"I've brought coffee," said Farnham, "and the paper."

Nic pushed himself blearily upright. "What? No more letters from my mother?"

Farnham denied this as solemnly as if he didn't know what sarcasm was.

"What about a caller? A young lady on the small side. Fair curly hair. Might have been interested in sitting?" Though Nic didn't really expect the girl to change her mind, Farnham's answer still disappointed.

"No, sir," he said. "But a young man did come by looking for employment."

From the carefully uninflected tone of Farnham's voice, Nic could tell he'd wanted to help. Spit and polish notwithstanding, his butler was a soft touch.

"Can we use him?" he asked, straightening the covers across his lap.

Farnham settled the tray before he answered. "The gardener is getting on in years, and Mrs. Choate could keep him busy in the kitchen for the winter."

"Seem likely to steal the plate?"

"No, sir. He was surprisingly well spoken. Must have gone to one of the national schools. He said his parents work at the gasworks near Regent's Park."

Nic pulled a face. The two great chimneys across the park did their bit to add another layer of foulness to the pall now smothering London. The working conditions were atrocious. No one who'd seen Doré's engraving of the works in South Lambeth could doubt it. Like one of the circles of Hell. Twelve hours a day. Seven days a week. He didn't wonder a boy would rather scrub pots than follow his parents there.

Pushing this disagreeable thought aside, he took a sip of Farnham's varnish-peeling coffee. The powerful brew inspired a pleasure no depression could obscure. Mrs. Choate had her virtues—an excellent pickle being among them—but Farnham made coffee fit for a man.

"Shall I hire him then, sir?"

"Mm?" said Nic, still wallowing in the drink.

"The boy. Would you like me to hire him?"

Nic shrugged. "Don't see why not. When Mrs. Choate returns from her sister's, I imagine she'll enjoy having someone new to boss around."

"Very good," said Farnham, and handed him the freshly ironed paper. Since the butler continued to hover, Nic suspected he was in for another of that worthy's lectures.

"Yes?" he said, not bothering to hide his annoyance.

"If you wouldn't mind my saying, sir—"

"And if I would?" Nic muttered.

"It has been my experience," Farnham pressed on, "that some light physical activity, or perhaps a visit to a friend, would do far more to lighten your mood than this . . . this torpor."

Nic narrowed his eyes. "I happen to like this torpor. As for my moods, they're an unavoidable outgrowth of my gift."

"I'm sure it's comfortable for you to think so, sir, but—"

"Farnham," said Nic, the warning razor sharp.

Like any old campaigner, the butler knew when to retreat. "Very well, sir," he said. "I'll be in my pantry should you need me."

As soon as he'd closed the door, Nic moved the tray and threw off the covers. Sparring with his butler might not be the twenty laps around the house Farnham had in mind, but it had put a bit of heat in his veins.

He finished his coffee as he dressed: trousers today rather than a robe. He thrust his arms into a clean, starched shirt, then frowned at the line of garish waistcoats that hung in his cedar wardrobe. Bother that. And bother shoes as well. He wasn't going anywhere, and no one was coming here.

He might, however, have just enough energy to send a note to his man of business. See if any new commissions had come in. What Nic wouldn't give for a trip to Paris! Not tomorrow, perhaps, but in a week or so—once he was back to his old self.

Too lazy to button his shirt, he clumped down the stairs with the tails flapping around his hips. "More coal!" he called as his bare feet hit the chilly marble inlay in the hall.

From the corner of his eye he saw a shadow flit in the direction of the kitchen. It couldn't have been Farnham because it didn't stop.

"You there," he said. "New boy."

The shadow froze, then reluctantly turned without coming closer. The boy's gangly shape inspired a nostalgic humor. Nic remembered being that age, all legs and elbows and fits of shyness. If it was shyness. The way the boy hunched into his shoulders made Nic wonder if he were expecting some sort of scold.

"Settling in all right?" he asked more gently.

The shadow mumbled something that probably meant yes.

"You don't have to be afraid of us," Nic assured him. "I know Farnham seems a bit regimental, but as long as you try your best, he'll more than do right by you."

"Yes, sir," said the boy, then started edging farther off. "I'll just fetch that coal you wanted."

The sudden rapping of the doorknocker did nothing to call him back.

Bloody hell, thought Nic. Can't train anyone these days.

Fortunately for his mood, the figure on the stoop called forth an immediate smile.

It was the maid from the night before. The single spot of color in the mist, she wore a hideous tweed coat over an even more hideous orange dress. Its skirt was stained and the ruffles around its hem draggled as if they'd been stepped on. Indeed, they might have been. Both coat and gown hung on their wearer like a sack. Last night she had not seemed this small. Now he saw she was a slip of a thing, not merely short, but tiny. Nor was her size the only trait he'd failed to appreciate by gaslight. He could not have missed her freckles, but her eyes, an interesting sunstruck umber hue, were as bright as the day was not.

Her hair, what he could see beneath her muddy brown knitted scarf, was quite remarkable. He'd guessed it was fair but hadn't expected this blazing mix of red and gold. Kinked by the weather, it was so curly and thick it seemed alive. Like faerie dew, beads of moisture clung to its rippling waves.

In spite of his ennui, his fingers itched for his paints.

"Don't tell me," he said, verging on a laugh, "Farnham tracked you down to jolly me from my gloom."

"I beg your pardon," said his visitor, drawing herself up. Nic had never seen a woman stand that straight. She looked like a little soldier with her shoulders thrust back and her jaw stuck out. Her nose, he noticed, had a funny turned-up ball on the end, like a forgotten bit of clay. Retroussé, a Frenchman would have said, but the word could not convey its winsome humor. A smudge of ash marred the skin of her freckled cheek. What a face, he thought. What a wonderfully unforgettable face.

Too bad he couldn't say as much for her name.

"Forgive me," he said as he racked his brains. "Obviously, you are here on your own initiative. Won't you come in and state your business? I shouldn't like a young lady to stand on my doorstep growing chilled."

Calling her a lady might be a stretch, for no true lady came to a gentleman's home alone. Nic had found, however, that most females, no matter how humble, liked to be spoken to as ladies. Unless they were ladies, he thought wryly, recalling how titillated Amanda Piggot had been by his supposedly common touch. But he had no desire to offend this young woman, not when she had most likely come to grant his dearest wish.

Despite his cordiality, his invitation seemed to unnerve her. Perhaps she wasn't as worldly as he'd thought. After a slight hesitation, she stepped past him into the relative warmth of his foyer.

"It is rather cold," she conceded. Her voice was low in pitch, boyish almost: a tinge of stable mixed with a hint of manor. This one, he thought with amusement, had aspirations. Clearly, his furnishings caught her eye. She strolled the circumference beneath the dome, pausing to study a statue of a sleek Egyptian cat. The treasure was carved in basalt and bore a gold-and-lapis collar around its neck. Her hand, gloved in coarse green wool, touched the smooth front paws.

She turned and, for one brief moment, looked as regal as the puss. Little duchess, he thought, his smile too broad to keep inside.

"I wish to know," she said, with that same self-possession, "if you're still looking for a model."

"I might be," he said, then broke into a laugh.

Unable to resist, he began to circle her. His hand caught the end of her scarf and unwrapped it as he went. She uttered a startled sound, but did not fight him, her eyes on his face as he slowly revealed her glory. Three long pins held her hair to her head in a messy lump. Feeling like a naughty schoolboy, he pulled them free. Curls fell, masses of them. Her hair was magic beneath the watery illumination of the skylight, the ends dancing with static, the color indescribable. Past her waist it tumbled, past her hips, a blanket behind which Lady Godiva could easily have hidden. His hands curled into fists. He wanted to paint her like that, naked on a horse, riding proud through the heart of town, making a triumph of what her husband had meant to be a shame.

Come to think of it, Nic needed a centerpiece for his next show. Something provocative. Something the jaded art world could not ignore.

"Take off your coat," he said, his voice hoarse with his urge to see the rest of her.

A wash of peony pink crept up her cheek. "I am not a whore," she said. "Just because my . . . my employer cast me off doesn't mean I'm anyone's for the taking."

"Cast you off?" Her words were a dash of cold reality. "Because of what happened to you last night?"

Hanging her head, she put the toe of one boot atop the other.

"Idiot," he said, and her head jerked in alarm. "Not you, love. Your employer." He cupped the side of her face, pitying her trouble with all his heart. Just once, why couldn't the men of his class respect the women in their care? "Did he try to force himself on you?"

Her mouth dropped and she blinked so rapidly he feared she was about to cry.

"Never mind," he said hastily, reluctant to face a scene. "You don't have to tell me. I just want you to know that no woman is less than a lady to me, no matter how she's been mistreated, no matter if she's worn ruts down the paths of Covent Garden. I have never forced a woman and I never shall."

With the pad of his thumb, he touched her trembling lower lip. She had a plain mouth but a pleasant one, its surface soft and pink. Naturally, now was not the time, but he wouldn't have minded kissing it. He'd do it slowly, he mused, and very, very gently. As if she read his thoughts, she shivered and pulled away.

Her eyes locked warily onto his. "Do you still want to paint me?"

"I do," he said. Deciding a casual tack was best, he examined his paint-stained nails. "I'd want you to board with me, of course."

"Of course," she agreed, a little too quickly. When he peered at her, she squared her shoulders in the way he'd already identified as her habit. "I'm not some quivering miss. I know what's expected of a model."

He smiled at her mixture of innocence and bravado—not that it was amusing, when one thought about it. Despite his assurance that he'd never force a woman, this poor girl was obviously prepared to bed him if she must. He touched her face again, following the hollow of her cheekbone toward her jaw. The artist in him took over from the man. Gripping her chin, he turned her head to catch the light from a different angle. She really was surprisingly dramatic.

"I'll pay you to pose," he said softly. "Whatever else you choose to give is just that: a choice. Unless you understand that very clearly, we can't go on."

She blinked as if he'd spoke in Chinese. "I do understand," she said, "and I thank you."

"Well, then." Suddenly buoyant, he tweaked the tip of her nose between two fingers. "Perhaps you'd be willing to take

off your coat and let me see what we've got to work with."
Her name returned in a tardy flash. "Mary, isn't it?"

"Yes," she said, fighting with her buttons. "Mary Colfax."

The name pleased him. Simple. Straightforward. Perfect
for a woman who'd be a challenge but not a trial.

Taking pity on her struggle, he reached in to remove her
awkward gloves. Though she swore under her breath, she let
him take them. Curious, he turned her hands between his
own. Her fingers were delicate, their nails clipped short, their
bases as callused as if she'd shoveled out the stable that
seemed to have supplied her original speech patterns. Oddly
enough, he liked her better for the roughness. This girl was
no layabout. When her coat was off as well, she thrust it at
him as if she loathed the very sight. Nic draped the worn
tweed over his arm.

"Now then, Mary Colfax," he said, feeling more satisfied
with the world, "why don't we drink some tea and discuss
your fee."

WITH A HEIGHTENED SENSE OF UNREALITY, MERRY
watched him hang the ugly coat as she pressed her fingertips
to her palms. They tingled from the way he'd probed them
with his thumb. How oddly he treated her: half woman, half
object. She could scarcely say which manner disturbed her
more. And of all things, he thought her father—her *father*—
had despoiled her. The duke of Monmouth was not that sort
of man, and yet her tongue cleaved to her mouth before she
could push the words out to defend him.

True or not, it was a convincing explanation of why a
maid might have been fired.

And it did seem to make Mr. Craven, who obviously had
a protective streak, more eager to take her in. Heavens, he'd
invited her to board with him! A stroke of luck, that, since
she hadn't known where she'd stay if he did not. Given how
conveniently everything was falling into place, it hardly be-
hooved her to correct his erroneous impression of her sire.

She couldn't reveal her true identity, after all. No matter
how debauched he was, Nicolas Craven would never com-

promise the daughter of a duke—at least, not an unmarried one.

She had thought her plan through most carefully. Not only was she going to accept his offer to paint her, she was going to let him paint her nude. That would be a scandal even her father could not suppress. She'd be utterly unmarriageable then, not just to Ernest but to any respectable man.

Yes, her father would be furious, but Nicolas Craven was wealthy and well known. Beyond a bit of unpleasantness, she suspected the man could defend himself. Certainly, if his swift disposal of her attacker were an indication, her brothers would pose no threat. In truth, they might have to worry about themselves. Still—she waved a mental hand—no mere artist would dare do serious injury to a peer.

Best of all, even if the duke decided to marry her to a commoner, a confirmed bachelor like Mr. Craven was certain to dig his heels in.

When the dust settled, Merry would have her freedom and Mr. Craven would have his art. His reputation might be a touch more notorious, but surely no harm lay in that. Artists like him thrived on notoriety.

The plan was, as far as she could see, without a single flaw.

Or almost without a flaw, she mused, as he led her down a narrow hall. The previous night's encounter had not prepared her for Nicolas Craven in the daylight. He wasn't just good-looking, he was gorgeous. Devilishly so, as if beauty could be a sin. His hair, which she'd simply thought untidy, was poetically long, a dark, smooth spill across his brow. The eyes she'd judged expressive downright smoldered in the light. They were gray and shining, like diamonds filled with smoke. And he was tall, almost as tall as her brothers, his shoulders as lean and broad as a statue from ancient Rome.

The fact that half his chest was showing did nothing to calm her pulse. Even as he walked before her, the sight was emblazoned in her mind. His shirt was in the American style, the kind that buttoned all the way down the tails. Naturally, with four not particularly modest brothers, she'd seen her share of bare male chests. But this male chest was different.

For one thing, Mr. Craven could have posed for an anatomy manual. His muscles looked as if they'd been laid in sculptor's clay directly on his frame. He had little chest hair, a mere smattering between his nipples, which—from the glimpses she caught beneath his shirt—were small and sharp. His feet were bare as well: long, strangely graceful feet. Merry was certain she'd never noticed a man's feet before. She found it disconcerting to notice them now, not to mention very personal.

Seemingly unaware of the flutter he had caused, Mr. Craven ushered her into a crowded Chinese parlor, where he rang for tea and savories. The servant who answered, a man he called Farnham, had a crooked nose and brush-cut iron-gray hair. A nasty scar slashed diagonally across his chin between the ends of his long mustache. Its skin puckered as if it had healed without medical care. Since he looked like an old pugilist, she wondered if he'd taught Nic the art of subduing strangers in the street. Happily, his manners were unobjectionable. The man glanced at her, no more than mildly curious. Beyond that, he seemed to make no judgment about her presence.

Of course, as an infamous artist's butler, he must have served more than his share of female guests.

As soon as the servant left, Mr. Craven lounged back in his chair, his chin propped on two fingers and a thumb, his legs sprawled out until his long, naked toes nearly touched her boot.

Unlike most men she knew, he seemed to feel no need to speak.

She forced herself to look down at her hands. Returning his gaze struck her as incautious. She didn't want to spoil her progress by giving him the wrong idea. It was one thing to hint she might welcome his advances, which, to judge by his behavior, required no more than showing up on his doorstep and being female. Actually giving in to those advances, however, was more than she wished to do. To her mind, the less real damage she did to her person the better. She didn't dismiss the possibility of one day having an affair, but she'd learned her lesson from Edward Burbrooke. The next time she offered herself, it would be to a man who wanted her as much as she wanted him.

She couldn't imagine that happening with Nicolas Craven.

"So," he said, crinkling his eyes in a manner that was, despite its urbanity, surprisingly sympathetic, "your life is about to start anew."

Had her story been true, Merry thought this was a very kind way to put it.

"I hope so," she said. "I've always wanted to have adventures."

"Good for you," he responded, his smile curling into his cheeks. His lips, she noticed, were thin and mobile. Their color was rich, as if they'd been stained by wine. Despite its gravelly timbre, his voice was soft. "Couldn't go home to your folks?"

"Dead," she lied, crossing her fingers in her skirt. "For a number of years."

"I'm sorry." To her surprise, he reached forward to squeeze the muscle between her shoulder and her neck. His grip was comforting, despite her lack of any need for comfort. "Don't worry, Mary. I'll make sure you have sufficient funds to keep you when we're done."

"That's very kind of you, Mr.—"

"For God's sake, call me Nic," he said. "And it's not kind, merely good business. I want the best models champing at the bit to work with me."

Merry grinned at the brass-bound edge of the Chinese table. "I imagine plenty of women would be eager to work with you, no matter what you paid."

He laughed, his thumb sliding past her collar to the sensitive skin along her neck. "Lord, I can't wait to get you in my studio."

His enthusiasm surprised her, though he'd said as much the night before. He genuinely seemed to want to paint her, plain old Merry Vance. She didn't know what to make of him, with his lingering touches and his smoldering stares and his "for God's sake, call me Nic." Merry's own manners were hardly priggish, but she had no clue how she ought to respond to his.

He treated her as if she'd been in his bed already.

Was this what Isabel meant by savoring his conquests bit by bit?

"Have I frightened you?" he asked, leaning so close she could smell the bergamot soap in which he washed.

"No," she said staunchly, though she could not suppress a shiver. "I'm looking forward to posing in your studio, Mr. Craven. I'm a great admirer of your work."

He sat back with a chuckle. "A great admirer, eh? Well, Lord willing, you'll have more reason to admire me before long. Maybe you'll even learn to call me Nic."

His implication was as clear as his wagging brows and yet she found she could not take offense. He was so good-naturedly rakish. More a wolf pup than a wolf. Her resistance to his charm began to melt like chocolate in the sun.

This man is dangerous, she thought.

Perhaps to her misfortune, the knowledge did not incline her to turn and run.

THE SAVORIES NIC HAD CALLED FOR TURNED OUT to be a meal of sausage and bread and cheese; hardly the dainty tidbits she was used to, but welcome all the same. Her nerves had for once gotten the better of her appetite, and this was the first solid food she'd eaten since the day before.

When Farnham returned to clear their plates—apparently, the other servants were on holiday—Nic showed her to her room.

It was tinier than her maid's chamber at home, with a single window overlooking the back garden, now a tangle of winter brown. The bed was narrow, the washstand chipped, and the Persian rug had seen better days. Dust grimed the painted baseboard, though the floor had at some recent time been swept.

Nic seemed to see nothing wrong in offering these amenities to her.

And why should he? she scolded herself. He had no reason to think she'd known better.

"It's very cozy," she said, forcing a smile.

"Well, the fireplace draws. And we never stint on coal. You're welcome to use as much as you like."

Hm, she thought, squinting at the loaded bucket. Was she expected to stoke the fire herself? She supposed she could manage. She'd seen housemaids do it often enough. To hide her consternation, she moved to the mantel. A painting hung above it, a nice one. If she recalled her "finishing" in art, it was a copy of Correggio's *Jupiter and Io*. The cloudlike god was as sooty and thick as London fog, which didn't stop the nymph he held from swooning in his misty arms.

Merry could imagine all too easily why Nic liked it.

"The water closet is across the hall," he was saying. "Nothing fancy, but you'll have it to yourself."

"I'm sure that will be fine," she said, though she wasn't sure at all. She nodded at the painting. "Did you copy this?"

He smiled and joined her. "Yes, I did. You have a good eye." He tapped the simple wooden frame. "I began my studies in Vienna. My master had a habit of tossing his students' paintings in the fire. This was the first of my efforts to escape the blaze. Ever since, I've had a fondness for Correggio."

"I suppose you studied all over Europe."

His expression grew distant. "I've seen a fair amount of it. Geneva. Florence. And Paris, of course, when politics allowed. It's good to know the world is bigger than the place you live."

"I've never been out of England."

He looked down at her, his gaze warming as he wound one of her curls around his finger. Those eyes of his . . . They were like molten silver, made even brighter by their short, dark fringe of lashes. She didn't know which moved her more: the kindness they held, or the banked erotic fire.

"Where would you travel if you could?" he asked.

She struggled to think with the heat blooming thick inside her. "The Forbidden City," she said. "Or maybe Rome."

He allowed her hair to spring free of his hold. "Rome

might be more practical than China, but I suppose you can go anywhere in your dreams."

His tone was so smoky, so suggestive, she felt compelled to step back. Here again was his persuasion, the sensual charm no woman could resist.

His mouth curled knowingly at her retreat, his eyes half-lidded with enjoyment. "I'll let you freshen up and rest then, shall I? We serve dinner at eight. You can eat with me, or Farnham can bring you a tray, whichever you prefer. It'll be simple fare until my cook returns, but I'm sure we'll manage."

"I'm sure," she agreed, her response embarrassingly ragged. She cleared her throat. "Thank you for showing me to my room. And thank you for taking me on."

His smile deepened, lending his eyes a glow that said the pleasure was all his. He stepped backward to the threshold, then laid his finger beside his nose.

"I'll see you later, Mary Colfax," he said, and closed the door behind him.

Reality struck like a cartload of bricks as soon as she was alone. She, who had never left the bosom of her family except to visit female friends, now shared a roof with a man she barely knew, a man who clearly considered her fair game for his amorous wiles.

"My-y," she said, the word sighing out on a long, low breath. Even she could scarcely credit she'd had the nerve.

She hadn't permitted herself to consider how she'd feel, not when she handed Isabel her packet of bogus letters to send back to Merry's mother, not when she snuck out of the mansion in her stolen dress and hired a cab to St. John's Wood.

She was alone with Nicolas Craven, alone but for a butler who probably saw more depravity in a week than she could imagine in a year. Knees weak, she dropped into a faded fan-backed chair. She felt as if she were galloping toward an unfamiliar jump on a half-broke horse, the hazards untested, the outcome wholly dependent on her and the creature's skill.

The intensity of her terror was a pleasure in itself.

*　　*　　*

DESPITE HER RESOLVE TO EMBRACE ALL CHAL-
lenges, Merry was dismayed to discover she had not planned
as well as she'd thought. She went down to dinner at five to
eight, still wearing her pitiful maid's dress.

She stopped in her tracks at the entrance to the dining
room, barely noticing when Nic rose. This room, a small but
perfect oval, was done up like a French salon from the era
of the Sun King. Soft, pastoral murals—not Nic's, she
thought—filled curlicued medallions on the walls. Gilt and
ormolu encrusted the furniture to the extent that she wondered if it was safe to sit. Everything looked antique, even
the ivory damask that draped the table.

She'd known Nic Craven was successful, but this eclectic
jewel of a home was more than she'd foreseen.

"Is something wrong?" he asked, standing beside his
chair.

Recalling herself, she touched the skirt of her orange
gown. "I have no clothes," she said.

She lied, of course. She had a steamer trunk full of clothes
sitting in the cellar of Isabel's town house. This trunk was
supposed to be on its way to Wales as part of her ruse to convince her mother she had gone. Since Nic didn't know this,
he looked her up and down, his eyes slanting, his lips curled
slightly at the corners.

She didn't understand how an expression so subtle could
be so predatory, or what he imagined lay under this baggy
gown. Certainly, nothing like what was there, or he wouldn't
have been grinning.

"We'll have to see what we can do about that," he said,
and offered her the chair across from his. When she took it,
he slid it under her with the ease of a gentleman born and
bred. "I have gowns I keep on hand for models, but I doubt
they'd fit you. You're a good deal slighter than most of the
women I paint. If you can survive till Monday, I know a
dressmaker we can visit. Very reasonable and discreet."

I'll bet, Merry thought, especially the discreet part.

Nic's eyes gleamed as if he'd read her mind. "I, of course,
would never force you to wear a stitch. Speaking as an artist,
I think the unadorned female form is a lovely thing."

Merry shot a repressive look from beneath her brows, but it only made Nic laugh.

"Little cold for that," she said.

Nic put his elbow on the table and tweaked her nose.

"You forget," he said, "in my house, we stoke the fires."

4

NIC LED MARY TO THE STUDIO AFTER DINNER. HE preferred his models relaxed and, over the years, he'd learned only one activity ensured that better than a hearty meal.

Mary looked as if she hadn't seen her share of those. Apparently, Nic could add "pinchpenny" to the duke of Monmouth's sins. Feeding his servants was evidently not his priority. She was skin and bones, poor thing, and had eaten every scrap Farnham set before her. Considering her appetite, her ladylike manners made him smile. This was a woman who had striven to improve herself.

The thought of helping her take the next step intrigued him. He suspected she would not waste the coin he paid her, though perhaps even she didn't know what sort of life she'd build.

At the moment, her mind did not appear to be on the future. He watched her circle his work space, her gaze wide and alert, her fingers stopping to touch whatever objects caught her eye. The sight caused an unexpected tightening in his groin. He wouldn't have minded having that attention, and those rough little hands, exploring him.

Until such time as that was possible, there was plenty for her to see. His studio was the largest structure in the house. Rising two stories, it was topped by a tin-lined dome that, during the summer, filled the space with golden light. Tonight, tall candelabra stood in for the sun, their iron branches vaguely medieval. His props ranged around the edges of the room, a mix of period furniture, exotic artifacts, and casts of classic statues. History was popular these days, preferably history that allowed one's models to go about lightly clad. Some might call it pandering, but Nic preferred to think of his choices as pragmatic. He had his say within the limits of what would sell. More often than not, as was the case tonight, what he thought would sell was also what pleased him.

Ignorant of the role she played in his musings, Mary trailed her hand along the edge of the big, stained sink where he washed his brushes. Out of the blue, as if some carnal switch had tripped inside his head, he pictured her sprawled inside the basin. The image was shockingly vivid. She was naked, wet, her legs dangling over the sides while he soaped her curly mound. He could nearly feel the softness of her secret skin; nearly hear the pop of the iridescent foam. A flush swept out like a fever from his loins. In seconds he was stiff, achingly so, just from watching her touch his things.

Who'd have thought a chit like this could rock him on his heels? Generally speaking, Nic's desire for a woman took time to build. His interest rose as he stirred their interest in him. Mary felt his pull, he knew, but had hardly reached the panting desperation he preferred.

Discreetly, before she turned around, he adjusted the sudden rearing of his cock. He'd rather she didn't know what she'd done to him just yet. Unfortunately, no rearrangement could hide the change. Swollen and tight, his shaft felt thicker around than her slender wrist. The thought of comparing the two, side by side, made him want to groan. Cursing the inconvenience of the male physique, he pulled out his shirt and let it hang. Better she think him a sloven than a satyr.

She came to a halt before the stage. "Do you want me to pose here?"

"Yes," he said, wondering if she could hear the bated hunger in his voice.

If she did, it didn't show. She lifted her ugly ruffled skirt, stepped up, and waded through a heap of tasseled cushions. Her ankles were as neat as he'd ever seen, and clad in unexpectedly nice boots. When she turned, he schooled his face to blandness.

"Who," she asked, "do you want me to be?"

A hoyden, he thought, his erection reaching the point of pain. A brazen debauchee.

"Just yourself," he said aloud. "I'm only sketching you tonight. I want to familiarize myself with your features."

She made a face at that and he realized she had no concept of her appeal.

"Sit," he said gruffly, "and make yourself comfortable."

Rather than watch her, which didn't seem wise in his current state, he retrieved his supplies from the cabinet by the sink, wincing a bit as his trousers pinched him on squatting down. Luckily, a block of sketching paper and charcoal was all he'd need. Her coloring was a challenge he preferred to tackle on its own. For tonight, gaining a knowledge of her form would be enough. Then he'd know how he wanted to use her.

As if there were any doubt of that.

Rolling his eyes at himself, he positioned a stool, then lugged one of the candelabra to the stage. Each of its tapers was backed by polished mirror. The gas was also lit, but the room was so large the sconces did not illuminate all he wished. He wanted bones tonight, bones and planes and shadows thrown by curves.

By the time he'd adjusted the light to his satisfaction, Mary sat cross-legged on a cushion with her weight propped on her arms. She'd been watching him. Her face was as curious as a child's.

"How old are you?" he demanded, suddenly suspicious.

"Twenty," she said, adding cheekily: "How old are you?"

"Thirty-one," he muttered.

She forgot her borrowed manners long enough to snort. "Practically decrepit."

"Baggage," he said.

She grinned as if his insult pleased her.

He almost lost his breath. Her grin was wide and infectious. Open and ageless, it did not increase her beauty so much as make him want to laugh. A precious gift, that, one few people had. Ignoring how much he'd like to see her grinning in his bed, he settled onto the stool. Luckily, his attraction ebbed in the oblivion of work. She squirmed more than an experienced model, but at least she did not sulk. With swift, sure strokes, he filled page after page and tossed each one aside. Finally, when his neck began to crick, he told her to stand and have a stretch.

"Are we done?" she asked, locking her hands before her chest.

Something about the way she pushed them caught his eye. She had muscle with her skin and bone, possibly interesting muscle, muscle he could barely see beneath that sacklike gown. He longed to rip it off, but suspected he'd scare her silly.

"Nic?" she said.

He shook himself. "Whether we're done is up to you. Are you too tired to sit any longer?"

She shrugged and again he sensed that hidden, fluid strength. He made up his mind. "That dress is driving me mad," he said and quickly undid the buttons of his shirt.

She gaped at him. "What are you doing?"

"Giving you my shirt. You can put it on behind that screen."

She peered dubiously at the wall of painted Chinese silk, but took the shirt when he thrust it at her. As she walked around the barrier, she held it gingerly by the collar.

"Mary," he said, forcing her to look at him, "wear the shirt *instead* of your chemise, not over it."

Pink crept up her cheeks. "I knew that."

Nic did not believe her for a minute. In spite of all she'd been through, Mary glowed with innocence like a girl fresh from her bath. He hoped she wasn't sorry to be here, that posing for him didn't feel like another step on the road to ruin. For many women, the slide from model to whore would seem a short one. Not that Mary had many options, especially if Monmouth had been too mean to give her a good character. No. She hadn't much choice but to come to him.

An old anger rose, as dark and bitter as the dregs of Farnham's coffee, even deeper for being turned partly against himself. He shoved his vexation away, but couldn't help thinking her former employer a bloody sod. He wondered if Monmouth had forced her or if he simply hadn't been very skilled. Mary certainly didn't act like a happily bedded woman. Perhaps the duke had a problem with performance. Some men preferred to blame that on their partners. Maybe that was the reason the bastard had let her go.

By the time she emerged with his shirt hanging over her drawers, he was fuming at the arrogance of his kind. A woman was not a handkerchief to be discarded once it was torn. Nic couldn't deny he'd parted ways with his share of partners, but never since his youth, never, had he left some poor young innocent to the mercy of the Fates!

Fortunately, Mary's reappearance dispersed his anger like a wind. Those drawers must have cost her a good month's pay. They were frilly and foolish, hanging to her knees in a lavish cascade of lace. Beneath her stockings, her calves were a ruddy marvel: tight and round and strong.

"Turn," he ordered, demonstrating with his hand.

She turned and his breath caught in his throat, part artist's pleasure, part man's. His shirt was loose, of course, but with the candles shining through it, at last he could see her shape. As he'd suspected, she was as slim as a wand. Her bottom demanded cupping, her shoulders a reverent sigh. She looked an athlete: a young Greek girl maybe, and very nearly a young Greek boy. She had breasts, though, small and unbound and perched so high on her ribs he doubted they'd hold his lightest paintbrush in their lee. She wore no corset.

Indeed, it would have been a crime against nature if she had. If ever a body defied the need for crushing, it was hers.

"Beautiful," he breathed, and she blushed to the roots of her marvelous red-gold hair.

He had to chuckle at her expression.

"Ah, Mary," he said, "you'll believe me before we're through."

MERRY WRIGGLED IN HER UNFAMILIAR BED, UNable to push the image of the shirtless painter from her mind. She'd been flushed the whole time she posed—and not with embarrassment. Nic was an eyeful: his tightly muscled chest, his long, sinewy arms, the sloping curve at the small of his back where his trousers hung on his narrow hips. He made her mouth water and her hands itch to touch.

Dangerous or not, Nicolas Craven left her stunned.

Naturally, she knew the cure for her condition. Merry's parents had never succeeded in sheltering her, hadn't even tried too hard with three rowdy boys to worry about. She knew the functions of the human body as well as, or better than, many matrons. The infamous Dr. Acton would never convince her women did not feel desire, or that easing it would harm her. She'd heard too many strapping stable boys brag of their addiction to the "solitary vice" to believe it diminished one's vigor in any way.

But to touch herself tonight seemed ill-advised.

She would think of him if she did, would dream she held that long, bare back and gazed into those smoky eyes. She could not afford the fantasy, not if she wished to emerge from this enterprise intact.

Merry wanted more than to be a notch on someone's bedpost.

With a groan of frustration, she rolled onto her back. Though the narrow mattress was piled with covers, her nose and toes were chips of ice. A steady gray sleet spit against the single window and a draft whistled heartlessly through its chinks. She'd tried to start the fire before retiring but her only reward had been a sickly puff of smoke.

Never having been further from assistance than the near-est bellpull, these discomforts were outside her experience. Up till now, she hadn't realized how spoiled she was.

This, she told herself, was the stupidest prank she'd ever pulled.

Loneliness ached inside her like the fading clang of Sun-day bells. She missed her motherly old maid and her broth-ers and her horses and the sweet smell of herbs that scented all her sheets. Lord, what her father would say if he could see her now! Tears welled in her eyes but almost before she'd pressed her arm across them, she threw the self-pity off.

Merry Vance was not a quitter.

Just because her plan proved difficult didn't mean she ought to give it up.

"I won't give up," she muttered, forcing herself to leave her nest of blankets. She nearly crawled straight back. Her chemise and drawers were no match for the icy air. Goose-bumps sprang up along her skin, marching from ankle to neck and back again. Her breath was misting in the moon-light. Something suspiciously like a whimper left her throat.

Pretending she hadn't heard it, she stomped determinedly to the grate and knelt before it. This fire was going to catch whether it wanted to or not. Just as she'd seen the house-maids do, she twisted screws of paper between the coals. Match after match was sacrificed to her vow to see them light. When the coals began to smoke, she simply coughed and waved her arm.

She didn't realize how thick the air had gotten until the door banged open behind her.

"Jesus," said Nic, his candle blurred by the haze.

Goodness, Merry thought. That's a lot of smoke.

As soon as he saw she was all right, he strode to the win-dow and heaved it open. She inhaled in protest at the blast of frigid air and caught an unfortunate lungful of floating soot.

Nic crouched down and held her shoulders while she coughed. "What were you trying to do? Burn the bloody house down?"

Merry's teeth chattered. "I was c-cold. I was trying to light the fire."

"Well, it might help if you'd opened the flue!"

"Oh," she said, mortified. "I, uh, guess I forgot. How silly of me."

"I'll say. Why didn't you give up when it started to smoke? And what is all this paper doing in here? You're smothering the fire."

Merry could only hunch her shoulders in a shrug. She could hardly admit she wasn't sure what a flue was, much less how one opened it. Something in the chimney, she thought, and stifled another cough. Despite her embarrassment, she couldn't help noticing Nic was bare from the waist up. The side he'd pulled her to during her coughing fit was smooth-skinned and toasty warm. As if he knew how good he felt, he snuggled her closer. His ribs pressed her arm, moving evenly as he breathed.

She knew the moment his awareness of her shifted, because the rhythm of that movement changed. Apparently, being alone with a scantily clad woman affected even a jaded rogue like him.

"Here." He moved to his knees behind her, his long, lean body spooning hers. "Let me show you how to find it."

He took her hand, cupping its back with his palm and guiding it up the chimney's maw. Merry's heart began to pound. He was so close his jaw brushed hers, its bone sharp, its skin appreciably smoother than her brothers'. When he nudged her hair back with his nose, a shiver skittered deliciously down her spine.

"Here's the handle," he said, his lips next to her ear. His fingers wrapped hers around a rusty metal hoop. He pulled and jiggled and she heard a muffled thunk. Air rushed down the shaft. Like magic, a tiny flame sprang up from one of the coals.

"There," he said, "now the fire can breathe."

Too bad Merry couldn't say the same.

Though he drew their arms back out, he remained on his knees behind her. His sleeping trousers were something a native of India might wear, silk with a twisted cord to tie them at the waist. Feeling her shiver again, he chafed her arms, then hummed low in his throat. The sound of his pleasure was sweet as honey.

"I never had to light the fires," she said, wanting to distract him. "I always worked in the laundry."

Nic smiled against her cheek. "No woman should have to light her own fire unless she enjoys it."

Heat washed Merry's body. She knew he wasn't talking about a fire you built with coal. He was talking about the pleasure she'd refused to give herself before.

The concept rocked a place inside her that had never moved before. That a man might know, and approve, and perhaps even want to watch what women did . . . She couldn't catch her breath. It came in shallow, ragged gasps. She knew he must hear, must guess what his words had done. He made a sound, low and rumbling, and rubbed his front against her like a cat. At once, her spine lost all its starch. His narrow, silk-clad hips slid slowly behind her own. Tiny hairs stood on her arms. He was aroused. His erection strafed her bottom, the friction light but unmistakable, as if he meant to tease them both. The ridge of his sex pulsed behind the silk, its motion enticingly erratic, its heat as humid as a summer day.

Merry struggled for control.

"I've always—" She drew a startled breath as he dragged the rounded tip along the parting of her cheeks. "I've always thought a woman should cultivate independence."

Nic chuckled, the sound a seduction by itself. "To be sure, independence is an admirable trait, but when a man has the strength and the will to offer a woman aid, why shouldn't she accept?"

As he spoke, his longest finger drew a circle on her hip, a deft, suggestive circle that made her want to move his hand a few more inches to the left. With all her strength, she fought a groan. Nic didn't make it easy. The tip of his tongue curled out to flick her ear. "Wouldn't you like my aid, Mary? Wouldn't you like me to ease your needs?"

"I told you, I'm not a wh—"

"Sh," he soothed, before she could say the word. "I remember what you told me and you know what I answered. Nothing will happen between us that you don't wish."

He was rocking her now, hugging her gently with arms and thighs and chest—even the arch of his graceful neck. She wanted to turn in his arms and lift her mouth to his. She remembered the night he'd rescued her and the urge she'd felt to put herself in his hands. Then her longing had been for safety. Now it was for risk. She knew his kiss would be sweet, knew it would sweep her into a mindless joy. Only the thought of all the women who'd succumbed to his charms before gave her the strength to draw away.

"At the moment," she said, pushing to her feet as steadily as she could, "I wish you would leave my room."

He laughed at her tartness and got to his feet as well. Meaning to appear stern, she crossed her arms beneath her breasts. To her dismay, this simply drew attention to the painful tightness of their peaks, pulsing against the muslin, hardened by more than cold. *Look at me,* they seemed to say. *Look at what you've done.* No doubt the part of him that had teased her bottom was shouting the same refrain, but Merry refused to heed its seductive call. Nic smiled, sleepy-eyed, and licked his index finger's pad.

Now what, she wondered, does he mean to do with that? His arm reached toward her, the dampened finger aiming for her breast. Knowledge welled with molten heat. He meant to touch her nipple. He wanted the cloth to cling to her skin.

With a muffled gasp, she shrank out of reach. If Nic was contrite, it did not show.

"Are you sure you want me to leave?" he purred. "I could warm you until the fire takes hold."

He slid the hand she'd evaded down his front, over his breastbone and muscled belly, over the cord that tied his sleeping trousers. They were gray, she saw, with a tiny figure in russet red. She bit her lip as his hand slid lower still, palming the arrogant jut of his erection. To save her life, she could not have looked away. Her breath stalled as he cupped himself and rubbed, a strong, voluptuous motion that pushed the whole of his sex against his front.

Lord, he was . . . it was . . . impressive the way he handled himself so frankly. His fingers squeezed his sack while his thumb worked a lazy circle beneath the crown. He'd grown so long his tip was caught under the cord. The silk clung damply there, outlining the flaring shape. She was staring so hard her eyes were burning. He did not appear to care; in truth, he seemed to savor her attention. He also seemed to know just how mesmerized she was.

"If you don't want me to touch you, you could watch," he suggested, his voice even rougher than before. "See if you like the way my body works."

In that instant, she wanted to watch more than she wanted to guard her pride. This man was beyond any rule she'd ever known. Free of inhibition. Ignorant of shame. She knew instinctively he'd take her places she'd never dreamed.

She spun to face the mantel. "I'm sure you'll manage fine without me."

He did not take her retreat as a rebuff. How could he when her voice was choked with lust? His hands found her upper arms, his thumbs sliding under the puffy sleeves of her chemise. It was her own garment, cut close to her figure to fit the season's narrow gowns. Usually grateful for its lightness, now she felt unbearably exposed. Tingles spread outward from his caress as his chin nudged her hair from the nape of her neck. His lips whispered like satin there, his breath like silent steam. Her very vertebrae were shivering with delight.

"Everything feels better when you watch," he said, his gravelly voice enough to melt her by itself. "You've no idea how hard you make me with a look."

The claim was nonsense, but that didn't stop her from yearning to believe. "You promised," she gasped. "You said you'd do as I asked."

"I said I'd do as you wished," he corrected. He lapped her shoulder with the flat of his tongue, catching a traitorous drop of sweat. "I think you wish this very much."

"Please."

Nic seemed to sense the sincerity of her plea. He hesitated, then withdrew, pausing only to close the window on his way. It was an odd kindness, one that unsettled her as much as his honeyed words.

She suspected he knew just how tempted she'd been to let him stay.

WITH THE CANDLE TO LIGHT HIS WAY, NIC PADDED to his room, down the gold, Morris-papered hall and the narrow stairs, past the still lifes and empty chairs. With one idle corner of his brain, he noticed the boots he'd set out for cleaning had disappeared. He couldn't imagine why anyone would collect them in the middle of the night—unless the new boy was trying to avoid him.

Strange, he thought, shaking the mystery off as he sat down on his bed. His gaze wandered inexorably to the ceiling.

Mary's chamber sat directly above that ornate plaster rose. When he'd woken to the smell of smoke, he'd experienced a wrench as terrible as the one he'd felt when he'd learned of Bess's passing. Not another, he'd thought. Not another death he could have prevented.

The relief of discovering she was safe must have unhinged his mind. It wasn't like him to push a woman. Entice her, yes. Push her, no.

He wanted her more than he could explain.

She was spirited, true, and he liked the thought of teaching her to see her beauty. He had no doubt she'd be a firecracker once he overcame her past experience. But why did he want her enough to risk frightening her off? What did his body read in hers, and obviously crave from hers, that his mind could not perceive?

He didn't for an instant believe the cause romantic. He'd learned long ago he was capable of affection, even attachment, but love? Not Nic Craven. Not for him the scourge of poets.

Rather than dwell on the puzzle, he slid back into bed. His body pulsed beneath the weight of the winter bedclothes but he resisted the urge to ease his discomfort.

Maybe his body wanted him to change his modus operandi. Maybe that was the message behind his reaction to Mary Colfax.

Let yourself want, his body might be saying. *Let yourself wait.*

Nic, after all, made his women wait. They seemed to like the end result. Perhaps he, too, ought to sample the joys of panting for release.

He shifted on the pillow and closed his eyes, but his mind would not behave. He could feel the skin of her neck beneath his lips, the cool, electric crackle of her hair. Despite his resolution, he hoped he wouldn't be waiting long.

MERRY WANTED TO SEE THE SKETCHES, BUT NIC WAS being vexing. He held them above his head and made her jump like her brothers used to when she was small.

"Bastard," she fumed while he laughed at her. He wasn't quite as tall as her siblings but he was quicker.

"Tut-tut," he said, switching hands. "You'll never pass for a lady with that filthy mouth."

When Merry ran the other way, he dodged behind a fake Egyptian chair.

"You can't have known many ladies," she panted, "if you think they never curse."

"Now, now, Duchess. I've known a few more ladies than you."

The nickname startled her. She hid her reaction with a huff. "Just give me the pictures, Nic. I know they're only sketches. I promise I won't use them to cast aspersions on your genius."

"My genius?" His eyes danced with laughter. "Oh, I like the sound of that. Almost as much as I like having you chase me around my studio."

She called him another dirty name. He grinned and wagged the pages just out of reach. "What will you give me for them, Mary?"

That stopped her. Merry liked to bargain. She put her hands on her hips. "What do you want for them?"

He tilted his head and raked her with a gaze of lascivious speculation. If chasing him around hadn't warmed her, this look certainly would have. A fresh prickle of perspiration heated the shallow valley between her breasts. He'd loaned her another shirt today and she knew it did little to hide her reaction. His eyes darkened, then lifted reluctantly to her face.

"I should demand a kiss," he said, "a slow, wet, steal-your-breath-till-sunset sort of kiss."

He licked his upper lip and Merry clenched her fists against a shudder of arousal. She'd be damned if she'd let him see how well she could imagine what he described. Her efforts were futile. Nic grinned as smugly as if she'd moaned.

"Alas," he continued, "a kiss might be considered a violation of our agreement. So I'll simply suggest that you pose nude."

"Nude!" she exclaimed, forgetting this was what she'd been hired for. For that matter, it was what she'd counted on having to do.

Nic examined his nails. The sky outside still glowered, but the fog had cleared and the studio windows cast a silvery aura around his form. He cut an elegant silhouette, his hair glossy, his profile sharp and fine. His dress might be Bohemian, but no one could fault its make. The slashing hollows of his cheeks gave him an air of tragedy. Here was a figure for a portrait, a Hamlet perhaps, or an ancient elven king.

His words, however, were anything but tragic.

"I could throw in a veil," he offered slyly.

"I'll give up the shirt," she countered. "And *I* get to arrange my hair."

"Done," he agreed and held out his hand to seal the deal.

Rather than shake it, Merry snatched the pile of sketches from his hold. Considering how quickly he'd done them, their detail quite amazed.

"Hm," she said, studying them. In some of the images, a few swift lines had caught the shape of her shoulder or her hand. In others, interlocking smudges of black and gray brought her features into the round. All the drawings were magical, and all were unmistakably almost her. This was more than the self she saw in the mirror; this was the self Nic saw: slightly foreign, plainer in a way but much more inter-esting. His simplest scribble had a mysterious vitality. She touched a glimmering profile, half expecting the girl in the sketch to wink.

He's brilliant, she thought, but what she said was: "Does my nose really look like that?"

He came to stand behind her. "Precisely like that."

She looked up at him in surprise.

"I never lie," he said. "Soften perhaps, but not lie."

She narrowed her eyes. "Not with the tools of your trade, you mean."

"Not with anything." He pressed his hand to his well-formed chest. "I am an honest Casanova."

"Hmpf," she said, because she didn't know what to make of this curious claim. Could an honest man succeed as a se-ducer?

He touched the tip of her nose with something like affec-tion. "Don't let it worry you, Duchess. Just strip off that shirt and we'll get to the business of the day."

He laughed when she slipped behind the changing screen, but Merry would not disrobe in front of him. Even with the concealment, her fingers shook as she opened his baggy shirt. She'd never bared her breasts for a man, not even on a dare. She hadn't expected to feel so vulnerable. For once in her life, she was grateful for her horrible hair. As thick as it was, she had no trouble covering most of her front behind its curls.

"You still there?" he called, as she huddled behind the screen.

She squeaked in alarm when his chin appeared over the top.

His smile was as kind as she'd ever seen it. "If you're not ready to do this, it can wait for another day. I know you've never modeled without your clothes."

"I can do it," she said and tried to square her shoulders. Despite her best efforts, they remained where they were, hunched protectively into her hair. Her eyes sent him a plea she didn't mean to make. Nic read it as easily as he did her fear.

"You know," he said, "I've seen plenty of naked women."

She nodded and blinked hard. "Hundreds," she agreed. "Maybe thousands."

"And you know I won't attack you just because you've taken off your shirt."

She nodded at that as well.

"Nor will I say insulting things. Or even think insulting things. For one thing, you're my model. For another, I like women. And for a third, you're very pretty. Neat as a pin," he added when she grimaced with disbelief. "Like a greyhound or a well-bred filly." His teeth flashed in a brilliant grin. "What do the Americans call those spotted horses?"

"Appaloosas," she said.

"Yes," he mused. "You're a pretty Appaloosa, and I'd be honored if you'd let me capture you in paint."

This comparison, at least, she could swallow.

"Oh, all right," she muttered, and stumped gracelessly around the screen.

Nic made no comment on her appearance, merely directed her to climb onto the sawhorse he'd erected in the middle of the stage. A rug draped the crossbar with a man's jumping saddle slung over that. Merry clutched her hair to her bosom as she clambered on. Silly, she knew—her breasts weren't anything to go barmy over—but she couldn't help herself. Though the stirrups were too long, she refused to bend over to adjust them.

"Your horse is too skinny," she said, unimpressed with his substitute, "and if you paint me astride, you're going to scandalize your critics."

Too late, she remembered that a scandal was to her benefit.

Nic looked up from squeezing blobs of paint onto his palette. She wished he ground his own colors. She would have liked to watch. But she supposed a modern artist didn't bother with romantic fancies, not when he could buy those convenient collapsible tubes. Besides which, Nic was romantic enough. Any more romantic and she might slither out of this saddle in a heap.

His eyes gleamed as if he knew the tenor of her thoughts.

"Are you certain Lady Godiva didn't ride astride? And on a skinny horse?"

"A horse would have to be dead to be this skinny." She cocked her head at him, belatedly registering what he'd said. "I'm supposed to be Lady Godiva?"

Her skepticism fed his amusement. "You have to admit you've got the hair for it."

"The hair maybe, but—"

"Hush," he said, one Prussian blue finger to his lips. "I'm the genius here."

Some genius. Even she knew Lady Godiva was supposed to be a siren. Made a bargain with her husband, as she recalled. He'd lower local taxes if she'd ride naked through the street. He thought she'd never dare but he was wrong. The townspeople were so grateful they all closed their shutters while she rode, except for a tailor who became the original Peeping Tom, for which impudence he was blinded. Merry had a hard time imagining her body blinding anyone, but she did feel daring, dressed in nothing but her hair and a pair of lacy drawers. And who knew? Maybe the real Godiva had been plain. Maybe the painters made her pretty.

She shifted in the saddle, uncomfortably conscious of her presence inside her skin. Her hair lay thick and warm across her breasts, brushing their tightened tips with every breath. Her thighs began to sweat where they gripped the saddle. Could Nic see? Could he possibly guess how oddly arousing she found her own display?

He didn't seem to. He was mixing colors now, squinting at her, then at the paint. She knew from the night before that, to him, she nearly ceased to be a person as soon as he started work. His concentration fascinated her, and also soothed her nerves. How could one be embarrassed, after all, when one's breast or thigh was merely another object to depict?

"Wait!" she said, as he lifted his laden brush. His brows rose in inquiry but she couldn't let him do this. "You have to get a sidesaddle. Lady Godiva was a noblewoman. And a real horse wouldn't hurt, either."

"Stickler for accuracy, are we?" Nic's tone was droll. "Don't worry, Duchess. This is just a study. To see if my concept works. If it does, I'll buy you a sidesaddle. And a horse—though God knows where we'd pose you."

"A white horse," she insisted, her memory of the legend clear.

"Brat," he teased and tossed his beautiful hair back with a laugh.

COME MONDAY, NIC TOOK HER TO A DRESSMAKER on Princes Street. To Merry's relief, it was no society haunt, not even a proper shop, but a private home in which the business was conducted. The proprietress was a shrunken old woman with a thick Parisian accent. Her hands were cold as she measured Merry and clucked. She reminded her so eerily of her mother's dresser she was afraid to open her mouth for fear the two women might be acquainted.

While this was going on, Nic waited in a tiny parlor by himself. Entirely a gentleman, he did not suggest he watch her being fitted, nor give instructions beyond a vague encouragement to "give her what she needs."

This presented a problem. Though Merry knew, despite her disinterest, precisely what the duke of Monmouth's daughter needed in her wardrobe, she had no idea what a maid turned artist's model might require.

Reduced to hazarding a guess, she ordered three plain warm dresses, an assortment of underthings, and two pairs of silk hose. These were not perhaps necessary, but even Merry could not bring herself to clothe her legs in scratchy wool.

Once she'd made her selections, everything was brought out for Nic's approval. The procedure made Merry feel peculiar, like a mistress instead of an employee. She didn't enjoy the feeling, but she supposed the old lady's assumption was understandable.

Nic showed no such discomfort. As if he vetted women's dresses every day, he examined the patterns and fabric. Merry tensed as his brows drew together above his nose. She wondered if, in her ignorance, she'd ordered too much, but he simply rubbed his jaw and nodded. Then he lifted his gaze to the bent old woman's. "Do you remember the royal purple you showed me last month?"

"Of course," she said with a businesswoman's smile. "A lovely silk velvet."

"We'd like something in that for evening. Off the shoulder and not too much bustle. But I leave the style to you. You know what I like."

"Indeed," agreed the seamstress, "and perhaps a matching cloak?"

Nic turned on his heel to look at Merry, a sharp, elegant motion that took her by surprise. His eyes were considering but soft. "A real coat, I think. Warmly lined. A dark tweed. Chocolate, if you have it. Or Chinese green. And velvet lapels. Black."

"Very good," said the seamstress. From her respectfully inclined head she obviously sensed that he was done.

Merry didn't speak until the assistant showed them out the door. "I need an evening gown?"

"You might," he said, his expression amused but uninformative. She fought a trickle of alarm. She hoped he wasn't planning to take her out in public. The last thing she wanted was to be spotted before her ruination was complete.

"And a coat?" she added as he whistled for a cab.

"Now that you need. The one you have is ragged."

He handed her up the steps of the old four-wheeled growler, his manners as impeccable as any son of noble blood. Merry had noticed this poise of his before. Had he been coached to do these things? Perhaps he'd hired a tutor. Perhaps, as an artist, the extra polish helped him attract a more affluent clientele.

He settled opposite her in the forward seat and stretched his long, lean legs to the other side. "If you feel awkward about accepting these garments, you could leave them behind when the job is through. Of course"—he grinned like a boy with his finger in the jampot—"you're so tiny no one else would ever fit them."

An unexpected warmth blossomed in Merry's chest. Why, he's worried about me, she thought. And doesn't want me to feel I'm taking charity. How sweet it was! And how comically unnecessary. Her father could buy a hundred velvet gowns and never miss a shilling.

She pressed her glove to her mouth to keep her laugh inside. "Thank you," she said, obliged to turn her twitching face to the window. "You're very kind."

It was beyond foolish, of course, but she found herself wondering just how long she could draw her employment out.

THEIR DAYS SETTLED INTO A PATTERN THE RETURN of the servants did not break, since the staff never bothered Nic unless he called them. A motley lot, their presence spoke volumes about his openness of mind. Merry doubted her mother would have hired even one of them. The butler, whom she'd met, was too rough in appearance for so visible a position. The cook had the interesting habit of preparing what she thought Nic ought to eat rather than what he asked for. The maid was pert, the elderly gardener could barely hobble around, and the newest member of the staff, a gangly teenaged boy, hid his face with a succession of ugly scarves—like a monster from a tale by LeFanu.

Happily, Merry's room was swept and her linens washed without her having to ask. She'd surmised her position was similar to a governess, but hadn't known what protocol required. Either the servants knew or had gotten their instructions from Nic. He ruled them like a genial if absentminded king. She could tell they were proud to serve him, as if his standing in society enhanced their own. Certainly, they viewed the facilitation of his art as their foremost responsibility.

The center of this eccentric little empire, Nic would rap on her door each dawn to catch the light, grumpier than she, even after his morning coffee. She'd pose until darkness fell or his hand grew too stiff to hold the brush. He spent most of his time doing studies. *Esquisse,* he called them, after the French. She gathered they were a sort of practice painting in which he worked out color and composition for the real painting to follow. He did them either on canvas or heavy paper coated with white size, depending on how many canvasses he'd prepared the night before. His supply didn't last long, so quick was he to discard some in disgust, often scraping a painting down mere minutes after beginning it. Each time he did, the back of Merry's neck would tighten as if she'd done something wrong.

He didn't like to converse while he worked, but finally she couldn't keep silent anymore. "Why must you destroy these pictures?" she demanded. "Why not save them and choose the best when you're done?"

He raised his brows as if she were simple, but he answered. "I'm not like the old-style painters who start with a dark ground and work toward white. I begin with white and lay progressively darker shades on top. Because of this, I cannot rework as much as they do. My initial composition must be right."

That may have been true, but Merry knew a half-mad perfectionist when she saw one.

His mood turned increasingly inward as the days progressed, leaving her so stultified with boredom she barely noticed when he had her pose without her drawers. For an active young woman, the job was torture. The only advantage to the monotony was that sometimes she could trick him into answering her questions. Not often, though. Most of the time, his distraction made him curt.

"Where did you grow up?" she'd ask.

"North," would be his surly answer.

"Who sent you that letter this morning?"

"No one," he'd snap, then stride over to adjust her chin.

He kissed her sometimes when he did this, a brusque smack on her lips that left her humming from head to toe.

She was miffed to discover she could be silenced by a kiss, especially a kiss like that, but at least she knew she wasn't invisible.

"Must I entertain you?" he moaned, one unusually restless day. He was frowning at the canvas, an expression she'd learned might mean anything at all.

"I only wanted to know how old you were when you saw your first naked woman."

"Twelve," he said and drew a stroke that seemed to ease his glare.

Merry held her breath and struggled not to move. His answer, brief as it was, hinted at a story she wished to hear. She watched him nod in satisfaction at what he'd done. Now, she thought, ask him. "Who was she?"

"Housemaid. She was washing up in her room."

"Is that when you decided you wanted to be a painter?"

To her surprise, he lowered his brush and laughed. "You think I do this because I'm depraved."

"Of course I don't!"

"You do." His grin was utterly infectious. "Finally found a job where I could ogle naked females. But you're the one who gets hot and bothered when she takes off all her clothes."

"I am not!"

"Aren't you?" He set down his palette and walked around the folding easel. He was a messy painter, his shirt stiff with old stains, his arms and fingers every color of the rainbow. Without a care for mussing her, he lifted her off the posing saddle and slid her down his front.

Merry was too startled to struggle or perhaps, if she were honest, too interested in seeing what he would do.

His body was warm and hard, his thigh easing between her legs until she straddled its muscled length. If she'd ever forgotten she was naked, she remembered it when she felt that smooth black wool against her most private parts. The sensation of vulnerability was mysteriously appealing. His hand curved over her bottom, sticky with paint. He smelled of turps and linseed oil, a scent she knew she'd forever associate with him. As he pulled her closer, his sex began to stir.

"You're wet," he said softly.

The truth of the words brought a blaze of color to her face.

"You're hard," she shot back, rather than cede the point.

His head bowed toward her ear. "Not yet, Duchess. But I'm getting there."

The feel of him changing sent a shiver down her spine. He was stretching inside his trousers, against her hip, growing longer, growing thick. She heard him growl and then his teeth sank lightly into her neck. His hand, the one that wasn't wrapped around her bottom, skimmed her ribs and slipped beneath her hair. Her breasts were trembling with her heartbeat, with the intensity of all he made her feel. When he molded one in his palm, she couldn't suppress a whimper. His hand was larger than her breast, a stark reminder of his masculine advantage.

"You're hard, too," he whispered and feathered her nipple with his thumb.

Her back arched. His touch inspired more pleasure than she could bear—plucking her, playing her, stroking round and round while she struggled to be still. His thigh flexed between her legs and she went liquid deep inside. She hitched against him, once, but it did not help. She wanted his mouth on her, wanted him to lay her down and drive inside. In that moment, she wouldn't have had the strength to stop him.

But he was not a man to rush these matters. He brushed her hair aside with gentle fingers.

"How lovely you are," he mused. "Your nipples match your rosy-golden curls."

Without warning, tears stung the corners of her eyes. For years she'd been known as the plainest deb in London. She'd made a joke of it herself. But hard as she tried not to care, it wasn't easy knowing that no one, not even her parents, thought her pretty. "Ragamuffin" was the kindest term her father had ever used. And now this man, this artiste, spoke as if *she* were a work of art. The effect it had on her was extraordinary, as if he'd looked into her heart and fed it the meal it most desired, the meal it had been starving for all her life. She couldn't stifle a pang of regret when he set her on her feet and stroked her hair back down her breasts.

Smiling faintly, he lifted a sticky vermilion lock. "I've gotten paint on you," he said. "Perhaps you'd better wash."

Only pride enabled her to retreat. "Yes," she said, ignoring her body's protest. "I'd better."

Her earlier conversation with Isabel could not have been clearer in her mind. *Likes them panting after him, I'll bet,* she'd said. Merry hadn't met her employer then, but she'd guessed more truly than she'd known. Worse, if she didn't guard herself better, she'd end up panting as pathetically as the rest.

LAVINIA VANCE AND HER YOUNGEST SON WERE SHARing a silent breakfast, her sole attempt at conversation having met with a muffled grunt. For once, she wished she were more in the habit of talking with her children. At least then she'd have a distraction from her worries. But Peter seemed to have worries of his own. His mind plainly elsewhere, he glowered at the tablecloth while she pushed her eggs around her plate and wondered if the letter Merry had sent from Wales would suffice to keep the elder Althorp off her back. Her daughter's tone had been softer than she'd expected, expressing regret for harsh words and a certain nostalgia for times she'd spent with Ernest when they were young.

Surely Merry wouldn't mention him if she weren't rethinking her position.

Her second son wandered in as she tried to convince herself this was true.

"That's some frown," he said, loading a plate at the parlor sideboard. "You keep thinking that hard, you'll hurt your brain."

For one astonished moment, Lavinia thought James was addressing her, but then Peter shot a rude gesture at his brother from beneath the table, where he must have thought it would be concealed. Her pang of resentment took her by surprise. My children don't even see me, she thought.

But that was just as well, wasn't it, considering the secrets she had to hide?

"I didn't know you were in town," she said to James, tilting her cheek up for his kiss.

"Just for the day. Lissa's got a bee in her bonnet about this cradle she saw at a shop in Mayfair. Says it's been preying on her mind and I simply have to buy it." He grimaced. "You'd think the child was due to pop out tomorrow."

"Well, it is her first," Lavinia soothed and patted his hand. "I was just telling Peter we got a letter from Merry in the morning post."

Startled, Peter looked up from his plate. He hadn't heard a word. Again, she felt that tiny screw of hurt. She knew her children didn't share her interest in fashion or society, but she hadn't realized they blocked out everything she said. Or was she being too sensitive? Clearly, Peter had other things on his mind.

James set down his plate and took the seat next to his brother. "How is our little devil?"

"Fine," she said. "Apparently, Wales is rainy this time of year."

James grunted at this intelligence and tucked into his food.

"Are you going to write back?" Peter asked.

She strove to answer lightly. "I planned to this afternoon. Shall I send her your regards?"

"Better send her Ernest Althorp's," said James. "I saw him at the club yesterday. Looked all pale and stoic. Barely unclenched his jaw enough to say 'hello.'" He stuck half a biscuit in his mouth and chewed. "Damned if the fellow isn't in love with her after all."

"He couldn't be," Lavinia gasped, setting her coffee down with a clink.

Peter gaped at her. She realized she had not sounded very motherly.

"I only meant I'd be surprised," she said more mildly,

"because Althorp is so sensible. Reining Merry in will be difficult enough without letting sentiment cloud his mind."

"Maybe he can't help himself," Peter said. "Merry's a good egg and not half as plain as you make her out to be. I don't see why he couldn't love her."

Lavinia's throat tightened at the challenge in his voice. Did he really think she regarded his sister as unlovable? And if so, was he right? Had she come to believe the lies she'd been whispering in people's ears?

If she had, she'd sunken further than she'd known.

"We all love her," she said firmly enough to make James glance up from his food. "I was simply pointing out that Ernest Althorp is not a man known for passion."

"Got that right." James chuckled around a bite of ham. "Not like Peter here with his danseuse." He switched his voice to falsetto. " 'Oh, James, she's a little doll!' "

At that, whatever disapproval Peter harbored toward his mother was forgotten in his attempt to shove his brother off his chair.

Their tussling brought back memories of other mornings. Once upon a time, they'd sat around this table every day: Merry, the boys, her husband. What a noise they could make, like a flock of starlings—especially Evelyn, who'd never lost his habit of speaking on top of everyone else.

One day soon only she would sit here. Or she and Geoffrey would, when he didn't leave early for his club.

Lavinia pressed her lips together. It wasn't like her to be maudlin. She spent time with her family, more than she cared to on occasion. Certainly, there was more to her life than a noisy breakfast—far more. At the moment, however, she could not think what that was.

NIC'S MOODS HAD TAKEN A TURN FOR THE WORSE. Merry should have been grateful, she supposed. He hadn't so much as flirted with her in days. Unfortunately, the reprieve came at a price. He frowned more, snapped more, even threw his brushes across the room. Their workday grew shorter and what work he did seemed listless. Nothing she said could cheer him.

One morning, she woke not to his impatient rap but to the sound of someone beating rugs off the balcony down the hall. She stumbled into the corridor, half fastened and panicked she'd overslept, to find only the maid and the eternally scarf-wrapped kitchen lad. Though he tended to scurry out of sight as shyly as a barncat, this morning his hands were too full of dusty carpet to escape. He did, however, hunch his presumably hideous head into the wool.

"What time is it?" she asked.

"Close on noon," said the sturdy maid. "We're sorry for waking you, but Mr. Farnham said we had to get this done."

"Noon!" Merry pressed her hand to her bosom. She never slept till noon. Nic mustn't have come by at all. "What happened to Mr. Craven?"

"One of his black fits," said the maid. "Likely sleep till dinner, then drink hisself back to bed."

Merry's throat tightened. "Is he ill?"

"Not ill, miss. Just ill-tempered from his work not going right. Makes him crawl into his hole like a prickly badger." The maid laughed. "Mr. Farnham says a whack on the rump'd do him more good than sleep."

Merry was accustomed to servants knowing their master's business. As a less than dutiful child, she'd often used their intelligence to her advantage. This maid's bluntness shocked her, but she supposed the staff considered her too close to their level to guard their tongues. Though the sensation of being taken for one of them was odd, it was not unwelcome. Clearly, her ruse was working.

"Maybe you could jolly him out of it," the maid suggested, slanting a smile at her. "The master likes his bit of skirt."

The kitchen boy released a muffled cough that did not sound amused. When Merry looked at him, the skin above his scarf had flushed the color of a plum. He was beating the carpet so hard the dust he raised threatened to engulf them all.

"I'll see if he's hungry," Merry said, tearing her gaze from the boy who so obviously didn't want to be seen. "Maybe Mrs. Choate will have something to tempt him."

But Merry didn't have to see the cook. Mr. Farnham shoved a tray at her as soon as she reached the landing on the stairs.

"Here," said the frazzled butler, "see if you can pry him out of bed."

Nonplussed by the order, Merry took the tray and headed toward Nic's door.

"Don't knock," Farnham advised. "He'll just ignore you."

With some trepidation, she took his advice. She wasn't at all sure she was ready to encounter her employer in his bed. Hand shaking, she reached for the knob.

Once it was open, she simply stood and looked around. His room was different from the rooms she had grown up in, simple and uncluttered. He'd hung no paintings here, not even his own. Her curious gaze found white walls and dark wood trim and on the ceiling a plaster rose from which descended a lovely blown-glass chandelier. The carpet was old but good, its colors so dark she could barely make out a pattern.

And then she took in the bed. Nic lay in it, a long, blanket-covered lump. His sleeping presence was enough to warm her face. More than that, though, the bed was huge. Japanese, she thought, from the pattern of squares and circles that formed the frame. No hangings draped it. Instead, six slim posts supported an elegant wooden roof. The structure resembled an open cage, as if Nic were a circus animal no one thought was very dangerous.

That, of course, was patently untrue.

Feeling very much as if she intruded, she noisily cleared her throat.

The lump in the coverlet moved. "Bloody hell," Nic swore. "Can't you keep your nose out of anything?"

Ignoring the sting this inspired, she set the tray on his bedside table and stood between him and a beam of sun. This was a trick she had learned from her occasionally hard-drinking brothers.

"Mr. Farnham is worried about you," she said.

He jerked at the sound of her voice, but did not emerge. "Just want a rest. Till my brain starts working again. Would have done it before, but then *you* came. Bloody Godiva."

Merry ignored this accusation just as she had the first. "One of the servants suggested a whack on the rump might do you good."

Nic's head surfaced from his cocoon. Though his eyes were clear, he gave every appearance of having been in his cups. His skin was pale and his hair hung over his face in a tangled mop. "You try it and you'll be sorry."

She smiled at the threat. She'd heard that from her brothers, too. "Perhaps if you shared what was troubling you, you'd feel better."

"No, no, no," he groaned, rolling onto his back with the pillow clutched to his face. "It's my picture and my problem, and I'll solve it my way."

"By hiding under the covers like a two year old?"

The pillow whumped her in the chest. Before she could catch her breath, Nic bolted up and the blankets slipped down. Her eyes widened. He wasn't wearing his Indian pyjamas. In fact, he wasn't wearing anything. She could see the halves of his bottom, smooth as cream, and between them the faintest down of black rising to lick his spine. A hollow shadowed the flesh behind his hip, evidence of a muscle as strong as it was spare. Merry swallowed hard before looking up. Nic pointed toward the door as if his arm were made of steel.

"Out," he rumbled, his voice as suited to anger as seduction, "before I give *you* a whack on the rump."

The words were comical but she sensed he meant them. Apparently, she could not dismiss his threats the way she did her brothers'. She goggled a moment, then backed away. Merry hadn't been spanked since she was ten and, given how hard Nic had thrown that pillow, she suspected she wouldn't enjoy it.

She sagged in relief as soon as she closed his door.

How peculiar he was, threatening to beat her just because she wished to help! And how different he seemed from the considerate man he'd been before. The change had to be more than artistic temperament. From what she'd seen, his work had been thoroughly acceptable. Perhaps this painting didn't have the depth of her father's portrait, but it hardly warranted him retreating to his bed.

Hard as she tried, she could not understand. Nic was successful, respected. His creations hung in the finest homes. Surely he couldn't doubt his talent. Why wasn't he satisfied? What drove him to seek perfection? Was that what genius was: a search for something no one else could see?

In spite of everything, she yearned to go back and ask. To soothe his brow perhaps, and reassure him he'd find his way.

Fear kept her from it, but not fear of failure. No, she was stopped by her all-too-vivid memory of his sleep-warmed body rising from those rumpled sheets. If she gave in to the urge, she feared his brow would not be all she soothed.

NIC PULLED THE BLANKET BACK OVER HIS FACE. HE told himself he was glad Mary left. He'd only have been brutish if she stayed. The old fury had him in its claws: at himself, at life, at the stupid blobs of oil and pigment that could not catch the magic in his brain.

What had any of it been for if he couldn't paint? He didn't fool himself that his sacrifice had been the greatest. That honor belonged to the boy and Bess. Her life. Cristopher's happiness. All so Nic could learn to make his little daubs.

He had nothing to offer them. Not then. Not now. He was a mere pleasure seeker, a pitiful excuse for a human being. The only value he possessed was in his hands. If they failed him, he might as well rot in this bed forever.

Caught in the downward spiral, he let himself think of his boyhood friend. The way she hummed when she worked. The way the sun streaked her golden hair. By God, Bess had been young. Seventeen. Fresh from her parent's farm, the smell of hay still on her skin.

Coming to work at Northwick had been her grand adventure.

You're a marvel, Nic, she'd say as they lay together in the

grove, her work-rough hand sliding down his shirtless chest.
I never knew a boy could be so nice.

Her kisses had tasted of fruit, sweet and sharp and far
more experienced than his. The first time she pressed her
tongue between his lips, he'd trembled as if the earth had
shuddered on its axis, overwhelmed by wonder and gratitude and a lust as sharp as whetted steel. For months, they'd
played at the preludes of love: two strong, young bodies
teasing each other hotter with a look, a kiss, a brush of skin
on skin. He remembered backing her against a tree one day
and thinking he'd die if he'd didn't come.

Do you want me to touch you? she'd whispered. *Do you
want me to take you in my hand?*

He'd spilled the minute she slipped her fingers inside his
linens. She hadn't even had to rub him. Despite the violent
bliss of his release, he'd wanted to weep with embarrassment.

Don't worry, she'd cooed, kissing the shame away. *You'll
learn to last and then I'll teach you what women like.*

The gift she gave him had no price. A precious thing. A
thing no man should ever dare to steal. Not ever.

She'd soaked the bed in blood, they'd said. Had to burn
it when she was gone. Hard to imagine the creature who
gave those life-affirming kisses could ever die.

Moaning, Nic rolled onto his belly. Bess had been his
Waterloo. The beginning of his fall. But when he ground his
face into the pillow, the kisses he imagined were not hers.

NIC'S BLACK FIT, AS THE MAID CALLED IT, STRETCHED
to two days, then three. He slept the way other men drank,
throwing himself into it as if he wished to drown. He had
what meals he ate sent to his room, so Merry had no chance
to speak to him at the table. She wondered how a body could
stand that much sleep, and began to look back on the boredom of posing with nostalgia. Desperate for distraction, she
played checkers with the cook, helped the maid clean a
gasolier, and evaded the butler's suggestion that she "stretch
her legs" in the neighboring park. Merry's peers were more

likely to frequent Hyde Park than Regent's, but it wouldn't be impossible for her to encounter someone she knew.

Even if she was climbing the walls, she couldn't risk being seen in London, not while her scheme seemed so close to falling through.

"He *is* going to finish my painting, isn't he?" she asked Mrs. Choate from her perch on a counter in the kitchen.

The cook was stirring a pot of soup on the iron range, her hair steamed to wispy curls, her motherly face pink. "'Course he is. Always does. Like my gran used to say, with every gift comes a curse. To my mind, these moods are the master's curse—never mind what Mr. Farnham says."

Merry rubbed her nose to hide her smile. The butler and Mrs. Choate had a more or less friendly rivalry: the one never agreed with the other if he could help it.

"Your picture will be special," the cook predicted. "The pictures he gets his fits over always end up the best. 'Course, like as not, he'll be down in the dumps again once it's finished, but far be it from me to tell an artist how to act."

"Maybe I'm not inspiring enough," she said, a worry that had been pricking her of late.

Mrs. Choate smiled at her through the steam. "Don't fret yourself over that. The master sees things other people don't, but that doesn't mean they aren't there. If he says you're Lady Godiva, I reckon you must be."

Merry's doubt expressed itself in a sigh.

"I think you're pretty," piped a voice from the scullery. It was the kitchen boy, who'd been in there scrubbing pots, so quiet they'd forgotten he was there.

"Well, bless me," said Mrs. Choate, laughing under her breath. "It speaks."

"Thank you," Merry called, but the boy might have sunk into the ground for all the response she got back.

Mrs. Choate rolled her eyes. "There's an odd duck," she murmured. "If freaks were fortunes, that one would own the world. Only thing he wants to talk about is Mr. Craven. Is he strict and do I think he's honest? Yesterday he asked old Max if he thought the horses liked the master!"

"Well, that is . . . I mean, people say that is the measure of a man: how he treats his animals and his servants."

"But why should a kitchen boy want to take his employer's measure? You'd think he'd be more concerned with what he's paid."

Merry had no answer but she did have another question. "*Does* he have a scar?" she whispered, remembering the omnipresent scarf.

"Spots is my theory," said Mrs. Choate. "But he works like the dickens, I'll give him that."

Merry wished she could say the same. Whatever the cook assured her, it was beginning to look as if her scandalous naked painting would never see the light of day.

Of course, if Nic continued to struggle, maybe she should take that as a sign her ruination wasn't meant to be. It wasn't too late to head it off. She could get herself to Wales; pretend she'd been with Isabel all along.

The prospect lured her. She could evade everything she dreaded: the embarrassment, the risk, her father's wrath. Not to mention Nic, who surely posed the greatest threat of all.

Social ignominy she could live down. Even a parent's fury would, in a decade or two, simmer back to its native affection. But to give one's innocence to a rake! Never mind hers was not a snowy innocence; the loss of one's virginity was still a matter of some moment. To give it to Nic—handsome, seductive, profligate Nic—seemed an invitation to despair. Three years had passed since her rejection by Edward Burbrooke, and she still cringed at the memory. She shuddered to think what Nic's rebuff would do.

Nic was so much more than Edward. He was heated oil and poppy smoke and damned nice when he put his mind to it. Nic said the words she'd always longed to hear. So what if she didn't believe them. He said them like they were true.

He was strange. She could not argue that. But Merry was strange herself. If she hadn't been, she would have married Ernest in a heartbeat. She wouldn't have been so drawn to risking everything she had. And for what? Adventure? Excitement? A taste of forbidden sins?

A sensible girl would have taken to her heels. A sensible

girl would have said: to hell with independence, I'm scampering home where I'll be safe.

Sighing, Merry kicked the old oak cabinet with her heels. She knew she wasn't sensible. Never had been. Never would be. The best she could manage was clever. Hopefully, when it came to Nic, she hadn't been too clever for her own good.

6 ❧

NIC FELT ODD WHEN HE AWOKE, AS IF HIS HEAD were filled with pulsing cotton instead of brains. The effect was not of brandy but of sleep and he knew that, heavy though his limbs might be, his body had no more slumber in it.

His refuge had kicked him out and barred the door behind him. He could lay here a few hours more but he would not recapture the oblivion he craved.

Rather than try, he swung his legs to the side of the bed and sat up, his elbows on his knees, his palms scrubbing slowly at his face. He had eaten and bathed during his periods of wakefulness, but his hair was nearly as bad a tangle as his model's.

He'd dreamed of kissing her, of her smooth, sleek limbs entwined with his. It had been a pleasant dream, sensual and slow, one whose memory buzzed along the surface of his skin. Perhaps she'd come into his room while he slept. He wasn't certain, but he thought he remembered someone light perched on the edge of the bed. He'd thought she was really there, but when he opened his eyes—or believed he opened them—he saw a ghost of himself as a boy, staring sadly toward the window as though he knew what tragedies lay ahead.

"You help other people," said his younger self, without turning his head. "Why won't you let them help you?"

"They deserve help," he responded, just as if the conversation made perfect sense.

The boy considered this. "Maybe you deserve help, too."

Everything faded after that, a dream lost in a dream. The encounter did not trouble him. Nothing much could when he was sleeping.

A soft tap brought his head out of his palms.

"Yes," he said, his voice croaking from disuse.

Mary peeped around the door. "You're up."

He quelled the sudden leaping of his heart. "Awake anyway."

She stepped in with a tray of coffee and fruit and toast. A flush crept over her freckles as she caught sight of his sex lying lax and unguarded between his thighs. Her eyes darted away and then back. The return flattered him, brief though it was. Flattered his manhood, too, for as soon as her gaze fell on it, it abruptly spurted longer. There was a wake-up call, he thought. Mouth curling with his first smile in days, Nic pulled the sheet fully over his legs. He'd forgotten what an innocent she could be, though not such an innocent that she'd shrieked.

Color recovering, she set the tray on the bedside table, then shifted both to his side. The ease with which she moved his furniture impressed him. What a little Amazon she was! With half an ear, he listened to her babble about Mrs. Choate putting chocolate in his coffee to get back at Farnham for ordering her not to cook anything fancier than toast.

"Don't care," he rasped, "as long as it's strong."

She poured a cup and handed it to him, her funny little face puckered with concern. She watched with great attention while he drank. Some small corner of his soul, a corner he was in no state to examine closely, decided it liked her care. The sense of well-being that suffused him owed as much to her furrowed brow as to the drink.

"I dreamed of you," he said, "that you sat on the bed and held my hand."

He watched her eyes, but she betrayed no sign of embarrassment, as she might have if it were true. Her brow puckered harder. "Would doing that have been wise?"

He laughed, this time at himself. His own snappishness had discouraged her from coddling him. "I'm sorry I was rude to you," he said. "And sorry that you worried. I can be a slug, I'm afraid, but I didn't mean to scare you."

"You didn't scare me. Only hurt me a bit because I wished to help."

He looked away from her expression, which was suddenly too sincere for comfort. Best not to encourage that.

"You're helping now," he said, putting a bit of carnal honey into his voice. He patted the mattress beside him. "And you could help even more if you wanted."

Instead, she stalked to the door.

"Huh," she said, with a spark that pleased him. "I know you're feeling better if you're on about that again."

"I'll have you yet, Duchess."

"Better go back to sleep then," she retorted, "so you can have me in your dreams."

He smiled. In *her* dreams, he suspected, she was nearly his.

IF MERRY HAD BEEN A MOUSE, NIC WOULD HAVE been the cat crouched in wait before her hole. They sat in the muraled French dining room, relaxing with coffee after their meal. Or Nic was relaxing; Merry merely strove to look as if she were. She watched him flick an envelope along his jaw. His gaze was considering, his pose a sprawling slouch. They'd returned to the studio today. Nic had thrown out just three studies, more in resignation than disgust.

She supposed this was cause for celebration, but she had the distinct impression his mind was more on her than on his work. For the first time since he'd had her bare her breasts, she'd felt self-conscious as she posed, as if the air were pressed too close to her naked skin. All day he'd stared at her not as a painter but as a man.

He'd touched her more often than he had to, adjusting her arm, her knee, the fall of a curl across her breast. Even now, fully clothed, she felt as if she were naked. His gaze was no leer but it seemed to strip her nonetheless. He knew what lay beneath her gown.

And he knew what his attention did to it.

She squirmed in her chair and turned her eyes to the trembling surface of her coffee. Pull yourself together, she thought. You're a toy to him: forgotten as soon as played with. This man couldn't possibly want her as much as she wanted him.

The fire hissed in the grate, the only accompaniment to the scrape of paper along his jaw. Merry could barely see his evening beard but she could hear it. The reminder of his maleness made her tighten deep inside.

"It seems," he said, his voice shockingly intimate in the quiet, "that I've been invited to a party."

He leaned across the table, one forearm stretched until his hand rested a tiny distance away from hers. She clutched her cup, but the warmth of this almost-touch was stronger than the warmth of the steaming drink. She told herself not to draw back. That would betray how strongly she was moved.

"A party?" she said, pretending to sip her coffee.

The tip of his finger brushed her hand. "Yes. And Farnham will box my ears if I don't get myself out of the house. I thought you might like to come."

"Me?" She was so startled she didn't notice when he took her hand, only that now he cradled it in his own.

"Yes." He stroked the delicate skin beneath her wrist. Sensation skittered outward from the touch. His gaze, both direct and intense, held her as much a prisoner as his hands. "I despise going alone. They're all couples. Old friends of mine."

"What sort of friends?"

His mouth twitched at her suspicion. "Let's see. Three

artists, one former actress, a coatgirl and a Jewish banker—
if that meets with your approval."

"No one else?" she said, thinking this sounded unlike anyone she might know. "Your friends will be the only ones who
are there?"

"Not a soul besides," he assured her. "They're all perfectly agreeable. Well, maybe not perfectly, but they make up
for it by being entertaining. Say yes, Mary. I want to show
you off."

"Me."

He carried the back of her hand to his smiling lips. "Yes,
you. You could wear the velvet gown."

"I could wear a hundred velvet gowns and I still
wouldn't—"

His tongue wet the valley between two knuckles, silenc-
ing her skepticism. Her skin cooled, then tingled as he repeated the shameless lick. His tongue was sharp and agile, a
bruised rose-pink that matched his mouth, that matched—
she suddenly, vividly recalled—the head of his waking sex.
She'd never thought of someone's tongue as being obscene
but his most definitely was. Other stories overheard from the
stable boys returned to haunt her: places they'd claimed experienced lovers liked to suck. She felt as if Nic's mouth
were on them now. To make matters worse, his nails began
scratching lightly across her palm. The caress had a singular
effect, sending chills up her arm and down her breasts; forceful chills, like an electrical experiment. Heat gathered in her
sex, its flesh beginning to contract and expand in synchrony
with his strokes.

"What are you doing?" she gasped, trying to pull away.

"I'm taking liberties. And I'm going to take another each
time I hear you speak as if you were not pretty." Looking up
at her through his lashes, he licked her hand again.

"Stop it!" she ordered, her emotions too confused to tug
very hard.

Rather than release her, he let her pull the back of his hand
to her breast. He rubbed her lightly there, one finger swing-
ing back and forth across the swell. "I'll stop," he said,
"when you agree to come."

The final word jolted through her, a soft, hot spear. She knew he didn't mean come to the party. He meant "come" as in "climax" and no doubt not alone. The blood of arousal flushed his face and lips, which had parted for his breath. He looked so beautiful he made her heart clench. Next to him, she was a hideous, freckled troll.

"Say you'll come," he said, softer now, rougher. "Say you'll come and meet my friends."

"I don't see why you want me to."

"I told you." One hand rose to stroke her cheek. "I don't like to come alone."

"Do you ever?" she whispered, remembering the night he'd slammed into her smoke-filled room, the night he'd cupped his sex and rubbed it while she watched.

His eyes gleamed in the gaslight, soft, gray jewels; windows, perhaps, but only to more mystery. His pupils were black as jet.

"Sometimes I do. Sometimes my needs are too pressing to wait. But then I wish I had someone with me."

"Someone?"

His thumb smoothed her brow. "I should like the someone to be you, Mary. I think you know that by now."

Before she could gather her wits, he released her and rose, reminding her how tall he was, how slim and spare. Though he'd scrubbed, tiny flecks of paint clung to his nails. The imperfection did not matter. His hands were all the more beautiful for this evidence of their skill.

"Tomorrow night," he said. "We'll leave at seven. Cook used to be a lady's maid. I'm sure she'd be happy to help you dress."

She should have resented his command. More to the point, the risk of going out should have drained this creamy pleasure from her limbs. Instead, reeling in mind and body, she sagged in her chair and admired his retreating form.

His bottom was narrow and firm, the muscles moving with his strides. With far too much ease, she could picture it laboring over her.

I'm at his mercy, she thought.

If he decided to take her now, she would not have the will to stop him.

SHE'D RECOVERED FROM HER FATALISM BY THE TIME the following evening rolled around, probably because she hadn't seen Nic all day and was able to rally her resistance. Rather than have her pose, he'd left her to bathe and primp and, as he put it, do whatever it is women do. Merry took this for the nonsense it was. She had no doubt he knew precisely what women did.

Mrs. Choate, the former lady's maid, was indeed a help, not only hooking her into the purple gown but also arranging her hair in a fashionable chignon. Her curls, for once useful, required no crimping to decorate her brow.

"I keep my skills up," said Mrs. Choate when Merry expressed her admiration at the effect. "In case they're needed."

She refrained from asking how many times they had been. She knew the answer would just depress her. Spirits dampened by the thought, she declined Mrs. Choate's offer to powder down her freckles.

"You'd have to powder everything," she said. "I'd rub off on whatever I touched."

"S'pose you're right," sighed the cook. Together they surveyed her reflection in the rust-flecked mirror. Merry felt odd dressing up in this humble room, odd and precarious, as if she were more in danger of being marked an imposter now.

The velvet gown, while bold, was as flattering as anything her mother would have picked. The bodice was dangerously low, but it had to be in order to show off what decolletage she had. As was the fashion, the skirt was smooth in front, its luxurious fabric pulled into a fall of ruffles at the back. Having spent much of her recent life wearing nothing at all, Merry had never been so aware of the imprisoning nature of modern dress. Tiebacks beneath the skirt kept it from spreading and its narrow width made it difficult to walk, especially with the dragging fantail train. Even the weight of the dress was burdensome. Despite this, she could not regret being shown to her best advantage. She might not be the beauty Nic claimed but, by God, she was as fine as cloth could make her. She felt a different woman tonight: not who she'd been before, not who she'd pretended to be, but someone else entirely.

Someone who could seduce a man, she mused, then shivered prophetically at the thought.

Nic seemed happy with the results. "Bang up to the mark," he said as she descended his curving marble stairs.

Merry barely registered the praise. In his black tailed coat and trousers, he took her breath away. Now that he was dressed more like men she knew, she could better judge his figure. His shoulders were broad and straight, his hips as narrow as a dancer's. His waistcoat—almost as snug as her bodice—glowed in peacock blue embroidered with silver flowers. No man of her acquaintance would have been caught dead in such garish garb, but on Nic it seemed fitting. The color lent a hint of azure to his silver eyes. He'd combed his hair back from his brow, and the tempting, touchable waves spilled over his collar at the back. Their russet highlights gleamed as if they'd been oiled.

"You blind me," she said with a crooked smile.

He tucked his thumbs under his lapels and swelled his chest. "Can't let you outshine me."

"As if I could," she said, but there was no bitterness in her tone, only enjoyment at their banter and the pleasant shock of his splendor in evening dress. She couldn't recall having had so handsome an escort in her life.

They rode to the party in a small, closed carriage that was driven by the gardener and pulled by a nag so old and slow she could only have been hired out of pity. The night was misty and moonless and the foolish horse shied at everything that moved, including the swaying lanterns they'd hung on the carriage to light the way. Fortunately, they hadn't far to go, just a few streets north to a line of bijou cottages near the Eton and Middlesex cricket ground.

Nic sat next to her on the single seat, his scent mingling with hers in the tiny space. The effect was like a drug. With difficulty, she restrained the impulse to lean into his shoulder and close her eyes. When they drew to a halt, he put his arm on the sleeve of her new green coat. In spite of her vow to maintain a level head, her pulse began to skip.

She wondered if he meant to kiss her.

"I probably should warn you," he said, "that my friends can be a trifle wild. There's no malice in them, but if anyone says or does anything to discommode you, come to me and I'll see they stop."

Merry's eyes widened, wondering what he meant by "wild." Not debauched surely. Not licentious or depraved. Just how "discommoded" might she be? Would she be forced into the position of giving her unworldliness away?

I shall have to guard my reactions, she thought, and not let him see if I am shocked.

Sensing her nervousness, if not the cause for it, Nic pressed his lips to her furrowed brow. His voice was a velvet murmur in the dark. "I know you can take care of yourself, but I'd be honored if you'd rely on me."

His words simultaneously soothed her nerves and increased her caution. How alluring he was, and how unlike anyone she'd known. She felt dazed as he helped her from the carriage to the footpath, his kid-gloved fingers tight on hers even after she'd stepped down. "I shall make it clear," he warned, "that I intend to claim you for my own."

Thus saying, he led her down a short brick walk to a picturesque wooden door. Designed to resemble a country cottage, its planks had been painted the same vivid blue as Nic's waistcoat. The door opened before he could knock.

Light spilled out, outlining a woman's voluptuous form. She was garbed in a gauzy, flowing gown that was either a very informal tea dress or an elaborate negligee. Artistic, Merry supposed it would be called, in the style of the Pre-Raphaelites. The woman wearing it was taller than ordinary, but not towering, with soft brown hair and the loveliest oval face Merry had ever seen. Her eyes were so blue they were nearly purple. She could have modeled for a Madonna were it not for the lushness of her mouth, and the fact that her lips were painted poppy red.

Now this, Merry thought with as much awe as dismay, is how a temptress ought to look.

"Nic!" the vision cried, opening soft white arms. "We thought you'd never come."

The pair embraced like old friends, rather close old friends, pressing their cheeks together and smiling into each other's hair.

Though she tried to hide it, Merry's body tensed. She wondered at Nic bringing her to the home of an old lover when he obviously intended to seduce her. Were the manners of his set so different from hers? Or did the difference lay in who Nic thought she was: not the daughter of a duke, but a ruined maid?

At last, after what seemed like an eternity, he pushed back from their hostess. "Anna," he said, his voice warm, "as always, you steal my breath."

Anna patted his shoulder and turned to Merry. Her smile dazzled. "You must be this shameless flatterer's friend."

"Mary Colfax," she said. Anna seemed to expect neither bow nor curtsey, so Merry did not bend. Indeed, she wasn't sure she could have. Her spine had gone as rigid as a poker.

Anna dimpled as if her stiffness did not exist. "Come in," she said, her hand slipping gently behind her elbow. "Everyone will be so pleased to meet you."

Her coat was taken by a pretty parlormaid, her gloves by Anna herself. From this Merry knew the evening's manners would be informal. Indeed, the guests' behavior upheld her guess. Scattered about a comfortable, earth-toned parlor, they consisted of three couples besides Merry and Nic. The other women, one fair and one dark, sat on the arms of their partners' chairs and leaned familiarly into their sides.

That alone would have given her mother vapors.

Two of the men were painters like Nic. Sebastian Locke was a tall, sardonic blond with a small goatee. His companion, introduced only as "Lovey"—the coatgirl, Merry guessed—was plump and fair and given to giggling for no cause. Gerald Hill, the second artist, was shorter and more earnest. He had the flushed cheeks and defensive manner of a man whose pride is easily bruised. To Merry, his partner was much more interesting. Her name was Evangeline. She was slim but bosomy and had an arresting, angular face, the left side of which was slightly higher than the right. The anomaly made one want to stare at her, though hardly in horror. She was striking but badly dressed in colors that, even to Merry's eye, did not suit her at all. The style of her muddy gown was mannish: high-collared, aggressively plain, as if she were daring people to admire the way she looked. Though she sat with Gerald Hill, her gaze kept straying to Sebastian Locke.

Here is one, Merry thought, who hasn't learned to hide her infatuations.

The final gentleman, Leopold Vandenberg, was older than the others. The first sight of him allayed most of Merry's fears. He seemed the essence of all that was conservative. Dressed soberly, he wore a full beard, streaked with gray. No amount of expensive tailoring could disguise the middle-aged thickening of his waist. Though his eyes were kind and his face intelligent, he could not have been considered handsome.

It did not take a genius to surmise he was the banker.

To Merry's surprise, he was also the lovely Anna's patron. But perhaps she should have expected the pairing. The lovely Anna struck Merry as a practical woman.

Once the introductions were complete, Sebastian Locke ran his gaze so boldly down her dress she felt like an object in a shop.

"Well, old boy," he said to Nic, "I see you've been holding out on us."

"Of course, I've been holding out." Nic's voice was light but he wrapped a protective arm around Merry's waist. "Your habits are too dissipated for any sane man to do otherwise."

"Nonsense." Locke's eyes remained on Merry even as he caressed his companion's flaxen curls. "You and I have supped from the same dish before."

This was too much for Nic. He stiffened and drew a sharp breath to speak.

"Stop it," Anna scolded, before he could respond. "I won't

have you two gnawing that bone in my house. Besides, you'll embarrass Miss Colfax."

"That I should hate to do," said Locke with a mocking bow that took in her and Anna. "Please, Miss Colfax, say my thoughtless words have not offended you."

"Indeed not," Merry responded crisply. "I've no doubt you're only interested in me because I came with Nic."

Nic released a muffled laugh, which the dark Evangeline echoed without restraint. "She's got you there, Sebastian. To a T."

Sebastian glared at Evangeline from under golden brows, an attention that seemed to please her. Sensing the current, Gerald Hill pulled her hand onto his knee.

A skein of forbidden interest unfurled in Merry's breast. Was this what Sebastian meant by supping from the same dish? Gerald didn't seem eager to share, but she wondered what more she'd see before the evening closed. The possibility of witnessing genuine immorality both frightened and intrigued her. Caught up in her thoughts, she shivered as Nic drew his finger around her ear. His voice was intimately low.

"Don't dare him," he warned.

"I wasn't," she gasped, aghast that he could think she would.

Nic chuckled and tweaked her nose. "You should see your face, Duchess. Like the proverbial moth. But he and Evangeline would eat you alive."

She frowned but did not argue. The others were staring at them with interest, wondering perhaps if they were having a lovers' spat. The curly blonde sprawled lower on the couch. "I like her hair," she announced, as if someone had intimated they did not. "It's like a little lamb's."

Her declaration broke the tension in the room. Sebastian laughed, his sulky face transformed to dazzling boyishness. He pulled the glass from his partner's hand. "No more wine for you, Lovey. You're soused."

"Am not," she pouted, but snuggled against him as he kissed her hair.

Considering its prelude, dinner was more agreeable than Merry would have guessed. The food was fine French fare, served with equally fine French wine. Better than the meal, though, was the flattering care with which Nic treated her. Like a chivalrous knight, he fed her morsels from his plate, touched her cheek and hand, even fetched one of Anna's cloaks when she grew chilled.

Propriety did not matter. For once in her life, she felt a princess—with Nic her handsome prince. Perhaps it was the wine or the heat in his eyes or the sensual atmosphere of the night, but giving him what he wanted no longer seemed unwise.

"You devastate me," he murmured over the rim of his crystal glass. He had turned toward her in his chair, his knees bumping hers. When she looked down, her gaze found his hand resting on his thigh, his thumb touching the curve of an unmistakable erection. His mouth turned up at her involuntary gasp. He'd wanted her to see, to know he was aroused.

Merry felt as if something warm and plump had been slipped inside her sex. The others were talking amongst themselves, but if any glanced over they would guess what he was doing.

"All yours," he breathed as his thumb swept slowly up and down. "Every hot, hungry inch."

"*If* I want it," she said, then spoiled the effect by choking on too large a swallow of her wine.

He patted her back. "Little fraud," he teased close to her ear. "You know you're dying to cram me deep inside you."

His words were too true for comfort. That his behavior was outrageous did not matter to her body. By the time dessert had been cleared, she was lightheaded with arousal. The postprandial separation of the sexes would have offered a break, but Anna, apparently, did not observe that custom.

They adjourned together to the sitting room, where Nic pulled her crosswise into his lap and pressed the rigid evidence of his interest into her hip. She could feel it through all her petticoats, could almost hear it through her skin.

When Gerald Hill tried to light a cigar, the other women shouted him down.

"Even I," said Leo Vandenberg with his faint Austrian accent, "am not bold enough to smoke in Anna's house."

"And he paid for it," she said, patting his shoulder without shame.

Merry used the cover of the other's laughter to nuzzle her prince's neck. Nic's arms tightened. When she looked into his face, his eyes were molten. *Brat,* he mouthed, and pressed a kiss to her tingling lips. The tip of his tongue left a small wet mark behind.

"Aw," said the blond girl, "look at the lovebirds."

"Cockatoos," quipped Sebastian and Merry blushed.

He made what she'd done seem both sordid and exciting.

"Why don't I show the ladies the facilities?" Anna suggested. "And while we're gone, you gentlemen see if you can't elevate your minds."

"More profit to ask us to elevate something lower," Sebastian said to the amusement of the men.

Anna rolled her eyes at Merry as if they belonged to a common sisterhood. To Merry's surprise, she realized she wouldn't have minded if they did.

But that was before Anna drew her alone into the library. Like the sitting room, this was a place a man would feel at ease. At present it was cold, for the fire had burned down long ago. Merry pulled her borrowed cloak closer and looked around. Though small, the number of books the room held astounded. From floor to ceiling they were shelved, even sitting in crooked stacks beneath the windows. A man's black slippers lay before the smoldering grate. The stitching hoop that sat on a table nearby suggested Anna might have embroidered them herself. This struck Merry as a homely task for a mistress to undertake, but Anna was no ordinary mistress. From the clutter and wear of the decor, she concluded this was the couple's private sphere.

"I suppose you're wondering why I brought you here," said her hostess.

Merry was curious but waited for the other woman to explain. Anna fingered a fold on her gauzy overskirt. Her skin was cream-colored, her hair a glossy oak. Even her hands were feminine: plump and soft with perfect oval nails.

Merry tried not to picture them pricking Nic's naked back.

Finally, Anna spoke. "It's none of my business," she said.

"But you're young and obviously impressionable. Decency compels me to offer you this advice." Again Merry said nothing. Anna released a breathy laugh. "All right, perhaps you're not as impressionable as I'd thought."

"You want to warn me about Nic," Merry said, "because you know him better than I do."

"For donkey's years." Anna's smile was wry. "And in all that time, he's never kept a woman more than a month."

"Not even you?"

The question was petty but Merry did not call it back. A hardness entered Anna's face that had not been there before.

"Not even me," she said blandly, and Merry knew she'd hurt her pride. She felt a twinge of shame. This was a woman who, had circumstances been different, she would have liked to befriend.

Unaware of her regret, Anna continued. "I know whereof I speak," she said. "And little as I imagine you want to hear it, you'd do well to heed my words. Nicolas Craven is a rake. I don't deny he's charming or that he can be kind, but he does not have it in him to give a woman his heart. Not even for as long as it takes to fuck her."

With all her strength, Merry hid her blanch of shock.

"You're right about his charm," she said, in her chilliest, most duchesslike voice. "And his kindness. More to the point, though, since he fucks so very well, perhaps one shouldn't complain if he keeps his heart."

Anna stared at her, then burst into startled laughter. "By God, you're a cool one. If I hadn't seen the way you look at him, I'd believe he'd met his match. But you're a girl, Mary, a warmhearted, starry-eyed girl and all Nic's kindness will only break your heart the harder."

"That's not your concern," Merry said, wishing she could draw herself as tall as the other woman.

"No," Anna sighed, "I suppose it's not. And who am I to warn you against breaking your heart? If nothing else, it will make a woman of you."

Was that what made a woman? Merry had never thought so, but maybe . . .

She shook her head before the idea could form. No. Anna

herself admitted Nic had failed to give his heart to her. Perhaps her disappointment colored her opinion. In any case, Merry was not going to let a warning from Nic's old lover spoil the nicest night she'd ever had.

Just once, she wanted to be the princess she'd always dreamed of being.

7

Even if Merry would rather have gone home, pride demanded she brazen the evening out. Her pulse still ragged, she returned to the sitting room and paused inside the door. She felt better as soon as she spotted Nic, though his pose was strange for a man in the midst of company. He sat on the floor in front of a large leather chair, his legs stretched before him, his head resting back on the empty cushion.

To Merry's eyes, he seemed more elegant than ever.

"You should come to Venice with us in March," Sebastian was saying. "I'm sure you could pick up a few commissions."

"I have my show at Tatling's in March."

"Well, la-di-da. A show at Tatling's."

From Sebastian's tone, Merry concluded he had not been invited to exhibit at the exclusive London gallery. Rumpled and vaguely feral, Sebastian sat across from Nic on the long brown sofa. His forearms rested on his knees with his hands clasped in between. He seemed restless and dissatisfied, but vulnerable as well. With a gentle smile, Nic stretched one boot to tap his fellow artist's shin.

"Give it a few years, old man. By then the galleries will be fighting to hang your work."

Sebastian wagged his head. "I wish I were as sure as you."

"Hah," barked Evangeline, "I wish I believed I had a chance in hell of ever being hung. But we know what people think of female artists."

"You're an artist, too?" Merry asked.

Everyone looked up at her in surprise, making her feel very much the outsider.

"Only according to my gran," said Evangeline, after a brief, uncomfortable pause.

"And me," Nic added in the same soft tone he'd used to reassure Sebastian.

"I always tell you you've got promise," Gerald put in, clearly aggrieved to be ignored. Evangeline shot him a scornful look that said what she thought of his opinion. "Well, I do," he insisted.

The couple made faces at each other while Nic beckoned Merry closer. He patted the chair behind him. "Sit with me," he said in a hot, rough voice that made her forget to care whether she belonged. "I missed you while you were gone."

Restraining the impulse to look around and see if Anna was close enough to hear, Merry slid into the chair in her narrow purple gown, then coaxed Nic's head to rest back on her knees. He smiled up at her, fond and sleepy-eyed, and pretended to bite her leg. Merry took that, too, as a token of victory. Maybe she meant no more to him than other women, but she flattered herself at least she meant as much.

"Where's Anna?" Sebastian asked, with the air of one who wishes to liven up an evening. "I think we need a story."

Anna chose that moment to reappear. "Of all the nerve. First I make you supper. Then you expect me to sing for it."

"Leo's Frenchman made the supper," said Sebastian. "And as hostess, you're obliged to entertain your guests."

Rather than contradict him, Anna turned to Leo. The older man had the armchair by the fire. Plainly, he was content with the comforts of his life. He seemed happy to indulge any manner of foolishness from his mistress's eccentric friends.

"Do as you wish, my dear," he said. "You know I always enjoy your tales."

His approval decided her. She crossed the Turkish carpet with its bold, dark shapes of red and brown, and perched her uncorseted form in the circle of the banker's arm. The fire gleamed on her loose chignon, a wood fire that smelled pleasantly of cedar and autumn leaves.

"Very well," she said, composing herself, "I shall tell the tale of the queen of the fey and the randy shepherd lad."

Despite Merry's jealousy of Anna's many charms, and the thought of how she'd once used them on Nic, the prospect of hearing something risqué pulled her forward in her chair. None of her brothers had shown a fondness for lewd books— for any books at all, truth be told—and Merry had long wanted to read one, if only to discover whether their authors knew more than stable boys. She held her breath as their hostess began.

"Queen Mab," said she, "was no puppet on a throne. She ruled the fey with an iron will and an eagle eye. No detail was too small for her royal notice, no task too humble for her delicate hand. Thus it was that when a shepherd and his flock wandered into forbidden lands, Mab immediately flew down from her pearl-encrusted palace to investigate.

"Now, as everyone knows, some faeries are as large as you and I, while some are as small as enchanted mushrooms. Mab was of the larger sort, and quite the most beautiful faerie who ever lived. Her hair was black, her eyes green, and her breast as snowy as a dove's. Her wings sparkled with dew-drop rainbows wherever they caught the light. Naturally, she could not allow a mere human to gaze upon her glory so, as she approached the intruder, she cast an invisibility spell to hide herself."

"Invisibility," leered Sebastian. "Imagine what a fellow could do with that!"

Evangeline snorted and rolled her eyes, but Anna ignored them both.

"The unsuspecting shepherd, no doubt bored by his duties, was napping beneath an apple tree. Mab was able to draw quite close without disturbing him."

"And he was handsome," Merry said, beginning to see where this was leading.

"Quite," Anna agreed, her eyes sliding coolly to Merry's face. "With wheaten curls and a scent like hay on a summer day. Mab didn't fall in love with him, of course. A faerie who gives her heart to a human must forfeit her powers. She did, however, immediately fall in lust. How could she not? The shepherd was as graceful as that statue by Michelangelo in the Louvre."

"Better equipped, I should hope," Nic said as he rubbed the back of his head against Merry's legs. Helpless to resist, she combed her fingers through his hair.

"Much better," Anna assured him. "I'm not implying Mab did anything so crude as disarrange the shepherd's clothes but, suffice to say, before she left the slumbering lad, she knew all of him to the inch—relaxed and at the ready. You see, she was so taken with him she sent him a dream of herself, posed in her diaphanous faerie gown, her nipples like cherries, her curves and dips a marvel no man could see without rising to the occasion. In the dream, she let him kiss one breast and herself drew one ivory hand up the tender inside of his thigh.

"This, however, was all the contact she permitted. He had not earned the right to more, not even in a dream."

"And when he woke?" Sebastian prompted.

Anna smiled. "When he woke, he thought he'd grown a hammer between his legs. No mortal man ever suffered such a cock-stand. It throbbed like the earth's own heart, long and thick and as glowingly red as a blacksmith's fire.

"Being a sociable sort, and not realizing his dream had been a true faerie visitation, the shepherd hobbled home as fast as he could, grabbed the first milkmaid he saw, and proceeded to churn her into a froth behind the village pub."

"I can guess what Mab thought of that," Nic said, prodding Merry's skirt again with his head. He'd drawn his knees up as Anna spoke and she suspected he was aroused. Feeling flushed herself, she stroked the cords along his neck. Her reward was a momentary closing of his eyes.

"Mab didn't like it at all," Anna said. "Here she, the queen of the fey, had deigned to let a mortal see her secret charms and what did he do but pour the lust she'd stirred into the first coarse vessel he found.

"Seething with fury, Mab cursed him. Even as the shepherd labored over the sighing maid, the queen took her revenge. From now on, she vowed, tup as he might, this scoundrel would not know completion's bliss until he turned his lust where it belonged."

"Ouch," said Gerald.

"Ouch, indeed," Anna agreed. "Cursed though he was, the hapless fellow's mighty instrument did not soften in the least. If anything, it grew in stature and demand. By this point, the well-sated maid was pushing him off her in disgust. Maddened by desire, the randy shepherd sought relief from every woman in the town. Young, old, handsome or hideous, he thrust his sword in every sheath. All to no avail. The faerie's curse had taken root. Give pleasure he could, even take it, but the ultimate joy was forever just out of reach.

"Finally, the women hid when they saw him coming. A truly tireless lover, these damsels discovered, was not a comfortable thing.

"Thrown back on his own devices, the shepherd tried to relieve the pain himself. For hours it seemed he wanked his monstrous prick until he feared both for it and his weary arm.

" 'I have been cursed,' he concluded, his mind clearing for a moment in exhaustion. 'That faerie I saw in my dream must have been real. Mayhap if I return to what I was doing when this began, I can find her again and beg her to release me.'

"Holding firm to this purpose, the shepherd—hobbling even worse than before—retraced his steps to the faerie mound. Again he lay under the apple tree and again, though without much hope, he composed himself to sleep. His effort was rewarded. As soon as he closed his eyes, the queen of the fey returned. Dazzled by her beauty, the dreaming shepherd fell to his knees. He knew he had found the source of his trouble. Between his trembling thighs, his organ buzzed as if it harbored a nest of maddened bees.

" 'Forgive me, queen of queens,' the shepherd pleaded. 'I am not worthy to kiss your wondrous toes. If only you'd tell me how I offended you, I'd do whatever is in my power to make amends.'

"Naturally, Mab was not pleased he could not guess what he had done, but knowing how men are, and impressed by his humility, she took pity on him. 'You must give me what you wasted on other women,' she said, 'and you must not cease until I say.'

"Scarcely able to believe his luck, the shepherd fell upon his beautiful tormentor. How his skin burned as he ripped aside her gauzy clothes! How his heart thundered as she clasped him to her breast! His need seemed to triple at the thought of finally achieving his culmination. As soon as his raging rod plunged into her tender grotto, the faerie said the words that dispelled her curse. At once the shepherd knew that he could come but, no longer the fool he'd been, he remembered Mab's admonition. He must not cease until she allowed it. He had no doubt that if he failed, the vengeful creature would curse him again, quite possibly with something worse. Gritting his teeth and shuddering with effort—for he was precious close to spilling as it was—the handsome young shepherd gave his all to the haughty queen.

"At last, after many painfully close calls, she sighed with pleasure and shivered delicately in his arms. 'Now,' she said, lifting her snowy hips against his own. 'Now you may claim your prize.'

"The shepherd could not wait a second longer. With a roar that shook the ground, he exploded in release, spewing his pent-up seed like so many gouts of fire. The bliss was unimaginable, for the faerie had enhanced it by magical means. The crisis left him boneless when it passed. He had not even strength to lift his eyes. Knowing he could not hold her, the faerie pulled free of his embrace.

" 'That will teach you,' she said, 'not to spend on a maid a passion fit for a queen.' "

Gerald was the first to recover from the silence that

gripped the room. "Bravo," he said, clapping loudly. "Your best ever."

Anna inclined her head as everyone echoed his praise.

Merry clapped as well, though she hardly knew where to look now that the spell had broken. She didn't wish the others to see her face, but couldn't help wondering how the tale had affected them. She knew it affected Nic, for the hand he'd wrapped around hers was damply hot.

He's infected me, she thought. Soon she'd be as depraved as he was.

But her reaction held more than titillation. For all its silliness, Anna's story made her sad. Two people who could have touched hearts had wasted their chance: one out of pride, and the other out of lust. Was that to be Merry's fate when she ventured into the world of carnal pleasure?

She could not say "if" anymore, only "when." Right or wrong, Nic had won her over. Worse, he seemed to know it. Grinning up at her, he pulled her knuckles to his mouth. "Ready to go?" he whispered.

Merry hesitated, then nodded with a blush. As always, he knew the question she'd really answered. Triumph gleamed in his smoky eyes.

She hoped with all her heart it was a triumph they could share.

NATURALLY, THEY COULD NOT LEAVE AT ONCE. NIC knew Mary wouldn't be comfortable with everyone guessing why they went. So he waited, itchingly impatient, through one last glass of Madeira. To his immense gratification, Mary's flush had not faded by the time he rose and stretched. He fancied he could hear her body humming with awareness. She hadn't met his gaze since Anna finished and that, oddly enough, aroused him most of all.

He knew she wanted to hide the hunger in her eyes.

He made their good-byes and ushered her out the door with as much haste as was seemly—perhaps a bit more. Anna lifted one brow at him when they left, but he honestly couldn't care. For once, he knew how his women felt.

He had to have her. Tonight. This minute. Sooner if they could manage it.

He swung her into his arms outside the door, thanking God old Max had brought the carriage round.

He practically tossed her onto the narrow seat.

"Nic!" she cried as she landed. He followed in an instant, pulling her sideways onto his lap. The carriage was icy, her body warm. Her startled hands flew to the breast of his winter coat. They belonged there. On him. All over him.

"Kiss me," he said. "Oh, God—*God*—put your mouth on mine."

Too eager to wait for her compliance, he clasped her head and forced his mouth to hers. She gasped but did not resist, and Nic abruptly felt as desperate as that bloody shepherd. Her lips were soft, yielding. He pushed inside and claimed her with his tongue. She tasted of wine and lust, of carmine red and throbbing violins. His throat closed on a moan. Deeper, he thought, and then: Damn, I could devour her. The kiss was rough, but his usual restraint had fled. To his relief, after her first stiff moment of surprise, she kissed him back, her strong, lithe arms wrapping his head and ribs, her tongue both sweet and greedy.

His heart pounded wildly in his chest. This kiss was so good. Too good. She pulled him into her mouth as if she could not wait for him to breach her. When he drew on her just as strongly, her sigh was a paean of agreement. She felt what he felt. She wanted what he wanted. Images swept through his mind, things he'd seen as her painter and now wished to see in bed. Her blush. Her breasts. The curve of her derriere. To touch her . . . To be given the right . . . He could not think. He wanted her until he hurt.

Her chignon began to fall. With a groan of pure sensual pleasure, he tore the pins away and buried his hands in the rippling mass of curls. Her hair was cool and thick. He found her scalp and rubbed, loving the way her breath caught in her throat, the way her neck seemed to lose its prideful starch.

"Mary," he said, his voice like gravel, "do you know what you do to me? Can you guess how mad I am to have you?"

He could not wait. He wrenched off his coat and opened his bursting trousers, drawing his erection from the tangle of sweaty cloth. He was heavy with arousal, leaden. The stiff, aching length fell against the purple velvet that draped her thigh. Merry gasped when she felt its living weight. Like magic, her cheek blazed with heat beneath his lips. Nic reached for her glove.

To his amazement, she pulled her hand away.

"Touch me," he said. "I want your fingers on my cock."

"But the coachman!"

"Fuck the coachman."

"But—"

He kissed her to silence. He was too near to getting what he craved to care who else might see. Max would not turn around in any case. Max was too well trained. Sinking deeper into desire, he nuzzled the bend of her neck and gloried in her sigh. She smelled wonderful, of vanilla and woman, of sweat and musk. His body wanted to absorb her through its pores. He slid his hand down her coat sleeve and tugged her wrist.

"Come on, Mary. I want those little calluses on my skin."

"Nic," she said, a laugh in it, "we haven't left Anna's yet. We're standing in the lane."

He cursed more creatively this time, and tried to steady his breath. Long before it calmed, he rapped on the window to rouse their dozing driver. "Max," he ordered, "take us home. And Lord help you if you stop for anything on the way."

Mary was still giggling when the carriage rumbled forward.

"You weren't supposed to notice that," he said, as disgruntled by her presence of mind as he was pleased by the yearning way she stroked his lapels.

She slid her hands behind his neck and laced them beneath his hair. "I take it I'm supposed to be overcome by passion."

"Yes," he huffed.

She tilted her head at him, her face in shadows, her eyes glinting with amusement. "Kiss me again, and we'll see if you overcome me."

His body leapt but he did not move. "If I kiss you again, I'll take you in the carriage. I admit, I'd be happy to do it, but it isn't what I'd planned for our first time."

"Oh, you've planned, have you?"

"Only since the moment I laid eyes on you."

Pleasure gurgled from her, a sound he'd never heard her make, one only the most confident woman could. The music warmed him deep inside. Wanting, needing to be closer, he pushed her skirts up her legs and turned her until she faced him on his lap. Her knees slid to either side of his hips, their progress stopped by the back of the leather seat. He scooted forward to bring her closer. Oh, that was better. Her gown was a tangle between them but beneath that only her drawers stopped the press of his raging flesh. Her warmth bled through the cloth, a humid warmth, perfumed by her arousal. He knew if he reached to touch it he would not stop.

Instead, he waited for her to touch him. Down her hands fell. From his shoulders. To his waist. Her thumbs rested on either side of his abdomen. She looked at his erection, rising thick and high between them, its thrumming surface lit by flickers of misty light. She bit her lip and then her hand was there, there on the upswung curve behind the head. Her thumb steadied him, then tightened. He tensed and fought a groan. The clasp felt shockingly good on his naked skin. She still wore her new kid gloves, their surface cool, their stitching a teasing rasp. Later, he thought. Later I'll strip her bare.

Her fingertips strafed the flare as if it were a harp string.

"If you won't kiss me," she murmured, "do you think I might kiss you?"

He had no power of speech to answer, just a groaning sigh.

She responded by brushing her lips across his own.

This was the kiss he'd dreamed of the day she'd showed up on his doorstep: a sweet kiss, a slow kiss. Her lips were a whisper over his, then a press, then a shy, wet exploration that ventured no further than the delicate skin above his teeth. He shivered under the silky tease as long as he could bear, breathing harder, twining tighter. He didn't want to scare her but his pulse was pounding so hard his skin was shaking. She wasn't touching his erection. She'd abandoned it to stroke his face with tender hands and even that sent sparks spangling down his nerves.

Finally, he couldn't stand it.

"More," he said, when her mouth began to wander down

his jaw. He stroked her neck above the collar of her coat. "Open for me. Let me taste you."

Her pulse stuttered under his fingers as she lifted her face to his. Her eyes were huge, unsure, but she did not object. "Like this," he whispered and went deep, wanting to drown in her, wanting to drink her in. He sighed, long and low, and pulled an answering sigh from her. Her hands moved from his face to his back, wrapping him as he wrapped her. The pleasure of the simple embrace surprised him. Despite the urgency of his need, he felt suspended in the moment, happy to spend the hours till sunrise in her arms.

Then the carriage wheels ceased crunching on the gritty drive and a different sort of tension took hold of his partner's limbs.

"We're home," she whispered.

Nic did not move except to lick the peak of her upper lip. "Nervous?"

She nodded with shyly lowered lashes and the conflagration inside him rose. He didn't know which made him ache more: her schoolgirl blushes or her boldness. He was going to enjoy this, really, truly enjoy this. He slid his hands down her back until they filled the hollow above her bustle.

"I'm not letting you back out now," he warned, "but I'll make you happy you gave in."

She gaped at his effrontery. Then she laughed.

"Tuck yourself in," she ordered, more breathless than reproaching. "Unless you want your servants to see a good bit more of you than they should."

He grinned at that, did as she advised, and kicked open the carriage door.

HE CARRIED HER OVER THE THRESHOLD LIKE A PRINCESS in a tale. The house was empty this time of night, the gas turned low, the shadows still.

"Light as a feather," he teased, bouncing her in his arms as he carried her up the stairs.

The action made her blood course faster through her veins. Light she might be, but to toss her like that meant he must be strong. The memory of his naked chest slid through her mind. She gripped his arm and felt his muscles through his sleeve. She wondered how he'd got them since he'd never done anything resembling exercise in front of her.

"At last," he said, shouldering through his door, "I have my sweet Godiva where I want her."

The light from the hall sconce lit the nearer objects of the room. Her eyes went to his huge Japanese bed, one corner of which stood out from the shadows. The door swung wider. Her body tightened. The bed loomed as big as a cricket ground, the posts like spears, the quilt a stark white field of snow. She pictured herself lying across it, impaled like a dying soldier, and shuddered involuntarily in his arms.

He laughed and kissed her temple. She thought he would toss her onto the bed and ravish her; she wanted him to, really, because she didn't wish to think too hard on what lay ahead. Instead, he carried her to the adjoining bath chamber and set her down. He lit a candle for her, then stroked her fallen hair.

"I know you've a shy streak," he said. "Do whatever you need to be comfortable. I'll wait. All night if you need me to."

She hoped the light was too dim to show the sudden moisture in her eyes. Anna was right. His kindness was a danger.

"I should hope I wouldn't take all night," she said as flippantly as she could. "Shyness is one thing, but insanity is quite another."

He laughed before backing away. "All night," he repeated.

His growl gave the promise an entirely different meaning.

Left to herself, she removed her clothes and washed up and tried to subdue the trembling of her hands. She wanted this, wanted him. Who better to introduce her to the secrets of the bed chamber? Most of all, she couldn't go back on her word once she'd implied she would give in. Female or no, that would have been dishonorable.

There's nothing to fear, she assured herself. After tonight, she couldn't doubt he wanted her. In that, at least, they were equal. She spared a moment to wonder if he'd notice her virginity. Perhaps she should pretend she hadn't actually been despoiled. Of course, if he knew she was a virgin, he might not want to take her. She screwed her eyes shut and shook her head. The last thing she needed was to complicate her lie. Besides, if her mother's exasperated warnings were reliable, she had nothing to worry about. She'd climbed too many trees and ridden too many horses astride to be left with anything more than a virgin's ignorance.

Inexperience, she corrected with a firm, outward breath. True ignorance hadn't been an issue since she was twelve.

I'll let him take the lead, she thought, and he'll never guess a thing.

HE'D TOLD HER HE WOULD WAIT, BUT IT WASN'T easy. Hours seemed to pass since he'd set her trembling on the blue-and-white Delft tile. His straining ears caught the rustle of silk and linen, the splash of water in the sink.

He lit candles—not too many—and turned down the covers on the bed. The sheets were fresh and smelled of Mrs. Choate's lavender potpourri. He doffed his coat and shoes and waistcoat, smoothing them over the back of an armchair as if they were a woman's skin. He wore one of his poet's shirts tonight, with flat, box-pleated ruffles on the cuffs. He unbuttoned the garment to his breastbone, then stopped.

Still no Mary.

He pressed his hand to his diaphragm and willed himself to calm. He'd done the right thing, letting her ready herself. She wouldn't change her mind. And if she did, tonight wasn't the night he was meant to have her. He could wait. He'd always been able to wait.

Oh, Lord, he prayed, casting his eyes to the ornately plastered ceiling. Please don't make me wait.

The door clicked open and he spun around.

She'd taken off her clothes. Every stitch. Even her hair was pushed behind her shoulders, which she'd squared in the challenging way he'd grown so fond of. Despite his amusement, the sight of her drove the breath straight from his lungs. He sank to the edge of the bed. She seemed magical standing there, an otherworldly sprite with the light flickering over her slim, feminine curves and her high, rose-tipped breasts. The triangle of curls between her legs glinted like antique gold. He wanted to run his fingers through it, wanted to part it and bare her treasure.

He gestured her toward him, coaxingly, reassuringly, and won two forward steps.

"You don't have to stare at me like that," she said. "You've seen it all before."

He smiled and shook his head. "Not like this. Not when I knew I'd be inside you."

She bit her lip and stopped, but she was close enough that he could catch her hands and pull her between his open thighs. She was shivering. He rubbed her from wrist to shoulder, hoping to warm more than her skin.

"Don't be afraid," he said, holding her worried gaze. "Making love to me won't be like it was with—" He stopped because he didn't want her to remember. "This will be pleasurable, Mary. For both of us."

"I hope so," she said, almost too soft to hear. "I'm not very experienced."

The confession touched him. That she could harbor any doubt as to his pleasure was quite ridiculous. At this point, shameful as it was to admit, he'd have enjoyed himself if she did no more than lay there and spread her legs. Laughing silently at the depth of his own lust, he hid his face between her breasts. They were silk against his evening beard, small and firm and kissable.

"Ah, Mary," he groaned, his hands slipping up her back as he reveled in the soft perfection of her skin, "the only experience you need is the kind we'll make together."

She gasped when he took her nipple in his mouth, then again when his hands slid down her back to squeeze her bottom. She was a feast for his touch, her skin like satin, her every muscle firm. He suckled her gently, teasingly, flicking the butter-smooth pebble with his tongue. The way she squirmed and shivered made him feel as if she'd never been touched this way before.

And maybe she hadn't. Maybe he was the first to take the time.

"Nic," she said as he found the hollow behind her knees and made them wobble. "Nic, I want you naked, too."

He stood so swiftly she almost lost her balance stepping back. "Don't do that," she scolded. "I need room."

He spread his arms, the picture of innocence, and won a grudging smile.

"Arms up," she ordered, and slid her hands beneath his shirt. "Why you didn't wear your American buttons tonight, I can't imagine."

He couldn't help laughing. God knew why, but her grumping made him happy. He bent forward so she could pull the shirt over his head. The cuffs caught on his wrists and she swore like a sailor as she struggled to undo them. The brush of her fingers, the way she bit her upper lip in concentration, made his breath huff like a train. He wanted to kiss her again, to penetrate every orifice she possessed. His chest was damp by the time she reached up to smooth his hair, a procedure that required her to go up on her toes. Nic was no giant, but she made him feel like one. Her breasts jiggled temptingly against his ribs before she stepped back to consider what she'd revealed.

"You're right," she said, one tapering finger to her jaw. "You do look different now that I know I'm going to have you."

His laugh burst out but the sound became a choke when she reached for the waistband of his trousers. "Careful, Duchess," he warned. "You wouldn't want to pinch anything valuable in those buttons."

She froze, then clucked when she realized he was teasing. She made short work of the placket, as if she were familiar—not to mention comfortable—with unfastening gentlemen's clothes. It was yet another contradiction in the puzzle that was Mary. Younger brothers? he wondered. Or perhaps her duties in the laundry? He didn't think she'd spent enough time with Monmouth to grow easy with this procedure. Nor could he doubt her claims of inexperience.

At least, he didn't think he could.

With the same unsettling efficiency, she shoved every-thing to his ankles and looked up at him from her crouch. Nic tensed. He didn't generally worry about his body; too many women had called it comely for him to waste time on that. Nonetheless, as Mary tilted her head and studied him, he found himself hoping she was pleased. He was certainly hard enough to flatter, whatever she thought of the individual con-figuration of his sex. He was high now, like a boy with his hand on his first breast. The head pulsed just beneath his navel, its foreskin drawn so eagerly back he felt as if he were stretching in two directions. When Mary's hand slipped up his thigh, his balls actually jumped in excitement. He thought she might touch them, hoped she might, but her fingers stopped at his hip and fanned across the bone. Again he felt that roughness that had piqued him. Hot tingles of sensation streaked down his legs.

"You should have lit more candles," she said. "I can hardly see you in this light."

His laughter shook his belly and his sex. He pulled her to her feet and kissed her. "I'll light them all," he said. "Every one I own."

Then he pulled her tight against him. She cried out as their bodies met, stretching up to hold him, to fit them more inti-mately together. Blood rushed to his skin in licks of fire. He groaned and lifted her and turned to lay her on the bed. She clutched him so closely he had to lower them both to the mat-tress together. He pressed her down beneath him, knowing he might be heavy but unable to resist. Her smallness drove him wild, but her strength made him fearless. He felt as if he could crush her, savage her, and she would only moan for more. She moaned now as he ran his hand down her curves, molding her, squeezing her, thrilling to the equal force with which she squeezed him back.

"Yes," he breathed as she gripped his buttocks. "Hold me as closely as you want."

Her mouth opened on his neck, hot, panting, and he knew she needed more.

He slipped his hand between them to find her wiry golden

curls. Once past them, her sex was as soft as he'd dreamed, as warm and wet.

"Oh," she gasped as he slid his finger up the melting satin crease.

He swallowed the piping syllable in a kiss, easing his finger inside her, easing his thumb to the center of her joy. Her limbs went lax, then taut, and then she poured a moan of hunger down his throat. Her sheath was a clinging cushion against his finger, tight but very welcoming. The thought of how she'd clasp his shaft made him coil like piano wire on a peg.

Wait, damn you, he ordered his pounding prick. Let her come before you test how warm her welcome is.

He pulled back from the kiss. Her eyes opened wide, clearly wondering why he'd stopped. "I want to watch," he said. "I want to see you take your pleasure."

Her back arched—a trembling, involuntary stretch—and he knew his request had deepened her excitement. Her eyes were dark, her hair a glorious tangle on the sheets.

"You always . . . want to watch," she said, so aroused she couldn't get the words out on one breath.

"Everything," he agreed, and slipped a second finger inside her. She was so narrow it almost wouldn't fit. With another sighing squirm, she pushed against him, driving him in to the webbing of his hand.

She laughed at his sharp inhalation, but her laugh was no steadier than her limbs.

"Touch me," he said, his voice like a match rasping sun-warmed brick. "Put your hand on my cock."

She touched him. This time her hand was bare, her palm damp, her fingers hot where they wrapped the thudding skin. Who'd have dreamed such strong, work-hardened hands could be so delicate? He thought he'd burst as she held him. Her touch was that good, that necessary. He swelled impossibly beneath it, overcome by a gratitude as deep as it was unprecedented. He'd needed this more than he knew, needed *her* more than he knew. His hips rolled forward, moving him in her grip, subtly, just enough to shift the skin along his shaft. The effect nearly shattered him.

"Shall I rub it then?" she said, as tentative as a girl.

The offer sent a blaze of heat across his face. He gritted his teeth and shook his head. "I couldn't take that now. Just hold me. There, under the crown. I want you to feel what happens to me when you come. I want you to feel my veins swell. I want you to count my racing pulse."

Her fingers tightened almost painfully as she arched again at his words. "I'm sorry," she said, forced to release him. "No one's ever made me feel this way."

He could not doubt it. Her head rolled from side to side, rustling her hair against the sheet. He could see she was near her limit. "Don't fight it," he said. "Just let go."

"I have to—" she gasped and her hips began to rock.

He quickened the motion of his hand until her eyes squeezed shut with embarrassed bliss. "Yes," he urged. "Take it. Take what you want."

Her conflict was a pleasure for him to see: her need betraying her shyness, her cries tight and keening in her throat. She was flushed in the candlelight, her breasts trembling, her nipples blood-kissed stones. Her legs twitched as her crisis neared. Her hands fisted on his back. Leaning closer, he looked down to watch his hand, then up to watch her face. He would not miss this. Not for anything. Her sheath began to flutter, gripping, releasing, pulling his fingers deeper. He pressed up against the throat of her sex where she'd feel it most and she broke with a violent shudder, her actual climax silent but intense.

For long moments she shook, arched up like a bow with her veins showing blue and fine against her neck. She was lost to him, but locked to him as well. He would have painted her like this if he could. The image was one he would have prized. It ended, though, as all sweet things must.

As he petted her down, she brushed her fingers along his shaft. His skin tingled for a moment, then suddenly felt twice as hot.

"I forgot you," she confessed. Her eyes fluttered slowly open, her smile curling into her flushed and freckled cheeks.

He kissed the dint at the tip of her nose. "Forgive me if I consider that a compliment."

She laughed and flung her arms around him, a gesture of thanks so natural and exuberant it made his throat feel oddly tight. He cleared it and pulled back, then brushed his thumb across one rosy-golden nipple. His hand was wet, fragrant. He lowered his head to lick the shining mark it had left behind. Mary quivered in response.

"Now," he said, "let's see if you're ready for the second course."

MERRY WAS AFRAID SHE'D NEVER BE READY, NOT for the devastating intimacy of his touch, not for the sound of the bed creaking as his weight moved over hers, not for the hot, wet press of Nic's naked skin.

Nic, she thought, his name trapped in her throat. The happiness he inspired was a kind of ache.

He'd been so generous, so knowing. She wanted to hold him tight and never let him go. Knowing the urge was foolish did not dim it in the least. The touch of his fingers parting his way for entry was enough to melt her anew.

She wasn't ready for this. Couldn't be ready.

"Sweet Mary," he whispered, fitting himself against her most private flesh. "Say you want me. Say you need me inside you now."

She groaned. He was silky hot, his tension both threat and promise. He would fill her, ease her. And then he would leave her empty.

"Say it," he urged, half plea, half growl.

She closed her eyes and gripped the sweating muscles of his waist. How could she deny him? She wanted everything he said. "I want you," she whispered. "I want you inside me now."

He pushed at once and moaned, his thickness slipping inside her like buttered steel. She felt the shape of him forcing her to give way, making room for itself, jolting a little inside her as her body clung and then relaxed. She could feel his pulse now, pattering against her own. More, she thought, enchanted by the heat and movement, by the astonishingly personal invasion. *Oh, more.* But then he stopped and hung above her on his forearms. A bead of sweat ran down his neck.

"Okay?" he asked through gritted teeth, shuddering when her body clenched in rising greed.

"I want more," she whispered, too shy to say it loudly.

"Jesus." He groaned, almost laughing but not quite. She feared she'd done something wrong. To her surprise, he rolled onto his back with her above him. "You'd better do it, Duchess. You're so damn tiny I'm afraid I'll hurt you."

Too tiny? she wondered. She liked how he felt stretching up inside her, but who knew how it felt to him? His grimace when she wriggled worried her. She braced on the straining tendons of his chest. "I'm not hurting you, am I?"

He laughed in earnest then, until he shook inside her. "You really don't know much about men, do you?"

Her cheeks burned with embarrassment. "Well, I—"

He silenced her with a gentle finger to her lips. She looked at him more closely. His face was flushed and his pupils nearly swallowed his smoky eyes. He might not have been panting but he was close. Of a certainty, he was not unhappy with his lot.

"It's all right," he said, still amused. "You're tight is all. Delectably so. Perfect, if you want to know the truth. I just want to make sure you're comfortable."

"I am," she said and worked herself down until she held him full and hot within her.

He swore and gripped her hips as if he didn't know whether to hold her off or yank her closer. Merry could have sworn herself; the shock of his presence was such a marvel. She'd thought what they'd done before was intimate, but this! They were joined now, flesh to flesh. A wave of strange sensation swelled inside her, part dizziness, part excitement, filling her body just as he filled her sex.

This was better than a moonlit gallop across a moor.

"Nic," she breathed, his name a prayer. Driven by a compulsion she couldn't resist, she dropped her hand. He shuddered when she touched the place where he pressed inside her.

"Don't move," he rasped, his sex flexing, stretching. A

vein jumped wildly beneath her hand. "Do not for God's sake move."

But he was the one who pulled her down and wrapped her close, who rolled them to their sides and slowly began to stroke.

"Closer," he said. Crooking his arm under her knee, he pulled her calf over his ribs. When he had her as he wanted, he ran his hand down her thigh to cup her bottom. His smallest finger curled into the valley there, stroking, tickling, making her blush and heat. Then the finger came to rest against the pulsing place they joined.

So, she thought, with a secret inward shiver, he can't believe it either.

"There," he said, "that's where I want you. That's where I need you most."

When his hips cocked forward, pressing him even deeper, she realized he hadn't just opened her completely, he'd also made it impossible for her to interfere with what he did. His arm held not only her leg in place, but her bottom and hip as well. He was controlling her movements, bracing her for his thrusts, keeping her to his lazy push and pull.

She was helpless and could not even mind. Each thick, slow stroke seemed to drag her deeper under his spell. His rhythm, his breath, was hers. When he gripped her bottom, her nails scored his back. When he coiled and thrust harder, so did she. In everything, they were together, bound by his will like solid ropes of gold. He shifted angles, going deeper, faster. The sense that he was losing control excited her. Need rose in a gathering wave. He felt it, too. His expression was harsh now, his motions wild.

"Fuck," he said, the word a soft explosion as his hips jolted hers. "Tighten, Mary. Pull me in."

It was what her body wanted most. She tightened, her very soul opening for the thrust. He swore at the strength of her pull, rigid, slamming into her with desperate force. "Mary," he cried. "Oh . . . God." She rode the edge, aching, needy, and then the storm crashed over them with a fury. She knew when he came because he stiffened and gasped in shock. The evidence of his climax threw her over. They shook in tandem, clinging like the last survivors of a wreck. The release was too sweet to bear. She buried her face in his neck and felt him do the same.

When the madness faded, a lull swept over her, but it was not a lull of peace.

She was sorry then. She wished she'd told him how special this night had been, that no other man had known what she'd given him. She wished the name he'd called her had truly been her own, wished she hadn't lied to and misled him. The deception seemed a betrayal not only of him but of her deepest self.

This little rite of passage, this loss of her virginity, had meant more than she'd expected. If she'd told him the truth, maybe, just maybe, she wouldn't have gone through it alone.

Neither of them spoke. Merry could feel herself shaking in his arms, hard, as if her body meant to rattle itself apart. No matter how little she knew about the act of love, she knew she wasn't supposed to react like this.

Finally, Nic stirred. "Good Lord," he said. "You must be freezing. Stay here. I'll build up the fire."

"No!" she cried, unthinking. "Don't leave me."

He stiffened at her plea, one brief, irretrievable moment. She knew she'd misstepped even as he chuckled and rolled her underneath him where she'd be warm.

"Mary," he said as she hugged his waist and hid her face against his chest. The word was a gentle scold she pretended not to hear. Alas, Nicolas Craven was not a man to let a woman live in a dream. He kissed the top of her lowered head.

"Be careful who you cling to," he said, soft and full of doom. "Men like me don't trade in hearts. In fact, men like me don't have them. Better save yours for someone who will cherish it as you deserve."

Well, Merry thought, if that condescending twaddle didn't cool her misplaced ardor, she didn't know what would. Blinking back what she told herself were tears of fury, she wriggled out from under him and sat up. Glaring, she shoved her curls back from her face.

"You should be so lucky," she huffed.

"No doubt," he agreed, and lazily scratched his chest. He lounged on his side like a sultan, his head propped on his hand, his still thick organ beginning to stretch and bob. With an effort, she wrenched her gaze away.

"I am not in love with you," she said. "Not even close."

"Good," he said. "See that you stay that way."

When she scowled at him, he merely cocked one brow. Infuriated, she climbed altogether out of the bed, the better to remove herself from temptation. "I'm going back to my room now."

His eyes narrowed. "Are you?"

"Yes, I am!" she snapped and turned to go.

She had the door halfway open when he slammed it shut before her. His hands caged her against the wood, his tall, lean body a wall of heat. His aggression excited her, though she tried to hide the sudden leaping of her blood. Instead, she tossed her hair in defiance, wishing she could whip him with its length. Nic blew a cloud of it from his face. When he spoke, he sounded angry.

"I'm not done with you."

"And when you are?"

"When I am, I'll let you know."

His arrogance made her sputter. He didn't seem to care how angry she was, didn't even seem to know. He lowered his head and sucked the tender skin of her nape against his teeth. She should have kicked him then, should have ducked under his arm and slipped away. She shouldn't have shivered, or wobbled on her knees, or turned to melted sugar between her legs.

"I don't want you to do this," she said, but he slid his hand down her belly to find the lie.

"Mary," he groaned, and somehow the sound of longing broke her will to hold him off. He knew it, too. His breathing quickened. She felt him at the small of her back, growing long again, growing thick.

"Spread your legs," he ordered, already nudging them with his own. "I want to take you from behind."

"Here?" she gasped. Was this a thing people did? Make

love standing up, as if they were animals, as if a bed were miles away?

"Here," he said, probing for entry. "*Here.*"

He slid into her as he said it, blunt and swift. Caught unprepared, she braced her arms against the door. He grunted, moving already. This time he was not lazy. This time he took her with single-minded haste. His hands were iron on her hips, his voice a honeyed rasp that spoke of things a lady should not hear. If Merry had ever doubted it, she knew she was no lady now.

Caught in the strangeness of the act, she watched her feet, planted wide, and his between them, the same long, naked feet that had unnerved her when they met. His tendons tightened as he thrust. His toes curled. He was working hard to get inside her, making the floor creak underneath. The boards where the carpet ended were dark and highly waxed. When she realized she could see their reflection in the shine, a gush of warmth slid down her leg. Nic groaned in appreciation. Their bodies sounded wet as they slapped together, not just outside, but in.

Wet, she thought, the word a tickling flutter in her sex. Wet with seed. Wet with cream. She pushed out with her bottom and silently begged for more.

He gave her what she needed, locking their hands in conjoined fists against the rattling door, shoving into her so hard he nearly lifted her off her feet.

"Yes," he crooned. "Oh, Mary, you're on fire."

Though she bowed her head and closed her eyes, she could not hide from this truth.

NIC WAS ODD. THAT WAS THE ONLY EXPLANATION
Merry had. Perhaps other men did trap their lovers against
the wall. Perhaps they, too, delighted in watching their
women's pleasure. But when Nic stood her in his claw-
footed tub to instruct her in the use of Dr. Allbutt's cleansing
syringe, she knew a few of the bats in his belfry were unique.

Murmuring reassurances, he lifted her foot to the curving
rim and helped her insert the perforated nozzle. Gentle and
sure, he might have been a physician but for the subtle quick-
ening of his breath.

"Sorry," he said, when she jumped at an unavoidably personal touch. "Should have remembered to lay in a supply of
sheaths." He frowned. "Don't know what got into me. I always plan ahead."

The reminder that there was an "always" did not thrill her.
Nor did the possibility this night might have consequences
beyond abandoning her virtue.

"I want you to know," he said, his eyes on the careful motions of his hands, "if anything happens . . . well, I'll take care of you."

Bemused by his euphemistic language, she pondered what he meant by taking care of her. Not marriage, she didn't think. Not that she wanted marriage. No, indeed. If that were the case, she wouldn't have turned to Nic in the first place. Still, whatever he was offering—financial support most likely—it was more than many men would. His own brand of decency, she supposed.

Oddly touched, she stroked the shadowed hollow of his face. "I'm not completely alone in the world. I have friends."

His laugh was wry. "Not friends who'll come pounding on my door, I hope."

If only he knew, she thought, doing her best to push the guilt away. Given his history, Nic must have faced irate relatives in the past. Surely hers would be no worse. It was even possible that, with her to calm them, they would be better. Aside from which, she saw no point in leaving the job half done. Ruined though she was, the public portion of her undoing was incomplete.

"I haven't told them where I am," she said, the half confession uncomfortable on her tongue. "I'd only notify them if, as you said, something happened."

He sighed and kissed her brow. "Ah, Mary, I'm a beast to make you worry. I meant our first time to be perfect."

"It was," she assured him. "I've never known anything like it."

She held his gaze, willing him to read her secret. For a moment, it seemed he did. His brows pulled together as if he were perplexed. Then, shaking his head against some thought, he smiled and cupped her cheek, once again the pleasant, worldly rake.

"You won't mind my French letters," he promised. "I have them specially made by a firm in Kingsland. They're sheep's intestine, double-layered and superfine. When they're wet, you can hardly tell they're there."

In spite of herself, she began to laugh. What would her mother say if she could see her daughter now, standing naked in a tub discussing prophylactic sheaths with a man who'd just slipped an irrigator up her quim? Even her best friend, Isabel, would be horrified. One might employ such instruments, but one would never discuss them, much less involve a man so intimately in their use!

"Nothing embarrasses you, does it?" she said.

He bent to dry her with a towel. "Sensible people can't afford to be embarrassed. Protection is part of the business of love."

Her neck tightened. How easy it was to forget he did this all the time, to believe what they shared was rare. She firmed her jaw. "You're right," she said. The business of love might be pleasant, but it didn't necessarily touch the heart.

NIC LAY ON HIS BACK, ABRUPTLY WIDE AWAKE. Something had disturbed him.

If a sound had roused him, he did not hear it now. Mary slept quietly by his side, curled away from him with her head pillowed on his outflung arm. He knew some men wouldn't let a woman stay the night, but he'd never minded—as long as they didn't want to stay all the time. In any case, her presence was not what had woken him.

Something I forgot to do, he thought. Or something I did do but shouldn't have.

The answer elusive, he eased his arm out from under Mary's neck. She made a tiny whimpering noise as he caught a snarl of hair, then subsided with a fetching wriggle.

Nic smiled. Her little freckled arse stuck up higher than the rest of her, a curve as profound as the hills of Rome. Helpless to resist, he ran his hand down the silken slope. The noise she made then was decidedly grumpy. He'd worked her hard this night, too hard no doubt, though she'd been with him sigh for sigh. Giving her shoulder a last caress, he let her be.

More than time you played the gentleman, he thought, but it was hard to regret a moment. She'd been like a child on Christmas morning, virginally tight, whorishly wet, delighted by each and every pleasure they unwrapped.

Maybe too delighted.

His mouth turned down as he remembered how she'd clung to him at the end. Of course, he'd held her rather tightly himself. Couldn't help it. That first climax had been a spine-wringer. For Mary, who appeared not to have had a half-competent lover before himself, the effect must have been dramatic.

Chances were, that was why she'd become emotional. He needn't assume she was falling in love, no more than he was.

He'd been stupid, though. Unforgivably so. He, of all people, knew better than to endanger a woman's health. He never forgot to use his sheaths, never forgot to have them on hand when he thought he'd need them. And he had thought he'd need them. For weeks now.

He didn't really believe Mary was pregnant, but the forgetting, that troubled him.

An image slipped into his mind. A child. Fat and bowed of lip. Golden curled. Snub-nosed. *Freckled.*

Shuddering, he thrust the covers off his body. No children. No, no, no. One Craven bastard was enough. His skin abruptly tight, he used the nearest post to swing up and out of bed. Time to work. He'd avoided that painting long enough.

This decided, he padded barefoot down the stairs, one fraction of his mind dedicated to the foolishness of donning no more than a robe in the dead of winter. The lion's share of his awareness was in his studio already. He sensed he was close to the answer, that the pressure of almost knowing was what had shaken him from his rest.

The sconces flared bright as he lifted the glass and lit them. With light to see by, he stood the half-dozen canvasses that had survived his latest purge against the wall. Each showed Mary riding a large white horse through a small medieval town.

The angles and the pose changed in the pictures. Some showed more of the buildings, some less. The horse didn't look half bad, despite Mary's warning against working without a model. The perspective was fine, and the play of light and color. Overall, the compositions were unobjectionable. He did not doubt he could sell them.

And every one bored him to tears.

They had nothing beneath their technically perfect surface. No blood. No heart. No glimmer of the lively woman they portrayed.

"Blah, blah, blah," he grumbled and fought an urge to toss them in the fire.

He wouldn't find the answer by hiding from his mistakes. He had to face them down, to stare his own stupidity in the eye.

Mary was the key: her spirit, her strange, unfashionable allure.

He plunged his fingers into his hair and pulled until the ends tugged at his scalp. He remembered how she'd responded the night he'd said he wanted to show her off at Anna's party.

I could wear a hundred velvet gowns and I still wouldn't—

He hadn't let her finish because he'd known how the sentence ended in her mind.

I still wouldn't be pretty.

He could almost hear her say it, could almost read the half-challenging cry that lay beneath.

Who says I can't be pretty? Who says!

Mary was a fighter, God bless her. Whatever her insecurities, some part of her refused to accept the world's opinion of her looks. Some part rebelled like a child thumping its heels against the injustice of adults.

Adults who, in this case, were quite, quite wrong.

Beauty often hid where the common man could not see it.

Nic could see it, though. That was his gift: to see it and to show it.

His arms fell from his head, slapping his silk-robed sides. The pressure inside him grew. What had she said when he accused her of being too eager to give her heart?

You should be so lucky.

He nodded at the memory. He should be so lucky. That's how he wanted to make the people who saw her portrait feel. He wanted to rub their noses in her gorgeous, sunny self.

Wanted to make them long to know her. Wanted to shove her peculiar beauty in their . . .

The hair at the back of his neck prickled, then stood up on his arms like grass in a sudden wind. He froze, blind to everything but the image crystallizing in his mind.

Yes. He had to shove her in their faces. Literally. He had to flatten the picture's depth. Brighten the colors. Sharpen the shadows.

A chill shivered down his spine as he grabbed a blank canvas and stood it on the easel. The chalk was in his hand almost before he knew he'd wanted it.

In three quick strokes he drew the tailor's window. This frame within a frame would make each viewer the Peeping Tom, the one resident of Coventry who could not resist a look. The tailor's room he'd leave in darkness, the better to blind them with the noonday light outside. Through this blaze would ride Godiva, close enough to touch. Her eyes would flash, her smile seduce. No lady, she, no slave to convention. She'd meet each gaze directly and dare the world to disapprove. *One night with her,* the men would think, *and I'd die a happy man.*

And the women . . . Well, maybe the women would cluck their tongues and maybe they would smile, inside, where they knew they shared Godiva's power.

Nic felt as if a god had seized his arm. The sketch seemed to draw itself, quick, sure streaks of umber brown. There the curve of Mary's cheek. Here the prancing lift of the horse's tail. All along it had been waiting for him to find it. And then it was done. His hand fell like a puppet with its strings cut. He was breathing as hard as if he'd run down the street he'd drawn. The picture seemed a miracle and yet he knew the source of every line. From each of his discarded efforts he'd saved a scrap of good. A turn of the head. A balance of light and dark. He might tinker yet, just to be sure, but for all intents and purposes, the portrait he would paint was sitting on this easel.

He smiled at it, ghost though it was, his eyes welling with the immensity of his relief. He had broken through the wall.

From this point on, the rest of the work was play.

*   *   *

MERRY SMOOTHED HER SKIRT FOR THE DOZENTH time and cursed her trembling hands. She'd woken early to an empty bed and had crept, thankfully unseen, to the privacy of her room. There she'd washed and dressed and stared at herself in the rusty mirror.

Her reflection told her nothing beyond the fact that her hair was now completely hopeless. She looked no more a ruined woman than before. Her eyes did not sparkle with secrets, nor her cheeks burn with shame. If anything, she looked pale.

Despite which she was convinced the moment anyone saw her they would know.

He'd been inside her. He'd made her spend with pleasure until her breath whined out like tortured steel. He'd left his seed on her, his scent. The memory of his thrusting, eager shape had been imprinted between her legs.

Surely this was not an alteration one could hide.

Disgusted, she turned from the mirror. What did she care if Farnham guessed, or Mrs. Choate? They could not think the worse of her. This was only what they'd expected all along. She was plain Mary Colfax here, not Lady Merry Vance—neither one of whom should have been prey to such simpering fears.

She'd enjoyed herself and so had Nic. She would not be sorry. With one last tug on her bodice, she ordered herself downstairs.

Nic waited at the bottom where he bounced on his toes with unusual excitement. He wore one of his painting shirts, the ruined linen starched and ironed by the scrupulous Mrs. Choate. The collar lay open at his neck, baring a wedge of smooth brown skin she longed to touch.

She wondered when she'd feel she had the right to caress him as she pleased.

Oblivious to her desire, Nic kissed her briskly on the cheek. "Glad you're up," he said. "Come eat quickly. I want to work. Today is going to be a good day, Mary. Very, very good."

She let him pull her to the Chinese parlor where a breakfast of rolls and ham and coffee awaited on a lacquered tray.

As she ate, he chattered about short perspectives and frames within frames and the necessity of challenging the viewer to become a participant in the picture. Fortunately, he required no response, for little he said made sense to her. His gestures were sharp as he paced the crowded parlor. Watching him—his energy, his intensity—made her heart beat faster in her chest.

"Now everything will be easy," he said. "Now we'll get somewhere."

As happy as she was for his breakthrough, the suggestion that he'd soon finish the work dismayed her. Whether he realized it or not, she'd have no justification for staying once he was done. Her father might conceivably forgive a brief adventure, but not an ongoing liaison. Merry wasn't sure she'd forgive that herself, not with a man who did not—no—who could not love her.

"Nothing to it now," he declared, and snapped his fingers on a laugh.

She struggled to swallow a bite of roll.

He was too euphoric to notice her dampened mood. When she finished her meal, he pulled the tray aside and scooped her into his arms. His hold felt different from the night before: more possessive and yet more casual, as if he'd lost any fear she might object. He carried her through the house that way, merely winking when the maid tittered behind her hand.

"Nic!" Merry protested, wishing she were silly enough to hide her face against his neck.

He chuckled and kissed her nose. "Can't be shy. We've gone beyond that, you and I."

Apparently, he also thought they'd gone beyond letting her undress herself. His sole nod to modesty was closing the studio door before he attacked her buttons. The winter light, cool but clear, poured through the windows as he peeled each barrier in turn. He murmured praise to her, then laughed at the state of her hair.

"Now this," he said, "is going to slow me down."

He sat her on the fake Egyptian chaise and brushed her

curls himself, working with surprising patience from tip to crown, one thick section at a time. When the tangles were gone, his strokes made a sound like a horse being curried, rhythmic and gentle, as if he meant to put her in a trance. In minutes, the waves of honey gold began to shine.

"Like that, don't you?" he said as she melted beneath his care. "Perhaps I should do this every morning."

His hand slid around to cup her breast. Merry bit back a moan. She sensed he wanted her arousal for the painting, rather than for himself. Nonetheless, his breath hissed through his teeth when he found her stiffened nipple.

"I'd like to mark you here," he whispered, one finger circling the swollen areola. "I'd like to suck you hard and paint the bruise."

She went liquid at his words, at the tiny tingling fireworks of his touch. He groaned, then kissed her shoulder with biting force.

"Don't tempt me," he said, rising to tug her hands. "I can't afford to waste the daylight."

"I wasn't tempting you."

He smiled with glowing eyes. "Trust me, Duchess, you tempt me just by being."

"You want me to believe that so I'll look sexy while you work."

He slid his palm down his paint-smeared shirt to the nascent ridge between his legs. Gently, shamelessly, his fingers rubbed it fuller. "I could prove how much you tempt me."

"Hah," was all she managed to get out, one glimpse of his "proof" having robbed her of her wits. She wanted him with a keenness the night before should have exhausted.

Fool, she thought.

But her traitorous body hummed as he helped her up to pose.

DAWN HAD BARELY BROKEN THE NEXT DAY WHEN Nic stuck his head in Farnham's pantry, a room that contained not just shelves and the silver safe, but also his butler's sitting area.

"Sir!" said Farnham, clearly startled. With the faintest of blushes to darken his slashing scar, he slapped the paper he'd been reading closed. "I was just about to iron this."

Nic laughed at having discovered his starchy servant in a misdeed. "So. This explains the extra fingerprints on my *London News.*" He cracked his knuckles, then took pity as Farnham began to sputter. "I'm teasing, man. I don't care if you read my paper, not even if you do leave fingerprints— which you haven't. I'm hiring a hack for Mary to ride in Regent's Park. I want the new boy to hold his head."

The butler set the paper carefully aside. "I believe young Thomas is assisting with the laundry today. Mrs. Choate says he has a strong arm. I, however, could certainly help you hold a horse."

Nic considered this. "No. You're too big. You might block the view. Or the light. I need the boy. The laundry will have to wait."

"'Wait'?" said Farnham in a tone that suggested waiting was not advisable.

Nic hadn't the faintest idea what washing clothes entailed, nor did he care, especially when he itched to sketch Mary on that horse. "Is that a problem?" he said, his brows lifting in full expectation of having his wishes met.

Though the butler winced, he did not disappoint. "No, no," he said. "I'll order dinner from the bakeshop and Mrs. Choate will be able to finish as she'd planned."

"Good," said Nic, the issue settled. "Have the boy meet us in the garden in half an hour."

He whistled as he strolled away, feeling sharper of mind and lighter of spirit than he had since the day he left his childhood home. Then he'd been starting his career. Now, if this picture lived up to its promise, he was about to enhance its luster.

Besides which, Mary would be thrilled with his surprise.

"THRILLED" WAS NOT THE WORD MERRY WOULD have used, especially when Nic borrowed a pair of the new boy's breeches for her to wear.

"I need to see your legs," he'd explained as she held them up in dismay. "I've decided you'll sit astride. But don't worry. We'll cover your top with an old reefer coat. No one who sees you will guess you're not a boy."

Merry was not so optimistic. She'd worn breeches in public on a number of notable occasions. Her appearance in them now was less than a good disguise.

"But my hair," she said weakly.

"Braid it up and stick it in a cap." He grinned as if he'd offered her a treat.

She hadn't the heart to spoil his fun.

When the new boy saw her in his knee breeches, he turned the color of a strawberry, the flush creeping over his omnipresent scarf, green today, with a crooked black stripe.

She didn't know if her appearance were the cause, but the lad seemed more turtlelike than ever, shrinking into the layers of wool as if he wished to disappear. When she realized he was there to lead the horse, she was tempted to fall off laughing. She hadn't needed anyone to lead her since she was four. Mary Colfax, of course, was another story. A city girl like her, and a poor one at that, had probably never been on a horse's back.

With that in mind, she tried to look as awkward as she could.

To her surprise—for she hadn't expected Nic to know one end of a horse from the other—he had hired a decent mount, a tall, gray mare with an elegant conformation. Though she wasn't as fine as Merry was used to, something inside her eased to feel a real horse underneath her.

The boy was easy with the mare as well, rubbing her muzzle and feeding her bits of carrot from his hand.

"You there," Nic called. "New boy. Take care you don't spook her with that scarf."

"Thomas," said the boy with a muffled sigh, then tucked the trailing end into his coat.

At a plodding pace better fit for a centenarian, Thomas led Merry and the horse through the gate to Regent's Park. From there they clumped past St. Dunstan's Chapel and around the boating lake. Finally, on a quiet stretch of lawn near the wintry remains of the botanical garden, Nic directed them to stop. Even now, with a frosting of snow on the ground, visitors strolled the park. Workmen hurried to jobs, servants walked dogs, and nannies from Cumberland Terrace guided their bundled charges toward the zoo. Two smartly gowned young ladies cantered past them but, to Merry's immense relief, they didn't give her or her companions a second glance.

She caught the tail end of their gossip as they swept by: something about purple gloves and an unfortunate yellow hat. She couldn't help wondering if their wearer were someone she knew.

For a moment she was split in two, yearning toward her old life yet dreading it as well. She might not know who she was in Nic's world, might indeed be falling on her face, but at least she was free to choose her way.

When Nic reached up to stroke the horse's neck, her gratitude warmed her smile.

"This spot will do," he said, his eyes crinkling back at her. He jerked his head at the bright, ice-skinned lake. "Plenty of ambient light."

By now, she was used to this being important. She watched as he set up his folding chair and propped his sketchbook on his knees. He grinned at her once before he started, then was lost to the world-swallowing distraction of his art. The most astonishing grimaces crossed his face, as if these contortions helped him draw. Like a cellist, she thought. Only by using his whole body could his passion infuse the work.

Young Tom, who had never seen this performance, was even more mesmerized than she.

"Hold her steady," Nic said, when the boy's fascination caused him to slacken his grip on the bridle. "I'll be at this for a bit."

A bit turned into a quarter hour, then a half. Apart from shifting her weight from one hock to the other and trying to nibble Tom's lumpy scarf, the mare didn't seem to mind the inactivity. Merry entertained herself by watching Tom. Cowed by his recent scold, he was sneaking looks at Nic whenever he thought the artist wouldn't catch him.

"He won't bite," she whispered from the corner of her mouth, "even if he did forget your name."

Her words startled the boy into looking at her and then she was startled, too. His gaze struck her like a curlew's cry, a piercing tangle of emotion. His eyes were a sweet spring blue, older than she expected and much, much sadder; adult somehow, though they were not a man's eyes yet. Lashed with starry, light-brown spikes, their clarity amazed. With eyes so lovely, few would mind whatever horror his scarf was hiding. Or maybe they would. Maybe the haunting beauty of his gaze would make the ruin seem even worse.

"Yes, miss," he said, and lowered his smooth young lids.

Color washed his forehead, pink as a country rose. She wondered if he were embarrassed that she'd addressed him. Would it embarrass a boy to speak to his employer's mistress? Assuming that's what she was. Merry wasn't sure there was a name for what she'd become to Nic.

At least, not a name she'd want to use.

"DO YOU RIDE, SIR?" ASKED THE BOY.

Nic glanced at him in surprise. The boy—*Tom,* he reminded himself—hadn't said a dozen words since they'd left the house and none at all since they'd dropped Mary at the ostler's door. He supposed he asked because Nic had been running his hand down the mare's left foreleg. It was a habit from his youth, one his mother had insisted on.

You bring them back the way you take them out, she liked to say. *And if you find a problem, you tell the groom. A care for the creatures that count on you is the measure of a man.*

He'd only forgotten once. The horse came up lame and she'd made him muck out bedding for a month. He could still remember his humiliation. The stable lads had known they wouldn't be punished for taking advantage of the young master's fall from grace. They'd worked him like a navvy. At the time, Nic had hated every minute of the backbreaking work, but now the memory inspired a rueful smile.

The marchioness had known how to teach a lesson. Still did, he imagined.

"I used to ride," he said, smoothing the horse's wind-blown mane, "when I was a boy."

"Did you like it?" Tom asked.

Nic wondered at his boldness. The boy wasn't looking at Nic but the tension in his gangly frame led Nic to believe his answer was important. Why that should be, he couldn't guess, but who knew what crotchets boys that age got into their heads?

"I liked riding fine," he said, "but I liked drawing better."

"Guess you liked that better than anything."

Nic squinted. The boy's tone was oddly challenging. Did he think a real man ought to favor horseflesh over paint?

"Yes," he said, still confused, "I liked drawing better than anything. That's why I became a painter."

Tom nodded as if this were no more than he'd expected. His hand stroked the horse's neck. "Guess you've still got the eye, though," he said. "Best-looking horse in the stable. Must have cost you." His glance slid to Nic then back away. "The maid said you bought Miss Mary dresses, too."

Nic's temper pricked. "See here," he said, "if you're try-ing to cast aspersions on how Miss Mary earned those dresses, you can just—"

"No." The boy lifted one hand in denial. "I was merely noting that you're generous with your coin."

Merely noting! thought Nic, amusement outweighing his anger. Those national schools must be doing a better job than he'd suspected. "Angling for a rise then, are you?"

"No, sir. You've been generous with my salary, as well."

"That's Farnham's doing."

When the boy shrugged, his eyes disappeared into his scarf. The habit suddenly overwhelmed Nic's curiosity. What was Tom hiding that he thought no one but him could bear? Nic had believed him too shy to interact with people, but the way he'd spoken today revealed a considerable, if peculiar, self-possession. Maybe all Tom needed was a little encour-agement to open up. Nic wouldn't have minded if he did. He'd never wanted a lot of starch among his staff.

He touched Tom's arm, about to press him, but the narrow

shoulders twitched and the boy spun away. He spoke with his head hunched determinedly down.

"I'd better check on Miss Mary," he said, moving toward the cobbled yard. "She's been alone a bit. Might be a rough crowd out there."

Nic laughed softly through his nose. Far from casting aspersions on her character, it seemed young Tom had also seen what a prize "Miss Mary" was.

10 ❧

MERRY COULDN'T BELIEVE HOW QUICKLY HER portrait had progressed. Nic worked like a man possessed, or at least like a man who didn't need food or sleep. At his insistence, she warmed his bed, but on many nights she was the only one doing so. When they did make love, he wasn't truly with her. Oh, his skill was as formidable as ever, and she couldn't deny she enjoyed herself, but somehow—without his full engagement—that enjoyment was not enough.

His distraction would have hurt if she hadn't been concerned for him. Where was the man who'd gone into raptures over a cup of coffee? Who made flirting an art form? Who considered the catnap a form a prayer? He seemed almost to be punishing himself with his current devotion to toil, though for what she could not guess.

She kept waiting for the real Nic to return. She didn't know how to be with this one and yet she could not bring herself to leave. He seemed to want her there, seemed to welcome, however distantly, her presence beside him in the night. He always pulled her close, always kissed her hair and sighed as he relaxed.

She worried that this small bond was enough to hold her. Her heart was too soft when it came to him, too soft by far.

One night, as he slept, he muttered a woman's name. *Bess,* she thought, or possibly *Beth.* It didn't even anger her. Instead, she wondered who the woman was and why her memory troubled her lover's sleep. She would have soothed him if she could, but his manner did not invite it. His Art was all to him now. Merry was merely a convenience.

NIC PAUSED AT THE DOOR TO THE LIBRARY, HIS news forgotten in the image that met his eye.

Mary sat by the window, a book on her lap, her profile turned to watch the carriages pass outside. Her hair lay over her shoulders in sheaves of fiery gold, an extravagant contradiction to the primness of her pose. Despite being at leisure, her spine was as straight as a poker in the plain green gown, one of the few gowns she'd chosen at the dressmaker. Highnecked and gently fitted, its sole adornment was a stiff white ruffle at throat and cuff. Her knees were pressed together, her hands folded neatly on the book. She reminded him of schoolgirls he'd known, well-bred schoolgirls, who do not forget their posture when they're alone.

His heart tightened unexpectedly at her beauty. He thought his brush had caught her but it hadn't. Nothing could. For all the time they'd spent together, for all the intimacy they'd shared, this spirited young woman remained a mystery.

"Mary," he said softly, not wanting to startle her.

She turned her head and the look on her face made the floor shift strangely beneath his feet. Her eyes were huge. In the firelight, they shone like amber washed in tears.

He moved swiftly to kneel beside her, his knuckles white as they closed on the worn leather arm of her chair. "What is it?" he said. "What's wrong?"

Wistfully, she touched his hair. "I was thinking how much I'll miss you when I'm gone."

"Gone! Why should you leave?"

"The picture is finished, isn't it?"

He shook his head to clear it. "How did you know I was going to tell you that?"

She smiled. "You have varnish on your shirt. And you're looking at me again, as if I were really here."

"Oh, Mary. I never meant . . ." Stricken by his own insensitivity, he had to stop and reform the words. "I never meant to neglect you."

"I know. You were simply caught up in your work." Her eyes shimmered as she cupped his cheek, a mixture of affection and regret. "You're happy with it, aren't you?"

"Yes," he said simply. "It's the best thing I've done."

"Good." She nodded. "I'm glad."

"I thought you might like to see it. Then we could go for a nice dinner at the Café Royal. Take in a show. Celebrate."

For the space of a breath she was silent. Thoughts crossed her face he could not begin to read.

"I can't go out," she said.

"Can't?"

She lowered her eyes. Her stillness frightened him. Suddenly, he didn't want her to explain, didn't want to know what had saddened her. He laid his hand on her sleeve, stroking her arm through the emerald wool.

"We could stay in." He cocked his head and smiled. "I could make up for my neglect."

Her lips curled into her freckled cheeks.

"Let me," he coaxed. "Let me make it up to you."

The growl was one he'd used a thousand times—suggestive, seductive—guaranteed to make a woman melt. For the first time in his life, the sound stuck in his throat.

"Let me," he whispered, and this time it was a plea.

Her eyes lifted to his, fathoms deep, a darkness into which a man could fall. Emotion trembled on their surface. He could barely swallow past the thickness of his throat. He ached to hold her, to cover that soft pink mouth and make it sigh. *Say yes,* he willed her. Say yes.

"Yes," she said, and leaned in for his kiss.

* * *

"WE CAN START ANOTHER PICTURE," HE SAID. "There's no reason this one has to be the last."

Mary snuggled closer but did not answer. They lay before the library fire, clothing scattered, sweat drying on glowing, rug-burned skin. Their coupling had been a quick, groaning thing, over too fast to fully recollect once it was done. Mary's lightly boned bodice lay like a carapace on the chair in which she'd sat. He couldn't remember taking it off, but his hands still seemed to bear the imprint of her thighs. He'd shoved them apart to take her, the tendons that led to her groin stretching beneath his hold. She'd moaned his name as he'd pressed inside, and once more when she came. Now her breasts shook in the dying firelight. The pulse was strong enough to follow both up her throat and down the sweep of her shallow belly. The triangle of curls at its base was sticky, matted in tiny caramel spears. He found the sight peculiarly arousing, though he had no doubt she'd have been self-conscious if she'd known.

Then again, she might have been furious. Nic had forgotten the blasted sheath again and hadn't pulled out quite soon enough at the end. At least one gush of seed was in her—which didn't bother him half as much as not having taken the time to savor her wet and bare.

The reaction was unprecedented and highly irresponsible. Worse, he'd have risked it again in a heartbeat.

He wasn't handling this well, wasn't handling her well. Long minutes had passed since his searing climax and his heart still thumped in his chest. It should have been slowing the way it always did at the end of an affair.

He told himself he simply wasn't ready to let her go. The picture had distracted him. Otherwise, he would have had his fill of her by now. Give him a few more weeks and he'd say good-bye without a qualm.

He'd be damned, however, if he'd beg for a few more weeks.

Beside him Mary stirred, her lips pressing his shoulder, her palm smoothing shyly across his chest. Simple though it was, her touch caused his shaft to thicken. Her head turned, her cheek petal-soft and cool. Her mouth found the rising itch of his left nipple. She'd never kissed him there before. The brush of lip and tongue was streaking fire. This was what he hadn't got enough of: this loss of her inhibitions, this victory over inexperience.

"When is your show?" she asked.

Nic fought a gasp as her teeth grazed skin. "Next Thursday."

Her hand trailed down his side to stop provokingly at his hip. When, he wondered, had these callused female fingers become the ultimate objects of his desire? Her thumb stretched to feather the edge of his pubic curls. He bit his lip, wanting her to take the leap herself. Just touch me, he thought. You don't have to ask permission. You don't have to worry you'll do it wrong. Just put your bloody fist around my cock. He held his breath in anticipation. Ridiculous, he thought, aghast at the depth his lust. Perfectly ridiculous.

"I'll stay till then," she said.

At first, he was too preoccupied with the position of her hand to comprehend. When he did, he opened his mouth to argue, then carefully shut it.

He had till Thursday. Four days to focus all his skill on her. Four days to wipe out his neglect. He rolled toward her, one hand sliding beneath her hair to knead her neck, the other stroking her silky back. She arched under his palm. She sighed.

He did not doubt he could change her mind.

SEBASTIAN LOCKE STOOD, STROKING HIS SMALL GOA-tee, before the finished picture. He had a tall person's habit of slouching into his hips—though this, naturally, could have been his idea of acting Byronic.

Whatever his pose, and despite the sleepy narrowing of his eyes, his attention was keen. His lips were pursed with concentration.

"These glazes are very thin," he said.

"Yes," Nic agreed.

He'd used the sheer layers of color to create the vibrancy he desired. Though he knew the effect he'd achieved was good, he found himself biting the side of his thumb. Sebastian's eye was sharp. This was one of the reasons for his dissatisfaction with his own work: he could see what needed to be done better than he could do it.

"Left off her freckles, I see," he said, with a teasing lift of one fair brow. "Too much of a challenge?"

Nic shook his head. "They made the picture look too busy."

"Mm." Sebastian returned to his perusal. His eyes drifted from the crown of Mary's hair to the place where her breast peeped coyly through the waves. "Mm," he said again.

Nic lost his patience. "For God's sake, Seb, just tell me what you think."

Sebastian laughed. "You bloody well know it's good, old man. I thought I'd try to give you more response than that."

"Should have been a damned critic."

At the mutter, Sebastian's smile distorted the curve of his blond mustache. His face might have been designed for just such saturnine expressions. "Those who can't do, eh?"

"I didn't mean it that way. You can do. Very well."

"Nic, Nic, Nic," Sebastian tutted, "always the kind one." He tapped the side of his jaw. "You say you *just* finished this?"

"Last night. You want to touch it to prove it's wet?"

"No, no. I don't doubt your word. I'm simply surprised." He slanted Nic an ironic glance. "Usually, when you finish a big project, you don't send for me to take a look at it. You crawl into your bed and hibernate."

Nic juggled the handful of coins inside his pocket. "This painting is different."

"So I see."

Knowing his friend was waiting for him to prod again, Nic stubbornly held his tongue.

"Oh, very well." Sebastian surrendered with a husky laugh. "It's brilliant. You've broken new artistic ground—for yourself, certainly, and possibly for more than yourself. These colors make me drool, as does your scrumptious little Godiva. The fact that you made that scrawny creature look so fuckable is a miracle in itself. When Alma-Tadema finishes turning green, he's going to slap your bloody back."

Nic let his breath out in relief. Bubbling with the sudden release of tension, he rocked back on his heels. "Mary begged me to get a sidesaddle, but I just couldn't make myself do it. Ruskin will have a fit. Probably call me a menace to society."

"You've invited Ruskin to your show?"

"Of course." Nic grinned. "A man like me looks forward to being a menace."

Catching the grin, Sebastian squeezed the muscle of Nic's shoulder. "It's good," he said, his gaze for once warm and open. "It's very good. I'm wondering though . . ."

"Yes?"

Sebastian's eyes tilted at the corners as if he were holding back a laugh. "You're looking particularly hale and glowy. So I'm wondering if your mood isn't due more to your current light of love than to the successful finish of your work."

The back of Nic's neck prickled with alarm. If his friend took it into his head that Mary was important to him, he'd pursue her with every wile he had. He'd always been competitive and the steady rise of Nic's career just made it worse. Mary might not be important to Nic the way the other artist thought, but she didn't deserve to be embroiled in Sebastian's games.

"What do you mean?" he said, forcing a casual tone. "Why would Mary Colfax have anything to do with how I feel?"

"Oh, I don't know. Maybe the way you looked at her at Anna's, as if you were the starving wolf and she the tender sheep."

"We hadn't slept together then."

"Ah," said Sebastian. But he didn't seem convinced.

"I like her," Nic said, striving to sound reasonable. "I like women."

Sebastian pressed his thumb consideringly to his lips. "I know you do. It's the secret to your success."

"Quite. And there's no reason to think this is any different."

His friend studied him, one arm crossed beneath the other arm's elbow while his thumbnail tapped his teeth. His thoughts were hidden behind their customary veil of banked amusement, but Nic could guess what he was thinking. He fought an urge to squirm. Everything he'd said to Sebastian was true. He did like women. All women. If the sparks he and Mary struck were unusually bright, well, that was a happy coincidence of compatibility. It didn't mean his feelings were serious or that her presence had anything to do with the improvement of his usual post-painting disposition. The picture was a personal landmark. Any artist would have been ebullient.

Finally, Sebastian broke the silence. "You should ask her to join us in Venice after the show. The countess has invited us to stay in her palazzo."

"Us?"

The other man's grin was devilish. Nic knew at once what it must mean. "You're taking Evangeline, aren't you?"

Sebastian's mustache twitched. "Her affair with Gerald Hill seems to have run its course."

"Oh, Seb." Nic scrubbed his face in resignation. "You know you should leave her alone. Neither of you are good for each other."

"You have your poisons," said Sebastian, thoroughly unrepentant. He lifted a fan-ended scumbling brush and twirled it deftly around two fingers. "You could come without Mary if you prefer. I know Evangeline wouldn't mind. Be like old times."

"God forbid," he muttered, recalling how the pair liked to entangle him in their dramas.

"Now, now," Sebastian scolded, "it wasn't all Sturm und Drang."

"No," Nic admitted. It hadn't been all storm and stress. The trio—Sebastian, Anna, and Evangeline—had taken him under their wing when he first arrived in London. His schooling had led him all over Europe. He'd had passing acquaintances but not friends. After he lost Bess, he hadn't had the heart to make them. Sebastian's warmth, and that of the others, had brought him back to the human fold.

A love that generous, that lifesaving, should never cause regret.

Now Sebastian laughed. "Remember how we'd sneak into Anna's plays, then sit up all night talking in her dressing room? Idiots, all of us, thinking we knew the meaning of life and art, so poor we had to pool our money for a meal."

"I remember." Nic brushed his friend's jaw with the back of his fingers. Nic had been proud of his poverty, proud of never touching his father's tainted coin.

Sebastian sighed. "I miss those days."

"Well, I don't miss half starving," Nic said, though he did miss the lightness of all their demons. They'd been amusing then, more eccentricities than burdens. When one was that young, nothing seemed incapable of being healed by time. He was older now and not so optimistic. Sometimes he thought their knowledge of each other merely strengthened their power to hurt.

"I miss it," Sebastian said, his voice suddenly hoarse. "I miss when we all were equal."

The confession moved Nic to the burning brink of tears. Sebastian could be a sly, deceitful bastard but, by God, he could also strip the truth to its hardest bone.

"We are equal," he said just as roughly. "There's more to measuring a man than the opinion of the world."

His friend laughed through his nose. Recovered from the moment of sentiment, his eyes held their old, self-deprecating glint. "Just say you'll think about Venice. You and I haven't drunk ourselves stupid in ages."

"I'll think about it," Nic promised.

To his surprise, he knew he would.

NIC HAD GONE OUT—TO VISIT HIS TAILOR, HE said—leaving Merry free to sneak into his studio. He'd never forbidden her to come alone, but that wasn't why she had waited. She couldn't stand for anyone else to witness her first view of the painting. Not Farnham. Not Mrs. Choate. Certainly not Nic. So great was her anxiety she'd evaded all his invitations to look at it with him. Hadn't peeked at the thing in weeks.

Just in case.

He said he never lied. Not in words and not in paint. He would show her as he saw her.

She wasn't sure she could bear it if she were ugly.

Mouth dry, her gaze slid to the curving bank of windows. The sky was pale but clear, and the bedraggled pines dripped with the recent thaw. Spring was coming, though she wouldn't be here to see it. How melancholy that knowledge was. How it weighted her heart like lumps of stone. She'd been here six weeks. Six amazing weeks that felt like one.

Merry shook off her sadness. She hadn't come here to brood or to procrastinate. The sun was shining through the windows, warming the scent of drying paint, lighting the tall pine easel that stood like a gallows in the glare. That easel held her portrait. Unframed. Uncovered. Less than an arm's length on any side. A small thing, really, to inspire such fear.

The word made her square her shoulders. Her skirt swept the dusty floor as she strode past Nic's armless Venus, past the half-used roll of canvas and the jumble of period props. She closed her eyes and pressed her lips together. Then she stepped around the painting.

Her breath caught in her throat, a gasp of shocked surprise.

His sketches had not prepared her. The picture was gorgeous. So bright, so vivid, the color struck her like a blow. She had a childish urge to lick it, as if it were a dripping fruit. The picture glowed, and she glowed in it.

She glowed.

Godiva was her. Down to the dint on her nose and the kink of her horrid hair. Those were her knobby knees. Her wiry arms. Her naughty, laughing eyes. Apart from the omission of her freckles, he hadn't flattered her in the least.

Despite which, no mirror had ever made her look so radiant.

"My," she breathed, her hand to her throat, her eyes filling even as she broke into a laugh. For the rest of her life she'd remember this moment.

She was beautiful. The way he saw her, she was.

This was a gift she'd never expected to receive. Better than her purple dress. Better than the sensual indulgence he'd poured over her these past few days. Better even than her first ride on a pony.

Most of all, though, this was a gift that demanded one in return.

11 ✒

THE SUN WAS STILL HIGH WHEN NIC RETURNED from shopping. He'd meant to seek Mary out, but hadn't expected to find her in his bedroom.

"I want to thank you," she said.

Since she sat on her heels in the middle of his mattress, wearing nothing but his favorite brown dressing gown, Nic had a sneaking suspicion what form her gratitude would take.

Smiling, he tossed all but the smallest of his parcels onto a chair. If she felt the need to thank him, his work of the past few days must be bearing fruit. His body tightened pleasurably, though he pretended to be confused. "Thank me?"

She nodded, her expression conveying both diffidence and determination. "For the painting. I looked at it this morning. It's very beautiful. No one has ever made me see myself that way."

"Ah." He lowered himself between the bed's two central posts—the doorway, as it were, to his magic cabinet. Thanks

for his artistic skill he had not anticipated. He drew one finger up her paisley silk–clad thigh, then hooked it beneath the
hastily knotted belt. Mary rewarded him with a squirm. In a
mood to tease, he tugged at the tie but did not pull it free.
"What if I think you're the one who should be thanked?"

"You've been thanking me. Ever since you finished."

Amusement slid through his chest like warm spiced wine.
"I'm glad you noticed. But these past few days haven't been
a thank-you. They've been a bribe."

"A bribe?" Her breath hitched as he mouthed her neck. He
followed up the advantage by sliding his hand inside the robe
to cup her breast. Her body jerked an instant before her nipple stiffened against his palm.

"My lovemaking is meant as an incentive, to make you
want to stay."

"Because you're not done with me yet."

The words possessed a nagging familiarity. He pulled
back from nuzzling her collarbone and peered into her face.
"What do you mean?"

"The first night, when you"—her color heightened—
"when you took me against the door to keep me from leaving, you said you weren't done with me."

His body heated at the memory, but he forced himself to
match her serious tone. He drew his hand from the melting
softness of her breast. "I never lied to you, Mary. I told you
this would end."

"I know." Her red-gold lashes fanned down to veil her
eyes, but she did not seem upset. She smoothed his robe
more neatly down her thighs. For one irrational moment, the
calmness with which she greeted his reminder vexed him.
Most of the women he'd known had tried their best to hold
him. Her gaze lifted again, steady and inscrutable. "I merely
wondered: since you say you're not done with me, what is it
you want that you haven't gotten? That's what I'd like to give
you tonight. As my thanks."

"Your thanks," he repeated.

"For making me look so beautiful in the painting."

"I painted you as I saw you."

"I know." The grin that lit her face made his ribs feel strangely bruised. "That's why it's wonderful."

"Well," he said. For the life of him, he couldn't account for the extent to which she'd discomposed him. He glanced down at the paper-wrapped package he'd carried to the bed, the pièce de résistance of his campaign to change her mind. "I suppose this means you don't want your present."

"A present! For me?" She erased any doubts he might have had by snatching the bundle from his hand. The paper tore beneath eager fingers as she uncovered the object wrapped inside. "Oh," she said, holding it up to catch the light. The bottle was round and fat, the glass cobalt blue with a branch of almond flowers molded on its belly. "It's so pretty."

"It's oil," he said, pleased by her delight.

Her nose wrinkled in confusion. "Oil?"

"Not for cooking, Duchess. For massage."

"Oh," she said, then again, with a lascivious rise and dip. "Ohhh. For massage. I'm sure I can put this to good use."

"I'm going to use it on you," he clarified, reaching to take it back.

Eyes dancing with mischief, she hugged the bottle to her breast. "No, no, no. You gave this to me. That means I can do with it as I please and what I please is to please you."

Lust poured like hot, thick treacle through his veins. His trousers, normally well fitted, drew tight with the hard, tenting jab of his erection. He'd thought of oiling her, of smoothing his hands along each inch of satiny, freckled skin. He'd dreamed of it as he perused the apothecary's shelves, imagining how she'd sigh, growing heavy inside his clothes.

That arousal was a spark compared to the bonfire he felt now. He was hot all over, his skin fevered, his pulse drumming hard between his legs. A sense of alarm accompanied the heat. He could not recall wanting anyone this badly—certainly not so far into an affair.

Mary, naturally, took note of his condition. Her nipples pushed against the dressing gown, a response that fanned his need.

She eyed his prodigious bulge with a humor he wished he

shared. "I see you like the idea of being oiled. Of course"—
she put her head to the side, almost resting it on her shoulder—"you'll have to instruct me. So I know precisely what
you like."

"Precisely?" he rasped.

"Precisely," she confirmed, then caught her upper lip in
her lower teeth. No gesture could have conveyed her nervousness better, or her resolve to overcome it. A delicious
pang speared upward through his cock, making the tip feel as
if it were being pinched.

"I'll tell you what I wish," he said, a whisper as soft as it
was rough.

"Would you—" She swallowed and began again. "Would
you show me?"

His eyebrows rose before he could stop them. She wanted
him to show her?

"I liked when you did that before," she said, the words
falling over each other in embarrassment. "That night when
I couldn't get my fire lit and you . . . touched yourself. I liked
that and I thought maybe you wouldn't mind doing it again.
You know, without your clothes on."

The smile he was fighting pressed his lips together. "You
liked that."

She nodded earnestly. "I thought it was exciting."

He had to lower his head or give himself away. "I don't
know, Mary. I'd have to be very relaxed to do something like
that in front of you."

"Oh, I can manage relaxing you." She waved her hand in
dismissal. "No harder than rubbing down a horse—or, er, so
I've heard."

His laugh came out a snort. He felt like a horse, a randy,
mare-sniffing stud who'd been locked in his stall for days.
He rose from the bed and faced her. "Shall I undress then?"

"Oh, yes." She shifted around on her knees to get a better
view. "That would be very helpful."

His eyes crinkled. "How flattering you are."

"Nothing of the sort! Only a nun wouldn't want to watch."

But she was flattering. His grin broadened as he disrobed.
He could not have had a more attentive audience, or one

more appreciative. Without hesitation, he offered her his enjoyment of his own body, his love of being watched. He
knew she shared that love, no matter how reluctant she was
to admit it. Tonight, for her, he would hold nothing back. Her
eyes were like saucers when he touched himself through his
clothes, squeezing the weight between his legs as he'd done
for her once before. That he knew she liked, for she squirmed
from side to side and clenched her hands atop her thighs.
Watching her watch him was almost too arousing. He had to
cut his fondling short for fear of slipping over the edge.

When he peeled his shirt slowly over his head, she
blinked to clear her vision. Thumbing his nipples into promi-
nence set her jaw agape. And she actually gasped when he
pushed his trousers down his legs.

"Look at you." She spread her hands as if drawing attention to a wonder. "Who could tire of such a show?"

"Not you, I hope," he said and climbed into bed to kiss
her.

Her body was warm and pliant, her mouth a clinging
haven for his tongue. He rolled her beneath him and gloried
in the press of flesh on flesh. As always, her firmness undid
him. He slid his hand around the peach-ripe curve of her bottom, tickling her hair, seeking the tactile evidence of her lust.
When he found it, a soft, feminine noise broke in her throat.
That was a sound he would never tire of. Sighing with delight, he wriggled his finger deeper.

Before he could explore her fully, Mary put both palms on
his chest and pushed.

"No," she said, "I'm supposed to be pleasing you."

Only those words could have stopped him. Amused and
painfully aroused, he let her push him onto his back, let her
spread his limbs out from his sides and tuck a pillow beneath
his neck. She sat back on her heels between his legs. Currents
of air brushed his groin, making him feel even more naked,
even more sensitized. His shaft surged up and down as it
were trying to reach her.

Mary seemed satisfied with her handiwork.

"That's better," she said, cradling the cobalt bottle between her breasts. "Now I can touch you as I please."

He could barely speak through the constriction of his throat. "That's what I've been waiting for. For you to do as you please. That's the thing I've wanted but haven't gotten."

"Oh," she said and laughed softly, "how fortuitous."

They smiled at each other, a hushed, hanging moment that felt—oddly enough—like friendship. For all his experience, Nic had not known this before. The feeling was good and warm, but it hurt a little, too, as if there could never quite be enough of it. Her eyes glittered briefly and then she grinned, full out, her face creasing with silent laughter. Her arm rose and tipped the bottle. The oil dribbled onto his breastbone. Warmed by her body, it rolled over his skin like cream.

She rubbed it toward his shoulders with her palms, sweeping around his pectorals, circling his jangled nipples with her thumbs. "I love your chest," she murmured, as if every tendon in his body had not gone taut. "Your muscles are so lean, and you don't have too much hair to see them."

"Pleased to oblige," he gasped with the ragged ghost of his voice.

Her strokes were long and strong. Once the first shock of contact faded, her hands seemed to stretch his muscles and pull them loose, easing tensions he hadn't known were there. She soothed the sides of his neck, then the back, then drew tight, oiled hands down the length of his tingling arms. When the pads of her fingers slid over his palms, his toes curled toward his feet.

"Good?" she whispered.

He groaned and closed his eyes. Her hands were magic: not too soft, not too hard. She seemed to have an instinct for his anatomy, knowing just where to dig to find a hidden knot. His erection eased but did not disappear, a pleasant throb now, a hunger that could wait. She shifted back to massage his legs, lifting them one at a time to work the muscles underneath. He shivered when she found the sweet spots on his feet, her thumb sliding firmly between each humming bone.

"Ah, Mary," he sighed, his spine arching uncontrollably, "this is heaven."

She kissed his instep, then laid down his leg and braced her hands on his thighs to scoot in closer. Roused from his stupor, Nic pushed himself upright. From heavy, pleasure-glazed eyes, he studied the architect of his bliss. Mary had tied her hair back with a ribbon, but her efforts on his behalf had inspired a predictable disarray. Tendrils curled wildly around her face. Her lips were soft, her freckles blurred by a wash of pink. She looked a wholly sensual creature, a woman awake to her sexual self. He'd wanted to see her like this since they met.

"Now," she said, "this is the part where you show me what you like."

Her fingertips feathered the bone at the top of his thighs, half tease, half nervous gesture. He knew he'd have to tread cautiously from now on.

"You want me to touch myself," he said, measuring the effect of every word. "You want me to put my hand on my cock and masturbate while you watch."

Her cheeks flamed scarlet but she did not deny his claim. "Yes," she said firmly, "but *I* want to finish you."

"And you'll follow my instructions?"

She squared her shoulders. "To the letter."

Her pluck inspired both admiration and humor. "You needn't, you know." He touched her heated face. "Not if I ask for something you don't like."

She opened her mouth, then licked her upper lip in hesitation. "Could we pretend I had to? I think I'd feel more at ease."

Nic squinted in surprise. Mary's request was unexpected, to say the least. He'd seen more than a little evidence of her will. That she would want to take orders from him—even in play—stirred his interest deeply. He was careful, however, not to let his amazement show. A sexual wish was a fragile thing. It had to be treated with respect.

"I believe I would like that," he said and held his hand out for the oil.

MERRY WASN'T CERTAIN SHE COULD EXPLAIN HER own behavior. She only knew that, for their final time together, she wanted to surrender something more profound than her virginity. That had been a scrap of flesh. This was a piece of her soul. Offering it was reckless, perhaps, but she'd always regretted the things she hadn't done more than the things she had.

With a quiver of anticipation, she tipped a puddle of oil into his palm. He curled his fingers over it in protection.

"Look at me," he said, his voice darkening the way it did when he was aroused. "I want you to know what your eyes can do."

She looked at him: at the flush on his prominent cheekbones, at the pulse beating visibly in his neck. His chest rose and fell as she took in the whorls of sheer black hair, the coppery discs of his nipples, the small, sharp points within. His borrowed robe lay heavy on her breasts but she did not want to remove it. All these weeks she'd posed for him . . .

Let him be naked, she thought. Let him display himself for me.

His gaze locked on her face as he clenched the hand she'd filled with oil. His sex had relaxed while she massaged him, but now—within the space of breaths—it rose again, lengthening, thickening, until his fist hung over a pulsing crest. The marvel of his body's transformation made her hold her breath. He had not lied. All she had to do was look at him. He tilted his wrist. Oil ran out in a golden thread. It hit the stretched red skin, spilling over, spilling down. His second hand caught it at the bottom.

The scent of almonds perfumed the air.

"Watch," he said, as if she needed to be told. "Watch how I touch myself."

The fist he'd closed around the base pulled slowly, strongly upward, moving the loose outer skin onto the bulbous head. As soon as the tip slipped free of his hold, his second hand followed, oiling him even more. Again he did this, and again: the motion smooth, the pressure tight, until his erection shone like polished wood. Then he stopped and let Merry stare.

Her heart knocked in her chest. His shaft was fat and dark, flushed now along its length and vibrating with excitement. She could see every texture, every individual dip and swell.

His penis could not be mistaken for anything but a part of the human body. Not marble. Not jade. This was living flesh, inextricably linked to the basest, most primitive functions of the male.

Its very meanness made her love it. She'd never seen anything more personal in her life.

"It's beautiful," she said, and the sack beneath his organ jumped.

"I'd like you to help me," he said, sounding as if his throat were filled with gravel. "Wrap your hand around the base. I want you to hold the skin taut while I rub."

He had read her unspoken desire, her unbearable urge to touch. She reached for the root of him, shaking now, almost afraid to do as he asked. He inhaled sharply when she wrapped him in her hand.

"Now push," he said, making it an order. "Stretch the skin back toward my balls."

She pushed until she bumped the swell of his testicles, using her strength to stretch his satiny outer skin, trying to match the force she'd seen him apply. He shuddered in her grip, but did not wince, and she knew she had not hurt him. She could not doubt he liked what she was doing. His brow and lip had beaded up with sweat. A thrill of power streaked up her arm. She was doing this to him: with her hand, with her eyes. Her sex pulsed, tight inside, as if a fist held her as well.

"Yes," he said, the praise a growl. "Now watch."

She could not help but watch; he was so close to her, pleasuring himself while she held his skin in opposition to his strokes. She didn't know why this increased his enjoyment, but it very clearly did. His body was tense, his respiration rigidly controlled. The music of his breath flowed through her like the act of love. In and out. Draw and blow. Old paint, green and yellow, clung beneath the nails of his graceful fingers. She watched where they rubbed, where they tightened until the tips grew white. The twisting rivers of his veins stood out from the flush of his phallic skin. She followed their rise up the thickened underridge, over the flaring neck to the smooth pink tip where they disappeared. His forefinger dug into a wrinkled fan of skin beneath the crown. His shaft quivered. His thighs twitched. There, she thought. That he really likes. Quivering herself, she pressed her lips between her teeth. His blind little eye was weeping a pearly tear.

She gasped for air. "I want to do it. I want to pleasure you."

He stopped, then released himself and put her second hand where his had been. Sensation jolted through her. He was hot. Pulsing. Slick from the scented oil. She pulled as he had pulled, not as smoothly perhaps, but with just as much concentration. Apparently, her technique was good enough. He sighed deeply and let his head roll on his neck. His shaft was like a hardened muscle, stiff inside but with a bit of give. Determined to do her best, she tightened the V of her thumb and forefinger when it crossed the sensitive spot beneath his crown. He responded to her touch the same as he had to his.

When she lifted her gaze, she found him watching her, his gray eyes quiet but intense. His skin was swarthy with arousal. His lips looked swollen, though they hadn't been kissing hard. When he licked them, she felt as if he licked her.

"You want something," she said, with an instinct as old as time. "Tell me, Nic. Tell me and I'll try to do it."

He hesitated.

"Tell me," she insisted, and swept her thumb across his crown. "Order me."

He laughed, a mere rush of breath. Then his face hardened.

"I want you to kiss it," he said. "I want you to take me in your mouth."

The words were gruff, not precisely an order but close. They created an image as stark as it was shocking. Surely she couldn't do this, couldn't draw that ferocious organ into her mouth. She wanted to, though. As soon as he said it, she grew wet.

Pretend, she thought. Pretend you must do what he says. Then whatever happens, however awkward you are, he has only himself to blame. Despite the injunction, she did not trust her voice. She nodded instead, a quick jerk with her teeth clenched tight together.

At her agreement, Nic's breath rushed out so swiftly his belly hollowed beneath his ribs. With the choppy motions of impatience, he shoved a pair of pillows behind his back. "Do it," he said, more forcefully now. "I want to watch you suck me."

She did not close her eyes. Chin trembling, she lipped the flare, then slid the silky crown between her lips. The taste, the feel was indescribable. Softer than soft. Smoother than smooth. His fingers slipped between her knuckles, then covered the hand that held his shaft. His palm was warm and steadying. He'll tell me, she thought. He'll tell me if I do it wrong.

"Take a little more," he whispered, his thighs suddenly shaking. "I promise I won't . . . push too far."

When she did as he asked, he sighed as if she'd granted his dearest wish. He was hot in her mouth, alive. He tasted of almonds, of salt and skin. It seemed natural to lick him, to suckle this tender fullness to the limit of their hands' grip.

He gasped at the change of pressure, then stroked the tangle of her hair as if tempted to grab it. Even if this had not given him away, she would have sensed the rise of his excitement in the leaping of the flesh beneath their hands.

"Tighter," he said, compressing her sweaty fingers with his own. "Don't let me come."

She hadn't known she could stop him, but the thought that she could hold him on that edge seared her with aching fire.

"Here," he rasped, moving her hand to circle the top of his scrotum. "Squeeze and tug."

His testicles felt like two boiled eggs, odd and firm within the wrinkled skin. She had to pull them down, away from his body, to hold him as he asked. He grunted when she did it, then lifted his hips and pushed himself slowly into her mouth. His legs were drawn up, his heels providing leverage.

"Yes," he said, his own hand falling away. "That's good."

He drew back until her lips tightened around the flare. The tip of him was sleek and ripe. She licked it, circled it, gathering salt and shudders. When she dug into the little eye, he moaned and pushed again.

"Slow," he urged, though he was the one who moved. "Slow and easy."

But perhaps the advice was meant for him. He began to build a rhythm, gentle, careful, but with a tension behind it she could not miss.

He's making love to my mouth, she thought, amazed and aflame with the power he'd placed in her hands. He trembled like the victim of a fever, inside her, against her, fighting with all his strength to prolong the pleasure, to protect her from the violence of his need. She couldn't remember feeling anything so exciting.

"Don't swallow," he whispered. "Get me wet."

She let her saliva paint him, let it wrap him in liquid bliss.

"Yes-s," he said, a drawn-out hiss as his buttocks tightened on the sheets. "Oh, yes."

He was as lost as he'd ever been to his work, his eyes drifting shut, his fingers kneading and releasing in her hair. She was lost herself: to the pleasure of giving pleasure, to the lingering push and pull, to the smell and the taste and the stunning sense of trust. He'd surrendered himself completely. She could not disappoint him. With her free arm braced outside his hip, she let her head sink even lower. Her body began to sway.

"Can't," he gasped, pressing hard against her palate. "Can't last much longer. You—" He inhaled sharply and pulled back. "You can let go. You don't have to finish me in your mouth."

But she grasped his shaft, holding the crest against her lip.

"I want to," she said, letting the words buzz his most sensitive skin. His eyes fluttered open and searched her face. His fingertips touched her jaw.

"I want to," she repeated and eased him back inside.

He groaned at the slow engulfment and again at the tight withdrawal. He left it to her then: to move, to pull, to rub and tease the spots she'd seen him rub himself. His hands fisted in her hair and her name was a prayerful curse. The taste of him was heady. She did not hurry but soon he swelled against her tongue, as smooth and hard as heated glass.

"Ah," he said, a panicked cry that trembled in his throat. "Ah, Mary!"

She was glad she held his shaft because he could not restrain that final thrust. He stiffened and pushed and came in pulsing bursts. She felt each spasm, each surge and twitch. The experience was both peculiar and enthralling. Never had she been so close to his pleasure. Never had she felt it as if it were her own. His thighs pressed her shoulders, then fell away. As tired as if she'd come herself, she leaned her head against his hip.

"Mary," he said, the sound rich and low. He stroked a curl behind her ear. "Come here where I can hold you."

She groaned, then wriggled upward to the stack of pillows. His arms came around her, easing her head onto his shoulder, a spot that seemed fashioned just for her. The rise and fall of his chest was like the rocking of a cradle. When he rubbed her back, she thought she'd drift straight off to sleep.

"Thank you," he said, and she couldn't help but smile at his heartfelt tone. "I'll see to you," he added, somewhat drowsily. "Just give me a minute to get my strength."

Merry didn't mind a wait, or even a dismissal. Despite her own arousal, she was content. She knew a different kind of satisfaction, one that drowned out everything but the present. Any concern for her departure seemed a distant thing. Yes, she would have to leave. She'd gotten what she'd come for. Tomorrow's show would ensure her public ruin. She didn't expect her parents' reaction to be pleasant, but she knew they'd be far more understanding if she did not stay with Nic. He himself had reminded her of the limits of their affair. If she didn't end it, he would. Better she should leave before she found herself losing not just her reputation but her family. Being a pariah she thought she could manage. Being disowned she could not bear.

But these were worries for another day. Tonight she had pleased him, and pleased him well. Maybe in the weeks to come she'd regret having given herself so freely. Maybe she'd wish she'd kept a tighter rein on her heart. In time, however, she was sure this night with Nic would become a pleasant memory for her scrapbook: wistful, perhaps, but not repented.

She was strong, after all, resourceful and resilient. She had never known a pain too great to stand. For goodness sake, how long had it been since she'd spared a thought for Edward Burbrooke? Ages, it seemed.

She refused to believe losing Nic would be any different.

NIC DIDN'T MEAN TO FALL ASLEEP—CERTAINLY NOT before he'd seen to Mary—but his well-pleasured body did not consult him. When he stirred again, the light outside was a dusky rose. Mary lay across him, her hair a tangled blanket for them both. Her pubis warmed his hip while the curve of her thigh nestled beside his penis. It was a lovely, abandoned sprawl, made even more meaningful by the fact that she was awake. Her fingers played lightly in his chest hair, the gentle touch almost enough to soothe him back to sleep.

"Mm," he sighed, a moan so happy he barely knew it as his own.

She propped her chin on her forearms and kissed his jaw. "Hello, sleeping beauty."

"Hello, waking beauty."

Even now, she wrinkled her nose at the compliment, making the bump at the end turn up. He pushed her curls from her endearing little face. Just looking at her made him happy, at peace in a way he hadn't felt for quite some time. The knowledge forced a decision he didn't see any way to avoid. No matter his long-standing dread of romantic attachment, no matter his fears of letting his lovers down: this particular affair was too rewarding to let go. Sebastian was right. Mary was good for him. And maybe, at least for now, he was good for her.

"I know that look," she said, meeting his grin with a furrow of suspicion. "You're planning something."

He wrapped his arms behind her waist. "Not planning precisely. Hoping. I'm not ready to let you go, Mary. I want you to come with me to Venice."

"Oh," she said, scarcely the response he was looking for. She pushed away from him and sat up. "Venice. That's— that's very flattering, but—"

"I could paint you there." He dragged his hand slowly down her breast. "In a gondola. Drifting down the Grand Canal. You said you never got to travel. Venice isn't the Forbidden City, but it's very beautiful. And we could go to Rome. That was on your list, wasn't it?"

"Yes," she said and pressed her palm to her heart. "Nic." Shakily, she laughed. "You don't know how touched I am that you remembered. Or how honored I feel that you'd want to keep me longer than you usually keep your lovers. I wish I could accept. I really do."

"You could if you wanted to."

"It's not that simple."

Abruptly grumpy, Nic sat up and pounded a pillow behind his back. "Is it the expense? Because, as far as I'm concerned, you've earned it."

"No." She shook her head, her eyes shining with regret. "It's not the expense. My reasons are personal."

"And that means?"

"It means I don't want to discuss them."

"You're tired of me." He didn't believe it, but he had to say the words. Her speechless response was all his pride could wish.

"Of course I'm not," she said once she'd recovered. "How could I be? Good Lord, most women go a lifetime without meeting someone as skilled in bed as you." Her chin drew up with the stubbornness he'd grown to love. "Staying simply isn't possible for me and I don't want to spoil our last night by arguing about it. Please, Nic, let's not end what we've shared with a fight."

Only a cad could have refused her. He cupped her slender shoulders, his thumbs smoothing the muscle, his fingers drinking in her skin.

"Anytime you change your mind," he said, "I'd be happy to take you back."

The promise was one he'd never offered in his life. For him, once an affair was over, it was over. The lapse might have frightened him if he'd actually thought she would accept. Instead, she whispered his name and slid her arms around his back. Her lips found his ear, then his cheek, then the deep, drawing welcome of his mouth. The kiss was another plea to remember what they'd shared, to keep their last night sweet.

Nic could not resist it. Forcing his anger away, he lost himself in what was easy, in what he'd always known he was good at.

He might not be able to keep Mary Colfax, but he could damn well make her miss him.

Tatling's, the picture gallery, had its premises on Bond Street. It was an old brick building, five stories tall and extremely solid in appearance. Lighter blocks of stone encased the display window and formed a medieval-looking arch around the door. The effect was one of respectability and discretion, both of which were bound to be tried today.

Her stomach queasy, Merry let Nic hand her down from the carriage. His face was set in a glower, as it had been all morning. She supposed she should have been flattered that her refusal to stay with him had put him out of sorts. Maybe later when this was behind her she would be. For now, though, his mood merely added to her tension.

She wished she hadn't promised she would attend. She feared last night would make a far better parting memory.

Of course, letting him come alone would have been a disgraceful display of cowardice. She had walked into his studio—indeed, she had walked into his arms—with her eyes wide open. The least she could do was stand by him to face the public consequences of her acts.

If she secretly hoped there would not be any today, that was only because she was human.

She lifted her skirts to cross the pavement. "Oh, look," she said, feigning a lightness she did not feel, "they've put one of your pictures in the window."

It was a modern scene of couples strolling down the new Thames Embankment. Fog softened the figures' edges while a curving line of gaslights swirled like specters in the mist. It was an eerie picture, as different from his Godiva as it could be, though Nic's touch was apparent in the skillful handling of the light.

"It's almost menacing," she said, "the way that fog rolls off the river."

Nic grunted, then seemed to think better of his rudeness. "Won't sell," he said, "though the brushwork's good enough."

I'd buy it, she nearly said, then realized anew he wouldn't believe she could.

I ought to tell him who I am, she thought. Her face went cold at the idea, but her fear was worse than pointless. If she waited, the discovery would be worse and, really, she had no more excuses. He wouldn't stop the show now; he had to fulfill his obligations to the gallery. If she told him, before someone else could, at least he wouldn't feel so much a fool.

Resolved, she touched his sleeve with a shaking hand.

"Nic," she said.

When he turned to her, his face immediately softened.

"I'm being a beast, aren't I?" he said, misconstruing her tone completely. "And you've done nothing to deserve it." The corners of his mouth turned up as he covered her glove with his. "I'm sorry, Duchess. I'm going to miss you more than I expected and my temper's gone to hell."

Blast, Merry thought, assailed with guilt at the irony of him offering her an apology. She pulled a breath of courage into her lungs.

"Nic," she began again, "there's something I need to—"

The gallery door opened before she could get the confession out.

"There you are," said a dapper young man in a sober suit. "I was beginning to wonder if you'd arrive before the crowd."

Her pulse still unsteady, Merry pulled herself together as Nic introduced Mr. Tatling. He was the grandson of the gallery's founder and, from what she could tell, a sharp individual in his own right. His eyes didn't even flicker at being made acquainted with Nic's model—though it was obvious from Nic's manner that she was more. Whatever his private thoughts, Mr. Tatling's bow to Mary Colfax was as respectful as any she'd received as Merry Vance.

"Enchanted," he said with a pleasant smile. "So glad you were able to come."

He led them quickly through the exhibition, which was spread among three rooms. Capacious and high-ceilinged, they were furnished in the style of a nice, upper-middle-class home. Looking around, she found nothing pretentious, nothing in bad taste—and just enough comfort to make visitors relax. Small floral arrangements enlivened a few of the polished tables, their colors clearly chosen to match Nic's work. Merry thought it all looked very welcoming, especially the waiting samovars of tea.

"We can shift anything you like," Tatling said, "but I think you'll agree this arrangement allows the pieces to complement each other."

Nic nodded his approval, then returned to the largest parlor, where the Godiva stood on a separate, gilded easel. He stopped in front of her and stared, two fingers pressed pensively to his lips. Mr. Tatling moved quietly behind his shoulder.

"Makes a nice centerpiece," he said. "As you might expect, we were quite elated when we unwrapped her. We're asking seven thousand."

Even Merry's jaw dropped at that.

"You're mad!" Nic exclaimed. "The most Leighton ever got was six."

Tatling shrugged, his eyes dancing with the excitement of

a salesman born. "Mr. Leighton didn't paint your Godiva. Besides, wealthy people like to brag about what they spend."

"Maybe so," said Nic, "but that's a bloody fortune."

The gallery owner's response was cut short by the tinkling of a bell above the door.

"Bother," he said, suddenly discomposed. "I was hoping Ruskin wouldn't come till later."

Curious, Merry turned to see the famous critic. Though dressed like a parson, he was a handsome man, slim and well-formed with thick red hair lightly touched by gray. Beneath his shaggy brows, his eyes were pale and burning.

Nic gave him a casual glance, then turned away as if his presence could not have mattered less. He guided her into an alcove and pulled her a cup of tea. "You had something you wanted to tell me?"

No, no, no, thought Merry. They were not going to have this discussion with that critic in the room. She'd heard stories about Ruskin: that he was so obsessed with female purity he hadn't been able to consummate his marriage. Seemed the sight of his wife's pubic hair had thrown him into shock. He'd thought women were like statues: smooth and perfect and free of the slightest sordid taint.

She finished her tea in a scalding gulp and set it down. The last thing Nic needed was to be distracted by her confession when he had to confront a man like that.

"I'll tell you later," she said, "after that critic leaves."

This answer amused Nic, but, for Merry, waiting for Ruskin to go was torture. Every time the street door opened, her muscles tightened into knots, wondering if this visitor or the next would be the one she knew. She could scarcely bear to watch who wandered near the Godiva. They'll know, she thought. Even if they don't know me, they'll know I'm the model when they see me next to Nic.

As if sensing her embarrassment, Nic did not introduce her to the people who stopped to chat. A few squinted at her, but no one said a word. She was glad she'd worn her plain green gown with the prissy collar. With luck, she might be mistaken for an employee of the gallery.

For his part, Nic was surprisingly at ease. He mingled

here as gracefully as he had among Anna's friends. If Merry had not known, she'd never have guessed his living depended on the patronage of the people to whom he spoke. Whether well-born or simply well-heeled, he behaved as if he were their equal, with neither condescension nor undue pride.

It was a side of his character she'd caught glimpses of before, one light-years distant from the tortured soul who'd torn his hair out over flaws no one but he could see. He's earned this self-assurance, she thought, because the memory of those struggles tells him he's done his best.

She'd known titled men who did not approach his quiet poise.

Even Ruskin did not throw him. The critic wound back to them after touring all the rooms, his parson's brow marred by a tiny frown.

"You have a fine grasp of realism," he said, his voice judicious and low and just a trifle pompous. "You'd do well, however, to cultivate a bit more spiritual meaning. Perhaps you could take a leaf from Mr. Holman Hunt's book?"

"Or Mr. Millais's?" Nic suggested just as gravely. He'd inclined his head so that only Merry could see the devil in his eye. She remembered then that Millais was the artist who'd married Ruskin's rejected wife.

The critic cleared his throat. "Of course. John Millais is also a great talent."

As soon as Ruskin left, Merry punched Nic's shoulder. "You're awful," she exclaimed. "That poor man!"

He didn't question that she knew the scandal, and why should he when it was so juicy? "Poor indeed," he chuckled. "Effie Ruskin was a treasure. In any case, I wouldn't have said it if he hadn't advised me to copy Hunt." He shuddered. "Lurid tripe is the kindest description I have for his work."

"Nonetheless," she said, even as a smile broke through her censure.

Catching the smile, Nic reached out to squeeze her hand. Whatever he'd meant to say was lost in an exclamation of concern.

"Good Lord, Mary! Your fingers are bits of ice." Oblivi-

ous to whoever might be watching, he stripped off her gloves
and chafed her hands against his chest. "What is it, love? Are
you worried you'll be recognized from the painting? You
shouldn't be, you know. If people think anything at all, it will
only be that I'm lucky."

If Merry hadn't been so overwrought, she would have
laughed. She was here precisely to be recognized. A thousand
times she'd imagined how she'd lift her chin to meet the first
pair of knowing eyes, how she'd dare them to say anything,
how she'd demonstrate with every line of her body that she
wasn't the least ashamed.

The only thing she hadn't imagined was how hard it
would be to do.

"I'm fine," she said, her jaw tightened to forestall a threatened chattering of her teeth.

Unconvinced, Nic brushed her cheek with the back of his
hand. "I'm sure Tatling would let you rest in his office."

She shook her head so hard, her chignon wobbled. "No,"
she said. "I'm not a coward."

And then the bell above the door rang, as if to prove the
lie. Merry jumped, then went cold from head to toe.

The duke and duchess of Monmouth were entering from
the street.

She could not catch her breath. It stuck in her throat along
with her heart, making it impossible to swallow. Of all the
outcomes she'd imagined, facing her parents was the last.
She'd thought someone else would carry the tale to them:
one of her schoolmates, or one of her mother's gossipy
friends. She'd thought she might have time to flee to Isabel
in Wales, so as not to be home while their outrage was the
fiercest.

How blind she'd been! How willfully, stupidly blind!

She should have guessed her father would be interested in
the painter who had so recently—and so skillfully—done his
portrait. As for her mother: what could be more natural than
that she'd wish to come along? Nic was society's darling, his
work as fashionable as Lavinia's sable-trimmed paletot.

Frozen in place, she watched the duchess hand that coat to
the gallery's pretty maid. A cloud of panic filled her breast,

one so alien to her experience she almost didn't recognize what it was. It felt like a heart spasm. In fact, she wished it were.

In a moment, her mother would turn, and her father, and—Lord!—there was Ernest behind them, her ever-hopeful, would-be fiancé.

Her nails were digging holes straight through her skin.

Oh, God, why hadn't she told Nic the truth when she had the chance?

Something snapped inside her that had never snapped before. She, whose courage had always been equal to any challenge, could not in the end face this, not now, not in front of Nic. Grabbing his arm, she dragged him bodily from the room, through the second gallery, and the third, to a door that led to a tiny scullery. Tea things waited in the dimness: dirty cups, tins of oolong and pekoe.

Nic rubbed his wrist when she let it go.

"All right," he said, his eyes worried, his mouth prepared to laugh, "why don't you tell me what's the matter?"

My parents are here, she meant to say. *I'm the daughter of a duke. I've been using you to ruin myself so they can't force me into marriage and I've probably embroiled you in a scandal people will talk about for years. If you're lucky, my brothers won't thrash you for it. If you're not, my father will try to run you out of town. I've been selfish, you see, and shortsighted and even though I thought I thought this through, it's painfully clear I didn't. You don't deserve this and I wouldn't blame you if you hated me forever.*

The thought of that, of him hating her, closed her throat around the words.

"I've changed my mind," she gasped. "I want to go to Venice."

She knew she was doing wrong, knew it in every fiber of her being. Running away was shameful, not to mention a mere postponement of the inevitable. In spite of which, as soon as she made the declaration, a terrible weight lifted off her shoulders. What matter if she'd have to face the same disaster later? Time was what she needed. To think. To plan. To be with Nic. Indeed, in that moment, delay seemed a gift from the Almighty.

Nic shook his head, his expression confused but tinged with dawning hope. Overwhelmed by a flood of conflicting emotions, Merry flung her arms around his neck.

"Please," she begged, "please let's go to Venice."

He slid his palms from the bend of her elbows up her arms. Merry bounced with impatience. "Goodness." He smiled. "You can't mean you want to leave this instant?"

"No," she said, her voice gone husky and suggestive, "this instant I want to go home."

She heard his breath catch, a small, flattering sound. His eyes darkened, and then his mouth took hers. It was a kiss so raw, so powerful, it literally made her forget everything but him. He crushed them together from chest to knee, his hands tight on her bottom, his arousal a burning ridge beneath his clothes. He rubbed it against her, groaning his pleasure into her mouth.

She could not doubt he was happy with her decision.

"Now?" he asked, a smoldering rasp against her cheek.

"Yes," she answered and tugged him toward the alley door.

He did not suggest they get their coats, nor say good-bye to Mr. Tatling. Nic was a creature of the flesh. When they emerged into the icy air, he simply laughed and began to run.

NIC CRAVEN'S PAINTING DISTURBED THE DUCHESS of Monmouth more than she could express, like something soft and wet being dragged across her skin. It was too aggressively sexual to view without a wince, its very beauty an affront. Horrid, she thought, though one couldn't say that without having heard the judgment of one's peers. They might decide such a stance was unsophisticated, and where would that leave her? Realizing her hands were clutched together at her waist, Lavinia forced them to relax.

Whatever she did, she must not cause a scene.

Even then, she could not tear her gaze away. Dimly, she was aware of the chatter that surrounded them. This picture, slyly titled "Godiva's Ride," was causing a sensation. Well-dressed men and women chirped with titillation or disgust. Or both. It was "Ruskin said this" and "Craven said that" and "Did you hear what Tatling is asking? I doubt even the prince would pay seven thousand!"

Beside her, her husband jerked at the sum. "Seven thousand *pounds*?"

Lavinia barely heard him. A tide was rising inside her that took all her strength to contain, a fury that bubbled up from her very core.

How dare Mr. Craven suggest women could live like this hoyden, this Godiva, and be the better for it? Lavinia knew for a fact they couldn't. Her one fall from grace haunted her even now.

A woman's sins were never forgotten.

Only men escaped reprisal.

Behind her, Ernest Althorp shuffled closer. She'd asked him along in order to share the news from Merry's latest letter—in the expectation, of course, that he'd relay it to his father. Merry was softening. Anyone who read her words could see it. Lavinia had been grateful for the alacrity with which Ernest accepted her invitation, not to mention his willingness to see, as she did, much cause for hope.

Now, however, his blocky masculine presence made her want to scream.

Men were swine. This stupid, lascivious painting merely proved it.

"Hm," said Ernest, peering thoughtfully around her, "looks a bit like Merry."

Lavinia turned her head to gape at him while a sensation like a hundred icy spiders crawled up her spine.

Ernest flushed beneath her stare. "Er, I mean, around the hair a bit and maybe the, er, nose. But of course it isn't her." He stood straighter and filled his chest. "Merry would never pose for a thing like this."

"No, she wouldn't," said Lavinia, her tone chill. She wasn't even sorry when he flinched.

Merry wouldn't. More importantly, Merry couldn't. Merry was in Wales. With Isabel. They'd received a letter just this morning. So that couldn't be Merry's nose or Merry's hair or the mischievous glint in Merry's eye. Lavinia's daughter was no siren. She was a horse-mad tomboy. A *freckled,* horse-mad tomboy . . .

Who'd ridden astride as often as she had sidesaddle . . .

Who'd been more than angry enough at her parents to do something truly rash . . .

Who'd depended on Isabel to cover up pranks before.

Good Lord.

The spiders skittered back down Lavinia's spine. She was breathing too quickly but couldn't seem to stop. Some time had passed since she'd studied her daughter's knees but, unless she was very happily mistaken, Godiva's knobby joints were a shocking good match for Merry's.

She took but a second to decide what she had to do.

"I'm buying this painting," she announced, her voice too high but level.

When her husband widened his eyes at her, she lifted her head and spoke with even more authority. "It's a masterpiece. Worth every shilling."

"I agree it's good . . ." Geoffrey hedged, but she hadn't the patience to hear him out. If Ernest was right, if this was a naked portrait of her daughter, she couldn't afford to let it sit here another minute. Even if it *wasn't* Meredith, she couldn't afford to. Someone else might remark on the resemblance. The duchess's situation was too precarious to weather the slightest breath of scandal.

She had to buy it and she had to buy it now.

"I'll pay for it myself," she said, shocking Geoffrey to a blank and blinking silence, "out of the estate my mother left me."

With the air of supreme entitlement she'd known how to draw on all her life, she took the portrait by its carved and gilded frame and lifted it from its perch. She heard the seam under her sleeve rip as she did, but cared no more for that than for the buzz of exclamations spreading around the room.

"Let me help you," said Ernest. He reached for the frame but she ignored him.

"Where's Tatling?" she called above the noise. "Tell him I'm offering eight."

The painting banged against her ankle as she carried it through the crowd, heavier than she expected and quite unwieldy. Lavinia cursed the thing in her mind. It couldn't be Merry, simply couldn't.

But if it was, she'd make bloody damn sure no one ever found out but her.

"CARE TO EXPLAIN WHY YOU MADE SUCH A SPECTAcle of yourself?" asked her husband, once their coachman dropped Ernest off.

His tone was calm but his arms were crossed over his chest and a muscle beat like a pulse beneath his beard.

Lavinia tugged her gloves farther up her hands. Her heart felt like a bird trapped in her throat. "I can't imagine what you mean."

"Can't you?"

"No, I cannot. I wanted that painting and I bought it. With my own funds, I might add."

"I'm not concerned about the money, Lavi. I think you know I'm happy to buy you what you wish. What I don't understand is your behavior. You haven't been yourself since Merry left."

"Don't be silly, darling. Who else would I be if not myself?"

Her airy laughter did not convince him. "Whatever is wrong, I wish you'd tell me."

"All I did was buy a *painting*."

He stared a moment longer, a shadow of worry behind his eyes. Before he could voice it, she turned away. She hated lying to him—truly, she did—but better a lie than seeing her world destroyed.

Too easily she remembered Althorp's grip around her neck.

13 ❧

IT WAS NIC'S IDEA TO MAKE A SEA VOYAGE. TRAINS were dusty and cramped, he said, and unreliable on the Continent. According to him, a week on the Mediterranean, on a comfortable commercial yacht, could not fail to entertain her.

No doubt this would have been true if Merry hadn't proved an ill-starred sailor. To her supreme mortification, no sooner had she stepped on board than her stomach began to lurch. By the time the gleaming ship had steamed into the Channel, she was a miserable, retching heap.

She could hardly imagine anything less entertaining—not to mention less romantic—than holding one's lover's head over a chamberpot.

She half wished Nic would neglect her. Instead, he took her condition in surprisingly good-natured stride, even joking they ought to steam for Egypt instead of Venice, since he'd heard the streets of Cairo were very dry.

"I am so sorry," she said, during a jelly-boned lull on the second day. Too weak to stand and too nauseated to lie down, she sat on the floor of their small but elegant cabin with her back propped against the lower bunk. She wore only her chemise and drawers, since Nic had stripped her dress some time ago.

Now he opened the porthole to admit a blast of chilly air, then tucked a blanket around her shoulders. "No need to be sorry," he said. "It's not as if you're doing it on purpose."

"But I'm never sick. Never. I feel awful for making you take care of me."

"I can tell." With a faint smile, he wiped her brow with a cotton cloth. "You shouldn't worry. I've nursed my share of sick people."

Merry felt unaccountably better when he lowered himself to the floor beside her; she was comforted somehow, as if his presence alone was strengthening. The thought made her nervous. She knew she couldn't afford to become dependent on a man like Nic.

"Hard to imagine you as a nurse," she said.

"Oh, ye of little faith." He lifted her hair and spread it on the bed behind her. "I assure you, I'm a regular Florence Nightingale to my friends. When I first came to London and fell in with Sebastian and Evangeline, neither could hold their liquor, nor judge which glass should be their last. I can't count the number of hangover potions I've prepared, or the hours of moaning and whining they forced me to endure."

"I haven't whined, have I?"

He kissed her temple. "Not even once, love. You're the best-behaved sick person I've ever met."

Merry sighed in relief, then wrinkled her nose. "It's still disgusting."

"Well, yes," he admitted with a chuckle, then hugged her gently closer. "But look at it this way. I've seen you at your worst. From here on in it can only get better."

"One hopes," she said and succumbed to the urge to lean her head against his chest.

Most likely she shouldn't have let it happen, but the steady thump of his heart lulled her to sleep.

THE NEXT DAY MERRY FELT BETTER BUT COULDN'T bring herself to eat for fear she would not keep it down. She hated being weak, especially in front of Nic. Even this he seemed to understand. He assured her he didn't think less of her and bullied her into drinking sips of peppermint tea. Merry loathed the stuff, but ever since their conversation of the day before, she'd been determined not to complain. That, at least, she could control.

On the fourth day, she tried to get out of bed and immediately lost her balance.

Nic turned almost as pale as she was. "That tears it," he said as he helped her back into bed. "I'm seeing if there's a doctor on this ship."

"Nic, I hardly think I need a doctor."

"You do, damn it." He huffed and pointed his finger at her chest. "I brought you onto this bloody tub. What happens to you is on my head."

"Fine," she said, too tired to argue, "but I promise not to blame you if I die."

"Don't even—" His voice was too choked to finish. She opened her eyes, touched by his concern even if it made her want to laugh.

"I'm just weak from too much lying around," she soothed. "I very much doubt I'll expire from mal de mer."

A sound broke in his throat that he immediately shook away. "Of course you won't," he said heartily. "I simply think it would be prudent to consult a doctor in your case. Perhaps you can be restored to your former self a little sooner."

As it turned out, the yacht was too small to employ a doctor. Nic did, however, beg a remedy from the cook, a drink composed of sugar, lime juice, and some salt.

The captain himself came to see her, a courtesy that seemed unnecessary to her, though Nic pronounced himself very grateful. Indeed, his gratitude was fervent enough to be embarrassing, even if the captain did take it with aplomb. He was an older, sun-bronzed man in a crisp gray uniform who peered at her eyes and clucked like a mother hen.

"I'm all right," she said faintly, struggling to sit up. "Haven't been sick in days."

"She hasn't eaten, either," Nic put in, hovering worriedly behind. "As you can see, she can't afford to lose the weight."

"Thanks so much," Merry snapped, which made the captain smile.

"I'll send down a bit of crystallized ginger," he said. "Nibbling that should settle her stomach enough to eat. Then we can try some soup and rice."

Merry bridled at being talked around like a child but managed to hold her tongue.

After the captain left, Nic laughed at her expression. "You look so fierce, Duchess. I suppose you aren't at death's door after all."

She scowled even harder, but his care had warmed her heart.

"TELL ME A STORY," SHE SAID AS THE RICE SETTLED uneasily in her stomach. Nic smelled of fresh air and peppermint-lemon tea. He'd squeezed next to her on the narrow bunk and sat with his arm around her back and his long legs crossed at the ankle. When he spoke his voice was guarded.

"A story about what?"

"Anything. You and Sebastian. What life was like when you were young."

"I'm not that much older than you, Mary. I imagine it was similar to what life was like for you. Knew the world was round and all."

"I didn't mean it that way. I meant where did you grow up? What sort of games did you play? Did you get on with your parents? Are they still alive?"

Nic squirmed perceptibly on the mattress. "That's a lot of questions."

"Then just answer one. I need distraction from my diges-
tion."

He smiled at that, though she could tell he was reluctant.
No doubt it wasn't fair of her to push, considering her own
lack of candor. All the same, she couldn't resist the chance
to pry.

Nic intrigued her more than ever.

"Very well," he conceded, shifting her head to a more
comfortable position on his chest. "I can tell you my mother
is alive. My father, however, was killed in a hunting accident some years back."

Merry stroked his shirt where it lay above his heart.
"How terrible for you both."

"Mm," said Nic, an odd, dry sound. "What's even more
terrible is that it probably wasn't an accident."

That brought her head up. "You can't mean he was *mur-
dered*?"

His mouth lifted crookedly as he stroked his finger down
her cheek. His eyes didn't so much look at her as beyond
her. Into the past, she imagined. She could tell he hadn't
liked his father enough to mourn him. Good riddance, his at-
titude seemed to say, which to her—a papa's girl if ever
there was one—was every bit as shocking as having one's
parent killed.

But at least this explained why he had not wanted to
share his past.

With a soft exhalation, he dropped his hand to his thigh.
"The man who shot him said he mistook my father's hunting cap for a grouse. Possible—though there was talk that
my father seduced his wife."

"Oh," she said, hardly knowing how to take this seamy
tale. What sort of family did Nic come from? "Surely the
matter was investigated?"

A flicker of amusement crossed his face. "I suspect the
local constabulary didn't look into the matter as closely as
they might. Neither my mother nor the purported adulteress
were especially eager for the truth to come to light. Besides
which, my father was hardly an innocent victim."

"Nonetheless," said Merry, aware she was treading on

shaky ground, "a man does not deserve to die for an indis-
cretion."

"No," Nic agreed, his face drawing tight in a look as dark
as she'd ever seen him wear. "Not for that."

Wanting to comfort him, she stroked the muscle ticking
in his jaw. "It was the woman's responsibility as much as it
was your father's. She wasn't helpless. She could have re-
pulsed his advances."

"I believe her husband thought the same. He took his
wife to Australia as soon as the inquest was over, as if they
both were transported convicts. Of course"—he released a
breath of laughter—"their hasty departure could have been
my mother's doing."

"Your mother is that forceful?"

"Forceful doesn't begin to describe her. To be fair, she's
almost always in the right. Has a keen sense of justice."

"I imagine that could be uncomfortable."

"Yes," he said wryly, then half drew breath as if a thought
were just then occurring to him. "Uncomfortable for her as
well, perhaps. Even with all her will she can't bring the
world up to her standards. She must suspect, now and then,
that she might be driving the people she loves away."

Mary opened her mouth to protest putting the blame for
his father's choices on his mother. Then she realized he
wasn't talking about his father. He was talking about himself. Nic was the one who'd run from his mother's judgment.

Before she could decide if this was a topic she ought to
broach, he smiled warmly into her eyes. "You were thinking
about your parents, weren't you, when you asked me about
mine? That if they were alive they might disapprove of what
you've done."

Since her parents *were* still alive and since there was no
might about their disapproval, she hadn't been thinking anything of the kind. Rather than admit this, she looked down at
her hands. "Maybe they'd be right to disapprove."

Nic made a soft, snorting noise. "You're thinking of society's rules, rules society itself does not follow unless they
are convenient."

"But one must live by some code of conduct!" Amazed by her own words, Merry pressed her fingers to her lips. The objection was one she had not meant to make, one she would have thought more suited to her father.

Happily, Nic did not take offense. His gaze serious, he tucked a fallen curl behind her ear. "What does your conscience tell you is right? To me, it is not wrong to take pride in one's youth and beauty. Nor do I think it a sin to share the pleasures of the flesh with a willing partner. What is sinful is cruelty to one's lovers, cruelty and lack of care."

She could not answer. Her mind did not disagree but her heart was swiftly reaching the conclusion that the pleasures of the flesh, at least for her, were not a concern for flesh alone. Like it or not, her emotions were engaged.

"Can it really be that simple?" she asked, the question slightly rough. She lifted her head to gaze at him but he did not gaze at her. Water-threaded light, pale as straw, danced across his skin, making his features seem by contrast very still. His eyes were soot-framed ash, his mouth a line of autumn rose. He looked both beautiful and sad.

"It can be that simple," he said, "if one remembers to be wise."

BY THE TIME THEY PASSED THE ISLAND OF CORSICA, Merry was able to totter onto the deck and watch the stars rise from the sea. The water was calm, an inky glitter that swept unmeasured to the sky. A single line of portholes lit the ship while a net of foamy waves parted around the prow. Nic held her to his side by the forward rail, warming her, steadying her. Her enjoyment of his company should have disturbed her. Instead, she drank it in. This trip had changed her, perhaps as much as her experiences in his home. For the first time since childhood, she'd been completely reliant on another person. Nic had neither begrudged her his care nor abused her dependence, and that had shifted the axis on which she turned.

She was living in the moment now, weak yet serene, as if her past had been swept away like the wake behind the ship.

Though she knew this was an illusion—the past was with her always—the effect was very real. She felt light and calm and, under that, a quivering sense of anticipation.

She didn't know what would happen next, didn't know who Merry Vance would turn out to be.

"I feel reborn," she said.

Nic chuckled, taking it as a joke. "Wait till you see Venice," he said. "Then you'll think you've gone to heaven."

14 ❧

THE SHINING BLACK GONDOLA SLIPPED FROM THE dock at St. Mark's Square into the shimmering mouth of the Grand Canal. The day was still, the water a luminous ruffled mirror. Watching the palazzos rise on either side, Nic felt the happiness only a surfeit of beauty could inspire. *La Serenissima.* He was in her arms again and she was as fascinating, as gorgeous, as crumbling and stained and changeable as ever.

No city had ever affected him like this one. Venice radiated a peace and a mystery time would never dim. He longed for his paints with an ache that was physical, but at the same time was content to have them packed away. Venice could not truly be recorded. Venice had to be experienced. One opened oneself, made oneself vulnerable, and then one soaked her in.

But perhaps he'd made himself too vulnerable, because

when Mary's hand closed over his, heat burned unexpectedly behind his eyes.

"It's astonishing," she whispered as if they'd entered a
holy place.

Blinking quickly, he turned on the narrow seat to smile at
her. "Are you comfortable? Not too cold? I'm afraid the
weather won't really warm up before next month."

"I'm fine," she said, her expression softly amused as she
pushed an errant curl out of her eye.

Oh, that hair of hers. Titian gold, the perfect shade for
Venice. In truth, all of her was perfect for Venice: her flaws
and quirks the gilding for her charm. Nic brushed his thumb
up the slope of her cheekbone and kissed her, really kissed
her, for the first time in a week. The gondolier chuckled with
a Venetian's tolerance for romance, but Nic wouldn't have
cared if he'd disapproved. Mary's kiss felt as much like
coming home as his first sight of the ancient city.

When he finally released her mouth, she was flatteringly
breathless.

"You're too thin," he said, touching her kiss-reddened
lips. "As soon as we get settled, I'm going to stuff you full
of biscotti."

Mary dropped her lashes like a courtesan, her mouth
curved and rosy, her hands folded primly in her lap. "Is that
all you're going to stuff me full of?"

He hadn't realized he'd grown hard until she said it, but
now he knew those demurely lowered eyes were measuring
his lust. His erection pulsed at her attention, growing hotter
and tighter at the thought of making up for its long neglect.

"No," he said, the answer a muted rumble. "As soon as I
get you alone, I'm going to cram you full of every inch of
me you can take."

"Good." Her grin went through him as potently as her
kiss. "I'll be looking forward to that."

He could not contain his laugh, or the joy that bubbled up
behind it. "Brat." He slung his arm around her neck. "Shall
I introduce you to the city in the meantime?"

"Oh, yes." She sat straighter on the scarlet cushion, her
eyes still glinting with carnal mischief. "I'm sure playing

tour guide would help distract you from the rather formidable size of your discomfort."

So he pointed out the sights as the young Venetian rowed them up the *Canalazzo:* the domed white church of Santa Maria della Salute, the crooked Palazzo Dario with its colored marble front, the Accademia where he'd studied as a young man, and the narrow *rio* that wound through the Dorsoduro district to his favorite small café.

"We'll go there," he said, abruptly afire to show her his youthful haunts. "There's a place in the *campo,* the square, where the city's cats laze in the sun. You can't walk up the steps without tripping over them. I used to spend hours there as a student, trying to catch them in my sketchbook."

"I want to see it," she said with a blissful sigh. "I want to see everything."

He could not miss the adoration in her eyes, but for once he did not regret it. He was too happy to be here. The canal was quiet, the city drowsing in the quiet hour after lunch. A single gondola trailed behind them with another passenger from their ship, too well bundled for Nic to tell if the figure was man or woman.

He was thankful for the solitude. For this one magical hour he didn't want to share Venice, or Mary, with anyone. He found himself wishing he'd leased a palazzo himself, or even taken rooms in a hotel. He'd made his plans so quickly after Mary changed her mind he hadn't stopped to think whether he really wanted to stay with Sebastian and Evangeline.

He'd been too jubilant to think.

In fact, he'd been more jubilant than wisdom would advise.

Suddenly uneasy, Nic worried his thumb against his teeth while the oarsman adjusted their course to avoid a *traghetto* ferrying a pedestrian to the opposite bank of the canal. The gondolier's motions were smooth, almost hypnotic, the sun flashing off the water and the oar, the prow cutting smoothly through tiny waves.

No, Nic thought, his elation had been perfectly understandable. Mary was a charming bed partner and companion. As pleasure loving as he was, it would have been more surprising if he hadn't been glad. Plus, there had been her bout of illness on the ship. A stone could not have failed to admire the pluck with which she'd faced it. She'd seemed so fragile huddled in that bunk—a child, really—putting on her bravest face as he watched her getting weaker, as her skin thinned and paled and her veins stood out in threads of lapis blue.

She'd frightened him, not only for the echo of memories he'd been running from for years, but for herself. He didn't want to lose *her:* Mary Colfax. Her light was far too bright to leave the world. He had no intention of telling her now, but if she hadn't finally managed to drink and eat, she might have died on that stupid boat.

Haunted by the thought, he shuddered against a chill that came entirely from within.

"What is it?" Mary asked. "What's wrong?"

He could only shake his head. He knew what moved him wasn't love. He didn't have that in him. This emotion was no more than the primitive male urge to protect those weaker than themselves. Or maybe she called to the artist in him. She was original. Irreplaceable. But he would have felt the same for a crumbling villa or a snippet of ancient song. What he felt wasn't love. It was simply high regard.

Despite the logic of this argument, he could not explain his tenderness away. Giving in to it, he smoothed her curls around her beautiful little head. "We're taking the train home," he declared, "and Perdition take the dust."

THE PALAZZO GUARDI ROSE FROM THE FLICKERING waters in a fantastical Byzantine-Gothic heap. Its facade was painted the soft brick red Nic informed her was *pastellone,* against which peaked and balconied windows stood out in grimy white Istrian stone. Marking a berth for the gondola to slip into was a line of Venice's trademark spiral-striped mooring posts. On their brief journey up the canal, Merry had seen these listing poles in every color of the rainbow. The Guardis' were a striking green and gold.

Both Nic and the curly-haired gondolier helped her onto the landing where a shallow set of steps led straight out of the water. As a perch, it seemed precarious. The second tread from the top bore the mark of a recent tide.

"Goodness," she exclaimed, "what do they do when it floods?"

Nic laughed as he paid the boatman. "The same thing their great-grandfathers did. They nail a board over the door and move upstairs."

Still smiling, he lifted a golden lion's head doorknocker and let it fall. After a short wait, a portly man in a suit admitted them with a bow. "Ah. *Signor Craven e signorina Colfax. Buon giorno.* I believe signor Locke is out, but the other signora is working in the *portego.*"

Nic nodded and thanked him in fluent Italian. Assuring the man they could find their way, he led Merry down a broad hall toward some ancient marble stairs. "That's signor Vecchi," he explained, "the countess's man of business." He waved at the doors they were passing, one of which was open to reveal a number of straw-filled packing crates. "For five generations, the Guardis have exported Venetian glass around the world. This floor serves as their warehouse and their office."

"They conduct their business from their home?"

"That's not unusual here, Duchess. Unlike the English peerage, Venetians are proud of being merchants. To them, the arrangement is practical."

Who would have thought it? she mused, then caught her breath as the musty, chilly stairwell widened into something quite extraordinary. Here, on a landing of colorful inlaid stone, four tall quatrefoil windows overlooked a sunny courtyard. Opposite this sudden flood of illumination, two flights of steps led grandly up from either side, their balusters carved in beautiful gray-white marble.

"One more flight," Nic said. "Then you'll really see a show."

The prediction was no exaggeration. Struck dumb, Merry panted to a halt when she reached the top. The central hall, or *portego,* was a vast, high corridor that extended from the front of the palazzo to the back. Rows of leaded windows lit either end. Between them lay an excess of ornament she'd never seen anything to equal. Garlands and festoons and gilt and more shiny patterned floors fought for attention from her confused and dazzled eyes. What surfaces weren't adorned with stuccowork had been skillfully painted to resemble it. Doors were embellished in this fashion, and lintels, and the frieze at the upper border of the walls. No less than six cut-glass chandeliers hung from the copiously frescoed ceiling, which itself was a maze of reality and trompe l'oeil.

The effect was both hideous and gorgeous, like a rose dipped in gold and hung with diamonds. Its sheer exuberance was all that kept her English aesthetic from revolt.

Dwarfed by this grandeur, but seeming at home in it, Evangeline knelt atop a tall wooden scaffold, obviously retouching the central fresco on the ceiling.

She cried out at seeing Nic and scrambled handily down, a process made easier by her simple white smock and loose brown trousers. Braided back, her straight dark hair framed the asymmetrical drama of her face.

Merry couldn't help thinking the outfit suited her a good deal better than the dowdy gown she'd worn to Anna's.

"Nic!" Evangeline exclaimed, pulling Merry's lover into a hug. "How glad I am to see you! Seb's been totally impossible. Maybe you can make him behave."

"I doubt that." Smiling wryly, Nic stroked the edge of Evangeline's paint-streaked hair. No image could have pointed up the interests they shared more clearly. To Merry's discomfort, Evangeline turned her head and pressed a lingering kiss into his palm.

"Nic," she said, her voice husky, "must you always be neutral territory?"

Nic pursed his mouth, but did not seem annoyed. "I've discovered neutrality is the safest position around you two." Turning back, he laid his hand behind Merry's shoulder. "You remember Mary, of course."

"Of course." Evangeline broke into a laugh. "Forgive me, Mary, but you should see your face! Like a little doe who's lost its mother." She pressed steepled fingers to her lips.

"You mustn't mind me and Nic. We've known each other forever. Our flirtation doesn't mean a thing."

Merry's brows rose in response. Nic's flirtation might not mean a thing to him, but she harbored no illusions about Evangeline's.

"Mm," said Nic, his tone as skeptical as Merry's thoughts, "a bit less of that, Evie. We've come for a nice visit, not to play your games."

"*Mi dispiace,*" Evangeline murmured, probably under the impression that Merry would not understand. The limits of her finishing school Italian aside, the apology seemed spurious. Evangeline's eyes were glowing with enjoyment.

"Shall I show you to your rooms?" she asked.

"Room," Nic corrected, his temper beginning at last to show. "Mary and I will stay together."

Merry was surprised to find herself blushing at his insistence, especially in front of a woman who, the last time they'd met, had been with a different man.

Evangeline, however, was made of sterner stuff. She smiled as if Nic's anger were a compliment. "The countess suggested I give you the red suite. There's a bedroom and a parlor. Hence my use of the term 'rooms.' "

Rather than apologize, Nic hummed as he had before. Like Merry, he seemed to know Evangeline had been hoping to get a rise. Unlike Merry, though, his annoyance had disappeared. To her, this was surer evidence of their friendship than any kiss.

"Where is the countess?" Merry asked as they followed a slightly more modest flight of stairs to the floor above.

Evangeline answered with a shrug. "Morocco, last I heard. I doubt she'll return to Venice until the *Festa della Sparesca.*" She smiled, fey and feminine, over her shoulder. "*La Serenissima* will be too cold for her old bones until then."

Though Merry had no idea when the festival of asparagus might occur—if that was indeed what Evangeline said—she received this news with a sinking stomach. Without the presence of the older woman, however irregular a countess she might be, Evangeline's wildness would not suffer any check. Obviously, the woman intended to seduce Nic. Whether he would resist was beyond Merry's power to guess. He seemed to have grown more attached to her of late but, in Nic's moral view of the world, attachment might not imply exclusivity.

She fisted her hands in her skirts as Evangeline showed them around their quarters, barely taking in the faded crimson silk walls and the huge canopied bed. She hadn't a leg to stand on as far as objecting went. She'd presented herself to Nic as a free spirit, eager for adventure. She'd sworn her heart was in no danger of being lost.

It wasn't Nic's fault she'd been lying.

To herself, as well, she thought with a burning shiver of awareness. She'd been destined to fall the day they met.

In his canny way, Nic was sensitive to her mood. "All right," he said as the door shut behind Evangeline with a thunk, "let it out before you burst."

Merry gritted her teeth. The last thing she wanted was to rail at him like a fishwife. One little complaint, however, was more than she could restrain.

"Never in my life," she said, "have I stared at anyone like a doe!"

Nic laughed and embraced her from behind. "She was trying to make you angry."

"Well, she succeeded!" She turned in his arms, her fury abruptly spilling over. " 'Oh, you mustn't mind me and Nic. We've known each other forever.' As if I were some sort of interloper! As if she owned you!"

Nic cupped her cheeks between his palms. "She's probably jealous."

"Jealous! She's a bloody—" She swallowed the insult and tossed her head. "Anyway, why was Mr. Vecchi calling her signora? I bet she told him she and Sebastian were married."

"As to that," said Nic with a small, uncomfortable sigh, "they are married."

Merry's jaw dropped even as she drew breath for her next rant. For a moment, her lungs wouldn't work at all.

"I know," he said, lifting his hands, "they don't behave

like man and wife. They consider what they have an 'open' marriage. In its way, for them, it works."

"But why even bother to marry?"

Nic pulled a rueful face. "They love each other. They simply love freedom more."

Merry began to speak, then found she couldn't. Freedom. Wasn't that what she'd claimed she wanted all along, how she'd pictured her later years: free to take lovers when she chose?

But not to *marry* them, she thought. Marriage was a promise to forsake all others. Or it ought to be. She hadn't realized she believed that but she did. Her brothers and her parents had taught her the value of commitment. For all its flaws, marriage was a matter of honor, of giving one's word and keeping it. Without being aware of it, she squared her shoulders.

It seemed the new Merry Vance wasn't quite what she'd expected.

Nic stroked her upper arms. "Do you want to leave? Find a hotel to stay in on our own?"

The offer startled her. Rather than give in to temptation, she shook her head. "I don't want to come between you and your friends."

"They'd understand. I want you to be comfortable."

"I am," she said, but her chin wobbled in spite of her efforts to keep it firm.

Seeing the telltale sign, Nic cursed under his breath and pulled her closer. She couldn't help curving into him; he was too warm, too caring—even if he didn't care as deeply as she did.

"I'm sorry," he said, his lips against her hair. "I didn't mean to expose you to the edge of Evie's wit. She fancied me once, years ago—at least, as much as she fancies anyone other than Sebastian. I think she hoped I'd save her from him: if I could make her fall in love with me, she could break her obsession with him. But those two are destined for each other, always circling, always taking little cuts. Whatever Evangeline thought she needed, it wasn't what I had."

"Were you sorry?" Merry dared to ask.

"Sorry?"

"That you couldn't be what she needed."

"Oh, Mary." His laugh was as arid as a desert. "In all my life, I've never been what anyone needed. But my heart wasn't broken, if that's what you mean. Even then, I knew better than to make promises I couldn't keep."

His arms tightened around her back, tense but possessive, as if his words stirred some conflict only her nearness could allay. You want me to need you, she thought, the knowledge as clear as the sun sparkling off the canal outside. You want me to need you because you need me, too.

She lifted her head and he met her gaze, his eyes troubled despite his smile. Don't say anything, she told herself. Just let this be and it might grow. Afraid to burst the fragile bubble, she dragged her hands down the slope of his back until their hips were snugged together. She forced herself to match his attempt at lightness. "You made me a promise, Nic. I trust you haven't forgotten it."

His expression turned sensual; practiced, the cynical side of her might have said, though his smile still warmed the blood coursing through her veins. "What promise would that be?"

"To stuff me full of every inch of you I could take."

"Ah. That promise." He bent and tugged her lower lip between his teeth. "Are you sure you want me to keep it now, when all of Venice lies before us?"

"Venice can wait," she said breathlessly. "I can't."

"Can't?" The word seemed to interest him as much as the mark his teeth had left on her mouth.

"Can't," she repeated, almost out of air. "I haven't held you in too long."

"Eight days," he supplied agreeably, his eyes heavy, his face beginning to darken, "and eight long, randy nights."

Her hands slipped over his bottom and squeezed his muscled cheeks. The crotch of his trousers grew measurably warmer. Inside them, his sex was hard and thick. "You've been a gentleman."

"More than you can imagine."

"If you'd stop being a gentleman now, I'd be very grateful."

"Would you?" His eyes danced as he gathered up the back of her skirts. A grind of his hips punctuated the question. "Would you cry with thanks while I pumped inside you? Would you quiver and sob and clutch me with your quim?"

She couldn't answer. He had found the parting in her drawers and, an instant later, the parting between her legs. She was wet for him, summer warm, as his touch skated over her sultry folds. The sound he made when he pressed two fingers inside her was like a lion's purr. His intrusion was just what she'd been craving. She squirmed over it, melted over it, and her voice broke on a sigh.

"So," he said, deep and rough, "my little Mary is no liar. She's weeping for me already."

He stroked her clutching walls, pressing the back of her passage, then the front. His knuckles nudged something sharply sensitive and she couldn't hold back a cry.

"Mm." He probed for the spot. "There's something good here, I see. Something worth exploring."

Merry gasped and tried to squirm away. "Don't, Nic. It's too much."

He chuckled but he stopped. "Maybe it's too much now," he said. "A bit later I'd wager you'll like it fine."

As if to prove he could make her like anything at all, his thumb slipped backward, oiled by the fluid of her lust. She jumped as it, too, probed her body, gathering a strange, tight tingle from a part she'd never thought to let anyone touch.

"Nic!" she gasped, a helpless protest. Or maybe it wasn't a protest. Maybe it was a plea for more.

Nic seemed equally aroused by the forbidden nature of his foray. His body was stiff, shaking palpably in desire. At her gasp of shock, he held her tighter, pushing deeper into her anus, setting his teeth to her neck and breathing hard. "Don't lie to me, Mary. And don't lie to yourself. Your body doesn't know what it's supposed to like. It only knows what it does."

She groaned as he rubbed her with all his hand. Heat

surged through her, a deep, prickling ache that swelled beyond the regions he could touch.

"Imagine this as my cock," he said, the words coming hoarse and thick as he rotated slowly with his thumb. "Imagine I filled you front and back."

Try as she might, she couldn't deny her yearning for the experiment he described. Would it hurt? Or would it simply be a new surrender? Certainly, she was not hurting now. Her pearl of pleasure felt like a tiny sun, pulsing frantically against the pressure he was exerting. Her body was enjoying this. Her body was on fire.

Which didn't mean she was comfortable doing more.

"The window is open," she whispered, her voice too unsteady for sound. "There's a breeze blowing over my bum."

He laughed and kissed her, deeply, wetly, as if he meant to fuse their mouths. The kiss was wilder somehow, more excited—whether because of their recent abstinence or from his unusual play, she could not say. Before she could ask, he lifted her off her feet, his fingers slipping from her to leave a throbbing emptiness behind. With a swoosh of wool and cotton, her skirts fell down her legs. He was carrying her. The breeze grew stronger, the smell of brackish water, the cry of hungry birds. He set her down on the little balcony, steadying her when she tottered on her feet.

She wanted him so badly she was weak.

"Look," he said, turning her to face the balustrade of stone. "Here's something I know you'll like."

At first she thought he meant Venice, spread before them like a drunkard's happy dream: water and sky and palazzos bridging the gulf between. Then her skirts crept once more up her legs.

"Nic—" She started to turn, but he caught her head and gently, firmly pushed it back.

"No." Soft as it was, his voice held a ring of command. A snap of cloth and metal announced the opening of his trousers. His feet sidled between her own, spreading them, spreading her. She shivered as the length of him burned her through her drawers. He was so long, so deliciously thick and hard. His breath came heavily as he spoke. "Venice was built to show off beautiful things. Here, of all places, why shouldn't you do what you like best? Why shouldn't we both do what we need?"

The balustrade pressed her belly where he'd crowded her up against it. A crinkling sound told her he'd taken one of his sheaths out of his pocket. She bit her lip. She wanted him to take her, wanted it enough to cry. No one could see, not really; the front of her skirts covered everything below her waist. And Nic was behind her. They would look as if they were embracing, as any lovers might. The chance that someone might guess, though, set her limbs atremble. Sighing, she felt him breach her drawers. The skin of his crown was hot, both delicate and firm. He teased it over her lips, then between them, then around the tiny spear of her clitoris. Her sheath clenched down on itself, trying to grab what it wished were thrust within.

"I'm going to fuck you," he whispered. "I'm going to make up for every night I did without. In front of Venice and the world, I'm going to cram my hungry cock up to your womb. And you, Miss Mary, do not have the will to stop me."

"No," she admitted with the last of her breath, "I don't."

He growled in answer. His first deep thrust drove a cry from her startled throat. By luck or design he'd found the tender spot he'd pressed before. She whimpered at the sharpness of the pleasure, at the thrumming stretch of him inside. He steadied her, and perhaps himself, with a tighter grip around her hips.

"Sh," he said, drawing back until his rim was caught inside her clutching gate. "You mustn't let anyone hear."

His warning made it that much harder to be quiet, no doubt as he'd intended. He knew her too well, her Nic. She felt fevered, her fear of discovery the peg that tightened the wire of her desperate need. She wanted him to slam into her without restraint, to drive her beyond the bounds of sense, and yet this taut control was more exciting still. She trembled as he cupped her pubis and thrust again, his finger finding her swollen bud just as the tip of him crossed those fateful nerves. The stimulation was almost more than she could bear, the pleasure so deep it felt like pain.

Nic laughed at her tortured groan. "Better," he said, reversing the dragging glide. "But not quite quiet enough."

"I'll show you quiet," she swore, but it took all her strength to keep her reaction to a shudder.

When she licked her lip, she tasted blood.

He did not mean for it to be easy. With each slow thrust, he caught the place again, pushing the ache deeper, making her want it more. Nor was he immune to the charm of their position. He thickened with every pulse until he had to gasp for breath against her cheek. His whole body was rigid, coiled tight against the powerful lure of release. Even the arm that wrapped her waist seemed to harden into stone.

"Faster," she pleaded.

"Slower," he breathed.

She reached back to grasp his hip. "Harder, then. Do it harder."

He said her name on a laughing scold. "Look at the city. Look at this beautiful, decadent city."

She looked, but all she could feel was him. The thrust of his penis. The heat of his chest. The throb and quiver of his blood. "I can't," she said. "I can only think of you."

He put his mouth beside her ear. "There are people fucking all over Venice. Whores, Mary, and wives and hard young men with barely hair enough for a beard. They're making love in boats and in bedrooms. In gardens and in grottos. In tangles of limbs no sensible man can count. They're groaning, Mary. They're tugging cocks and suckling breasts. They're sweating and slippery. Hot. Desperate. Trying to spill or wishing they hadn't just. The sheets of Venice are stiff with come, the thighs of Venice sticky, the arms of Venice full. And now we're a part of it. We're fucking Venice until she screams."

She saw what he said. The men. The women. The body parts drenched with seed. She could not wait for him. She came from the magic of his voice, not with a scream but with a moan. He gritted out a curse as the ripples of her pleasure gripped his cock. The tension in him changed. Suddenly his thrusts came harder; not faster, but with more force. He was battering her sweetest spot with every drive, blunt, smooth, turning one release into a violent, blissful string.

"We're fucking her," he gasped, his arm a stranglehold, his fingers digging into her softest flesh. "Making love as if we never . . . had . . . before."

With that, he followed her into the maelstrom, shuddering, silent, with convulsively tightening muscles and bursts of seed only he could feel. Something swept through her— maybe Venice, maybe him—sweeter than sweet, softer than soft, deeper than any orgasm she'd known. The feeling was chocolate and velvet and kisses rolled into one; comfort, if comfort could shake one like the earth. She sighed from the pit of her belly, half sad, half happy, and heard him do the same. His hold on her eased but did not fall away.

He feels it, she thought. He feels the magic, too.

"Lord, Mary," he swore, curling round her like a cloak. "You are the sweetest thing."

She was ready to tell him then. That she loved him. That she had lied. That she sensed his heart was a good deal bigger than he believed.

But when she opened her eyes, the sight that met them drove the confession from her brain. Someone had been watching them. A man stood on the narrow landing beneath the balcony: a tall, slender man with a golden beard and the gleam of knowledge in his eyes. It was Sebastian. Evangeline's husband. Nicolas's friend. His smile curled upward, slowly, sardonically, changing her flush of sweetness to one of shame.

She couldn't pretend he did not guess what they'd been doing.

He brought his gathered fingers to his mouth, then opened them, an ironic Italian kiss. His lips moved. *"Bella,"* she thought they mouthed. *"Bella signorina."*

He looked as if he thought she'd do the same with him, as if he were imagining it even then. Her body tightened and heated, a response she could not control. She might hate herself for it but she could not reason it away.

Attraction doesn't matter, she thought. It doesn't dictate what I do.

Nic stirred behind her, pulling gently from her body. "Cold out here," he muttered, clearly unaware that they weren't alone.

"Yes," Merry agreed and turned to push him into the room.

If she had her way, he'd never know they had been seen.

15 ❧

As always, Nic slept like the dead. Merry wished she could follow his example, but the day had left her with too many troubling thoughts. Instead, she lay in the dark staring up at the swagged baldachin canopy, listening to Nic breathe and wondering if she dared creep down the marble stairs to find a snack.

The cook would not be pleased. As they'd sat down to dinner, the countess's chef had burst into the dining room, bewailing the mysterious disappearance of a roast. Sebastian had laughed and told her Nic would buy another, but the servant had not been calmed.

"This means the death of trust," she had pronounced. "Someone in my *casa* is a thief!"

Unimpressed by her drama, Evangeline shooed her off. Sadly, the cook's departure didn't improve the evening's tone. Sebastian spent the meal grinning wickedly at his plate—most likely reveling in what he'd witnessed that afternoon—while Evangeline alternated between sniping at him and trying to get Nic to take her side.

"*You* understand the treatment a woman deserves," she said, which prompted a snort from her wandering spouse. When she glared at him he answered with a smoky look, full of history and suggestion. "The treatment a woman deserves," he drawled, "isn't always the one she needs."

Evangeline pretended to be annoyed by this, but Merry had no trouble guessing why she was flushed. Chances were Sebastian knew what made her body tick as well as Nic knew Merry's. In fact, after all these years, Sebastian probably knew his wife's susceptibilities better.

The thought of staying with Nic long enough to develop that sort of rapport was dangerously appealing.

Not that any of this crossed Nic's mind. He spent the evening in a daze, very much as if he were planning another painting. To her surprise, when she asked if he wanted to see whether the valise with his sketching implements had arrived, he merely shrugged.

At dinner he seemed to hear no more than half of what anyone said.

Between his abstraction and the others' war of words, only Merry gave the clam-laden spaghetti *alle vongole* the attention it deserved. If she'd had any sense, she'd have eaten Nic's portion, too. To hell with being ladylike; Merry's stomach had catching up to do.

Because she'd ignored it earlier, it was making demands on her now. With a grimace of resignation, she pushed off the covers and swung out of bed. The terrazzo floor, a special surface of crushed and polished stone, felt like ice beneath her toes. Cursing, she grabbed Nic's robe from the end of the bed and groped her way through the elegant, moonlit suite.

Their rooms were shabby but impressive, filled with heavy chairs and ancient chests, just waiting to clap her knees. The aqueous light confused the shadows, as did the numerous gilt-framed mirrors. Twice the small Turkish carpets tried to trip her, causing her to gasp and flail her arms.

It was too much to hope that Nic would hear her and get up.

As luck would have it, she met Sebastian coming up the stairs as she was tiptoeing down. She saw him before he saw her, but didn't have time to back away. The landing windows, with their interlaced ogee peaks, cast circles of moonlight across his head and shoulders. In one hand he held a bottle, in the other a basket of bread. He was trudging up the treads as if he were weary—a sympathetic figure until he saw her, froze, and wolfishly flashed his teeth.

He closed the distance between them in two long strides.

"I'm going for a snack," she said rudely enough to discourage anyone but him.

Smile broadening, he braced his legs to block her way. "Work up an appetite, did you?"

"I was sick on the boat. Cast up my accounts all over the place."

His throaty chuckle was a pleasure she didn't care to acknowledge. "If you wish to disgust me, you'll have to do better than that."

"And if you wish to attract me, you'll have to do better than these childish games."

He threw back his head on a silent laugh, his throat bared, his eyes creased appealingly at the corners. He recovered abruptly, tucking the wine beneath his arm so he could cup her cheek in his lean, long-fingered hand. She shivered at his touch, but not completely in distaste. "Come with me," he said like a seducer in a novel. "I have something special to show you."

Merry crossed her arms. "I'm sure you do."

This time his chest was all that shook with his amusement. "Nothing of *that* sort, I assure you. I could hardly expect you to decide your sexual future this soon after meeting me. Unlike Nic, my personality takes a while to grow on one. No, I've something else to show you, something of artistic interest that may shed light on the tangled web that is Nic and Sebastian and Eve. Besides which, I have prosciutto in this breadbasket, along with the most amiable sweet sparkling wine: Prosecco, Mary, the pride of the Veneto."

Her stomach betrayed her by rumbling loudly.

"You see?" Sebastian purred. "I *do* know what women need."

His beseeching smile, manipulative though it was, was too charming to resist. She did want to understand Nic better, which meant understanding his history with his friends. "No tricks," she insisted. "You'll show me whatever it is and let me go."

"Absolutely," he assured her. "I may not be as civilized as Nic, but I'd never take a lady against her will."

"SHE'S A GENIUS," HE SAID WISTFULLY, "A FUCKING bloody genius."

Sebastian had led her to a room in the palazzo's attic, one that had served for some time as an artist's garret: obviously Evangeline's. It was a cluttered, cozy space with exposed brick walls and dusty wooden flooring. A woman's shawl hung from a nail on one of the ceiling beams, and a volume of Browning's poems shared a rickety table with a paint-smeared palette. Not concerned with these homey details, Sebastian held a branch of candles before his wife's latest artistic effort. The flames wavered in what Merry guessed was inebriation.

The possibility did not frighten her as it might have with other men. Alcohol didn't seem to change Sebastian's personality to any discernible degree. She suspected he was too used to being foxed for it to matter.

"Nic doesn't hold a candle to her," he said, "and God knows a hack like me can't." Shaking his head, he swung the bottle at his side. "Fifty years from now the world will be ready to see her gift. Then they'll be sorry they ignored her."

Merry wasn't enough of an expert to dispute this. She only knew the painting was the strangest, most disturbing work of art she'd ever seen. It was a portrait of Nic and Sebastian and Eve—but just barely. Their figures looked like displaced shards of glass, the pieces shifted from one body to another so that breasts and eyes and hands jumbled all together. The colors screamed rage and sorrow and an odd, insinuating sensuality. "I'm ugly," the picture seemed to say, "but you know you can't look away."

The picture frightened her. It held a threat, or perhaps a warning, and even though Evangeline scarcely knew Merry, the message seemed to speak directly to her.

"It's powerful," she said, "uncomfortably so."

She could tell he was pleased with her answer. "Yes," he said, "I knew you'd understand."

His expression amazed her. Nic had claimed Sebastian loved his wife, but she hadn't believed it until she saw those tears of pride shimmering in his eyes.

She touched his arm before he could lift the Prosecco to his mouth. "Have you told her how you feel?"

The bottle descended with a slosh of sparkling wine. When he laughed, it sounded like a sob. "Too many times to count. She's afraid to believe me, afraid to admit she's better than either one of us. Oh, she pretends she hates how unfair the world is, that a woman is the equal of any man, but in truth, in secret truth, she wants Nic and me to be her heroes." He took a swig, long and thirsty, then saluted the extraordinary painting. "Ain't goin' t' happen, Evie. You've got more to say in your little finger than the two of us put together."

Nic has something to say, Merry thought. Maybe he says it more gently but he does.

She shut her mouth on the words. She suspected Sebastian knew this. And maybe, in secret truth, he needed his image of Evangeline to cut Nic down to size.

Fearing she'd learned more than she bargained for, she dried her hands on Nic's dressing gown and tried to frame her next comment with care. "Nic says Evangeline fancied him once."

"Hah!" Sebastian barked. "Not just once. She'd jump back in his bed the minute he invited her."

"You could stop her," she suggested.

Sebastian smiled, a lazy curl of mouth and mustache. "Maybe I could. But maybe I don't want to. Maybe I fancy Nic myself."

He wagged his fair, straight brows as if daring her to be shocked. Despite her best efforts, she could not hide the sudden hitching of her breath. Her heart had jolted as hard as when she'd tripped on the Turkish rug. Before she could gather her wits, he set down the candelabra and reached toward her with the wine bottle's neck. He wasn't offering her a drink. Instead, he drew the cool green glass down the hollow between her breasts. The tip of his fingers followed into the shadows. When he met her startled gaze, his eyes were amused but sympathetic.

"You could join us," he said, "square off our little triangle."

She shook her head, though the response wasn't as immediate as she liked. His offer held a dark attraction, one she knew better than to accept. "I couldn't do that to Nic."

"Who says Nic would mind?"

Oh, he was determined to shock her. Ignoring the implications behind his words, she firmed her jaw. "I couldn't do that to me, then. I won't watch Nic bedding someone else."

Sebastian's finger traced a path around the neckline of her robe, skimming the first slight swell of her breasts. Her nipples hardened beneath the silk but she refused to act ashamed. Sebastian wet his lips, then lifted his eyes to hers. "What if refusing to play meant you would lose him?"

Merry didn't believe Nic would stoop to this kind of blackmail but, in the end, it did not matter. "My answer would be the same," she said. "I was not born to share."

A grudging respect lurked behind the mockery of his smile. He didn't speak, merely turned back to the painting and took a drink.

She had the impression she'd been dismissed.

So much, she thought, for being fed.

"Where have you been?" Nic demanded as Mary draped his robe on the bed's twisting bottom rail.

She was naked beneath the silk. The bedside lamp threw her slimness into relief, slanting the shadows of her breasts along her ribs. His throat ached at her blend of fragility and strength. She was a faerie in the moonlight: elusive, mysterious. He'd woke half an hour earlier to find her gone and had been sitting up ever since. Every creak of the old building had heightened his consternation, every watery slap of the canal.

Twice he'd gotten up to search for her and twice he'd stopped himself at the door. Nicolas Craven did not treat women like possessions. His lovers were free to go when and where they pleased.

But he hadn't liked wondering where she was, or the suspicions it invoked. Of course, he liked her failure to answer even less. Suspicions notwithstanding, he'd fully expected her to offer an innocent explanation. Her hesitation told him that would not be the case.

"Well?" he prompted.

She smoothed the paisley robe across the rail. "Sebastian took me to the attic to show me Evangeline's painting."

Her voice was uninflected, but he was too experienced not to realize she was testing him. He'd known women who lived to make their partners jealous. To them, this proved how highly they were prized—a ploy he had always scorned.

To his dismay, this time the ploy was working.

Rather than betray his weakness, he gritted his teeth and waited. As he'd expected, Mary gave in before he did.

"He tried to seduce me," she confessed, "but I declined."

A fury swept through him that had nothing to do with any game she might be playing and everything to do with the perfidy of his friend. Sebastian knew what Mary meant to him, better perhaps than he did. At that moment, Nic could cheerfully have smashed his teeth straight down his throat.

"Is that so?" he said tightly, and even he could hear the anger in it.

"Yes." She looked at him, pride in every line of her body: a funny-faced, pint-sized queen. "You can do what you like and I can't stop you, but I've decided for myself. For as long as we're together, I'll only sleep with you."

Her declaration disarmed him. He gaped in astonishment, but she was not finished yet. "I trust you'd give me the courtesy of a warning," she added stiffly. "I don't think I'd want to stay if you intended to be intimate with someone else."

"I assure you," he snapped, "I have no such intention!"

"You don't?" Her queenly mien had fallen away as if it had never been. What remained was a vulnerable and sweet young woman.

Nic grinned at the change, warmed in places no fire could reach. Knowledge burst inside him then—silently, brilliantly—like an unsuspected star. He didn't know how he'd managed to blind himself for so long. This afternoon, on the balcony, he'd felt the glow they made together and had fretted at what it meant. Now he knew. He loved Mary Colfax, loved her as he'd never thought to love another soul.

To his astonishment, the revelation was not as awful as he'd feared.

Then again, he would have to think carefully before deciding on a course of action. His relief that she'd turned Sebastian down might have made him giddy. What, after all, did loving Mary mean? Would it change him? Would it last? He knew very well she cared for him. Might he disappoint her despite the unexpected openness of his heart?

Until he could answer those questions, he had better keep the sentiment to himself.

He could not, however, keep her at a distance.

"Come here," he said, putting out his arms. "Let me prove how easily you entertain me all by yourself."

Though she clambered onto the bed with the agility of a stripling lad, the way she snuggled into his arms was purely female. He stroked her cloud of hair behind her back, the pleasure of touching her strangely new. When she slung her thigh across his legs—a possessive gesture, if ever there was one—he hardened as emphatically as if she'd taken him in her mouth.

She hummed at the feel of him stiffening, but did not move except to wriggle and hug his waist. Like him, she seemed content, at least for now, to hold and to be held. Her cheek moved like a cat's against his shoulder. When she spoke, her voice was still unsure.

"Tonight, in the attic, Sebastian implied that you . . . that the three of you . . ."

Ah, thought Nic as her query trailed away. Old Seb tried to set them at odds by disclosing that bit of history.

"Yes," he said, deciding truth was the best response.

Her head lifted slightly from his chest. "Yes?"

"Yes, we all were intimate together." He let out the sigh he'd been holding. "Looking back, the choice seems foolish. How could such a thing not complicate our friendship? Someone always feels hurt, or jealous, or simply less loved than someone else. For a while, after it ended, I wasn't certain we would stay friends. We should have guessed what we were risking. But we were young. Proud of our wildness. Proud of flouting society's rules. I don't think any of us realized that who you share your body with is more than a matter of the flesh."

Mary's hold tightened on his waist. He heard her draw a breath but she did not speak.

"I've shocked you, haven't I?"

"I—" She laughed, a soft exhalation. "Yes, a bit. When I first met you, that night you saved me in the street, when you touched my face and asked to paint me, I thought, 'Here's a man who has no limits. Here's a man who's done things.' It attracted me."

"And now?"

She feathered her hand across his shoulder. "It still does. I think you're very brave."

He smiled at that, then turned on his side to face her. "It had nothing to do with bravery. Just the ability to be open to something new. Sebastian was my friend as much as Eve. I'm not certain I can explain what they gave me. I was a stranger to London and more alone than you can imagine. They welcomed me back to the human fold."

She was quiet for a moment, her hand curled between them on the sheet. He sensed no judgment in her, simply an effort to understand. "Anna came after them, didn't she?"

"Yes," he said, remembering how she'd taken him in when he could no longer stand between Seb and Eve and their sharp, sharp knives. They'd made him feel again, but Anna had made him sane.

"They were the important ones, weren't they?"

"The important ones?"

"Of all the people you slept with."

"Yes," he said, surprised by her insight and by the fact that he'd never defined it that way himself. "They were the important ones."

"You'll be my important one." She said this with a hint of defiance, but also with satisfaction. She was proud he would change her life.

He went hot at the knowledge: his face, his eyes, the skin across his chest. "Mary," he said, his throat so tight the sound would scarcely come out. He was painfully aware of her youth, of the honor she did him and the responsibility it imposed. He had never said such a thing to anyone, never had the courage she was showing now.

"Don't worry," she said, "it's all right if you only like me."

He couldn't let her believe that, no matter if he ended up disappointing her, no matter how little he wished to bare his heart.

"I more than like you," he said, then silenced her—and himself—with a deep, distracting kiss. Sharing his secrets had grown too easy. It was time to return to safer ground.

Otherwise, he might tell her more than she could condone.

LAVINIA VANCE'S PRIVATE DRESSING ROOM WAS filled with gowns and gloves and all manner of feminine things. Here she stored her jewels and her cosmetics and sometimes, when she chanced to be indisposed, she spent the night on the soft, pink satin lounge. Only her maid entered this jasmine-scented sanctuary, and even she did not possess the key to the old armoire.

It was the perfect place to hide the painting: her enemy, as she'd come to think it, the squawking voice of all her fears. Staring at it tonight, by the light of a single beeswax taper, she felt so overwhelmed she had to set the candle down and sink onto the tufted chaise.

She knew Godiva was Merry, knew it without a doubt. Geoffrey had Craven's address, of course, from corresponding with the artist about his own portrait. Unfortunately, once she'd screwed up her nerve to go there, the closemouthed butler refused to say anything except that his master was not in England. Left with no choice, she'd returned to the gallery, to try her luck with Mr. Tatling.

"Charming young woman," he'd said when she asked him about the model. "Name of Mary Colfax. Quiet, but surprisingly well spoken for a girl of humble birth."

The gallery owner had no idea how surprising it really was, nor had he questioned Lavinia's urgent need to contact his client. Her claim that she wanted to commission another work was enough to earn her the intelligence that the artist, along with his female friend, had left on a jaunt to Venice. He had the address if she cared to write.

Lavinia didn't, but she took it all the same.

Venice. So far away. How tempting it was to simply leave everything be. But Merry would return. Eventually. No doubt trailing clouds of scandal like noxious fumes. Lavinia could have strangled her if she weren't so worried for her well-being. And she was worried. Truly, she was. She merely wished her impossible daughter had spared a second's thought for someone else.

Worst of all—or, rather, not worst but certainly very bad—the letters from Wales were starting to dry up, almost as if whoever was sending them was trying to make them last.

"Didn't think about Isabel, did you?" Lavinia accused her daughter's maddeningly happy likeness.

But the painting could not answer, no more than it could tell her how to put Althorp off.

He'd had the gall to drop by the house that morning during breakfast. Geoffrey had not yet left for his club and was still lingering over his paper. Althorp accounted for his presence at that highly improper hour by saying he'd come as a favor to Ernest, to see if some files he'd been missing had turned up.

When Geoffrey informed him—rather coolly, Lavinia thought—that he'd returned them the day before, Althorp simply laughed.

"So hard to keep track," he'd said with his butter-smooth bonhomie. "I wonder that you let your daughter out of your sight. One never knows, after all, what one's family is getting up to behind one's back."

"Trust is always a risk," replied her husband, "but so is mistrust. A man must weigh the cost of both."

That, too, inspired amusement. "Too true," Althorp had chuckled. He turned to go, squeezing her shoulder as he left. Casual as it was, the gesture was a clear, unspoken threat, a flaunting of his long-ago possession. I can unmask you, it said, in front of whoever I choose. Whether that meant the world or just her husband she did not know, no more than she knew if Geoffrey had noticed the impropriety.

He had taken his leave soon after, studying her from the door as coolly as he'd studied Althorp. He appeared to be waiting for her to speak, possibly to confess. At the very least, he'd begun to question her friendship with Ernest's father. Her pose of innocence would be harder than ever to maintain.

With a swallowed moan, she pressed her fists to her aching brow.

She had to act, had to get Merry back, as much for her daughter's sake as for her own.

Peter will help, she thought with a sudden burst of inspiration. Peter would do anything for his sister. She'd give him an edited version of the truth: that Craven had seduced Merry and that they had to bring her back before her father, and everyone else who mattered, caught wind of what she'd done. Lavinia was certain her son could manage one indolent artist. If not, well, she'd give him permission to tell his brothers. With luck—which, admittedly, had been in short supply—Lavinia wouldn't just rescue her daughter from that horrid Casanova, she'd return her to the arms of her future fiancé. They'd hush up everything, *everything,* and the world would go peacefully back to what it had been.

Fortified by decision, Lavinia stood. It was late, but Peter was a night owl. She'd go to him now, before she lost her nerve.

She gave the painting one last, hard look.

"I'll save you," she vowed through clenching teeth, "whether you want to be saved or not!"

16 ～

JUST BEFORE NOON, NIC WENT DOWN WITH MARY to the dining room. There they found Sebastian and Evangeline, bleary-eyed and eating a silent breakfast. A cerulean glass chandelier hung above their heads, one of the famous *chioche* of Murano. Neither of Nic's friends seemed to appreciate the way its twisting branches cast gossamer threads of light around the peacock blue walls. Sebastian, in particular, appeared to have lost his rakish spirits—either as a result of overindulgence or of having failed to seduce Nic's lover.

Nic suspected a bit of both.

"'Morning," said Evangeline, her nose buried in the paper. For his part, Sebastian waved a hunk of toasted bread.

Since Mary seemed uncertain how to respond to their bad manners, Nic pulled out a chair for her at the opposite end of the oval table.

"Relax," he said as he headed for the sideboard. "I'll fetch you a plate of something nice."

"That's right," Sebastian muttered. "Treat the match girl like a queen."

Before Evangeline could add her tuppence to this topic, Nic covered her open mouth.

"Enough," he said, "from both of you. The way you've been acting, Mary will think I'm a few bricks short for being your friend."

"We were only—" said Evangeline, then stopped to glance helplessly at Sebastian.

"—only making trouble," Sebastian finished with a grin that said he expected to be forgiven, though beneath the confidence he did not seem quite sure. "Hell, Nic, we both think she's adorable. Far better than that puffed-up Lady Piggot."

Sighing, Nic let his hands rest on Evangeline's shoulders. Mary watched with widened eyes from the other end, clearly more intrigued than offended by this discussion.

"I am not your procurer," Nic said with a patience gained from a rewarding night in Mary's arms. "What's more, it's been some time since the three of us did anything like that together."

"But we can hope," said Eve, her expression a twin of Sebastian's.

"No, you can't," Nic corrected bluntly, "not with Mary and not with me." His grin broke out without his willing it. This joy was so sweet, so new he could not contain it. Seeing his smile, Mary turned her own down toward her lap. She *was* adorable in her snug sea-green gown with her tidy little figure and her upswept curls ablaze in the morning sun. She looked up, her cheeks pink with pleasure, and mouthed a "thank you" for his eyes.

"Lord save us," Sebastian burst out, "if I weren't queasy already, watching you two bill and coo would do the job."

"Drink your coffee," Eve scolded and lightly slapped his arm.

Obviously not sorry, Sebastian kissed the air at her.

Nic knew an end to their interference was the best he could expect from them for the present. Demanding they apologize to Mary would almost certainly be futile. Ignoring them both, he turned to fill his and Mary's plates.

No one spoke until he sat.

"Signor Vecchi came by this morning," Sebastian said, his eyes wary, his coffee cradled to his chest. "He said your servant arrived with your luggage and he put him in a room with the underfootman."

"My servant?"

"The boy who traveled with you."

"But Mary and I came alone."

Sebastian shrugged. "Perhaps it was an employee of the ship then, and signor Vecchi mistook his English. In any case, your luggage is here, waiting in the hall on the *mezzanino* until you tell the housekeeper what to do with it."

Nic rubbed the bridge of his nose. Should he bring his sketching things along when he and Mary went out, or simply be a sightseer? The latter, he decided. He suspected she'd had more than enough of watching him sit and scribble.

"You should take Mary to the Basilica San Marco and the Doge's Palace," Evangeline suggested. "I'm sure she'd enjoy the Tintoretto."

"Not to mention," Sebastian leeringly put in, "the cell where they imprisoned Casanova."

His tone was almost its former teasing self, but Nic regarded him with reserve. "I'll do what Mary wishes," he said.

He didn't care that his friends both rolled their eyes. He had a feeling the message that Mary came first had finally sunken in.

VENDORS CRAMMED THE PERIMETER OF THE PIAZZA of San Marco: cafés, sellers of mementos, everything a tourist could desire—if only she dared to pick her way through the hordes of pigeons. Not for nothing was this square called the drawing room of the world. Merry heard greetings exchanged in more tongues than she could name.

Despite these distractions, she was suitably awed by the grandeur of church and state. Getting lost with Nic after their tour, however, was even better. Venice was a small city. By a straight path, one could cross her in an hour. Unfortunately,

La Serenissima was not straight. She was a labyrinth of alleys and squares and narrow back canals that forced one to retrace one's steps or hire a boat. No matter how they tried, they couldn't find Nic's favorite café from his time at the Academy. In the days that followed, the search became a game where the journey was the reward. This was a city of traders, of jewelers and weavers and sun-browned boatmen. She never knew what they'd find around each timeworn corner. A market filled with shining fish? An ancient well with a rim of gargoyles? Perhaps a goldsmith would appear to delight them, or a binder of leather books.

She enjoyed the artisans best because Nic would go in to meet them. Without being told who he was, the workers treated him as a member of their fraternity, a fellow maker of beautiful things. They could tell from his questions, and from the respect with which he listened, that he was a man of discernment. With Nic to help her, Merry's Italian improved by leaps and bounds. In all her time at finishing school, she hadn't learned half as much, nor been half as stimulated.

Her mind, it seemed, was coming awake as pleasurably as her body, not with effort but from their rambling exploration. *Gianduiotto,* a fabulous mix of chocolate and hazelnut ice cream, was her word from the Campo Santa Margherita, while history and commerce were the subjects at antique shops like Aladdin's caves. A spyglass from one was wrapped as a gift for Mr. Farnham and a pretty tea set for Mrs. Choate. Every afternoon a new *barcaro,* or wine bar, welcomed them for a rest. The churches were a revelation, the people a lesson in how to live every moment well. Sometimes, overwhelmed, they simply sat on a mossy wall and gazed about, their shoulders brushing, their hands linked companionably in enjoyment.

Sebastian and Evangeline might have ceased to exist for all the notice Nic and Merry took of what they did. The bubble that surrounded them was too perfect to be pierced.

Merry had never been this content, nor seen Nic so at ease within himself. She began to believe, tremblingly at first and then with greater faith, that they might live happily as man and wife. In spite of the obstacles between them—not the least of which being the difference in their stations—they rubbed along too well for her to doubt they could succeed.

Ironically, this hope was the only shadow on her horizon. Once admitted into her heart, the desire to bind herself to him grew to a passion she hadn't imagined she could feel. Even a child, which she hitherto had no urge to bear, became inordinately appealing. She wanted to cuddle a baby with Nic's eyes, to teach him to ride a pony, to give him brothers and sisters and a great big box of rainbow paints.

Seduced by the beauty of her daydreams, she would drift off even as the wonders of the city spread around them.

"Where has my Mary gone?" Nic would tease, and she'd have to invent a lie.

She told herself these longings were nonsensical. Love had softened her brain and she was turning not into her mother but into a mindless broodmare. She began to tense each time he brought out his French letters, even though, as he'd promised, they didn't diminish her pleasure in the least.

Despite his defense of her, despite his apparent—and probably temporary—commitment to fidelity, he had not said he loved her. No promises for the future had issued from his lips. In truth, all he'd done was give her cause for hope.

She had to wonder if this were not his cruelest kindness yet.

SWEARING HIS FRIENDS TO THEIR BEST BEHAVIOR, Nic allowed Sebastian and Eve to escort Mary to the opera. He would have gone along, except he desperately needed the time to think. He could no longer fool himself into believing his feelings for Mary would go away. If anything, they had grown stronger.

This week had proven how well they could get along. Her simple presence made him happy, her quick mind and quicker humor, her fearlessness in exploring. The proprietors adored her, sensing no doubt a spirit as independent as their own.

He was almost sure he should tell her he loved her. In fact, he was seriously wondering if he should ask her to be his wife.

It was a momentous step, one that sent chills of terror down his spine, though the urge to propose intensified each time he tried to reject it. He wanted her with him, through good times and through bad. He could fear neither with her beside him. She made him feel stronger, kinder, more connected to his better self. With her, he could be redeemed. With her, his role in Bess's death could truly become the past. Once she married him, she'd never want for anything again. He had the means to both cherish and protect.

But asking her was not without risk. If she said no, would that spell the end of what they had? He knew how he felt when a woman turned too serious: as if he couldn't run away fast enough.

If Mary ran from him, he didn't know how he'd stand it. If he said nothing, at least he could hold on to what he had.

Tangled in this dilemma, he wandered absently into the library. It was a large room, as long as the whole palazzo, its corners bristling with stucco cherubs, its painted ceiling a vision of the heaven he hoped to find. The gas was lit, though it could not hold back the weight of Venice's night. That loomed clear and black outside the windows, its velvet back drop hung with pitiless diamond stars.

A muffled cough drew his attention to the center of the room. A boy of fifteen or sixteen, slim and straight, stood before a lectern on which a book of sailing ships lay open. His face was eerily familiar, though if Nic had met him, he could not remember where. He was staring at Nic with a seriousness beyond his years: a watchful, challenging stare.

"I'm sorry," said Nic, "are you a relative of the countess?"

The boy laughed, harshly, briefly, then stopped. "I'm your kitchen boy, Mr. Craven."

"My kitchen boy." Nic moved closer, squinting in confusion.

"I usually wear a scarf."

Nic's befuddlement cleared for a moment, then quickly closed in again. "Yes. Thomas, isn't it? We thought you had a scar."

When the boy spread his hands, Nic realized how unnaturally still he'd been before. "No scar," he said, his eyes never leaving Nic's. "At least, none that you can see."

"Then why—" Rather than get drawn further into things he didn't understand, Nic changed his question to one that seemed important. "What are you doing here? Surely Farnham didn't send you."

"I wanted to see Venice. But don't worry. I didn't stow away. I've been saving up. And I'll pay the cook back for that roast."

"That was you then. Sebastian was certain it was the cat." Nic's smile invited the boy to smile back, but his expression never changed. Closing the last few steps between them, Nic put his hand beside the boy's on the edge of the book of ships. This close, he could see a vein ticking at the boy's temple. Inexplicably, his own pulse felt as ragged. "Your parents don't work in the gasworks, do they?"

For some reason, Nic's guess called up a sheen of tears. Beneath it, Thomas's eyes were blue and clear. The flush that stained his cheeks made them glow even brighter.

"No," he conceded, "my parents don't work at the gasworks."

He seemed sadder than any boy his age had a right to be. Nic could only speculate what experiences had engraved that melancholy on his face.

"It doesn't matter," Nic said. "Whoever your parents are, whatever you did before you came to work for me, simply doesn't matter."

"I know it doesn't." The boy's mouth pressed together, then lifted wryly at the corners. "Because I know you don't give a damn."

Baffled, Nic pulled his hand back to his side. He did not understand this boy's manner and the mystery was making him uneasy. "Why did you follow us?" he demanded, his voice harder than he intended.

"I told you—"

"No, don't give me that Banbury tale about wanting to see Venice. Why did you follow me and Mary on the ship?"

The boy faced him, still flushed, though anger appeared to

have the upper hand. "I came to see what the great Nicolas Craven is really like."

"Do you want to be an artist, then? Is that what this is about? Because you don't need my permission to be one. That's something that comes from inside."

"And you'll sacrifice anything for it, won't you?"

Nic rubbed his forehead. The boy's hostility rolled off him in trembling waves. Nic couldn't imagine what he was getting at, but he was losing patience fast. As if he knew this, the boy turned away. Both his hands were pressed to the book now, white around the nails and so tense the lectern shook.

"Look," Nic said more gently, but the boy cut him off.

"Why aren't you with your friends tonight? I hear the Teatro La Fenice is quite a wonder."

By now Nic was certain he'd never had a stranger conversation. Hell, he thought, mentally throwing up his hands. If the boy wanted to know the great Nic Craven, why not answer?

"I needed to think," he said, "to decide if I should ask the woman I love to marry me."

The boy's lips whitened to match his nails. "The woman you love."

"Can't recommend it," Nic added, trying to be jovial. "Turns a man inside out, love does. Not that I have much right to complain, since I've never fallen in love before."

The boy's head came up, his eyes gone wide with shock. "Never . . . you've never . . . ?"

"Well, damn," said Nic with an awkward laugh, "you'd think I'd told you I just escaped from an asylum."

Like a shade being pulled down a window, the boy's expression closed. "Forgive me," he said stiffly. "I shouldn't have intruded. I'll leave you to your decision."

Nic could only gape as he strode away.

Kitchen boys were not what they used to be.

17

THE OPERA WAS MIRACULOUS. EXQUISITELY SUNG, grandly staged, it portrayed a tragic romance that struck Merry's heart a little too close to home. Loathe to cry in front of her companions, she told herself what she'd seen wasn't truly love. True love, the sort that happened in real life, was rarely that dramatic and doomed.

Nonetheless, she could not go directly upstairs to Nic, not with her feelings stripped to the bone.

Bidding Eve and Sebastian good night, she crossed the canal floor hallway toward the door to the high-walled garden in the back. Her steps quickened in anticipation. The air had been crisp tonight but not chill, and the stars had hung like jewels on an ebony cloth. As amusing as Eve and Sebastian were, she was looking forward to enjoying the heavens on her own. The stars would calm her, she thought, and then she'd be ready to go to Nic.

The last thing she wanted was to show him how she felt before he could face it.

The heavy garden door resisted her efforts to heave it open. Only when she threw all her weight against it did it surrender. Fearing she might not get back in, she wedged a Guardi shipping crate between the wood and its pilastered marble frame.

To her disappointment, she did not have the courtyard to herself. Someone sat hunched on the bottom step beneath the door, someone young and male. She began to back away, then realized whoever it was was weeping. The sobs were choked but unmistakable, as was the resentment with which they wrenched from the youthful chest.

Merry could not walk away. Whatever their cause, she knew those feelings well herself. What's more, she thought she recognized the young man's coat, a battered corduroy sack that stretched across the growing shoulders it contained.

What on earth, she wondered, was Nic's kitchen boy doing here?

Questions could wait, however, until she found out what was wrong.

She lowered herself to the bottom step and slung her arm around the weeping boy, just as her older brothers had done for her. The boy covered his face but was too miserable to move away.

"There," she said, her breast warming with humor and pity. "Thomas, isn't it? Whatever it is can't be worth drowning Venice over."

"My name is Cristopher," he snapped with an anger she didn't understand until he lifted his face to catch the light shining through the open door.

The air rushed from Merry's lungs. Free now of its scarf, the face he revealed was a younger twin of Nic's. The color of his eyes and hair were different, but he had the same jaw, same nose, even the same ironic lift to his brows. "My God," she said, hardly able to take it in. "My God, you're his spitting image."

Cristopher's tears spilled down anew. "He didn't know me. He looked straight at me and didn't know me."

"Who didn't know you?" she asked, but in the pit of her stomach, she knew.

"My father. The bloody darling of the art world. Couldn't recognize his own son."

"Did he know he had a son?"

Cristopher laughed and wiped his nose on his sleeve. "Too right, he did. He's been sending me a tenner every quarter since I went away to school. That's how I ran away, how I paid for a berth on the ship with you."

The story he told came out garbled, but Merry managed to sort it out. Though not a legitimate son, Cris had been raised by Nic's mother who, according to Cris, was something of a tyrant. Nic hadn't been home since Cris was four and, naturally enough, the boy had developed a yen to know his father. In order to get around Nic's aversion to seeing him, he'd disguised himself as a servant.

"I just wanted to understand him," he said. "Why he left. Who he was. Grandmother never said anything precisely bad about him, but I could tell he'd disappointed her. I had to judge for myself. When I saw how good he was to the others, and that they weren't perfect either, I thought maybe if he got to know me, he might see that having me around wouldn't be so bad."

Her own eyes burning, Merry stroked his tear-wet cheek. "No," she said, "it wouldn't be bad at all. You're clever and resourceful and very brave. If you were my son, I think I'd burst with pride."

He couldn't have been much younger than she was, but when he flung his arms around her waist, she did feel like a mother. She sensed he hadn't heard this kind of praise before, maybe hadn't known how much he needed it. All thoughts of scolding him for running away flew from her head. After all, twenty years old or not, she was in no position to throw stones.

She patted his back until he settled, until he finally drew an easy breath. Then, with a dignity much like his father's, he pushed back and dried his tears.

"He good as told me he didn't love my mother," he said, enunciating each word as if to prove he could face the truth.

"All this time, I thought that was why he'd never married: because he loved her too much to give his heart to someone else. I thought he couldn't bear to see me because I reminded him of what he'd lost. But he never loved her at all. He never loved anyone. I was telling myself a tale. He didn't come back because he never cared."

"You don't know that," Merry said, her voice husky with shock. "There may have been other reasons."

"What reasons?" he demanded. "Just tell me what other reasons could there be?"

He sounded as if, despite his disillusionment, he wanted her to supply them. Merry wished she could.

"I don't know," she said, hugging him again. "Maybe the reason is something neither of us understands."

She tried to believe the words but feared she, too, was telling herself a tale.

SHE FOUND NIC IN THE SITTING ROOM OF THEIR suite. He stood by the window, staring out at the night as he swirled a glass of brandy around his palm. His red-and-gold waistcoat, which matched the silk-papered walls, hung open around a snowy shirt. His trousers were rumpled, his hair unkempt. An evening beard shadowed the elegant hollows of his cheeks. He was the picture of Bohemian élan except for the line of worry that creased his brow.

For once she did not care what lay behind it.

I'm as bad as Evangeline, she thought. Illogical as it was, she wanted the man she loved to be a hero.

He turned when her heel struck the shining terrazzo floor. "Mary," he said, his smile unusually hesitant, "I was hoping you'd come back soon."

She couldn't answer like a normal person, couldn't ease into the trouble or be kind.

"Your son is here," she said, so tired it wasn't even an accusation.

The blood drained visibly from his face. If she'd ever doubted Cristopher's tale of woe, she could not now.

"My son?"

"Yes," she said, "the one you hired to scrub your pots."

"The one I . . ." The brandy snifter slipped from his fingers. He tried to catch it, but it fell to a Persian rug and split in half. "My God." His eyes widened with rising horror. "No wonder he acted the way he did. I spoke to him. Tonight. In the library. I had no idea."

"I have to say, Nic, I really don't understand that. Even if you hadn't seen him since he was four, all you'd have to do is look in a mirror to know he's yours."

"It's not what you think."

"I scarcely have to think. The facts speak well enough by themselves."

"You don't know the facts." He left the window to take her hands. "Cristopher doesn't know the facts. Not that they're praiseworthy as it is." He must have felt her stiffness, because he loosed her hands and ran his own back through his hair. "I'll tell you everything—if you want to hear it."

She met his gaze as steadily as she could. She wanted to hear, she did, and yet part of her could not give a damn. This man had abandoned his son. How long before he abandoned her?

"I'm not certain you should tell me," she said. "Yes, we've enjoyed each other's company, but can you honestly say I need to know?"

He made a swallowed sound of protest, then cupped her cheeks between his palms as if he meant to press his sincerity through her skin. "Yes," he said, "you, of all people, need to know."

Against her better judgment, she was flattered. *She, of all people.* As if she were different from the rest. But this could be the fatal secret to Nic's charm: that he made every woman think she was the exception. Wary, she pulled free of his hold and sat on the edge of a scarlet loveseat. Nic did not join her. His chest lifted on a breath. He closed his eyes, then opened them and spoke.

"I'm not who you think I am. I'm not who anyone thinks I am."

"You're not Nicolas Craven."

"I'm Nicolas Herbert Aldwin Craven, the seventh marquis of Northwick."

This wasn't remotely what she'd expected, but the minute she heard the words, they made a terrible kind of sense. She'd always marveled at the way he carried himself, at his lack of awe for men she'd supposed to be above him. He was a marquis, a *marquis,* a single rank below a duke. Good Lord, if her parents caught wind of this, they'd be crying the banns within the hour. But that didn't matter, couldn't matter. Marquis or not, Nic was no better marriage prospect than he'd been before. Head aching, she squeezed her temples and tried to think.

"What," she said, "does being a marquis have to do with not knowing your own son?"

"I have to tell it all," he said, "or you'll never understand."

"By all means." She motioned dryly for him to go on. "Tell it all."

Her sarcasm brought his head up. He hesitated, then forged ahead.

"My father was weak," he said, "though he didn't seem it. Outwardly, he was handsome and athletic. Most people saw him as a hale-fellow, well-met sort of man. I doubt they knew what a liar he was, or suspected how soulless he could be. Perhaps his arrogance seemed appropriate to his station. But my father's *droit du seigneur* ran deep. What he wanted, he thought he had a right to, no matter who he hurt to get it. No outrage was beneath him—not cheating, not theft, not rape— as long as he believed he would not get caught."

Nic's hand made a fist before his breastbone, the other wrapping around it as if he wished to hit someone. Fascinated in spite of herself, Merry waited for him to pull himself together.

"He feared my mother," he said with a quick, sardonic glance. "Of all the people in his sphere, only she knew what he was, and had known since she maneuvered him into making her his wife. She's a practical woman, my mother, a mere squire's daughter. She married him for his estate, then ran it better than any Craven ever had. For the most part, she let him go his way. Sometimes, though, she'd catch him in an act she couldn't stomach, usually an injury to someone too weak to stand against him. To her mind, my father could do what he liked to his peers. The servants, however, the tenants, or the young, she considered hers to protect. If he tried to take advantage of them, well, Hell knew no fury like Northwick's marchioness."

He laughed at that, but the memory did not cheer him. With a heavy exhalation, he sat next to her on the loveseat. "I had a friend among the staff, a laundrymaid named Bess. She was like a lot of servants who work outside the house: sassy and independent. She was a little younger than you. Eighteen, I believe, and I was fifteen. Tall for my years. A man, I thought, though mostly I was just randy."

Smiling faintly, he drew his finger down Merry's nose. "We took a liking to each other, the way young people will. Played at kissing. Cuddled behind the barn. It was forbidden fruit, I guess, to treat each other as equals when the world would say we were anything but. Bess was the first to teach me what women liked. In fact, before Bess, I barely knew what *I* liked.

"But we never went beyond that bit of play. Bess wanted to save her maidenhead for her husband. She used to tease me, saying I could never be aught but a toy to her. She was going to marry a dairy man and raise a herd of cows."

His sigh came again, deeper this time and longer. He rested his forearms on his knees. "I don't know if my father discovered what we were up to, but whether he did or not, Bess took his fancy. She was a pretty girl, fair-haired and buxom, with a laugh that could make a man stiffen in his smalls. My father caught her alone one day and forced himself on her. Didn't even try to seduce her, just took what he pleased and left.

"For all her sass, he knew she wouldn't dare complain. She was a laundrymaid. He was a lord. With a word, he could ruin her chance of working anywhere again."

At that, he seemed unable to go on, his jaw bunching, his hands locked together between his knees. Merry touched his wrist, then gently wrapped her fingers around the bone.

"Didn't she tell you what your father had done?"

He shuddered and shook his head. "No. I think she was ashamed. And maybe she didn't want me to confront him. She must have known it would come to blows. The temper I had then, I'd have made sure it did. She might have feared for me, or not wanted to set her friend and his father at odds, no matter what had been done to her."

"She sounds like a special person."

"She was. Special and strong and brave. I doubt anyone would have known if she hadn't begun to show."

"Your father got her pregnant."

"Yes." He squeezed his knotted hands. "Naturally, my mother suspected him. She knew his habits. But he was ready for her accusations. He spun a story even he thought might be true. He claimed the child was mine. People knew Bess and I were close. An estate like Northwick is like a village. Gossip runs rampant from barn to ballroom. My mother kept abreast of goings on, so he knew she would have heard."

"Wouldn't your mother have believed you if you denied it?"

"Yes," Nic said, "but I didn't deny it." He met her startled gaze with the resignation of a man who knows the worst confession is yet to come. Tensing, Merry drew her hand back from his arm. Nic rubbed the place where she'd held his wrist.

"My father and I made a devil's bargain. He knew how much I wanted to travel to Europe to study painting. I was mad for it, like a knight with his holy grail. My mother hated the idea. She'd married my father so her sons could grow up to be lords. A painter worked for a living. A painter was in trade. To her, I might as well have wanted to be a butcher.

"My father swore he could bring her round, but only if I confirmed his lie.

"I knew I shouldn't have done it. Knew even as he swore up and down he'd take care of Bess and the baby. Give her money. Hire a midwife. Find them a good place to live."

"Did you think he was lying?"

Nic rasped out a laugh. "It didn't matter if he was lying. I knew my mother would do all he promised and more, whoever she thought the father of the child. Bess was my friend.

I should have been there for her lying in. I should have stayed to make sure she was all right. I could have waited to leave until the child was born. But I was like him. I wanted what I wanted and I didn't care to wait.

"She said she understood. She told me to go, to be happy with her blessing. We'd never loved each other, either one. It was friendship between us, and a bit of fun. She told me to be the artist I was meant to be. And then she died giving birth to my father's son."

He covered his face, then dropped his hands as if he didn't deserve to hide. His eyes were red but dry.

"By the time I came home, Bess was gone and my mother had taken the baby in. No one had bothered to write me. I stayed at Northwick a month, until I couldn't bear the shame. I went to Paris that time and Rome and any place I could think of that was far. And then my father was killed in that hunting accident. My mother called me back for his funeral. Cristopher was four and hadn't the faintest notion who I was. Burst into tears the first time he saw me. My mother pressed me to take up the reins, but I couldn't be the marquis, couldn't assume the title my father had made a mark of shame." His hand clenched on his thigh. "It was my shame, too. I knew I'd never live up to their expectations. I'd already proven that."

"So you went to London."

He shook himself. "Yes, I went to London and began the career for which I'd left my friend to die."

"And you never told your mother the truth, not even after your father died?"

He snorted. "What would be the point? So Cristopher could have a dead bastard for a father instead of a living one?"

The simple bitterness of the statement broke through the guard around her heart. Nic had done wrong; she could not, would not deny that. To be sure, fifteen was young to expect a boy to carry the burdens of a man, but Nic hadn't come back later either, after he'd found his place in the world. No child should be abandoned by its parent, even if that parenthood was a lie. But, whatever his failings, Nic had not killed

Cris's mother. Moreover, she knew he was far from heartless toward his father's child. He might think he was, might have acted as if he were, but no man suffered the kind of guilt she saw Nic suffering unless he very much regretted what he had done.

He's afraid, she thought. Afraid he *can't* be a father. Afraid he'll fail Cristopher the same way he failed Bess.

None of this excused his behavior but maybe, just maybe, it meant the wrongs could be redressed.

Of course, Merry had a reason or two to want to believe that. If Nic discovered he could love Cristopher, that he could fulfill a responsibility and didn't have to run from it, then maybe he'd discover a wife was no harder to keep beside him than a son.

"You hate me," he said, sounding as if he half wished she did. "You think I'm despicable."

She looked at him, her emotions strangely still, or maybe not still but simply waiting, like a storm that can't decide which way to blow. "I don't think you're despicable. I think you're a coward."

He flinched as if she'd struck him, his eyes welling with tears he struggled to blink away. Part of her was awed that she had the power to wound him. The rest was merely sorry. Helpless to stop herself, she cupped his cheek, stroking the bristled skin, wanting to soothe just a little of his pain.

"You don't have to stay a coward," she whispered, her vision breaking in watered stars. "You could change if you wanted. And maybe you wouldn't have to change as much as you think. I know you care about people. Look how you treat Farnham and Mrs. Choate. Look how you love Evangeline and Sebastian. You forgive them their flaws, Nic—and their flaws aren't exactly tiny. You're loyal. You're generous. No one else would have hired a boy like Cristopher. Him and his crazy scarf. They'd have kicked him out on his arse."

"Farnham hired him," Nic said as he wiped her dampened cheeks. His hands shook as much as if her tears were his own.

"You *let* Farnham hire him," she said, "as I'm sure he knew you would."

Without warning, he pulled her into an embrace so tight she could barely breathe. "Oh, God," he said. "I love you so much it hurts."

She clung to him, let him drop his desperate kisses across her face. They didn't take long to deepen, settling over her mouth and sinking in as his hands slid possessively up and down her back. "Forgive me," he said, the plea husky enough to sound like a seduction. "Forgive me, Mary. Please."

She moaned as he carried her to the bedroom, as he cradled her against his hardness and breathed her name. He laid her down like a treasure. His touch was gentle, reverent, as if he sensed how fragile the bond between them was. Her mind began to drift with pleasure, but even then she knew: hers was not the forgiveness he had to earn.

18

WITH ONE LEG TUCKED BENEATH HER, MERRY SAT on the edge of the bed to watch Nic dress. One by one he pushed the buttons through his shirt, seemingly unaware of her attention or the comfort she took in watching him perform this simple task. This, too, was intimacy, as much as kisses or ardent words. It might not last, but it was sweet. She smiled as he smoothed his palm down the starched white cloth that molded so beautifully to his chest. The gesture spoke of satisfaction, both in the skill of his tailor and in the strength of his fine male form. He might not view his clothes as weapons the way her mother did, but his pleasure in them ran deep.

The reminder of home brought a tightness to her throat. Nic wasn't the only one who'd been running from things he feared to face.

But there was nothing she could do about that now. Not here in Venice, not with Nic so real and warm before her. Her gaze followed the hand that tucked his shirt into his trousers, picturing what lay beneath, remembering the way he'd taken her in the night.

After the first time, he'd been less gentle, his thickness forging strongly up inside her, his hands hard and sweaty on her wrists. "Lock your ankles," he'd gasped as the imminence of his finish forced him to fight for air. "Lock your ankles behind me and pull me in."

Now, catching her staring, he smiled lazily through his lashes. "Keep looking at me like that and we'll never leave the palazzo."

She smiled back but did not answer, not sure what she wanted; not sure what *he* wanted, despite the warmth he'd shown.

He'd said he loved her, but the words resisted sinking in. If he'd declared himself before she'd spoken to Cris, she would have leapt to say the same. Now she wondered if she should. She didn't doubt he had a heart, but having a heart wasn't the same as giving it to her, not truly, not fully, the way she'd given hers.

Whatever affection he might feel, he'd proved he wasn't a man who welcomed familial ties.

Troubled, and reluctant to show it, she pleated the folds of her sky-blue skirt between her hands. The dress was another gift from Nic, feminine as well as smart, with bands of black satin braid around the hems. She marveled that he could know her taste better than she did, and still not sense what was in her mind.

"We could take him with us," she said, not daring to look up.

Nic shrugged gracefully into his waistcoat. "Take who with us?"

"Cristopher," she said. "I'm sure he'd enjoy a chance to see the city."

He paused, clearly caught off guard, then finished fastening the navy silk. "He'll still be angry with me. I think I should give him time."

"He doesn't even know you know who he is. Do you want to make him wait, biting his nails and wondering if I've told you?"

"*I* need time, then. Time to decide what the hell I'm going to say. Christ, Mary." He raked his hair back. "What do I know about fifteen-year-old boys?"

"You know you were one."

"And a right young wreck I was, too."

"He needs you," she said. "He came all this way just to get to know you."

Nic's lips tightened, but a moment later his anger washed away on a pensive sigh. "You're right. I have to do something about him. And I will. Just not this minute."

"Soon," she insisted, pulling one of his hands between her own. His skin was surprisingly cold. She squeezed his chilly fingers. "Today."

He nodded curtly and bent to kiss her. His thumb stroked her temple while his fingertips speared the waves at the edge of her hair. His tongue slipped gently into her mouth, probing once, twice, before drawing wetly back. Merry's heart beat noticeably faster than before.

"Today," he agreed against her lips. "Today, but not right now."

To Nic, the day was a mockery of the contentment they'd shared before. Instead of embracing the city, they merely walked its streets. Sadness shadowed Merry's smiles. Meaning to make her a gift, he paid far too many lire for a pair of masks in the bustling alleys of the Mercerie. One was adorned with emerald feathers, the other painted in diamonds of red and gold. Hoping to make her laugh, he held the big-nosed, feathered half-mask before his eyes.

"We could return for next year's Carnival," he said. "See *La Serenissima* at her wildest."

She gazed at him from under gently lifted brows. A year is a long time, her expression seemed to say. Do you really think I'll still be with you?

Not wanting to hear the words out loud, Nic pointed out a coffee shop across the cobbled square. "There," he said, "let's warm up with an espresso."

Before she could answer, a group of schoolchildren tumbled into the *campo,* pushing and laughing, their voices like seabird's cries. They jostled her as they ran by and Nic had to brace her arm to keep her from stumbling.

"You're tired," he said, knowing he'd kept her out too long.

"A little," she conceded. "I wouldn't mind going back."

She didn't say what they both were thinking: that by dragging her around the city, he'd been putting off his promise to speak to Cris. He wondered if she knew her silence would scrape his conscience more roughly than any scold.

Chagrined, he led her to the nearest landing and hailed a gondolier. As they pulled away, clouds scudded over the red-tiled roofs, marking a change in the weather as surely as Mary's mood. All day he'd been seeing his actions through her eyes, not just what he'd done to Cris in Venice, but what he'd been doing all his life. Oh, he'd known he wasn't behaving honorably, but he'd never had such a vivid comprehension of the sin.

He'd wallowed in guilt, looking at Cristopher as the symbol of his shame, instead of as a person.

Now he realized his shame was worthless.

Only change mattered. Only fulfilling his obligations.

They poled from the Rio dei Fuseri to the Rio di San Moisè. Three boats could pass each other on these thoroughfares, and in places only two. The buildings' pale-gold brick closed in on either side, bridges sliding over their heads, flotsam bobbing around their upcurved prow. If he'd wanted, Nic could have reached out to touch the walls. This is my challenge, he thought, to push ahead no matter how cramped the way.

Despite his resolve, he wished Mary had said she loved him. If she'd believed in him, he knew he'd have found the strength to face his father's son.

But she didn't believe in him.

And if she didn't, why should Cristopher, who Nic had disappointed far worse than her?

With skin like ice, he helped her from the boat to the Guardi landing. The canal was low and brackish. He looked up at the windows of the palazzo. Glass winked in their ornate frames, the cloverleaf insets at the top throwing back the setting sun.

Maybe Cristopher wouldn't be here. Maybe he'd grown so disgusted he'd already left for home.

Mary touched his coat sleeve, her fingers fanning across the wool. "Don't worry, Nic. He wants to forgive you."

"But what if I let him down?"

Her laugh was a rush of air. "You'd have to work hard to do that. I suspect he'd be happy with crumbs."

A sudden rise of angry voices interrupted his response. They were English voices, loud and male and so aristocratic they sent a shudder down his spine.

"By God," one shouted, "there she is!"

Nic turned to see a wide, flat-bottomed boat lurch into the final slip. The three large men who rode in it immediately scrambled onto the tide-stained ledge. Behind him, Mary uttered a strangled whimper. He had just enough time to see her face turn white before one of the men barreled into him.

Mary screamed as they both went down at the impact. They would have rolled into the water if Nic hadn't stopped their slide by grabbing the nearest window's grill.

"Get her into the boat," ordered the man who lay atop him.

"Like hell!" said Nic, for which he was rewarded by a ham-sized fist smashing into his nose.

He heard his cartilage snap, blood spurting out in a quick, hot stream.

"Bastard," growled the man, and cocked his arm for another go.

Nic wouldn't have responded half as fiercely if he hadn't seen the others trying to shove Mary into their boat. She was struggling, but eventually they'd overpower her. Thanking Farnham with all his heart, he blocked the punch as he'd been trained, though the force of it ached straight through his forearm. The knee he drove into his attacker's crotch was more effective, and the uppercut to his jaw actually lifted him away.

Nic stumbled to his feet, bleeding like a pig, his mind such a boiling haze of fury he didn't hesitate an instant to take on the other two. The second man was dispatched into the canal by means of a well-placed boot to his arse. Then, as that one spluttered in the water, Nic grabbed the third by the collar and threw him face first against the front of the Guardi palace.

"No-o," Mary moaned, which he did not understand.

Ignoring her, he slammed her would-be kidnapper into the wall again. If Nic's nose was broken, he didn't see why someone else's shouldn't join it. "Who are you?" he demanded, sounding stupidly as if he had a cold. "And what the hell do you think you're doing?"

The man winced as Nic bent his arm up between his shoulders. Despite his discomfort, he did not seem afraid. "I could ask you the same," he snarled, his head twisted round so he could glare. "You must be mad taking her to Venice. Did you think no one would notice the missing daughter of a duke?"

"The missing what?" said Nic, beginning to be amused. "Good Lord, have you got the wrong girl!"

This, at last, surprised the man. He looked from Mary to Nic and back again. Something about the glance unnerved him. It was not a glance a person gave to someone he did not know.

Mary cleared her throat, her face as red as it had formerly been white. "This is my brother Peter," she said, "and the others are Evelyn and James."

"Charmed," said the one climbing out of the water, his tone much drier than his clothes. "Lord, Merry"—he peeled off his jacket and wrung it out—"you might have told him who you were."

A pressure was building inside Nic's head. He pushed back from the man she'd introduced as Peter. "What does he mean, you might have told me?"

Her neck bent as if a weight had pushed it down. If he hadn't known it was ridiculous, he'd have said she was ashamed.

"Mary?" he prodded, not liking this evasion.

Peter turned from the wall and tugged his crumpled coat. "Allow me," he said with a little bow. "Nicolas Craven, meet

Lady Merry Vance—if you aren't beyond such formalities now."

"Peter," Merry whispered, a confession all by itself.

Nic stared at her, the pieces beginning to fit together, no matter how little he wished to read them. "Lady Merry," he repeated numbly, "the duke of Monmouth's daughter. But why would you pretend to be a maid?"

"Yes, why would you?" said the man who'd tackled him: Evelyn, Nic believed. He could see the family resemblance now that he wasn't being pummeled: in the brush of strawberry-gold curls, in the ginger-speckled skin.

Still suffering from the knee Nic had planted in his groin, Evelyn groaned as he pushed onto his feet. "Why don't you tell us all, Merry? I'm sure James would like to know why he had to leave his pregnant wife to rescue you from a man who's obviously as much in the dark as we are—a man Mother is fully convinced seduced you, I might add, as if any one could make you take one step against your will."

Merry pressed her lips together, but could not hide the way they shook. "Mother and Father were going to make me marry Ernest. I told them we wouldn't suit, but nobody believed me. Mother fired Ginny, *fired* her, Evelyn. An elderly woman, practically a member of our family, shuffled off to God knows where just because I wouldn't toe Mother's line. I'm sorry I worried you, I really am, but can't you see I had no choice?"

"No choice!" her brother exclaimed. "No choice but *this*?"

Nic barely heard him. The ground was rocking beneath his feet and he knew his encounter with Evelyn's fist was not the cause. All this time he'd thought she was the honest one, the good one, the one whose example he had to live up to. He'd wanted to be better for her. Hell, for the first time in his life he'd given a woman his blasted heart. But Merry had lied to him. She'd posed for him, and slept with him, just to avoid a suitor she didn't like. He suspected her plan had succeeded beyond her dreams. She was damaged goods, after all, publicly damaged goods. He doubted even the fortune hunters would chase her now.

"Well," he said, dizzied and sweating, but determined to reclaim his pride, "what a revelation. I must admit you had me fooled."

He had to steel himself against the entreaty in her eyes.

"I'm sorry," she said, her hand held out to empty air. "It was wrong of me to involve you."

"Nonsense." Nic shrugged the apology off. "Begging your brothers' pardon, but we both had a lot of fun."

Her eyebrows drew together in a little pleat. "Nic, you know it was more than fun. I care for you. I have from the very start."

He wanted to scream with wounded rage. How bloody nice of her to care for him.

"All the better," he said, his jaw like tempered steel. "No point having it off with a man you don't *care for*—unless, of course, it gets you out of a nasty marriage."

"As to that," Evelyn added darkly, "we'll have to see what happens when you get home."

Nic shook his head in spurious pity. "Too bad, Merry. Looks like your brothers have made up their minds to save you. None of my business, though. I'll just gather up your things, shall I? See you get smoothly on your way."

"Nic." Her voice seemed to thrum inside his chest, low, like a cello's deepest string. "Don't do this, Nic. Don't turn what we shared into something dirty."

"You're the one who turned it dirty," he said, "the minute you used me to get your way."

He climbed the steps and grabbed the handle of the door. His fingers slipped, with blood, with sweat, but he forced the wood in with his shoulder. When she called his name, he pretended he could not hear.

Just as he pretended he could not hear her begin to cry.

NIC SENT THE HOUSEKEEPER OUT WITH HER LUG-gage. Hard as Merry tried to convince her brothers to let her at least send Nic a message, none were inclined to budge. "If I see that bastard again," Evelyn warned, "I'll smash his nose straight through his pretty head."

Her plea that Nic had never been at fault, that running to him had been her idea, did not soften them in the least.

"I swear," said James, who was still drying out, "if Mother hadn't made us promise not to tell Father, I'd look forward to him grinding that poncy rake into the ground."

With an effort, Merry refrained from pointing out "that poncy rake" had gotten the better of all three of them. "It wasn't his fault," she insisted for the dozenth time as they practically shoved her on the train at Mestre.

Through all this, Peter, her once trusty ally, had been silent. Now he spoke. "Yes," he agreed, "this wasn't Mr. Craven's fault."

She knew he meant that it was hers. Her eyes welled with burning tears. Peter's censure, mild as it was, hurt worse than the others' put together.

Blindly, she let him lead her into the private compartment, swallowing hard as he settled her into the seat beside the window. She touched his hand to keep him by her. "I know I've put you all to a great deal of trouble."

"Do you?" Peter's expression was unusually sober, as if her flight had aged him. "What you've done could affect us all. If word of this gets out—and it may, no matter how hard Mother tries to hush it up—Evelyn and James and their wives and, for all I know, their children will be breathing the dust from this scandal for years to come. You might not care for your honor, Merry, but you should have shown a care for your family's."

Her tears overran her control and she had to turn away. For some time she could not think, but only watch the mainland's factories slide into a haze of smoke behind the train. *Dirty,* she thought. *I turned it all to ash.* Nic's dismissive words echoed through her mind. "A lot of fun," he'd called what they'd shared, as if it were no more than a lark. She was almost certain he'd been trying to salve his pride. But even if he did still care, what hope could she hold out for their future? None that she could live with, not loving him as she did. If she couldn't settle for being his mistress, for a month or a year or however long it lasted, she didn't have a choice. She had to leave him.

She only wished she hadn't hurt him along the way.

Peter was right. Perhaps she'd had cause to rebel but, as always, she'd acted without thinking the consequences through. She'd treated the people she loved like obstacles to leap over or ignore. Worst of all, the minute she'd done enough to achieve her goal, she'd run like the coward she'd called Nic, compounding her sins for no better purpose than a few more days of pleasure.

Squaring her shoulders, she dried her cheeks with her gloves. What's done is done, she thought. Tears would avail her nothing now. She might have acted like a child but she'd face her punishment like a woman. Whatever choices she made from this point forward, she'd carry the weight of them on her own.

NIC STOPPED CLIMBING HALFWAY UP THE STAIRS.
Cristopher stood on the landing before the arch of the leaded windows. He was a shadow in the twilight, awkward, his arm extended behind him toward the corner, as if he'd been caught in the act of retreating into the dark.

Is this what I've done to him, Nic wondered, to this boy who was brave enough to leave everything he knew? Was the prospect of Nic's anger so awful he had to hide?

As he resumed his ascent, only the glitter of Cris's eyes tracked his approach. Blood throbbed in Nic's nose as if a steam engine had taken up residence in his head. He'd washed up in the kitchen and the unflappable signor Vecchi had snapped the cartilage back into place. All the same, he knew he looked like he'd been in a drunken brawl. The last thing he wanted was to talk about it; the first was to bury himself in bed.

With an inward groan, he forced himself not to trudge past Bess's son.

"Are you all right?" he asked, coming to a halt before him.

Cristopher nodded, white showing round his eyes.

Nic put his hand on his shoulder. "You should go home,"

he said softly, and the boy bowed his head. "I can give you money for a ticket if you need it."

"I don't need money." The words were a nearly inaudible whisper. "I only need you."

For the life of him, Nic could not respond. Why? he thought. Why do you need me when all I've done is let you down? Was his longing for a father so strong he'd forgive it all? Without meaning to, his grip tightened on the span of young muscle and bone. "I can't do this now. I'm sorry but I can't."

The boy swallowed and nodded and lifted the chin that was sharp just like his own. "Those men . . . ?"

"They were Mary's brothers. They took her back to her family."

"I'm sorry," said the boy.

Nic closed his eyes, but the pain didn't disappear. After a moment, he opened them and patted Cris's arm. "You can stay if you like. I won't send you away."

It was nothing, not even a crumb, but it was all Nic could manage. He felt the boy's gaze as he stepped past him to the next flight of stairs. Beneath his palm, the marble balustrade was as cool and smooth as glass.

He put his weight on it as his feet dragged up the treads, one step, two, each one a mountain in his mind.

Mary, he thought, then. *Merry*.

His hand made a fist, but his fingers would not hold it. They spread on the door to their suite and shoved at the inlaid wood.

Inside a decanter waited, an oasis of golden brandy. He poured a glass. Not too little. Not too much. Just enough to summon the gods of Lethe.

19

NIC MEANT TO GET OUT OF BED, BUT INSTEAD SAT slumped on its edge with his elbows on his thighs and his brow on the heels of his hands. Night pressed, moonless and dank, outside the windows. The day must have passed while he slept. All he wore were the same black silk-lined trousers he'd had on the evening Merry left. He wanted to take them off. He also wanted to eat, wash, then extinguish the lamp some interfering soul had set on the rosewood nightstand.

Of course, soon enough the flame would sputter out by itself. The wick was in need of trimming.

Trousers, he thought, his mind slowly ordering the tasks he wished to do. He'd pull on his robe, the robe that still smelled of Mary, then slip downstairs to the empty kitchen.

He had one arm through the sleeve when a shadow separated from the archway to the sitting room.

The shadow was Sebastian. He carried a tray on which Nic made out a decanter and two glasses.

"Thought you'd have to wake up soon." He lowered the chased silver platter to the bottom corner of the bed. Nic saw that it held, along with the brandy, a plate of fruit and cheese. His stomach grumbled at the sight.

Sebastian straightened and half smiled at him, his eyes traveling slowly down Nic's front. Abruptly conscious of his undress, Nic stuck his arm through the second sleeve and pulled the brown paisley closed.

"What do you want?" he said, his voice like graveled fur.

Sebastian poured a glass and held it out until Nic took it. "Evie and I thought you might be in need of entertainment. We met a young tenor at the opera the other night. He came for dinner. An adventurous lad." He cocked his head. "Perhaps you'd like to help us make him sing."

The flush that moved through Nic's body was more reflex than desire. With a sense of detachment, he let himself remember how it was to tangle too many limbs to count, to be mindless flesh, to forget oneself in drunken laughter and faceless warmth.

Unfortunately, he also remembered how disconcerting it was to catch a stranger's eye in the throes of pleasure, and how empty one could feel when that pleasure drained away.

Sebastian seemed to read his reluctance. He covered Nic's fingers where they curled around the glass. "We could send him home if you'd rather. Keep it just the three of us."

But the thought of being alone with Sebastian and Eve was even worse, like willfully stepping into a pit of quicksand he'd just escaped.

"Too old for those games," he said, not wanting to hurt his friend.

Sebastian's hand fell away. Folding his arms across his chest, he studied Nic like a boatman trying to gauge a stormy sky. "You have to forgive me eventually," he said. "After all, how many friends do you have in this world? Me, Evangeline, Anna. That's pretty much the sum. And don't add Farnham, old man. You pay him too much to know if he truly likes you."

But Nic hadn't been about to add Farnham. He'd been about to add Mary. She could have been a friend, once upon a time. At least, he thought she could have. But she'd left him. She'd used him. She'd seemed to love him but that had been a lie. The cruelest lie.

Hadn't it?

Pain beat dully between his brows but he didn't reach up to rub it. Nothing was clear to him, not even the anger he'd felt at her when she left. What if he'd been wrong? What if, in his hurt and humiliation, he'd made accusations that were not true?

But what did that matter now? She was gone. It was over. He couldn't have kept her even if she had loved him. A girl like Mary, like *Merry,* needed a man she could rely on. A husband. A hero. A reliable father for her children. Nic had already demonstrated he could not handle that.

"Nic," said Sebastian, still watching him, "I'm sorry I tried to seduce her. Sincerely sorry."

Nic shook his head. "Doesn't matter. You don't blame a cat for chasing mice."

"Maybe not, but you can blame a man. You had a right to expect better of me."

All Nic managed was a shrug. He was dead to everything tonight.

"You know," Sebastian said, with more gentleness than was his custom, "it wouldn't have worked between you and Mary, not in the long run. Women like that don't give their husbands the kind of freedom our sort need."

Nic said nothing, merely stared at the flickering depths of the lamplit brandy. The golden sparks were a match for Merry's eyes. His heart cramped in his chest. He didn't want the drink anymore, or the food. Come to that, he wasn't certain he could move.

STEAM ROSE FROM THE BATH, SHEER, SILVER CURLS that obscured his view of the brown-and-white tiled walls. The design was geometric. Greek, he thought, a squared rise and fall that lured him to close his eyes.

I could sleep right here, he thought, and let his lids sink down.

He woke to the feel of hands trying to haul him from the water.

"Idiot," said Evangeline. "Do you want to drown?"

Cris was helping her and Nic thought their presence must be a dream. If it was, it was a damned uncomfortable one. With Nic propped between them, they stumbled across the hall and dumped him in a chair.

Evangeline shook her head at him, her paint-splattered shirt plastered to her body by his bath water.

"You can go now," Cris said very firmly. "I'll take care of him from here."

To Nic's surprise, Evangeline nodded and withdrew.

He'd begun to doze when Cris threw a bath sheet across his lap.

"I don't know what you're still doing here," the boy snapped in exasperation. "Neither one of those lechers can keep their hands to themselves."

Nic slid lower in the soggy chair. "They're my friends."

"Could have fooled me."

"You don't understand them."

"Actually," said Cris, in a tone that reminded Nic of his mother, "I don't think *they* understand *you*. In fact, I'm not convinced you understand yourself. If you did, you wouldn't have let the one thing you wanted slip through your fingers."

Against Nic's will, anger began to clear the cobwebs from his brain. "I suppose you're going to tell me I should have fought to keep her."

"Nothing of the sort." Cris tossed his head. "She's far too good for the likes of you."

"I'm sure that explains why she lied to me."

"And you didn't lie to her?"

Cristopher's eyes were slits of hard blue steel. Annoyed by his defiance, Nic shoved himself upright in the chair. "She used me," he said, speaking as clearly as he could. "She never loved me at all."

"Huh," said Cris, "for a man who lives by his eyes, you're pretty blind."

"She was only trying to avoid a marriage she didn't—"

Rather than continue the argument, which he wasn't certain

of in the first place, Nic pushed to his feet and wrapped the
sheet around his waist. With a grimace for the wobbly feeling that plagued his knees, he stalked past Cristopher toward
the bedroom. "I don't have to explain this to you. You're fifteen years old. You couldn't know the first thing about it."

"Don't judge me by your own stupidity. I know more
about love than you."

The voice was following him. Nic stopped and turned at
the archway to head it off. "Oh, really."

Cristopher flushed but held his ground. "I know you don't
give up just because the person you love turns out to be im-
perfect. I know you don't pretend not to love a person just
because it would be easier if you didn't. I know you don't
hide in bed and pull the covers over you just because fighting for what matters takes some work. Mary was right to go
back to her family. You're a mess!"

"I wasn't a mess for her." Fully awake now, Nic jabbed
his thumb against the center of his chest. "I changed. She
made me change."

"Did a good job of it, too. Minute you face a challenge,
you're back to your old ways."

Nic bit back a curse no fifteen-year-old should hear.
"Leave me alone," he muttered and headed stubbornly for
the bed.

Cris grabbed his arm before he could crawl in. "If I did
what you deserved, I would leave you alone. You don't know
what you're missing, you stupid bastard. There's plenty of
people who'd be glad for a son like me."

Nic would have ignored him but for the tears he heard in
his voice, the pride that wanted to believe but couldn't quite.
Everything he said was true. Cris was bright and brave—
good Lord, was he brave—not only to come here on his own
but to speak his heart, and in full expectation of having it
trampled! He wasn't responsible for their father's sins. He
was a gift, a second chance that Nic had done his best to spit
on.

Just as, in the end, he'd done his best to spit on Merry.

He blew his breath out through his nose, disgusted by the
level to which he'd sunk. Cristopher obviously thought the

sound was directed at him because he pulled away as if Nic's skin had burned.

"No." Nic caught him back. "You're right. I am a stupid bastard and you are a son a man should be proud of."

Cristopher's jaw dropped. For all his bravado, he seemed not to have expected Nic to concede. Nic found himself smiling, something lightening inside him, delicate but *there,* like a flicker of sun seen from the corner of the eye. He put his hand on Cris's shoulder, rubbing the ball of it with his thumb. The feeling in his heart intensified, not merely light but warmth. His knees steadied.

What if the thing he'd feared most was the very thing that could save him?

Cris started to speak but Nic lifted his hand to stop him. He had to get these thoughts out while they were clear. "There's something I need to tell you, something I think you're old enough to know."

"Yes?" said Cris, abruptly wary.

"I don't know if this will make you feel worse or better. Believe me, it doesn't change what I owe you."

"Just tell me."

"I'm not your father."

Cris stared at him. "Not . . . but you look just like me!"

"That's because I'm your brother."

Cris shuffled haltingly to the bed. Moving like an old man, he lowered himself to the mattress. Velvet covers heaped around him, red once, but now a dusty pink. How many dramas had this bed seen? How many broken hearts? "Then your father . . . your father was mine." He looked up, emotions sliding across his face. "Grandmother doesn't know, does she?"

"No, and I'm not certain I want to tell her."

Cristopher grimaced as if picturing how she'd react. Given her sterling standards of behavior, the dowager marchioness was not a woman one liked to admit one had deceived. "If you're not my father," he said, pausing to bite his lip, "then I was wrong to be angry at you for not treating me like a son."

Gingerly, Nic took a seat on the bed beside him. "You had

every right to be angry. That's who you thought I was. Hell, I agreed to the lie myself. Some other time I'll tell you why. Right this minute all you need to know is that your mother was my best friend. For that alone, I should have been part of your life."

"Why weren't you then? If you knew that, why did you stay away?"

There it was. The heart of his failings. He had no justification. All he could offer was the truth.

"I was ashamed," he said, "for letting your mother down. I was young and scared and selfish and the longer I stayed away the harder it was to come back and face you. You didn't like me when you were little, you know. Just a big, scary stranger, I guess. It was easier to feel guilty than to do what I knew was right."

The boy mulled this over, quiet, serious, weighing everything all together. His thoughtfulness was a trait Nic could not trace. Bess had not had it. Nic certainly didn't, nor Nic's mother. Seeing it forced home the awareness that Cris was his own person, with his own unique feelings and experience. He was not a mistake, not a tragedy, not a burden, just a human being trying to find his way.

"What about now?" he said, once his deliberations were complete.

The fading daylight caught the golden peach fuzz on his cheek. For all his self-possession, Cris was still a lad. Nic must be careful not to imply promises he could not keep. Gathering his courage, he gripped his thighs through the bath sheet. "How would you like to go to Northwick? With me."

"Northwick?" Cris repeated, visibly struggling not to jump to conclusions. "With you?"

"Yes," said Nic. "It strikes me that I need to return to the place where I went wrong. See if my mother really does want me to assume my filial duties. I can't swear the attempt will work, but if I don't bollocks it up too badly, you and I can move forward from there. Unless you'd rather go back to school?"

Cris hesitated. For a moment Nic thought he would refuse, that too much damage had been done. Then his brother shook himself. "No, I'd rather be with you. I'd like to see if we can be family. If that's what you want."

"It is," Nic said. "At least I'd like to try."

Cris gnawed his lip again. "What about Mary? If you're set on fixing things, don't you want to fix that first?"

Nic considered this, not because he wanted to hurt his brother's feelings but because he knew only a careful answer would be believed. He wasn't sure what purpose running after Merry would serve, not as he was: all intention and no result. Now that he'd discovered whose daughter she was, he knew she needed neither his money nor his protection. Cris had implied she loved him, but love hadn't been enough to hold her, no more than pleasure. Until he had more to offer, he could not expect her to change her mind.

Aware that Cris was waiting, he squeezed his arm. "The situation with Merry is more complicated than it seems. In any case, yours is the prior debt. If I can't pay that, then what you said before is true: she's far too good for the likes of me."

" 'Complicated,' eh?" said Cris with a skeptical, purse-lipped smile.

Nic pressed his hand to his heart at a sudden memory. "My God, you're the image of your mother with that expression. She used to smile at me just like that when she thought I was talking nonsense."

Cris looked at the floor and then back up. His eyes pierced Nic like shooting stars. "You *did* love her," he said as if expecting a contradiction. "I don't care what you say, I know you loved her at least a bit."

Nic smoothed his brother's hair back from his brow. "Maybe I did. And maybe I still do."

THE DUKE OF MONMOUTH WAITED ON THE PLAT-form at Victoria Station, as tall and stern as a standing stone amid the flow of travelers. He wore a long black coat with a velvet collar, above which showed a silver-and-white cravat. His hat was high and straight, his walking stick clenched in the same broad hand that held his gloves. His expression was that of a general prepared for a battle he does not relish but can't avoid.

Merry hadn't known how much she loved him until she realized she couldn't run to his arms.

Naturally, her brothers were dismayed to see him, though he did not take them to task for trying to hide the truth. "You were doing as your mother asked," he said in response to Evelyn's stiff apology. "You aren't the ones who broke a trust."

"Yes, sir," said Evelyn, and they tactfully withdrew.

With her brothers gone, Merry had no choice but to meet her father's gaze. She could see beyond his sternness now: to confusion that his daughter would defy him, to hope that she could explain and, finally, to a love no amount of disappointment could destroy. He was as Nic had portrayed him long ago, the different sides of his nature like layers of vibrant paint: strong and weak, wise and foolish, prideful and forgiving.

She hadn't known it at the time, but Nic had given her a gift when he showed her how to see her father's heart, a gift she would need to get through the days ahead.

Fortified by a peculiar sort of pride, she put back her shoulders and stood straight. "Do you want me to explain myself here, Father?"

"Can you?" he demanded.

"Not as you would wish," she admitted. She smoothed the front of her coat, the coat Nic bought her, then forced herself to stillness. "May I ask how you found out where I was?"

"Hyde said you weren't with Isabel. Your mother filled in the rest. She recognized you from that painting. Bought it to protect you—much good as it did. Hyde told half the city before I could calm him down."

Merry bit her lip. The earl of Hyde was Isabel Beckett's husband. He must have discovered the truth about the letters. Merry hoped he had not punished her friend too badly as a result.

"I don't know what you were thinking, Merry, running off like that with a man you barely knew! The scandal's going to cost you dear enough. Hyde was livid at you for involving Isabel. Rightly so. He's convinced everyone will believe she's as wild as you are."

"I'll speak to him, Papa. Maybe I can—"

"You will not!" A porter turned his head at the furious denial. Her father lowered his voice and glared. "You'll not speak to anyone I don't approve beforehand. Honestly, that man might have done anything to you. You might have been killed and we'd never have known. Can't you imagine how desperate we would have been? We love you, Merry. We deserve more respect than this."

"I know," she said, tears spilling hotly down her face despite her resolve to hold them back. "I also know no amount of remorse can undo my actions. I only want you to understand one thing. Nicolas Craven never hurt me. He has his flaws, as do I, but he never forced me, never frightened me, never misled me about his intentions in any way." Her father's face twisted in protest but she would not let him interrupt. "He was a gentleman. Maybe not by your standards, but by mine."

"He is beneath you," spit her father. "Beneath any decent woman!"

"He is not," Merry said, her emotions calming with her words. "In his way, he's as good a man as you."

Her father didn't know what to say to this. Perhaps her quiet confidence had somehow unsteadied his. The crowd jostled them in the pause, porters pushing carts piled high with baggage, mothers herding children, men in dark suits striding swiftly with folded newspapers under their arms. The sheer Englishness of the scene assailed her. She was home again, though it would never be home quite like before.

Recovering, her father spoke. His words were gruff, reluctant, their brusqueness a mask for his concern. "I'm sorry to ask but I need to be clear on this. He did compromise you, didn't he?"

Merry met his eyes. Whatever the complexity of his emotions, her father's will was strong. If she wasn't careful, she'd put Nic even more in the way of harm. Only a fool— which, admittedly, she had been—would count on Nic's unsuspected title to stay her father's hand. In truth, she'd rather he didn't know who Nic was. A marquis was a person a duke could force into marriage, at least in her father's view of the world. She knew Nic would resist, but she'd brought enough ugliness into his life. If at all possible, she'd shield him from her father's wrath.

"In strictest truth," she said, "it would be fairer to say I compromised him."

Her father opened his mouth, then seemed to think better of asking a question whose answer he might not wish to know. Instead, he offered her his arm. His hold was stiff but steadying.

"Come," he said, "your mother will have more to say to you at home."

Merry's stomach lurched queasily toward her throat. As difficult as this confrontation had been, she knew the next would be even worse.

THE INTERVIEW WITH HER MOTHER WAS NOT PLEAS-ant, but she survived it. Unlike her father's quiet outrage, the duchess's hysteria struck no chord—not because Merry couldn't conceive of reasons for it, but because her mother's concerns seemed more alien than ever. Even before her time with Nic, Merry had cared more about people than position. The measure of a man, or woman, came not from titles or clothes or whether they knew which fork to use. It came from inside, from the soul. Merry knew her own soul was far from spotless, but what shame she felt was for being selfish. The experiences she'd shared with Nic, good and bad, she did not regret.

One regret, though, she could not shake: that she hadn't done more for Cris. As she lay in the bed of her childhood beneath her parents' roof, as she fought to feel like more than a daughter, she found herself dwelling on his dilemma. No doubt this turn of mind was illogical: their situations were more different than the same. Nonetheless, in the short time she'd known Cris, he'd touched her heart. In any case, it was less painful to think of him than of her and Nic.

So she wondered how he was and if he and Nic had come

to an understanding. She thought about things she might have said to help: that just because Nic was afraid to care didn't mean that he did not, that even if Nic was indifferent, this didn't rob Cris of worth. Cris would have to work harder, was all, to think as well of himself as he should.

In this, she and Cris were matched; Nic had not been able to love either of them enough.

NIC'S MOTHER WAS IN THE GREENHOUSE STACKING trays of seedlings. She wore a pair of soiled men's riding trousers and an equally soiled pair of boots. He'd forgotten how square her hands were, how strong and practical. Her waist was thicker than he recalled and her hair was definitely grayer. Other than that, she was precisely the same old warhorse.

To his surprise, he found the sight of her strangely dear.

She looked up when he made a quiet noise inside his throat. Her eyes were older, their blue more faded. The pain that flashed across them in that first unguarded instant took him aback. Up till then, he hadn't truly believed his absence hurt her. He knew how far short of her dreams for him he had fallen.

"Good Lord," she said, then hesitated as if she wasn't sure she was seeing true. "Nicolas, is it really you?"

"In the all-too-solid flesh." Though his voice was light, his hands were shaking. She'd always seen every meanness he'd slipped into. And she'd always demanded he try again. When he was young he'd resented her for it. Now he heartily wished he'd learned the lessons sooner.

She nodded, a curt dip of the chin that roused a thousand boyhood memories. "Finally decided to stop punishing me?"

He swallowed a surge of an old, old anger. This was not a rut he wanted to go down. "It was never my intent to punish you."

"Wasn't it? The boy's half convinced I drove you away. Least, that's what he tried to convince himself. I guess boys want to love their fathers no matter what."

Nic rubbed his hands over his face. He reminded himself

he didn't come here to fight. He would not let her push him to it.

"Maybe I was angry," he admitted as calmly as he could. "Maybe I left in part to strike back at you. There was more to me than my failings, but that was all you seemed to see. It was hard for me to be around that."

"I only wanted you to live up to your potential."

"I know," he said, "and you're probably the reason I'm not completely pathetic now. But your ideas about my potential are not the same as mine. I'm proud of what I can do with these two hands. I've brought something into the world that wasn't there before. Something good, Mother, not just something that will sell.

"On the other hand"—he paused for a long, deep breath—"you're right about my not fulfilling my responsibilities. I'd like you to help me with that, if you would."

"You're asking me for help."

"Yes. I need to learn to be the marquis."

"Need to?" she repeated.

Nic shoved his hands into his pockets and struggled not to clench them. "You always could strike to the heart of things."

"And you could always evade it." Her knees creaked as she bent to retrieve a glove that lay on the rough slate floor.

"Not this time. I've come to stay, for a while anyway. I brought Cris with me. He's waiting up at the house."

She stared at him, measuring his use of Cris's name. "I imagined it was you he went to when he ran away."

"Oh," he said. He shifted to his second foot. "I hadn't thought . . . But of course the school must have notified you when he went missing. I suppose I should have written you, let you know he was all right."

"I knew better than to expect a letter," she said so blandly his temper rose. If she knew better than to expect a letter, why was she always haranguing him by the post? And what sort of guardian let a fifteen-year-old boy wander off without raising every possible alarm? She hadn't known for certain Cris was with him. He hadn't known himself. Anything might have happened!

But he swallowed all that back. No doubt she knew better

than he how well Cris could take care of himself. Which of them had the right of it hardly mattered.

"I shall try to be a better correspondent in the future," he said. "What I'd like now is to take a share in running the estate."

"Just a share?" she said, judgment in the word.

"My share," he clarified. "And don't pretend you really want me to take over. You know damn well you like running this place as you please."

"I run it well," she said, her face going red with anger. "I've sweated myself to the bone to keep Northwick in fighting trim."

He smiled and she huffed at him, but they both knew he'd made his point.

"So." Eyes narrowed, she slapped the gardening glove against her thigh. "You still haven't told me why you 'need' to be the marquis."

Before he even spoke, the blush rolled hot and unstoppable up his face. "There's a woman," he mumbled.

For the first time since she'd seen him, his mother smiled. Her expression conveyed a mixture of gloating and affection. The gloating he expected. The affection he had not seen for quite some time.

Then again, maybe he'd been too defensive to see how much she cared.

"Not just 'a' woman," she crowed. "A woman couldn't get you to do all this."

20 ❧

No one came to see her, not even her broth-
ers' wives. Merry had been popular in her way; eccentric,
yes, but a companion most people enjoyed. Now she'd become a social leper. Despite her father's efforts to quiet the
earl of Hyde, whispers ran like wildfire through the upper
strata of society. Merry Vance had run away with a painter
and lived like a mistress in his home. She'd traveled with him
and slept with him and laughed in the face of every rule that
mattered—at least to them.

Merry didn't give a toss for the rules, but the rejection of
people she'd thought her friends could not help but wound
her.

Two notes arrived, one from Nic's friend Anna and another from Edward Burbrooke's wife. Both were kind but
since both had had relationships with gentlemen who
spurned her, she didn't much want to see either one. They

were too manifestly what she was not: women who held their men.

I chose this, she told herself. I might not have guessed how hard it would be, but I chose it.

Crying over the milk she'd spilled would gain her nothing now.

Left to herself, she spent long hours in the family stables, riding the horses, grooming them, soaking up their simple animal code of right and wrong. All she needed there were two strong arms and a will to work. Once the grooms gave up their efforts to stop her, she could not fear she would fall short.

Finally, the second week after her return to London, Isabel Beckett paid her a call. She seemed nervous to be there, but hugged her tight and long. Merry cried a bit, as did her friend. When they saw each others' tears, they laughed and hugged again.

"I can't tell you how sorry I am," Isabel declared. "Andrew was so angry when he found that last letter, he couldn't keep his fury to himself. I don't even know how many people he told. Only your father's influence finally convinced him to stop." Annoyance twisted her pretty face. "He tried to forbid me to see you, but I told him he'd be sleeping in the guest room until he let me. I knew he'd give in. To tell the truth, though, I didn't expect him to hold out so long!"

"Oh, Isabel!" Merry exclaimed, seeing the glitter of pain beneath her friend's outward triumph. Despite Isabel's complaints, Merry knew she liked her stuffy husband. "I'm the one who's sorry. I never meant to come between you and the earl. I should have guessed I might, but I swear I never meant to. Believe me, if you felt you had to avoid me, I'd understand."

"Phooey," said Isabel, with a toss of her sleek blond head, "what sort of friend would I be if I did that?"

A wise one, Merry thought, much too grateful to say the words out loud.

*   *   *

WHEN ERNEST JOINED THE TRICKLE OF VISITORS,
Merry received her former suitor in the Corinthian-columned
magnificence of the green salon—hardly a cozy venue but
one that reminded her in no uncertain terms just where she
was. Perched on the edge of a carved mahogany chair, poor
Ernest looked as if he'd rather have met her in a dungeon.
She couldn't help smiling at his chagrin. She was surprisingly happy to see him, almost as happy as she'd been when
Isabel came to call.

Friends were worth the world, she thought, especially
friends who stood by one when times were hard.

"You look different," he said.

"Do I?" Giving in to the urge to tease him, she smoothed
her hair like a skilled coquette. "Perhaps the scandal has lent
me an air of glamor."

Ernest wagged his head like a thoughtful bear. "No. You
don't look glamorous, you look pretty."

"Pretty, eh?"

"Yes," he said staunchly, then pulled a rueful face. "I suppose whatever that blackguard did to you couldn't have been
all bad. Unless"—he cleared his throat and drummed his fingers on his knees—"dare I impute your rosy glow to my
presence?"

The words were so awkward, so un-Ernest-like, Merry
had to bite her lip against a laugh. "You sound like a boy
who's been coached to flatter his elderly maiden aunt."

Ernest flushed to the roots of his flaxen hair. "I meant
every word. I'd like to think my being here makes you
happy."

"It does," she assured him. "These days my friends are
few and far between. If your gallantry didn't inspire my admiration, your bravery certainly would."

Ernest sighed as if her compliment filled him with gloom.
He released the grip he'd taken on his knee to place his hand
gently over hers. "I have to ask," he said. "Lord knows I've
come to accept that you don't love me, but I'd be a heel if I
turned away when you needed me most." He patted her fingers as if she were a frightened child. "Merry, won't you
agree to be my wife?"

For the space of a breath, she was tempted. Here was the most reliable man she knew. His passion might not be grand but it was steady. She doubted he had the imagination to want a wife who'd offer him more than fondness. She'd have to rein in her spirits, but she'd be accepted again. Forgiven.

Marrying him would, however, be the most abominably selfish thing she'd ever done.

Taking a moment to gather herself, she covered the hand that had covered hers and met his sky-blue gaze.

"Someone will love you," she said, "with all her heart and soul. You're too good and too strong for that not to happen. God willing, you'll feel the same for her. I cannot marry you and rob you of the chance to know that."

"But you need me!"

"I need you to be my friend, not let me ruin your life to fix a mess I made. For heaven's sake, you could kiss your political career good-bye if you married me now."

"Maybe the kind of career my father has in mind, but I've never been one for shaking hands and making speeches. I enjoy the work I do for your father better. Behind the scenes. Hammering down the details."

"But I thought— It was my understanding that Papa would sponsor you for the Commons if we married."

"Yes, and I probably would have gone along if this hadn't happened. Gone along and been miserable. You aren't the only one who's had time to think lately about what kind of life you want to lead, about what kind of person you want to be. My father will simply have to get over his disappointment."

His face bore a harder expression than Merry had ever seen him wear.

"Your father didn't want you to come here today, did he?" she guessed. "He wants you to sever our connection."

Ernest shrugged, his evasion telling her more than words about the state of things with his father. Wistfully, he touched one curl that had slipped free of her coiffure. "Are you certain I can't change your mind?"

"Quite," she said with her fondest smile, "though I cannot express how much your asking means."

Her certainty must have sunken in. He rose, not so much upset as disconcerted. He had braced himself for the sacrifice, and now it was not required.

"Very well," he said, "I shall not ask again. I warn you, though, I take my responsibilities as friend very seriously. In the days to come, you may see more of me than you like."

"Impossible!" she declared, and rose on tiptoe to kiss his cheek.

True to his nature, Ernest bowed stiffly and took his leave. As he shut the wide door behind him, another sound, subtle but unmistakable, caught Merry's suspicious ear: the swoosh of a skirt on a polished parquet floor. Someone had been standing behind the drawing room's second door, the one that led to the shuttered ballroom.

No servant would be there now, not with so little prospect of its use. In any case, the identity of the eavesdropper could not be in doubt.

Apparently, Merry's mother had not given up on saving her from herself.

LAVINIA DIDN'T LET HERSELF THINK AS SHE CLIMBED the curving stairs. She couldn't let herself think. If she did, she knew her nerve would desert her.

Althorp had lost everything. The match he'd counted on to raise his son's political stock was now a liability. To make matters worse, Ernest had defied him. She should have exulted to see her enemy brought low, but she knew how angry he would be, more than angry enough to lash out at her.

Her hand clenched against the pit of her stomach, sweaty, shaking, her tension a mix of fear and determination. When Althorp heard his son had been here, that he'd offered to save Merry, he would ruin her. He wouldn't care what he himself might pay by bringing the truth to light; he would simply want revenge.

Her arms still bore the bruises of their latest meeting, held before he—and everyone else— discovered what Merry had been up to with Mr. Craven. His anger had terrified her, for it seemed to have no limits. "This is your final chance!" he had roared, though the carriage in which they rode rolled through a public street.

"How can you do this?" she'd pleaded in desperation. "You yourself know the sting of society's censure. What did my daughter and I ever do to you that you would want us to suffer that same pain?"

His fury abruptly faded to cool amusement. "You left me, didn't you?"

"We were married, both of us. Besides, you cannot pretend you truly loved me."

She had never seen eyes so cold and dead. One gloved finger moved to stroke her cheek. "How skilled you are at lying to yourself. What you and I shared was nothing so mundane as love. But I see you've forgotten how you trembled with excitement when I made you crawl to me on your knees, how you moaned when I took you so forcefully you'd be tender inside for days. I could have refined you, Lavinia, could have taken you to heights your blockish husband cannot imagine. What's more, deep in your heart, you know it. You were made for me, though you haven't the courage to admit it." His voice sank to a growl that rasped her nerves. "Even now, if I touched you, I know I'd find you wet."

She gasped, unable to speak or move. It wasn't true. She would not let it be. He was sick and depraved and she was nothing like him!

He smiled as he read the panic in her eyes. "Yes, tell yourself I'm a madman. Then you can deny everything I say. It does not matter anymore. You are useful, Lavinia, weak and useful. You can help my son to the future he deserves."

"Ernest wouldn't thank you," she dared to say, "if he knew what you'd done on his behalf."

Althorp's brows rose. Though he lounged against the squabs, Lavinia suddenly felt as if she were choking. "Is that a threat?" he said, his tone deceptively soft and casual. "If it is, I warn you, I'll crush you like a grape. Betray me to my son and these past few months will seem like child's play."

"N-no," she stammered. "Never. I wouldn't—"

He silenced her by drawing his hand down the front of her throat. The seat springs creaked as his shadow loomed closer, his mouth, his breath. She had frozen like a mouse before a snake. He nipped her lower lip, then her upper, the sensitive flesh left stinging in his wake. *Yes,* thought something inside her too primal to control. She whimpered as he kissed her roughly, crudely, and again as he tore away.

The kiss had not lasted more than seconds but her skin pulsed wildly from scalp to toe.

It's fear, she told herself. It's only fear.

"Fail me again," he said hoarsely, "and you'll wish you'd never been born."

But she wished that already. She couldn't live with this constant dread: couldn't eat, couldn't sleep. Her clothes, her pride and joy, hung on her like sacks. Her hands were constantly atremble. Worse than the fear, though, was the shame. Look what I've done, she thought. Look what I've done in the name of protecting my position.

She stopped in the upper hall, overcome by a revulsion that nearly made her ill.

She had betrayed a woman's most sacred charge: to love and protect her children. She could see now how wrong she'd been to try to force Merry and Ernest together. Merry's new dignity proved it.

Her daughter had come back from Venice changed. As stubborn as ever, but changed. Inside herself she was quiet, certain of her moorings, as if no matter what challenges lay ahead, she knew that she could face them, that she would be true to her personal sense of right and wrong.

Now Lavinia had to do the same. It was her only hope in all the world. She doubted it could save her reputation or her marriage, but perhaps it could save her soul.

Drawing a breath for courage, she knocked on the door to her husband's study and waited for him to call her in.

When she entered, he sat behind the broad oak desk with the shining red porphyry top. His smile, weary but welcoming, pierced her guilty heart. She'd forgotten how pleased she'd been to win him, not merely because he was a duke, but because he'd been so much a man. No beauty like Merry's painter, her husband's looks had been good and plain—a foil to her own, she'd thought, never dreaming how ugly she could become.

"Lavinia," he said, and pushed a stack of papers to the side: estate business, she imagined, or perhaps even business for the government. Geoffrey had always been good at cultivating alliances, not a subtle man, but respected. If he hadn't been, she doubted Althorp would have wanted their daughter for his son.

I should have gone to him at the start, she thought, newly horrified by her stupidity. He might have hated me, but he had the power to protect us all.

Now he tilted his head in inquiry at her silence.

"I must speak with you," she said.

"Yes?"

She swallowed. "Ernest offered for Merry again. Against his father's wishes."

Geoffrey's face tightened in what might have been disapproval. Whether it was directed at her she didn't know. "From your tone, I assume she refused."

"Yes. But that's not why I'm here." Though her hands were icy, runnels of sweat dripped down her rigid back. She bit her lip, then let the words out in a rush. "Ernest's father is blackmailing me. I—I had an affair with him. Years ago. He threatened to tell you if I didn't make certain Ernest succeeded in his suit. He thought if Merry wed Ernest, you'd throw your influence behind his son's career."

"But I already support his career. He's my secretary, for God's sake. I've given him loads of responsibility. As much as he can handle."

"Althorp wanted more than for Ernest to be someone's right hand. He thinks his son should be prime minister."

The expressions that crossed her husband's face were genuinely strange. Whatever his emotions were, outrage was not among them. He stood slowly, coming around the desk to lean against its front. If Lavinia hadn't known him so well, she'd have said he was stalling.

"Well." He rubbed the length of his bearded jaw. "There's an ambition—though if he expects to chivvy Ernest into it, he doesn't know his son as well as he thinks. May I ask why you decided to tell me now? Or is it because if you don't, you believe Althorp will?"

Lavinia fought the urge to drop her eyes. "Yes," she admitted, "partly. But it's also because I can't live like this anymore. I hurt her, Geoffrey. My own daughter. I spread rumors about her. Made sure everyone knew how difficult she was. I scared off her other suitors to ensure she'd have no one to choose from but Ernest." Her chin trembled at her husband's jerk of shock. "I know it was wrong of me. I can't tell you how dreadfully ashamed I am."

For a long moment, Geoffrey simply stared at her. Then he sighed. "Ah, Lavi, what a pair of fools we've been."

"What do you mean?"

He paused again, his eyes for some reason not just sad but bitterly amused. "I knew about you and Althorp."

Lavinia felt as if the floor had dropped a foot. "You knew?"

"I can even tell you when. It was the year I headed that committee to push funding for the underground through the House of Lords. I thought those tunnels would shape London's future, make her the strongest, fastest city in the world. Looking back, in my obsession to see the legislation pass, I neglected everything else. I took you for granted, love. I simply assumed you'd wait."

"Good Lord," she said, scarcely able to take it in. He'd known. All this time he'd known.

"Yes." He reached to smooth her hair. "When I saw what was happening, I realized I'd misjudged. I don't know what I'd planned to say to you, but you must have broken off the affair almost as soon as I stopped spending that time away. I decided it would be easier if I didn't confront you." He laughed without sound. "I told myself I was doing it to spare your feelings. To be honest, though, my pride didn't want to admit you preferred another man."

"Never!" Lavinia said, catching his hands in hers. She hadn't preferred Althorp. Couldn't. "I was stupid, and perhaps a little lonely, but I never preferred him to you. He wasn't even kind except at first. As soon as he had what he wanted, he let his true nature show."

Her husband squeezed her hands. "I'm sorry, love. You shouldn't have had to go through that alone. In truth, I'd begun to think, lately, the affair might have started up again. I confess I'm relieved to hear it was only blackmail."

Lavinia shuddered. Only blackmail! "I'm afraid he may make good on his threats. Now that Ernest has stood against him, he may decide he has nothing left to lose. He could tell everyone what we did."

"Oh, Lavi, I'm sure he was only bluffing. Say what you like about Althorp, his sense of self-preservation is finely honed."

"But you didn't see how angry he was!"

Geoffrey cupped her face. "He wouldn't want Ernest to know. Me, yes. I think he's always resented the privileges people like us enjoy. But he wouldn't tell the world. He loves that boy. No doubt he's angry Ernest isn't avoiding Merry, but the thought of his son hating him would destroy him."

"I don't know." Lavinia shook her head, remembering Althorp's choler, remembering—despite every desire to forget—his brutal kiss. "Oh, I wish I'd never met him! Most of all, I wish I could undo what I've done to our daughter. If I hadn't pushed her so hard, she might not have run away."

"Hush." Geoffrey moved his fingers to her lips. "Merry made her own choices, but none of that matters now. If she's turned Ernest down, she's truly on her own. She needs us to be strong for her, not to waste energy on 'what if.'"

His gentleness overcame her and she hid her face against his chest. His body was solid, his arms more comforting than any arms she'd known. Whatever twisted feelings she did or did not have for Althorp, when Geoffrey's hold closed around her, she knew she loved the man she'd married with a strength that was almost pain.

"We have to tell Merry," he said, "in case Althorp is as irrational as you say. It wouldn't be fair to let her hear it from someone else. Besides, she deserves to know what you did to run off her suitors. If there's any chance of her finding someone else, she'll need some confidence in her charms."

Lavinia closed her eyes and held tight to the back of his coat, unable to suppress a surge of resentment. She'd said she was sorry. Was it really necessary that she abase herself so completely? It wasn't as if her daughter had been drowning in suitors to begin with. And what if she told her brothers? They'd all feel sorry for Merry then, and they all would hate Lavinia.

"I'm not certain I can face her," she said. "She's going to be very angry."

"I'll help you," he said with a tenderness that shamed her. "Together we'll get through this."

Lavinia didn't see how telling the truth could be anything but awful. For the moment, though, in the soothing shelter of his arms, she let herself believe she would survive.

21 ❧

THE CARRIAGE SET NIC DOWN AT THE CORNER OF Pall Mall and St. James Square. From there, he strode swiftly through a misty summer rain. Men hurried by him on the pavement, their uniformly black umbrellas bobbing like crows' wings above their heads: clerks and bankers, he suspected, eager to reach their homes. Exhaling softly in relief, he slipped from the bustling stream and up the steps to the duke of Monmouth's club.

His was the largest on the street, two long floors of arched windows with a heavy, garlanded frieze to top them off. Given the grandeur of the place, he wasn't surprised that the Cerberus at the door—a mournful undertaker of a man—was not happy to see Nic's sun-browned, canary-waistcoated, slightly dampened self.

"The duke will see me," he said and handed the man his card.

Nic's tension over the coming meeting was so great he

couldn't enjoy the celerity with which he was admitted once the man returned. He buttoned his coat as they climbed the marble stairs. Merry's father didn't need to see his eccentric dress.

Monmouth himself met him at the door to a lofty, book-lined room. Other gentlemen sat inside, reading, smoking, or quietly playing cards. As if to forestall Nic's entry into this sanctum sanctorum, the duke immediately gestured down the hall. "We can speak in the visitor's room," he said, both his voice and manner stiff.

Though he was sorry to see the reaction, Nic couldn't blame him for it. He had, after all, despoiled the man's daughter.

As they entered a dingy parlor, a waiter wheeled in a drinks trolley, then withdrew and closed the door behind him. The furniture, an assortment of chairs and knickknack tables, was clearly cast off from the rest of the club, its cushions worn, its wood marred with cracks and stains. With deliberate rudeness, Monmouth poured himself—and only himself—half a tumbler of whiskey. He carried the drink to the single window and gazed down at the carriage traffic in the street. Sensing he ought to let his host collect his temper, Nic waited for him to speak.

Monmouth swallowed a mouthful of liquor, then turned his head to face his guest. His expression was hard, his eyes keen but unreadable. "I marvel that you have the nerve to come here."

"I would not have," Nic answered, "were it not for the urging of my heart."

"Your heart," Monmouth repeated, his gaze sharpening even more. His glass hung halfway to his mouth, the subtle vibration of the fluid all that showed he was not as calm as he appeared.

That, at least, Nic and he had in common.

"I am in love with your daughter," Nic said. "I would like to ask you for her hand."

Monmouth set his drink on the sill with a quiet click. He was breathing hard, head down, both hands clenched in fists.

Nic knew what was coming as soon as he saw the duke inhale.

He did not, however, do anything to evade the explosive punch.

The force with which it connected staggered him. His vision blurred, the pain seeming to spike straight through his brain. Almost immediately, his nose began to bleed.

"Well," he said, handkerchief pressed to the flow, "I see where your sons get their gift for scrapping."

Monmouth seemed shocked by his own behavior, though he did his best to hide it. "I will not apologize for that," he said. "My daughter may be . . . in difficulties at present, but she need not stoop to marrying a painter, no matter if he has claimed the privileges of a spouse."

"No apology required, I assure you. I earned this broken nose, as I'm sure I earned the one I got from your son. What I have not earned is your scorn for the way I make my living. I have not been honest in every aspect of my life but in my art I've always given full measure, as you yourself have cause to know."

"You ruined her!" Monmouth insisted, red springing fresh into his face. "I don't care what she said about it being her idea. You took advantage of my daughter. You're older than she is and should have had more sense. And if you think offering to marry her makes it better, you are mistaken. I'll not have my daughter leg-shackled to some commoner, to a filthy rake with paint under his nails!"

Monmouth's anger filled the air like burning ice but Nic did not shrink from it. He had earned the right to stand as this man's equal, not because of his birth, but because he'd finally proved—to himself if no one else—that he was ready to pick up the mantle the former marquis had dropped. Thanks to his mother's idea of training, Nic's muscles were hardened from manual labor, his fingers stained with ink from hours of slaving over Northwick's books. His heart felt stronger, too, in ways he had not expected. After all these years apart, he and his mother had been strangers, much like he and Cris. Now he thought—with work and patience—they all might end up as friends.

He was richer for that, and more confident. When he answered Monmouth's accusation, he did so with as much dignity as he could, considering he had a square of blood-sopped linen squashed to his nose.

"Most of what you say is true, and promises of reform mean nothing until I prove them. But I believe I can convince your daughter I am in earnest. What's more, I believe she would be happy to let me try."

"People will laugh at her," Monmouth said, though less heatedly than before. "They will say she is desperate if she marries you."

"Most likely," Nic agreed, "though I do not think her a slave to pride. Still, she is a rare woman. She deserves the best, including a titled husband if she cares to have one. That is why I'm going to tell you something I haven't told anyone but Merry in fifteen years. I am not a commoner. I am the seventh marquis of Northwick. For personal reasons, I did not claim the title until now. Sharing it with Merry cannot erase what I have done, but I trust no one will say she has married beneath her."

Monmouth stared at him, every bit as stunned as Nic expected. "She did not tell me," he said once he'd found his voice. "I cannot believe she did not tell me."

Nic could believe it, but having his guess confirmed filled his heart with admiration. "When your daughter and I parted," he said, "she remained in some doubt as to my feelings. I imagine she did not want to see me forced into a marriage she wasn't certain I would welcome."

"Are you saying she loves you, too?"

"I believe that to be the case."

Monmouth blinked. "Well," he said, patently at a loss.

Turning back to the rain-spotted window, he stroked the neatly groomed edges of his beard. He was once again the man Nic had painted: proud but human, wanting to do right but uncertain what that was. After a seemingly endless pause, he offered Nic the drink trolley's bucket of shaved ice.

"Grab a handful," he said gruffly. "That nose is going to swell."

"Thank you," said Nic, relieved to finally be able to tilt his head back.

"She did defend you," Monmouth grudgingly admitted. "Practically swore she held you down and had her way. S'pose it's time we let her make her own decisions, since that's what she's likely to do in any case." He sighed with a resignation only a parent could express. "You may call on us tomorrow. If my daughter wishes to see you, I will not prevent it, but neither will I argue on your behalf."

Nic lowered the ice to thank him, but Monmouth forestalled him with a look, half warning, half amused. "My daughter can be extremely stubborn, Mr. Craven. Convincing her to give you a chance will be up to you."

"A chance is all I ask," said Nic, and left the duke with a formal bow.

TOO RESTLESS TO SLEEP, MERRY TOSSED IN HER lightly sheeted bed. Tonight her sisters-in-law had thrown a dinner party at Evelyn's town house, and she'd been the honored guest: an apology, Lissa confessed, for being so slow to show support.

Merry had been touched but also troubled, because they'd invited Ernest, too.

His estrangement from his father was taking an obvious toll. He had circles beneath his eyes and his hair was almost unkempt. Rumor had it Althorp was furious over his son's continued loyalty to Merry—over other disappointments as well, though Ernest could not know that.

The duchess's confession had shocked Merry but, in a sad way, did not surprise her. Maybe her mother did love her. Maybe the tears she'd shed so copiously were a sign of remorse and not just regret that she'd been caught. Whatever the case, Merry suspected she'd always guard her heart against her. Forgiveness might come with time but probably never trust.

At Merry's insistence, her brothers were made privy to the truth on the grounds that they, too, might need to brace themselves for more scandal. Though their mother's tears seemed

to weigh more persuasively with them, even they were regarding her with reserve.

Knowing one's mother had had an affair was bound to
change a son's opinion.

This was part of the reason she hesitated to share the
whole story with Ernest. Despite her mother's pleas not to
risk enraging Althorp, her father had left the choice to Merry.
"You're the closest to him," he'd said, "and perhaps we've
all kept too many secrets. If you think he'll be better off, then
he should know." But would Ernest be better off? Would
knowing free him from dancing to his father's tune? Althorp
probably didn't deserve a son like Ernest, but did Ernest deserve to hate his father? He'd shown some spine already.
Maybe that was enough.

Still undecided, she'd found him alone in Evelyn's parlor.

With a grimace for being caught brooding, he set a minia-
ture of Evelyn's wife back on the mantel. "I've never seen
my father like this," he said without preamble. "Why can't he
respect my choice to support a friend? He flies into a fury
one moment, then shuts himself up to drink the next. I swear
he's aged ten years in the last two weeks. I've tried to talk to
him but he refuses. If I didn't know better, I'd swear he was
afraid of me."

Merry stroked his sleeve. "Maybe he is."

Ernest stared at her. "What do you know, Merry? What
does everyone know that they aren't telling? Your brothers
have been strange to me all night, your mother won't meet
my eye, and your father asked if I needed a vacation."

Merry sighed. "I want you to think before you answer. If
your father had done something awful, would you truly want
to know?"

"Something awful to you?"

"Only indirectly. And what he did, he did for you."

Frowning, he pulled her to sit on the couch. "Tell me," he
said, and so she did. The white-lipped self-control with
which he listened cut straight to her heart. She apologized for
being the one to tell him but he thanked her.

"If I have to hear it," he said, "I'd rather it come from my
best friend."

That cut her, too, that he considered her his best friend. She stared at her knotted hands. "What will you do?"

"I don't know. If I tell him I know, he may take it out on your family."

"But you shouldn't have to pretend!"

"My father and I spend a lot of time pretending. This wouldn't be anything new."

A history lay behind those words that she, his supposed best friend, had never guessed was there. This is wrong, she thought. Someone should know and love the whole of who Ernest is. Of course, if by chance he had feelings for her, that someone should not be Merry.

"Talk to Peter," she said in her firmest voice. "He could use some cheering since that opera dancer threw him over. Besides which, he's developed a bit of sense lately. It wouldn't hurt for him to practice it on you."

Ernest smiled. "I shall keep that in mind," he said with a touch of his old resilience.

It wasn't a cure, she thought later as she punched a stubborn pillow beneath her head. It was, however, a sign they'd both stepped onto the long road back.

MERRY HAD FINALLY DROPPED OFF TO SLEEP WHEN a muffled clatter startled her from her doze. Someone was in the sitting room, apparently breaking in. Could Althorp have decided to take a new revenge? Heart in her throat, she rolled out of bed and grabbed a poker from the fireplace, then crept silently to the door. She was just drawing breath to scream when she recognized the figure stumbling up from the broken flowerpots.

Heat flashed between her legs, a searing wave that spread quickly up her breasts. Their tips hardened so swiftly she couldn't restrain a blush.

Absence seemed to have made more than her heart grow fonder.

"Nic!" she gasped as he brushed the remains of a begonia from his thigh.

With a rueful laugh, he helped her light a lamp. "This isn't how I intended to make my reappearance."

He was dressed like a working man in baggy trousers and a sacklike coat. Despite his damp and rumpled state, he looked twice as elegant as any person of her acquaintance.

"What are you doing here?" she asked, her voice husky from more than sleep. "And what happened to your nose?"

He touched the sticking plaster that wrapped the bridge. "Present from your father, who—once he'd vented his displeasure—gave me leave to call on you tomorrow. I, however, discovered I couldn't wait." Before she could ask him what that meant, he kissed her, hard and quick at first, then slanting his mouth to sink hungrily in. After a moment, he broke for air. "Oh, I missed you," he said. "I can't even tell you how much." Again he kissed her and again he cut the foray short. "Tell me you forgive me for not returning sooner."

"Well, since I didn't expect you back at all, I—"

He silenced her with a deep, seductive penetration of his tongue.

"Since I—" she tried again, then lost her train of thought. His fingers had spread around her bottom to lift her against the startling bulge of his erection. Heat alone seemed to have dried the cloth that stretched across it. By contrast, the cover of her nightdress did little to hide her dampness from him.

With a smoky growl, he rotated his hips into the thin foulard. "Missed me, too, I see."

"Yes, but—"

"Sh. Tell me later." His lips opened on her throat and her head dropped back without her will. She couldn't have spoken if she wanted. All she could do was cling. "I know you had to leave me," he said, the words a heated whisper near her ear. "You couldn't have stayed, not the way I was. Not to mention your family must have been mad with worry. Just try to understand I couldn't come back until I was sure I had something to offer."

"What?" she said, breathless and shivering. "What are you offering?"

His next kiss was the sweetest yet, deep but soft, his lips

gentling, his hands gentling, his body folding around her like a blanket of love and care. Long before she'd had enough, he released her with a deep, sighing moan that shot straight from her ear to the pulsing tissues between her thighs. Cradling her face in his hands, he gazed at her with concern. "Tell me this first, love. How are you getting on?"

She laughed with what remained of her breath. "Better than I was when I thought a marauder was breaking in."

"I mean, has it been very bad for you?"

"Because I came home a fallen woman?" She smoothed his wet hair back with her fingers, the feel of the silky strands a restorative to her soul. He was here and, for now, everything was well. "I won't deny having shed a few self-pitying tears, but there have been bright spots as well as dark. Isabel has been a rock and Ernest, bless him, actually proposed again."

"Tell me you didn't say yes."

His horror warmed her woman's pride. "Of course I didn't. How could I? Ernest deserves better than a woman who cannot love him with all her heart." Colored by the memory of the talk they'd shared in Evelyn's parlor, this declaration was possibly a bit too passionate. Nic was peering at her, his eyes narrow, as if *he* wanted to be loved with all her heart. She lowered her chin to hide her budding smile, then looked at him through her lashes. "I should warn you that in visiting me you risk your own reputation. I don't know if you've heard, but I'm a terrible influence on everyone I meet."

Nic grinned. "I could have told people that. But you're serious. Oh, Merry, tell me everything."

Suddenly able to see the humor in her predicament, she explained about Althorp's ambitions for Ernest and the lengths to which her mother had gone in order to satisfy his blackmail. Unlike her, Nic was not amused.

"Good Lord," he said. "Your own mother. You must have been devastated."

"Not as much as you might think. I always knew she didn't care for me very deeply. Awful as it sounds, discovering what she'd done freed me not to care for her. Papa has rallied the family round, united front and all, but I have to admit I'm rather enjoying how much my disgrace has embarrassed Mother. Her so-called friends are a bunch of cats. They're reveling in the chance to revenge themselves on her for all the times she lorded it over them. Childish of me, I suppose, but there it is."

"Surely you want to see her punished more than that?"

She pulled up her shoulders in a shrug. "Maybe being who she is is punishment enough. She was fighting to protect things I don't think truly matter. In the process, she lost much of her family's trust. And, to be fair, when I ran away that day at Tatling's, I was just as cowardly. Unfortunately, I'm not convinced she's changed in any lasting way. Perhaps she's incapable. So we smooth out the surface and go on. I can't regret what's happened. If she hadn't done what she did, I'd never have turned to you. I'd have missed out on memories I'll always treasure."

Nic was silent then, his fingers fanning the skin beneath the ruffled sleeves of her thin silk gown. As absent as it was, the caress sent tingles down her arms. She'd forgotten how much he could make her want him.

"I took Cristopher back to Northwick," he said. "We spent the summer learning how to run the estate. Actually, that was for me more than for Cris, but my mother bullied him, too, when she got the chance." He pulled a breath into his lungs and raised his eyes. "I've taken back the title, Merry. I told your father this afternoon. He gave me leave to court you."

Emotions washed through her: awe, happiness, followed by a sobering twinge of doubt. If guilt were his only motivation, she didn't want this gift. She put up her chin. "I won't be another responsibility."

His expression softened. "You're not a responsibility. You're a blessing. I changed because I wanted to be worthy of you, but if you refuse me, I won't go back to what I was. I'm ready for this, love. I want to give you what I've learned to be."

"You truly want to marry me?"

She could not keep the disbelief from creeping into her tone. He smiled, the understanding in his eyes threatening to make her cry. He pressed his hand over his heart. "I'd be deeply honored if you'd marry me. I love you, Merry, and I admire you. If you agree to have me, I'll spend my life showing you how much."

"I want to run a stud," she blurted out.

A smile tugged the corners of his mouth. "So long as you mean with horses, I have no objection."

"I don't believe a woman should sit at home looking pretty. At least, not a woman like me."

"Have you noticed I'm not objecting?"

She bit her upper lip, then laid her palm across the hand he'd pressed to his heart. His skin was warm, his fingers long and hard. She remembered how they could pluck and soothe and feather like angels' wings. Did she dare believe they could also support her dreams?

Burning with too many wants to name, she leaned toward him, letting her breasts brush the rain-dampened linen of his coat. Color washed his cheeks as he felt the subtle rasp of her hardened nipples, their darkening visible even in the lamplight. Beneath their hands, his chest began to rise and fall.

"Why don't you show me how much you admire me now?" she said.

He moaned deep in his chest, then tore off his coat and pulled her to him. "Oh, God, Merry." He kissed her hair, her cheek, the pulsing hollow of her throat. "Oh, God, will I show you!"

They fought to remove his clothes, jousting over buttons and peeling chilly, sodden cloth from warm, hair-roughened skin. Her hands were as greedy as his kiss, skimming over chest and belly, gripping knotted shoulders and squeezing his clenched behind. The hair that led silkily from his navel was an arrow whose compulsion she obeyed. Down to his abdomen, into the cloud of curls. Combing through them, she found the base of his rigidly swollen sex. His kiss broke on a gasp.

She smiled up at him, fey and bold. Up she drew her fingers, inch by inch, vein by vein, then down again to wrap him firmly in her hold. She tightened her grip just to feel his flesh resist. He was magnificent: hot and thick, a pulsing, animal thing. Wrapping one finger beneath the rim, she tugged him gently into the air. His shaft seemed to stretch to match her pull. When she swept her thumb across the slippery crown, he jerked as if she'd struck him.

"Do you like that?" she crooned. Her second hand found the fullness of his balls. Carefully, her eyes never leaving his, she compressed them between her fingers and her palm. His breath hissed like a kettle left too long on the fire.

Teasing him was simply too entertaining. She started to sink to her knees to tease him more, but he caught her beneath the arms and pulled her up.

"Bed," he panted, "quick!"

Hardly waiting for her to point, he scooped her up and carried her to her room, peeling off her nightdress as soon as he set her down. He knelt then, his mouth pulling strongly at her breasts, his hands painting beauty into her skin. Her limbs began to tremble as if he'd drugged her. If he had, he'd used a substance that magnified her sensations. She felt every expulsion of ragged breath, every flicker of lash and tongue. When he twisted the tip of her second breast between two knuckles, the resulting spear of feeling was so intense, she had to speak.

"Nic," she whispered, "my legs won't hold me."

He chuckled and lifted her onto the tangled covers of her bed. Climbing up himself, he stretched his muscled length against her side. His erection burned its shape into her hip while his hands poured fire over her curves.

"Let's see," he said, "if I remember how to do this."

Two agile fingers slid between her curls, parting silky, lust-oiled folds. Their pads dipped inside her, teasing, tickling, before finally curling in.

She pressed a fist to her mouth to mute her tortured groan. Centuries seemed to have passed since he'd touched her, millennia of aching need. Her spine arched strongly as he stroked, deeply, slowly, bowing her body off the bed.

"Yes," he said, beginning to shift lower, "I think my memory is coming back."

She felt his smile as he nuzzled her trembling flesh, then his teeth in a teasing nip. He laved her with the tip of his tongue, then settled in to suck the swollen bud. Any worry for his injury was forgotten as feeling rolled through her in rich, intoxicating waves. With one broad hand beneath her bottom, he tilted her hips to press her close.

The pleasure was almost too much to stand. Her body ached and tightened as his fingers worked magically inside her, heightening the effect of his mouth, of the rush of his breath and the cool, wet tickle of his rain-spiked hair. The muscles of his shoulders bunched beneath her hands. His breathing hitched and rasped. He seemed to want this climax as much as she.

"Wait," she said, the longing too huge to keep inside, "let me taste you, too."

He stopped. A shudder swept through him, betraying how much he wanted to comply.

"Turn," she insisted, urging with her hands. "I want us to share this."

He turned until she had him in her reach. With a moan of welcome, she pulled him into her mouth: his heat, his full-ness, his musky, throbbing silk. This was what she needed. This was what she'd dreamed of in the night.

They strained together, the position awkward but exciting, a challenge to concentration and control. Sweat rolled down their bodies, and fingers gripped harder than they should. Even that small pinch of pain was arousing. They couldn't control themselves, not completely.

Still fighting the lure of full abandon, Nic gasped out in-structions. "Not so far. You'll . . . oh, God. Don't make me come, love. Easy now. Slow."

She barely registered what he said. His groans were music, his involuntary twitches of response as stimulating as anything he did to her. She kneaded the muscles of his bot-tom, then pressed the puckered entry that hid within. He stiff-ened, violently, inside her mouth and out.

"Merry," he said, a hiss of smoldering sound, "you don't have to—"

But she knew what he wanted. She remembered what he'd done to her in Venice. She pushed, gaining a small but obviously pleasurable insertion. His warning changed to a groan. His spine rolled as if her touch had turned it liquid. She wriggled her finger and he thrust as if he could not restrain his reaction, filling her mouth, filling her being with nothing but the knowledge of his body's joy.

Even with that, with his erection stretched to bursting and his back bowed with desire, he still sent her over the edge before she could drag him with her.

She cried out. The climax was too sharply sweet to hold it in. Nic swore like a sailor, then pulled from her mouth and turned around. The bed creaked at the suddenness of his movement. She heard him curse again with impatience, felt him yank her thighs apart and fumble for his home. As soon as he found it, he thrust, one long, smooth stroke, before her quivers had a chance to fade.

He grunted, feeling her clench, and thrust again even harder.

He was bare inside her, his flesh to hers.

"Feel that?" he said, his nostrils flaring as his hips worked tighter still. "That's you and me, Merry. Nothing but you and me."

But even this failed to satisfy his need. He pushed his torso upward, his arms roped with muscle as he rose. His knees dug into the mattress. His thighs were so hard they might have been made of stone. He was big, his blood drumming against the stretch of her tender sheath. His crown seemed ready to breach her womb.

The sensation was utterly, meltingly delicious, as if his very life were held within her sex. Purring with pleasure, she dragged her palms down his back to press the sweaty dip at the base of his spine. He groaned as if she'd hurt him. She didn't know how to help except to let her legs relax even further to the side.

"Oh, Lord," he said as he slipped a fraction deeper. "That feels so good. I think I'll never move again."

He appeared to mean it. Still dazed from her orgasm, but coiling tighter by the second, she slid her hands around and up his ribs. His heart was thundering, the points of his nipples like little stones beneath her touch. She circled them, then pulled them gently by the tips. He inhaled sharply and breathed her name.

Lit by more than love or lust, his eyes burned in the dimness. She knew what he felt because she felt it, too. His need was raw, deeper than his body, deeper even than his heart, a desperation no one but she could fill. And she would fill it. She'd give him back the trust he was giving her.

"Nic," she said, her voice like brandy in her throat, "everything I am I share with you."

His face twisted with emotion. He didn't even try to hide the glitter of his tears. Her sex tightened in a spasm of pre-orgasmic bliss. He grit his teeth and swelled inside her. His shiver was a thrill that skittered sumptuously down her spine. Slowly, as if they both would shatter at a breath, he drew back through her body's hold.

"You," he said hoarsely, "make me whole."

He slammed into her then with wonderfully brutal force, hitting her high and hard. Two drives, three, his cock a velvet hammer. She thought he'd burst but on he went, working her, working himself inside her. He was completely beyond control, no polished rake but a creature of pure instinct. The cries he uttered were rough and rhythmic. Hungry. Sweat flew between them. Her sex felt deliciously bruised by his naked, pumping shaft. Her heart simply felt beloved.

She would fly, she thought, ready to weep with exhilaration. She would soar into the sun. Helpless to stop, she gripped his arms and came at the bottom blow of a stroke. A heartbeat later he unraveled with a groan, his hips shimmying against hers in quick, deep beats that locked and held as his ecstasy met hers.

He strained there, gushing, shaking, then let his weight sink slowly down.

She scarcely had the strength to wrap him in her arms.

"Very well," she said, panting out the words, "I will marry you."

His laugh rumbled against her breast. "Convinced you, did I?" He rose on his elbow to gaze at her, his cheeks flushed, his eyes shining with love and humor. With a musing smile, he wound one golden curl around his finger.

"I want to ask you something," he said, "and you needn't tell me unless you wish. That night, after Anna's party, that was your first time, wasn't it? You gave me your virginity."

Her fiery blush was all the answer he required.

"Lord," he said, "I'm a cur to be glad but I can't help it."

"You are a cur. Not to mention a dangerous seducer."

His dear, battered face grew serious. "From this day forward, Merry, I'm only seducing you. You gave me a gift that night, and I didn't even know."

She fought not to squirm with embarrassment and delight. "Well," she huffed, "I trust you know it now."

"Yes." He tweaked the turned-up end of her nose. "Now I'm lucky enough to know."

22

THE SKIRT TO MERRY'S GOWN WAS ALMOST TOO FULL to fit through her dressing room door. She managed it, though, squeezing into the sitting room while the mothers argued over what sort of flowers should decorate her headpiece. Like ghosts of weddings past, their voices trailed into her refuge.

"Orange blossoms," insisted Merry's mother.

"Nothing at all!" boomed the dowager marchioness. "My son isn't marrying some French tart!"

"Don't catch those pearls on the furniture," Ginny called, the only one to notice Merry's escape. The old nurse had been called back for the wedding, though she'd refused Merry's offer of a position in her new home.

In the months since her dismissal, Ginny had enjoyed helping her sister in her Devon tea shop so much she'd decided she really was ready to retire.

Merry smiled at the irony. It seemed even Ginny had prof-
ited from this mess.

Careful not to snag her skirt, she lowered herself to the
settee by the window. She'd never have guessed a wedding
could be this tiring—especially when everyone else was
fighting to do the work. The gown itself had proved a challenge to her less-than-stellar tact. In the end, the duchess
agreed to let Nic choose the design, but only if Madame
sewed it.

The result was lavish beyond her wildest dreams. The
overdress was a rich summer green, and the underdress a
froth of Venetian lace. The snug, sleeveless bodice was so
heavily encrusted with tiny pearls, she felt as if she were
wearing armor. More pearls spilled over the skirt in delicate
fronds and curls. A princess could have worn this gown or,
for that matter, an empress! Instead, it was gracing plain old
Merry Vance.

She felt both ridiculous and gorgeous, more of a spectacle
than she'd been since posing naked as Godiva. Interestingly
enough, her mother had given her Nic's painting—after ex-
tracting a promise they'd hang it "privately." Now, arrayed in
a dress that nearly outdid that undress, she didn't know
whether to laugh hysterically or burst into happy tears at the
thought of dragging this beautiful monstrosity down the
aisle.

When her mother saw the final fitting, she'd nodded and
tapped her chin. "I'll give Craven this," she said. "He knows
how to make a woman look her best."

"You should call him Northwick," Merry corrected gently, "or Nic if that feels more natural."

Her mother sniffed. "I'll call him Northwick after he's
kept you happy for a year. And I'll call him Nic when he
hands me my next grandchild."

She seemed not to realize how surreal such comments
were, as if—after all that had happened—Merry should now
believe her well-being was her mother's dearest concern. She
let the pretense stand for her father's sake but found herself
thinking less of her mother's sense with every day.

Nic could not warm to her at all.

Oh, he was polite, even charming, and Lavinia professed to like him, but he saved his true self, his honest self, for the people who really loved her.

To Merry's surprise, Nic proved more than just a ladies' man. After an initial bristly meeting, with various veiled references to his healing nose, all three of her brothers had succumbed to his worldly glamor. When they discovered he was also a good sport, their last resistance gave up the ghost. The possibility of a male-only fishing tramp to Scotland had been thrown out for discussion—after the honeymoon, of course.

"Bah!" Nic's mother had exclaimed. "As if men have the patience to fish well."

Merry had been leery of the dowager marchioness until she saw how determined the woman was to like her. Rough around the edges she might be, and certainly used to running things her own way. All the same, her candor won Merry's respect, along with her still awkward love for her son.

When Merry realized how easily the marchioness would fit in among the rowdy Vances, she did feel a little sorry for her mother.

Not sorry enough, however, to get between the mothers now. That was Isabel's job. Finally forgiven by her husband, thanks to some bargain that made her giggle whenever Merry asked what it was, she was doing diplomatic duty as Merry's matron of honor.

"Wouldn't miss it," she'd declared. "This is absolutely, without question, the most romantic and gossip-worthy match anyone's seen in years. Imagine that Lothario turning out to be a marquis! Half the females in London are kicking themselves with envy."

Merry had to admit to liking that, even if a fair number of those females knew precisely what there was to be envious of. But that was a knowledge she could adjust to. Nic's past was Nic's past. His future was what mattered and he'd entrusted that to her.

Pressing a fist to her burgeoning laugh, Merry tipped her head back and closed her eyes. Thank God her family didn't know the truth about all their guests, Sebastian and Evangeline in particular. They thought this marriage was irregular as it was!

The sound of a hesitant knock brought her neck upright again. Cristopher hovered in the doorway, achingly adult in his formal white tie and tails.

"Hello, love," she said, the endearment easy. "Come keep me company until the madwomen track me down."

He shot a wary look at the dressing room, from which sounds of debate still issued out, then crossed hastily to the cushion she'd cleared her skirt from to make room. Perching on its edge, he pressed his knees together like a nervous debutante. "I need to ask your advice."

"Ask away," she said, airily waving her hand. "Right about now, I'd like to feel old and wise."

He gave her a boyish, quicksilver grin, but quickly sobered. "It's about Nic. I know you and I get on, so I was wondering . . . I don't want to presume, but I was wondering if you think he'd mind if I spent my next holiday from school with you two."

Merry put a hand to her tightening throat. Before she could speak, Nic entered from the hall.

"Why don't you ask me yourself?" he said, his eyes so bright and his voice so rough Merry knew at once what his answer would be.

"You can say no," Cris said quickly. "I know I haven't—well, we haven't lived like family for very long, and you'd only just be married. I'd understand if you thought it an imposition."

By the time he finished stammering, Nic had crossed the room. He cupped the side of his brother's face, then bent and pressed his lips softly to his temple.

"My home is your home," he said, "as much as if you were my son. You don't need to ask. You only need to show up."

"Yes," Merry seconded, holding out her hand. "Visit as often as you like."

"If I visit as often as I like," Cris said, with a grin to match his brother's, "the marchioness might get lonely."

Nic pulled Cris into a bruising hug. "We'll have her visit, too. We'll make room for everyone."

Merry felt as if she were watching him slay the last of his demons. She was so proud she feared she'd burst her stays. Then her eyes welled over and she remembered where she was.

"Oh, look what you've done!" she cried as her sniffles fought with her laughs. Already, she could feel her nose turning pink. "I'm going to walk into that church looking like a rabbit!"

"My," Nic teased, "what a vain, vain creature you've become."

But when he pulled her into his arms and kissed her, she found her looks didn't worry her in the least.